CRITICAL ACCLAIM FOR
THE SHILL TRILOGY

"Sly, sexy and surprising, *The Shill* is a darkly comic Hollywood tale of a not-so-innocent out-of-work actress being groomed for larceny."—Wallace Stroby, author of *The Devil's Share*, *Shoot the Woman First*, and *Cold Shot to the Heart*

"[*The Shill* is] a fast-paced heist story filled with colorful characters and interesting plot twists."—S.W. Lauden, author of *Crosswise*

"[*Kill the Shill* is] a fast and hard ride into a con trick. Told by a writer who pulls no punches this does not disappoint."—Richard Godwin, author of *Wrong Crowd*

"Hell hath no fury like an actress duped. Revenge is the motivation, deception the means to get even in this exciting crime thriller."—Scott Adlerberg, author of *Spiders and Flies* and *Jungle Horses*, on *Kill the Shill*

THE SHILL TRILOGY

BOOKS BY JOHN SHEPPHIRD

The Shill Trilogy
Bottom Feeders
Deception Specialist
Tennis Noir (Anthology)

JOHN SHEPPHIRD

THE SHILL TRILOGY

THE SHILL, KILL THE SHILL, BEWARE THE SHILL

Crimson Gate Books

For Jennifer

TABLE OF CONTENTS

THE SHILL

CHAPTER 1

Work as an actress was sparse. Jane survived by a variety of dead-end, part-time jobs. This one, working for a private investigator, paid minimum wage.

Six months ago, on a foggy morning in L.A.'s beach community of Playa Del Rey, she sat in her Nissan waiting for the subject to emerge from his apartment. Her task was to videotape the man as proof he was physically mobile without the assistance of a wheelchair or crutches. Jane worked for Tim Peduga, an ex-cop turned PI who specialized in insurance fraud.

She arrived just before dawn and found a spot across the street from the apartment. She parked in front of a modern house under construction and hoped the contractors, when they arrived, wouldn't make her move. She could hear the rumble of jets from adjacent LAX airport in the distance.

Jane checked herself in the rearview mirror and hated what she saw. There were bags under her eyes, her forehead was breaking out and her chin looked puffy. Thirty years of age and these moments of self-doubt came more and more often now—a deep, dark depression knocking at the door.

Neighbors walked dogs past. A FedEx truck stopped down the street. She fought boredom by listening to celebrity podcasts on her iPod.

Finally the man emerged from his apartment. It was definitely the same guy from the photo she'd been given. He had shoulder-length curly black hair parted down the middle and a long, scraggly beard. She thought the only thing missing was a flowing black cloak and he could pass for Rasputin, the famed Russian mystic.

She powered the camera.

Even though the video was time stamped, she was instructed to shoot the front page of the *L.A. Times* first. Her boss Tim explained that a video time-stamp could be manipulated after the fact but a physical newspaper is undisputable proof. She supported the lens on the steering wheel and zoomed in.

Rasputin unlocked the door of a Toyota pickup and searched the cab before emerging with a pack of cigarettes. He smacked the pack of Marlboros on his palm and peeled back the cellophane, tossing the remnants into the wind. He produced a lighter and lit the smoke.

That's when he noticed her.

She averted her gaze, pretended to be busy with something below the dash while still keeping the camera trained. In the LCD viewfinder she saw him walk toward her. She dropped the camera and went for the ignition. The car sputtered and stalled.

He was closing in fast.

She locked the doors.

"Excuse me," he said angry. "What are you doing? Do I know you?"

She averted his gaze and tried to start the car again. No luck. *Piece of...*

He tossed the cigarette at her windshield and smacked the hood. "Were you filming me? You don't have the right!"

She pumped the gas as the starter whined but the Nissan would not fire. *Damn it!*

"Give me the camera, bitch!"

What'd he call me?

Jane defiantly flipped him off. She regretted it when it only enraged him more.

Red-faced, he ran around the car and rummaged through the

pile of construction refuse. He came back with a cinderblock raised over his head.

You've got to be kidding.

Jane ducked below the dash just before the windshield shattered. Chunks of broken glass rained down into her hair.

Over the cinderblock on her dented hood she could see him searching for something else to throw. She went for the ignition again. The car finally started with a mighty roar.

His eyes registered fear.

"Motherfucker!" she screamed. She threw it into drive and punched the gas.

Boom!

Rasputin flipped over the hood followed by the sound of his head hitting the pavement—much like a watermelon cracking open upon impact.

CHAPTER 2

Months later, dressed in frayed clown regalia, Jane performed a magic trick under the shade of a gnarled ficus tree. For the audience of children she held out an over-sized "die," the singular term for dice she made clear to the kids, and placed it in a black lacquer miniature cabinet. She closed the two doors and tilted the box to one side before she opened the adjacent chamber.

"See, it vanished."

She shut that door and tilted the box the other way—the children hearing a *thunk* as the die seemingly slid to the other half of the box. Opening the opposite door Jane said, "All gone. Show's over. Thank you very much."

The kids screamed in protest. They demanded she open both doors at the same time but she pretended not to understand them. When they had been teased enough, Jane opened them both. The die had disappeared.

"Not everything is as it appears," she said.

This was the final line of her magic routine. She reached into a nearby hat and pulled out the die as if it invisibly jumped through space.

Jaws dropped in amazement. It was her best trick, Jane's grand finale, an over-the-counter magic shop standard hailed "the sucker die box"—no sleight of hand required and the art of deception at her fingertips.

Later, as the rambunctious kids ate ice cream outside French doors, Jane packed her show away. Kneeling on a thick Persian rug in the master bedroom she paused to gaze at the antique four-post bed, its fine linen, silk pillows and a pure white duvet ironed to perfection. God, it must be nice to be this rich, to wake up in a bed like this. For a brief moment she could daydream until—

"That was great." The woman of the house was there with purse in hand. "Thank you *so* much. Brady and his friends loved your act."

Here was a woman who has everything, this tasteful house, a six-year-old boy, a family of her own. She was the lucky one who woke up every morning in this wonderful bed—obviously with a man who loved her. And worst of all, she appeared to be only a few years older.

"Two hundred dollars, right?" the woman said.

Jane nodded and continued to pack her show away. She felt deep envy, the feeling creeping up into her throat, copper to taste, bitter. She needed a drink of water but did not feel like asking. When she finally stood the woman handed her a check.

"I thought we agreed on cash," Jane said.

"I didn't have a chance to get to the bank. I can call my husband and have him drop by the ATM, but he won't be back until later."

Jane bit her lip. She *needed* cash. She could not wait for the stupid husband because she'd be late for class. Jane thanked the woman and took the check without glancing at the total.

Standing in the driveway, still dressed as a clown, Jane waited for her taxi.

She dug out her last thirty dollars and hoped it would be enough to get across town. Once there, she knew she could bum a ride home. This sleepy, tree-lined neighborhood north of Montana Avenue in Santa Monica was once dominated by single-story, pre-war craftsman bungalows. Jane could see that most had been torn down and replaced with two-story, imported-tile McMansions. She found the check to take a look.

No tip. *Figures.*

Jane wondered why the wealthiest people tipped the worst, or, as in this case, not at all. She hated having to rely on taxis but her car was in the shop again, this time a "broken timing belt," whatever that was. She'd nicknamed her car rusty-yet-trusty Nissan, but now it was held for ransom by Yuri her mechanic for six hundred dollars plus storage charges since he'd had it so long.

Not long ago she was working for Peduga Investigations when the crazy Rasputin smashed her car's windshield. Tim paid to replace the glass, plus a little more, and now Jane had nothing to show for it. She suspected Tim wasn't calling her for surveillance gigs anymore because of that incident.

Being a private investigator seemed flexible enough to allow for her acting pursuits, and Jane figured she could eventually hang her own shingle when she became a licensed PI. She'd done the homework and was collecting paystubs as proof for the required hours needed to get her license.

Then last month, just after the Nissan got out of the body shop, it betrayed her. She'd had to tow it to Yuri's and the tow alone cost her a hundred and twenty bucks.

But this job, two hundred dollars, would not liberate the Nissan. The money would go towards food, overdue rent and piles of laundry. She would revive her spent pay-as-you-go cell phone, and maybe tackle one or two of the minimum payments from the stack of final notices collecting dust. She checked her watch again. Where was that damn taxi?

Twenty minutes later, in the back of the cab, she peeled off the silly costume. Jane could feel the Arab's eyes in the rearview mirror.

"Can you hurry, please? I'm going to be late."

"I drive fast-as-can, lady. Don't want speeding ticket."

With a towel Jane wiped the clown-white off her face. She caught him peering again. She was used to men looking at her, ever since she was a teenager—eyes lingering, drinking her in.

She tried her best to ignore the cabbie, slipped on a white blouse and then removed her athletic bra underneath, a learned maneuver from doing quick-changes backstage in school plays. She stuffed her clown costume into her bag and finally dug out her sides, the script pages with her lines.

On the way to acting class, in clogged Los Angeles traffic, Jane studied her lines.

By the time the meter neared thirty dollars Jane still had more than a mile to go. She told the cabbie to pull over, handed him all the money and apologized for the lack of tip. She could sense his disappointment but there was nothing she could do.

Lugging her suitcase full of magic tricks, wearing a simple white blouse and wrinkled black linen slacks, Jane walked to class, sweating from the heat.

The shabby theater strip on Santa Monica Boulevard, lined with tiny ninety-nine seat theaters, was Hollywood's equivalent to New York's Off-Off Broadway. Under a marquee for Brecht's "The Good Woman of Setzuan" she rushed past a strung-out prostitute. Upon closer inspection Jane saw the hooker was actually a guy in drag, quite normal for this part of town.

The class had already begun, and Jane tried to slip in unnoticed. No luck. Jeremy Sands, her acting coach whose guidance supposedly had steered a well-known student to an Oscar years ago, stopped mid-lecture.

"Well, look who's late again," he said.

The group of acting students seated in the first few rows eyed Jane.

"I'm sorry, Jeremy."

"What's that on your face?"

"What?"

"That..." he said waving his crooked finger at her, "that hideous white stuff, darling. On your face!" Jane ran her sleeve across her forehead, a hint of residual clown white smearing off.

"I...uhm. I do birthday parties," Jane said quietly.

"I beg your pardon," he said with flamboyance.

"I was working. As a clown."

"A clown?"

"Sorry I'm late."

She noticed a new student in the class, an attractive man in a black turtleneck standing in the shadows. He was staring at her. Jane felt two feet tall.

"Everyone else seemed to make it here on time," Jeremy pointed out. "Face it, Jane, you're always late. Are you going to be late to the audition of your life?"

Jane said nothing, anger burning. She suspected Jeremy was mad because she was months behind in tuition. She remained silent, eyes downcast. She focused on the chipped paint in the concrete floor.

Jeremy let it hang there for an uncomfortable beat. "We hope not," he said, followed by a dramatic sigh. "Now, where were we? Heavens, I forget. It doesn't matter. Let's shift our energy to an improvisation exercise. Everybody participates, so please break up in pairs."

Jane was wiping the residual clown white from her face with a Burger King napkin when *he* approached.

"Try using this."

Looking up Jane found herself face-to-face with the handsome man in the turtleneck sweater offering his cloth handkerchief. Mid-forties, well-groomed, he was new to the class. She thought it strange a man carried a handkerchief in this day and age.

"Thank you," she said, reaching for it.

"Let me," the stranger offered. She hesitated, then Jane closed her eyes and let him dab her face. The cloth felt soft. She caught the scent of his cologne, or maybe it was aftershave, and breathed it in.

"I think I got it all."

"Thank you."

"I'm Cooper."

"Jane."

"Jane...?"

"Jane Innes."

"Cooper Sinclaire."

They shook hands. His grasp was firm. *Something about him.*

Cooper nodded towards Jeremy, "I think he likes you."

"I don't think so. He picks on me all the time."

"Need a partner?"

After class Cooper found her, said, "I know a great place where we can get something to eat."

"I don't know...I have to meet a friend," she said. This was her conditioned response, the excuse she'd often used when men hit on her.

"Cancel."

"Maybe some other time." She didn't know anything about him. He was older than any of the men she'd dated before.

"You must be hungry. Just a quick bite. No big deal."

He was so confident, so determined, and she felt uneasy. Jane caught herself twirling her hair. "Maybe next week, after class, we can get a cup of coffee or something."

"Tonight, and I won't take no for an answer."

She felt her nipples alert against her thin blouse. She hoped he hadn't noticed that she wasn't wearing a bra, but was pretty sure he had.

CHAPTER 3

White tablecloths, delicate flowers in tiny porcelain vases—Jane and Cooper shared a quiet corner in a quaint bistro tucked away in West Hollywood.

The waiter poured a sample of red wine. Cooper nosed the glass, tasted it, then approved with a nod. The waiter distributed equally and was off.

"Tell me about you," Cooper said, studying her.

Jane sipped and could tell it was a good bottle, not the under-five dollar twist-cap vintage she drank regularly.

"What do you want to know?"

"Let's start with where you're from."

Self-consciously she began to talk. She told him about growing up in Albuquerque, an only child with a single-parent mom. She told him about the semester at the University of Colorado when she caught the acting bug, about driving her Nissan out to L. A. to try to make it as an actress. She told him about her different odd jobs. He was especially intrigued by the work she'd done for the private investigator. She told him about the recent Rasputin incident.

"I'm banking hours so I can get my own license," she said. "You can't make any money working for PIs. You've got to be your own boss and bill the hours yourself. I figure it's a gig that will allow me the freedom and flexibility to work as an actress."

"Are there times," he asked, "that you impersonate people?"

"Never in person, but I've done it over the phone."

He waited silently until she explained.

"Once I pretended to be a career headhunter to gather information for one of our clients, a woman attorney who practices family law."

"Oh?"

"A deadbeat dad was skipping out on alimony and child support. They tried to garnish wages but he claimed to be unemployed. I got him to admit he was working under the table, and making a pretty good living. The phone call was recorded and he was subpoenaed to appear in court."

"How'd you get him to spill the beans?"

"I pretended I was really interested in his spa and hot tub business. Flirted a little. Built up his ego and earned his trust, I guess."

"How'd you do that?"

"Listened mostly. Let him brag about himself. Encouraged him. He took the bait."

"I bet you're good at it."

"I guess so. I'm an actress."

"Tell me more."

Jane was careful not to give him too many details. The double-wide trailers she and her mother lived in, the crazy boyfriends she endured, and the fact that she never knew her father. The waiter returned and refilled her glass. She talked about how acting was her complete obsession. All else was secondary.

"I can't seem to get a break," she said.

"It will happen. You're talented," Cooper said. "You're a lot better than everyone else in class."

"Thank you for saying that," she said, feeling a dash of confidence enhanced by the warming effect of the wine. "What about you? Tell me what you've done."

"What I've done?"

"As an actor."

"I'm really kind of new to it all," he said. "I thought it might be fun to try because I've always been a ham."

"But Jeremy doesn't accept just anybody. You had to pass his rigorous audition process to get into the class."

Cooper shrugged. "Sure."

"He must have seen something in you," she said.

"Maybe. I don't know. It's fun." He gave her a playful smile. "I live to have fun. How about you?"

She met his eyes for a moment, had an idea what he meant by that. She looked away without answering, smiled to herself. There was spark and sizzle—a thousand words conveyed in one brief, mischievous moment of silence.

The waiter appeared again with a sliced baguette and duck pate. When Jane took a bite she realized this was the first thing she'd eaten all day, other than three peppermint Lifesavers. Probably why the wine had gone straight to her head.

Cooper drove Jane home that night. His sleek Jaguar made it clear he was wealthy. She liked the smell of the leather upholstery.

When they pulled up outside her shabby apartment complex Jane felt the need to make an excuse. "I lost my roommate and I'm sort of in between places right now."

He made her feel at ease, insisted that he walk her to the front gate. When he asked to see her again Jane fumbled through her bag and gave him a business card with her picture on it, an actor's calling card. When Jane first came to Los Angeles, two years ago, she hired a photographer who specialized in creating eight by ten head shots for budding actors. The cards were part of the package.

"Call this number, it texts me," she explained. "I'll call right back."

Cooper raised his eyebrows.

"I don't have a home phone since this place is a temporary arrangement, and I'm in between cell phones right now because the reception is so bad on this block." The truth was Verizon had shut off her landline months ago, the heartless bastards, and there was no "talk time" credit left on her pay-as-you-go cell phone.

After an affectionate peck on the cheek, Cooper bid Jane goodnight and casually drifted off, a perfect gentleman.

Jane crawled into bed happy. She marveled how her day started out so awful but then, in the blink of an eye, turned so wonderful. For one magical evening she'd been able to forget her troubles.

She thought about him, tried to remember his scent, definitely in the mood. She imagined he was in bed next to her, and then the endless possibilities.

CHAPTER 4

Fancy dinners, jazz clubs—she ran out of nice things to wear and started borrowing clothes from her neighbor Carla.

Carla Gomez was from La Puente, a Hispanic blue-collar suburb east of Los Angeles. She worked as a bank teller and moonlighted as a hostess in a restaurant nearby. Jane didn't have many friends and considered Carla her closest.

Carla's clothes were more revealing than Jane would have chosen for herself, but they fit well and struck the right note for the upscale places Cooper took her.

"A little black dress is always in style," Carla told her. Carla also owned lots of high-heeled shoes. Jane had claim to only one pair of heels, so she was in luck.

In return Carla demanded all the romantic details. Jane felt giddy, like a teenager, talking about boys from school as she curled up on Carla's couch and filled her in.

"You're so lucky," Carla said. "A nice guy with bucks. That's it, girl."

Jane explained she felt Cooper was very patient, careful not to force himself upon her. Testing the waters, his kisses grew heavier and his hands explored, but he was always respectful, always tender.

"He got any cute friends?"

Cooper and Jane agreed it would be best to keep their dating secret from Jeremy and the acting class. Pretending not to be interested in him was difficult. She stole glances from time to time but after class left separately. They often met for a late dinner, just as they had on their first date.

She was falling hard.

One evening they went to a Beverly Hills nightclub, a dark and cozy piano bar. A jazz trio set the mood as the raspy-voiced female singer belted old-school standards, Peggy Lee and Billy Holiday. The patrons were much older, distinguished.

After a few scotches Cooper leaned in and whispered to her, "What do you say we cut out of here and stiff the waitress?"

"Why?" Jane asked, confused.

"For the thrill. This place is packed. She won't see us."

"Leave without paying?"

"Haven't you ever stolen anything? Shoplifted?"

"No."

"Let's give it a shot."

"We can't," Jane said, catching sight of the middle-aged cocktail waitress standing at the bar. "I used to wait tables and enough assholes—"

"—But it'll be exciting."

"I've got money," she reached for her purse.

"No, no, put that away. I was only joking." Cooper pulled a wad from his pocket. Jane could see there was a crisp hundred-dollar bill on top. Why would he want to stiff the waitress? It seemed so weird.

Cooper left a generous tip and they were off.

On the way to his car Cooper suggested they go back to his place for a night-cap. Jane had a pretty good idea where that would lead.

He had mentioned that he lived on the West Side so Jane was not surprised when Cooper drove to Marina Del Rey. But she was surprised when he parked and led her past the luxury waterfront apartments to the docks.

"You never said you lived on a boat," she said.

"Guess it never came up."

What a yacht it was. Jane was floored when she stepped inside. The boat was extravagant with polished wood, plush carpet and a good-sized galley.

"It's awesome," she said.

He went to the refrigerator. "Champagne?"

At the counter he popped the cork. She kicked off her heels, and standing behind him, slid her arms around his waist.

"Guess I'll have to call you Captain now, follow orders" she said, teasing, "and be your wench."

He turned and she devoured him with kisses.

It quickly grew more passionate. On the way to the bed Cooper ripped a few buttons from Jane's borrowed dress. She didn't care, groped his shirt and worked her hands down his hard torso. They undressed each other, both breathing heavily.

It was a nice surprise to discover Cooper's well-defined body. She ran her hands down his core, then wriggled her fingers through his pubic hair finding him rock hard.

They hit the sheets.

His skin was warm and soft. She could feel his muscles surge, entangled, quenching Jane's heated desire.

She wrapped her legs around him and they were in union.

It felt so right.

The next morning, after kisses and lattes made from the boat's cappuccino machine, Cooper drove Jane to her apartment.

"You're incredible," he whispered in her ear as they kissed goodbye. She watched him drive off, smitten.

The next day he made no contact with her. Jane tried his cell. She got his voice mail and left a message. Getting no response, and feeling vulnerable, she left another message.

By the time she left the fourth message Jane was miserable.

"Hey, I haven't heard from you so I hope everything's okay. Call me. Miss you."

She hung up hoping her voice was not too desperate, too

obvious. *Desperation is the worst perfume,* she once heard. Why didn't he call back?

Later that evening, and under protest, Carla drove Jane out to Marina Del Rey. The night was foggy, the streets damp.

"This is stupid," Carla said. "He's probably married and never told you. Probably got bratty kids, too."

"Maybe, but I have to talk to him."

They traveled down Lincoln Boulevard in Carla's Mazda and turned on to Tahiti Drive. Jane tried to remember where his boat was docked. She saw the familiar entrance and told Carla to stop.

"Will you come with me?" Jane asked.

"Hell no. You're crazy. Play hard to get, and let him call you. They always do, eventually."

"Come on, it's dark."

"You're such a wimp."

They got out and walked to the gated entrance. It was locked and there was no way to climb over. Then a gay couple came through, well-dressed guys in their forties obviously going out for the night.

"Hello, ladies," one of them said.

"I lost my key," Carla said.

"Sure you did."

"You don't believe me?"

One of them was Hispanic and he and Carla exchanged a few words in Spanish that Jane did not understand. Her charm prevailed. They shared a laugh and Jane caught the gate before it locked.

Approaching the docks she could see Cooper's yacht. The fog was thick. Cabin lights reflected off the black water. Jane moved cautiously, trying not to make any noise.

They peered into a porthole.

Cooper was inside working on his laptop.

"I see him."

Carla offered a nod.

Jane took a moment to collect herself and was about to board the yacht when she saw someone else—in silhouette.

Another woman.

The woman brought Cooper a cup of tea and affectionately fondled the back of his neck. Cooper kissed the woman on her hand and went back to his work.

Jane and Carla shared a look.

"See. I told ya."

"Shit!" Tears and a salty tang in her throat, Jane was devastated. She ran back and Carla followed.

CHAPTER 5

Jane had performed grand openings before. They did not pay as well as birthday parties but there was no other work on the horizon, and this was a three day gig. Clown-face painted in a frown to match her mood, Jane filled helium balloons outside the entrance of a new Costco.

As down as she was, Jane found it in herself to pantomime a silly story. A few kids stood stone-faced as Jane mimed that it took great strength to keep the helium balloon grounded. Jane reminded herself that every chance to perform is a gift, whether it was a B-movie, bad dinner theater, or occasional work as a clown. In the midst of this performance Jane's phone buzzed in her pocket. She snuck a peek at the display.

It was Cooper.

Her spent cell phone allowed basic texting but the voice calls were blocked until she could refill the account, so she took a break and then gave Cooper a call from the payphone in the lunchroom. As it rang Jane studied the State of California minimum wage placard near the phone.

"Hello?" Cooper answered

"It's me. What do you want?" she said.

"To see you."

"Where've you been?"

"I'm so sorry. I've been swamped with work. I really should have called you back."

"What do you want?"

"Let's get together. I miss you."

At that moment a handful of Costco employees entered, gossiping and laughing. Jane could see some were taken aback by a clown in their lunchroom.

"I've got to get off the phone, I'm working," she said.

"We need to talk,"

"I'm busy tonight."

"Look, Jane—"

"I've got to get back to work."

She hung up on him.

Jane stepped out of the lunch room and heard the pay phone ringing behind her. Jane tried her best to wipe her tears without smearing her painted clown face.

By the time she was outside her beeper buzzed, Cooper again. She ignored it and returned to her kiosk.

A small girl pointed and said, "Mommy, look at the sad clown."

An hour later Jane saw Cooper in his Jaguar cruising the Costco parking lot. How had he found her? Someone must have picked up the payphone back in the lunch-room and offered her whereabouts. "She's the clown passing out balloons."

Jane darted inside, abandoning her post, balloons floating to the heavens.

There's no way in hell he's going to see me in this corny costume.

At the lockers she got her clothes, changed in the restroom and left out back through the tire center.

Up the street Jane caught the bus, and on the way home wondered if she would be fired for leaving.

Back in her studio apartment, Jane opened the bottle of Bolla Chianti she was saving, swallowed a gulp and got into a hot shower. She finished a good cry under the spray and felt better. She slipped into her terry-cloth robe, combed her hair and poured more Chianti.

Not the first time her heart had been broken. But this time her feelings for Cooper were so intense, so real. She'd felt alive. Why does it have to hurt so much?

She turned on the television and was mildly caught up by a police pursuit. The news helicopter followed a pick-up truck in a reckless get away. Jane could recognize some of the freeway exits as the guy eluded capture. Someone knocked on her door. She turned down the volume and peeked out of the curtains.

It was Cooper. He caught sight of her. "Jane?"

"What do you want?" Jane asked.

"It's me."

"So?"

"Let me in so we can talk."

"No."

"What's wrong?"

She opened the door a crack, peeked out. "I saw you with her," she said with venom.

She could see his wheels turning.

"On your boat. Is she your wife?"

"My wife?"

"The woman I saw!"

"No, she's not my wife."

"You don't return my calls, and you're seeing someone else. I don't need that shit, all right? And I'm busy right now, so—"

"—Look, I just want to talk. Can I come in?"

"No. My place is a mess."

"Just give me a chance to explain."

"There's nothing to explain."

"Let me in and we can talk about it. I don't know what you saw, but it's not what you think. You need to know something. It's important."

Jane unchained the lock and stepped away from the door.

He let himself in and closed it gently.

She cleared fashion magazines from her couch so he had a place to sit. She debated offering him wine since she was drinking.

"Look," he said, "I'm sorry I didn't call you. And that woman you saw, she's not a girlfriend either."

"I've heard that before. Look, I don't play second fiddle."

"How can I explain it to you—?"

"—You don't have to explain anything." Jane took a healthy sip of her wine.

"She's an actress."

"Oh, Christ," she said, on the edge of tears.

He reached over and took the sleeve of her robe. "Please, bear with me for a moment," he said. "I'm sorry I haven't been honest with you. That woman you saw was an actress from another class. I'm in a few acting classes, not just Jeremy's, but for good reason. I'm searching for the right partner. Can you keep a secret?"

On television the cops fish-tailed the pick-up. The guy was out of the truck, running, vaulting a chain link fence. Cops and dogs closed in.

Cooper continued. "I'm searching for the right partner. If I don't find her I'm going to miss a great opportunity. I'm looking for a collaborator to pull a job."

"What kind of job?"

"An illegal job."

Jane said nothing.

"Listen, I'm not in real estate like I said. I'm looking for a partner to play the part of my wife in order to pull this thing off. It's going to be risky."

"And illegal. Got it."

"A con. A swindle involving diamonds."

"Diamonds?"

"I need a shill."

Jane knew what a shill was from her experience doing magic tricks but she questioned him anyway. "What's a shill?"

"A plant. A person who appears to be an outsider. Someone who seems trustworthy to the mark."

Jane also knew what a "mark" was—a term familiar in the magic trade. She tried to make sense of it all, said to him, "So you're a con man?"

"I prefer to be called a craftsman in the art of deception."

His big yacht, fine clothes, it was now clear. "The boat's not yours, am I right?" she asked.

"Leased. Look I'm sorry I lied to you. Sometimes I just—-It doesn't matter."

She studied him.

"Unfortunately you're only half of what I'm looking for. You're beautiful and you radiate such goodness. But I don't think you've got the nerve, the moxie. I'm not sure if I see it in you. That's why I'm still searching."

She studied her carpet not knowing what to say.

"I messed up." A hint of emotion was weaving into his voice. "I started to fall in love. I didn't mean for that to happen."

"That time you wanted to stiff our waitress," she asked, "was that a test?"

"Yes. You didn't pass, but you were honorable."

On television the cops had the perpetrator handcuffed and face down in an alley. He squirmed but was going nowhere.

"I really shouldn't have told you so much. I just felt I owed it to you. Can you keep my secret?"

"Yes."

"Promise?"

"I promise."

"Thank you." He rose and turned to go.

"How illegal is this thing you're doing?" she asked.

"I've said too much."

"Does this other girl, that actress on your boat, does *she* have the moxie?"

"I'm sorry. Goodbye."

He let himself out.

Jane sank into her couch. *A con man?* She was lost in the notion of it all.

On television the cops escorted the bad guy to their patrol car and the station returned to its regular programming.

On day two of her clown gig she found Clifford "Wizzbo" Nance at her balloon kiosk. She knew Wizzbo, heavy and balding, always in a pathetic costume. For the children he put on a goofy and comical act, but around adults Jane found him caustic and cynical.

"Clifford?" she said approaching.

"What are you doing here?" he said, eyeing the clown wig peeking out of her bag.

"I was about to ask you the same question."

"Haven't you heard?" He leaned in and burped, his breath smelling of beer. "You're fired."

"You're my replacement?"

"They say you freakin' up and split. What's with that?"

Anger flared but she tried not to show it. She turned on her heels and headed back to the bus stop.

"I say something wrong?" Clifford called out.

When Jane returned to her apartment she was shocked to see an eviction notice posted on her door. Eviction? How was that possible? She was only one month behind in rent.

She knocked on the apartment manager's door. Squat Mrs. Kovacs answered. She wore a sweatshirt featuring frolicking garden gnomes.

"What's this?" Jane asked showing her the notice.

"Yes, I know, Jane. There's nothing I can do." Miss Kovacs was from Eastern Europe, her accent thick.

"But I thought we had an agreement. I told you, I can pay half and make it up next month."

"It is not my doing, darling. The new property management company, they insist. They say you are behind in rent so often that you've broken your lease, and want you out for good."

"But I can make it up. If you just give me some time."

"The new property management, I tell them this for you, darling. But they say *no*, they say it is new policy. I'm so sorry, Jane. Are you hungry? I've made chicken dumplings. Come, please, come in and eat."

Jane said nothing more and returned to her apartment. Sitting on her couch, the eviction notice in her hand, she thought about what Cooper had said. He was searching for a partner in crime to do something illegal, he made that clear. But Jane was trained as an actress, and playing a part in his scheme could be the role of a lifetime.

His wife, this shill, it's a part. This is an acting job.

Cooper needed someone to play a convincing character. It would be a flawed character, an accomplice, but flawed characters are the best kind. And deep down Jane knew she could play this role. *I can bring the character to life.*

She picked up the phone to call Cooper but remembered Verizon had shut off her service. In the drawer where she kept her laundry detergent she found enough quarters for a phone call.

She walked to the 7-Eleven.

She waited until sirens cleared in the distance before calling on the payphone. She was planning on leaving a message but was surprised when Cooper answered.

"It's me. Tell me more about this job."

CHAPTER 6

Cooper said he couldn't talk business over the phone. He had sent a car service for her but the Lincoln she had ridden over in was gone now. Jane was punching Cooper's security code into the polished brass keypad of the gated entrance when she sensed the men behind her. They were watching.

Frantic, she punched the four-digit code a second time before the buzzer finally sounded. She entered. The heavy gate clanged shut behind her. She broke into a run until she reached Cooper's boat.

"I think those men are following me."

They walked casually by, one waving to Cooper.

"Hey, Coop," he said.

"Taking her out today?" Cooper called out to them.

"Catalina for the Avalon Blues Festival."

"Nice."

Jane felt foolish for not recognizing them from the night she was here with Carla.

"Louis and Jim," he said. "They've got the thirty-two footer."

She let out a sigh. "I thought they were...I was sure they were following me."

"They're quite harmless...um, a couple, if you know what I mean. Nice guys."

"My active imagination."

"Let's eat."

In the galley down below Cooper made tuna-fish sandwiches on toasted rye. Jane, sitting at the dining table, opened a manila folder. There was a photo of a man in his fifties, stocky with a rugged face. He wore a stylish business suit and scowled to the camera.

"He looks mean," she said.

"Wolff is not known for his kindness or sense of humor."

"His name is Wolff?

"Alexander Wolff, real estate tycoon. Moves fortunes."

"Moves?"

"Like Bobby Fischer, the chess player, that's how Wolff rolls. Aggressive strategy, with speed and a take no prisoners style. Rook takes knight. Sacrifice the pawn. Go in for the kill. As much as I skirt the law now and again, Wolff makes me look like a pure amateur."

"How much *do* you skirt the law?"

"I only go after those who can afford it."

"And Wolff can afford it?"

"In spades. He also brokers in bonds, precious metal, off shore investments, but real estate mostly. He owns high-rises all over the world, many in Hong Kong. Oil wells. And he loves horse racing. Owns a stable of promising thoroughbreds."

"Hong Kong? Is he British?"

"South African and very serious about his privacy." Cooper set the toasted tuna-fish sandwich on the table and took a seat. He poured her lemonade and continued, "He purchased a prized thoroughbred yearling last year in Lexington, Kentucky, and he's coming out here to race it."

Cooper produced a picture of a horse standing in an auction ring and said, "It's got considerable pedigree. His sire won The Dubai World Cup."

Jane sipped her lemonade and asked, "So how does it work, this scam?"

"I propose a diamond deal."

"Diamonds are a girl's best friend."

"Excuse me?"

"Marilyn's life was so sad, when you think about it."

"Who?"

"Marilyn Monroe."

"What's that have to do with anything?"

"It doesn't."

"Pay attention. I'll whet his appetite with real diamonds then swap out for phony, counterfeit stones. Afterward he'll be too embarrassed to go to the cops."

"How's that?"

"To not compromise his image as a world-class deal maker."

Jane took a bite of her sandwich, chunks of pickle mixed into the tuna salad. It reminded her of the way her mother used to make them. "What makes you think he'll go for the scheme?" she asked.

"For a con to work, the mark has to have one distinctive character trait." Cooper paused for dramatic effect. "That, Miss Innes, is greed. Alexander Wolff drips it from his pores, and he's got a monster ego. The horse racing proves he's a gambler. His greed will lead him to our trap. His ego will keep him from squealing afterward."

Cooper was so confident. She felt comfortable sitting next to him, like somehow she belonged there.

"Why me? I mean, there has to be other women... professionals."

"I considered that. But I'm betting he won't suspect you."

"Why not?"

"You have an innocence."

"I'm not all *that* innocent," she said.

Cooper pulled out another file and handed it to her—the image of a beautiful woman on a polo field, high cheek bones and long silky black hair. She was exquisite—could be in one of the fashion magazines back at her apartment.

"That's Alexander's fiancé," Cooper said.

"She's beautiful."

"Alexander Wolff is impossible to get close to. He's evasive and cold, very guarded. The best have tried, salesmen, bankers, nobody can get near. But Veronica is different, more down to earth. That's how we'll get to Wolff." He rested his hand on the top of hers. "That's your job. The entire deal rests on your ability to make her acquaintance, and then become her friend to earn her trust."

Jane studied the picture, trying to imagine what Veronica would be like in real life.

"Veronica is a biblical name," she said. "The woman who cleansed Christ's face at a station of the cross." Jane remembered that from catechism.

"I suppose. We've got to create a random, off-hand encounter. You'll befriend her and set up a dinner. I'll take over from there."

"Why would she want to be my friend?"

"Listen," Cooper leaned in, "that kind of thinking, wipe it out of your mind. You've got to be positive that she'll want to know you."

"Why?"

"I'm going to train you, make you absolutely convincing as a woman from a sophisticated background, having been privileged all your life. I'll tell you what to say and how to say it. She'll *want* to know you."

Jane studied the photographs.

"If you are going to do this," Cooper said, "then I have to make one thing clear."

She met his eyes.

"You've got to do everything I say, without hesitation. Do you understand? No matter what." He sat back waiting for her reply.

"I understand," Jane said. She finished her lemonade. Out of nervousness she chewed the ice. "I need six hundred bucks to fix my car, and another fifteen hundred to catch up on my rent."

"Your rent?"

"And I need three hundred and sixty for the phone company," she said. "And I owe my neighbor Carla about five hundred bucks."

"Don't worry about that."

"Then forget it!" Jane said, angered. "Find yourself another shill."

Cooper burst out laughing. "Hold on. Don't worry. I'll take care of everything. You're not going to need to pay rent because you'll be staying with me. And you won't need a car because we'll drive together. You're going to leave your old life behind."

"But I owe that money, and I want my car."

"Fine, but you can't drive it."

"Why not?"

"It will stick out. Remember, you're someone completely different, a refined young lady, royalty. You're right; you'll need some walking around money." He peeled off a few hundred-dollar bills from his money clip, laying them on the table in the condensation mark of her glass. "If it makes you feel better, I understand your scruples."

"What about my stuff?"

"We'll put your things in storage." Cooper picked up the money and held it out to her, meeting her eyes again. "Take it."

Jane hesitated. Deep inside something told her not to reach for the bills. But something tugged from the other direction. If she accepted his money she would be obligated, his employee. If she didn't she could still walk away.

"Well?" he asked.

Jane took the money.

The new bills were crisp. Jane took her wallet from her purse and placed them inside. "How much are we going to make?" she asked.

"Let's talk about that in the car. We've got some shopping to do."

CHAPTER 7

They drove over Mulholland Pass and dipped into the San Fernando Valley. Smog reigned and long-range visibility was low—a blanket of brown haze seemingly trapped forever.

"How much?" Jane asked.

Cooper rubbed his chin, teasing, as if deep in thought. "Hard to tell because math is not one of my strengths. I figure twenty percent of the take is your end."

"Why not fifty-fifty?"

"Because I cover the expenses, I've done all the leg work and I'm the boss. You're lucky to get twenty. I got five percent on my first job, and was grateful as hell."

Thirty minutes later Jane stood before an assortment of pistols neatly arranged in a glass case.

"Which one do you like?" Cooper asked.

She studied them, some black, others chrome. They stood in the showroom of the VIP Gun Club, an exclusive indoor shooting range housed in a reinforced cinderblock industrial park building in Simi Valley. She could hear occasional muffled shots fired beyond the diamond-plate steel door.

"I've never shot a real gun," she said.

"I don't expect you'll ever have to. But just in case, as insurance, you're going to buy one."

"I could never shoot anyone."

"Like I said, you won't have to."

"Then why do I need one?"

"For protection."

"Protection from what?"

"Think of it as an ace in the hole. Nobody needs to know you have it. It will give you a sense of security, and confidence. You'll always be in control. And if you ever get in a pinch..."

"Do you carry a gun?"

"When I'm working."

"Are you carrying one now?"

"We're not working yet." He glanced down at the case. "I say you give that Colt Auto a whirl," he said, pointing to a .32 chrome pistol with white pearl handles.

Jane considered the weapon. It looked harmless enough.

"It's small enough to fit in a purse," he added.

Moments later, standing in the indoor shooting range, the gun felt snug in her hand. The steel was cold and it was heavier than it looked. He taught her how to insert the clip, hold the gun, aim.

He'd bought ammunition and a paper target of a man's torso, a silhouette of a scowling hoodlum pointing a gun, the bulls-eye highlighted by black oval rings in the middle of the man's chest. Jane thought it sad that the paper target was of a human being, not a round target, like in archery. An automated pulley sent the paper target out to fifty feet.

"Okay. Give it a try."

Jane hesitated.

She had once shot a prop gun loaded with blanks in the movie she acted in, a low budget science fiction film titled *Gemini.* In between takes a professional gun wrangler swapped the pistols loaded with blanks with identical plastic ones for rehearsals and wider shots. But this weapon had real bullets. It scared her.

"Come on," Cooper urged her. "You can do it." He wrapped his arms around her.

She raised the gun, aimed and pulled the trigger.

It was loud, even with her earmuffs on. But after a while Jane got the hang of it. She was surprised by the power of the thing.

When they were out of ammo he led her back to the counter.

They registered the gun in Jane's name. Cooper explained that both the Brady Bill and California law required that the handgun remain at the store for two weeks after the purchase. The FBI would run a background check. Since she didn't have a criminal record she'd be allowed to return and pick up the gun in a "fortnight," the actual word he used. Jane knew that was a term from Shakespeare, heard that expression since working on *Gemini*. The director was nicknamed "Johnny Fortnight" because he had made so many low-budget genre films, most of them shot in just two weeks.

"It's called the cooling off period," the bearded old man behind the counter explained.

Cooper helped her fill out the paperwork then paid for the gun with cash. She had never seen him use cash before, only credit cards. Back in the Jaguar, he said, "Okay, now that we've got that taken care of, let's get you something to wear. Dress you up a bit."

"Dressed to kill?" she asked.

"Precisely."

CHAPTER 8

The silk felt cool against her skin. As the dress caressed Jane's torso when she moved the feeling made her quiver. She felt so sexy, aroused. She could not recall ever having worn anything so beautiful.

Cooper had taken her to an exclusive boutique in Beverly Hills. She was trying on a delicate evening gown in front of the mirror, backless, provocative, yet classy.

"What do you think?" Cooper asked, studying her.

"It's incredible!"

"You'll need heels with that." He turned to the haughty saleswoman, "She's going to need the right kind. And an evening wrap."

"Of course."

Jane knew her type, a middle-aged retail professional wearing Chanel No. 5—hair in a tight bun and skewered with an ivory chopstick.

"Just look at you," Cooper said. "Beautiful."

She looked in the mirror. The last time she felt like this was prom night.

The saleswoman returned with the shoes, then later a sleek designer business suit, skirt cut high. Cooper said he liked the way this "number" accentuated Jane's shapely legs. The saleswoman was quick to produce Italian leather black pumps.

Jane barely recognized herself.

As the saleswoman was busy ringing up the items Jane took him by the hand and led him into the dressing room.

"What are you doing?"

"Ssshh," she said closing the door.

Intoxicated, she unbuttoned his pants then worked her hands below his waist.

"Jane, I don't think…"

To silence him she bit his lip as playful punishment so it was clear she was leading this dance. She worked her mouth around the back of his ear.

She could feel him getting hard.

She stripped her panties off, dropped them at her heels.

"What about…?"

"That bitch can wait," she whispered in his ear.

She pulled his slacks down, and then his briefs. She propped one of her legs up on the bench and he grabbed her behind. His warm hands squeezed tight.

She wriggled until they found each other.

Jane stared at herself in the mirror, said, "Say my name."

"Jane," he whispered.

"Louder"

He complied.

"No. Louder. Say it so the saleslady hears."

Hearing him shout her name at this moment was incredibly exciting. He took charge, increased the pace. She let herself go.

She tried to watch herself in the reflection until the sensation became so intense and she had to close her eyes. The climax came quick and strong. It was *so good*, powerful—a release that brought tears. She bit his neck, her mouth wet. Cooper maneuvered her into the corner, pressing her bare ass against the glass, holding up one of her legs, driving.

This new position paid off in spades—a jackpot. She came again. He followed soon after. Bar none—this was the best orgasm she'd ever had.

CHAPTER 9

With Cooper's money Jane was able to pay her overdue tuition and Jeremy ceased picking on her. In class Jeremy showed little encouragement toward Cooper but took credit for Jane's newfound confidence.

"This boldness, the strong convictions," Jeremy said, "these fresh choices you've brought to your work, they complement you, my dear. And you wear them well. You are progressing well in my class."

Cooper and Jane shared a glance. Jane knew all this was Cooper's doing. He had reshaped her. He was the one who'd created the new persona.

Later that night on the boat Cooper gave Jane her new name: Kimberly VanCise. "Old money, Dutch-Catholic," he said. "That's you."

"Tell me more about her."

"Refined. Educated. She's graceful, cares for others, yet knows how to have a good time. She's unpretentious."

"What'd she study?"

"Russian literature. Know anything about that?"

"A little about Chekhov's plays."

"That's a start."

"Where'd I go to school?"

"Brown University. Ivy League but not too obvious. You got a Masters, but don't mention that unless it comes up."

"I got a Masters?"

"Your trust fund encouraged a higher education."

These few details sent Jane's imagination whirling. She asked, "What's your name going to be?"

"Charles VanCise."

"Like that. It's got a ring to it."

The next day Cooper and Jane moved her things out of her apartment and into a nearby storage unit. She paid Carla the money she owed, and told her that she was going out of town on an acting job. Close enough to the truth, really. Carla was happy for Jane and wished her luck.

Cooper and Jane no longer spent evenings out. He insisted she study her background, read Tolstoy and Dostoyevsky, and undergo rigorous training. He taught her to walk and talk. He spent hours on her table manners since, as he put it, "so much of the time we will spend with both Wolff and Veronica will be over meals."

Gone was their courtship; this was schooling.

One morning Cooper's cell phone rang. Jane looked on as Cooper nodded and listened intently. He got up and paced while on the phone. It was clearly the tip he'd been waiting for.

"Great. Thank you." Cooper hung up and turned to Jane. "Alexander Wolff is going to be here in three days."

"Veronica, too?

"Yes. We don't have much time."

CHAPTER 10

Alexander Wolff had reservations at the Bel Air. Jane knew the hotel was known for two things: a famous bar where countless Hollywood deals were supposedly negotiated, sometimes on the back of a cocktail napkin, and an exceptional spa that rivaled those found in the luxurious desert retreats of Arizona or Palm Springs. Cooper assumed Veronica would spend time in the spa. This is where Jane would make her introduction. When he insisted they do a preliminary scout of the location, Jane put on her new business suit and tied up her hair.

After driving up a tree-lined road into Bel Air they arrived to face a spiffy brigade of valets, tanned college-aged guys who could easily be fashion models, Jane thought. They opened Jane's car door and handed Cooper a ticket with white-toothed smiles.

What first caught Jane's eye was the hotel's expansive grounds and meticulous landscaping. They passed through the garden lobby and moved to the bar for a drink.

Cooper ordered for her. "The lady will have a cosmopolitan, and bring me a Woodford Manhattan, straight up." When the waitress left he turned to her and said, "As Kimberly, you'll order only cosmopolitans or Absolute Martinis. Don't ever ask for wine."

"But I like wine," she said.

"Not knowing wine reeks bourgeois. It's a dead give-away."

"I know my wine."

"Not the wine that Kimberly drinks. Trust me."

She figured he was right and asked "What's in a cosmopolitan, anyway?" having only read about them in fashion magazines.

"Vodka, cranberry, triple sec. It's what debutantes drink. You'll like it."

"Kimberly would drink it?"

"Since college. And also, forget those Lifesaver candies you eat all the time. Kimberly wouldn't do that."

"Okay," she agreed, knowing deep down she'd miss them.

When the drink came Jane sipped it with apprehensively but was pleasantly surprised. It really did taste good. All it took was this little detail, this sensory hit of flavor enhanced by alcohol and her character kicked in.

She was no longer Jane Innes. She was now Kimberly Van-Cise. It felt great. She sat up taller—a new persona.

Cooper asked for the menu from the hotel's restaurant and showed Jane not only what to order, but how to order it. He also said she must make a mental note of the first names of the hotel staff without having to rely on their name-tags. It would not only encourage them to remember hers, but imply that she stays at the hotel often.

Kyle Foster, a successful actor in his twenties she recognized from the movies, entered the bar with an entourage of friends, hipsters and all under-dressed for the place. They settled into a booth in the rear.

Cooper caught Jane checking them out. "You know him?"

"That's Kyle Foster."

"Who?"

"He's a movie star. He used to date Jessica Sanchez."

Cooper craned his neck. "I don't see many movies."

Jane realized Cooper was from another generation. How could he not know Kyle Foster? Veronica, their mark, was a good twenty years younger than Alexander Wolff judging from the photos Cooper had shown her. She glanced around the bar. With the exception of Kyle and his jean-clad friends, Jane could see most of the men were with women much younger. Were these men's second or third wives? Mistresses? That's the difference between the "haves" and the "have-nots," she thought.

It was the first time she'd ever thought of Cooper as being old.

"Finish up, beautiful," he said, "let's take a stroll." She liked that he called her beautiful.

They walked by one of the pools and he pointed out the exclusive bungalows adjacent to the main hotel.

"That's where Wolff stays," Cooper explained. "We can keep an eye on his room from the pool."

On their way out Cooper stopped at the front desk and con-firmed details of Wolff's reservation. Outside he tipped the valet a twenty dollar bill and minutes later they were in the Jaguar.

Gliding down the hill he asked, "So, what was her name?"

"Who?"

"Our waitress at the bar."

"This a test?"

"Were you paying attention?"

"Maureen. Irish name."

"You're going to do fine."

Jane put her hand on the inside of his leg, something Kimber-ly would do, as they rolled down the hill and out of Bel Air.

The next week Cooper spent a lot of time on his computer, and Jane practiced her new persona day and night. She walked in character, ate in character, spoke and laughed in character. Little mannerisms and details blossomed. Kimberly was starting to function on her own, surprising Jane sometimes.

The character was taking on life.

A FedEx package arrived, and Cooper received new credit

cards, all inscribed with an alias. Jane asked him how he did it but Cooper merely said, "You'll learn in time."

Finally the day came. They packed their things and moved into the hotel.

The room was the standard deluxe suite. But Jane had never stayed in a place like this before. The carpet was fine-weave wool, the bathroom marble, the fixtures gold-plated. As she was hanging her new clothes in the closet, her cell phone buzzed. She did not recognize the number so decided to check her voice mail. She picked up the hotel phone and was about to dial when Cooper stopped her.

"What are you doing?"

"Checking my messages."

"Not from this phone. The hotel keeps a record of every call."

"Oh, right. Sorry." Jane felt so dumb.

"Use my cell," he said giving her his phone. "We'll never use that phone, unless it's room-to-room, or to the desk. Understand?"

"Yes."

"Good."

Jane dialed and listened. It was a message from her mother.

"Hi, Jane, we're here in Los Angeles. Call me. I want to see you, honey."

Deflated, Jane sank into the bed.

"My mom, she's in town."

"Where?"

"In Pomona. At the Winter Nationals."

"What's that?"

"A drag race." Jane was so embarrassed. "Her boyfriend is on the Winston Cup Racing Team. They travel the circuit this time of year."

"Listen Jane, I—"

"Don't worry; I'm not going to call her back." She stood and went back to hanging up her clothes, feeling him watch her.

"I think you should," he said.

"Should what?"

"Call her back. If not, she'll worry. If she thinks you're missing, she may call the cops and that wouldn't be good."

"She'll insist on seeing me. I can't get out of it."

"I'm sure we can carve out time." Cooper checked his watch. "Wolff's flight has arrived. They should be here any time now. Come on."

Cooper led Jane into the bar and sat a table with a view of the front desk. Jane ordered a cosmopolitan. Cooper reached into his jacket and pulled out two rings.

"Put these on," he said.

Jane gasped. One was a wedding band, the other a diamond engagement ring.

"We're supposed to be married."

"Oh, right," she said. Tears welled up but she had to remind herself this was not real. Cooper was not proposing to her. This was all part of the role, and these beautiful rings were mere props.

As time passed her nerves got the best of her.

"You all right?" Cooper asked,

"Butterflies," she said.

"Butterflies?"

"In the stomach. Dress rehearsal."

"Oh." Cooper laughed. "Don't worry, we won't approach them tonight. We're just taking a look."

As if on cue Jane watched the bellman cross the lobby and step outside. Car doors slammed. Voices echoed. After a moment Veronica and Alexander Wolff made their entrance.

"There they are," Cooper whispered.

Wolff entered the lobby first. Jane could tell he was a man who'd spent most of his life in charge of things. The woman with him was hidden behind a tall, dark younger man with a shaved head carrying luggage—a bodyguard, Jane guessed.

Then she got a good view of the woman. Jane's first thought

was that Veronica was more beautiful in person. She was taller than she appeared in the photograph. As she walked she led with her hips in a fluid motion. Like a swan, or a doe—sensual. It reminded Jane of something she once had learned in acting class; that when breaking down a character the actor should make the choice to lead with either hips, head, or heart. Veronica led with her hips.

As quickly as they'd come, they were gone. The bell staff followed with carts of luggage.

Jane released a deep sigh.

Cooper turned to her. "What do you think?" he said.

"Bring it on," Jane said before downing the last of her drink.

CHAPTER 11

Jane was up early. The light was soft in their hotel room, the sheer drapes casting a faint glow. She could hear birds chirp outside and an occasional door slam down the hall. Jane settled into the plush sofa and was reading the complimentary *New York Times* when Cooper stirred under the duvet cover and sat up.

"You sleep alright?" she asked.

"Why?"

"You were tossing and turning all night."

Without answering he got up, scratching himself and staggering to the bathroom. "Order room service," he said before closing the door.

She could hear the shower turn on as she searched for the menu. Appalled at the exorbitant prices, Jane kept it simple. She ordered the continental breakfast for two which included a pot of coffee. Coffee was what she needed most.

Jane turned on the television. In silence, she and Cooper watched the morning news while eating breakfast.

"You might think about getting ready," he said.

Countdown to curtain, she thought.

Jane fell back on her training to transform into character as she changed into her costume. She did this now, concentrating on how Kimberly would dress herself. Cooper had ordered cotton drawstring pants and a Brown University sweatshirt.

Jane had washed the sweatshirt a few times to make it feel worn-in. By the time she eased into her sandals, she was ready.

"Good luck," Cooper said.

"You're not supposed to say that!"

"Why not?"

"You're supposed to say 'break a leg.' You should know that."

"Oh. What else am I not supposed to say?"

"A lot of things."

"Like?"

"The name of the Scottish Play in a theatre."

"What's that?"

"Shakespeare's *Macbeth*."

"Why not?"

"It's bad luck."

"Who says?"

"Forget it." She kissed him, a quick peck on the cheek—not her style, but the way she envisioned Kimberly would kiss her husband Charles goodbye.

Walking through the hotel she was a little nervous, which she knew was good—like an athlete before an event. She was ready for the challenge.

Jane strolled outside, crossed a bridge over a delicate koi pond, and entered the Asian-themed spa. A pleasant young woman with a perfect complexion greeted her at the reception desk, jotting down her name and room number. Jane declined the offer for a deep tissue massage and scanned the place. There were a few women lounging in the waiting area reading or watching television, but no Veronica. An attendant gave her a thick robe and directed her to the changing room.

At a full-length mahogany locker, Jane undressed and slipped into the robe before checking out the sauna, Jacuzzi and whirlpool. In an exercise room a yoga instructor modified the positions of her few students.

Still no Veronica.

Jane kicked off her sandals, disrobed and slipped into the Jacuzzi. The water was hot and took getting used to. She submerged her body in stages until she was neck deep and had a good view of the place. Jane closed her eyes. This is how it feels to be Kimberly.

Moments later Jane was startled to see Veronica moving toward the Jacuzzi wrapped in a terry cloth robe. She watched out of the corner of her eye as Veronica disrobed near Jane. She could see Veronica was in excellent shape, her back muscles shapely, and her legs long and firm.

Jane closed her eyes again, and opened them when she felt Veronica slip in the water on the opposite side of the Jacuzzi.

"Good morning," Jane said.

"Hi," Veronica said, adjusting her hair into a ponytail.

Jane casually glanced away, searching for a way to open the conversation, something off-hand.

But then Veronica spoke first. "I love these places."

"This one's really nice," Jane said.

"Have you ever been to Canyon Ranch?" Veronica asked.

"That's in Arizona, right?"

"Just outside Tuscon."

"I haven't, but friends say it's great."

"I highly recommend it."

Jane said nothing and considered her next move. Cooper taught her it was best not to lead the conversation, but steer it. Small talk was one thing, but she knew she would have to get to a more intimate place, a commonality between them.

"My husband's here on business…. what brings you to Los Angeles?" Jane asked.

"Same. My fiancé has meetings all week."

"Where are you from?" Jane asked.

"Cape Town, but I grew up in New York."

"Oh. Did you live in the city?"

"Raised upstate, but I met Alexander in Manhattan, when I used to live there."

She offered me his name. That was a good sign.

"Charles and I met in the city as well. At an auction at Christie's." Jane felt good that Cooper's alias rolled off her tongue so easily. "He outbid me for a signed first-edition of Jane Austen's *Pride and Prejudice* and I was furious. Then he asked me to lunch, the rascal. Do you make it to New York often?"

"Not as often as I'd like."

Jane made idle conversation about a number of things, all rehearsed—her supposed ski chalet in Sun Valley, her supposed education and travels. When Veronica broached the subject of movies Jane was glad. This was something she could talk freely about without having to fake it. They chatted about various stars and Hollywood gossip.

As they became acquainted, Jane found Veronica to be surprisingly laid back, and she seemed like a lot of fun. They moved to the sauna and then to the whirlpool. Finally the two retreated to separate showers. Jane finished quickly, and was dressed when Veronica emerged from the frosted glass stalls and moved to the sink.

When Veronica was brushing her jet-black hair Jane figured she'd take a stab at it. "Since we're both staying here maybe we should arrange a dinner some evening. My husband would love to commiserate with a fellow New Yorker," Jane said.

Veronica looked over in the reflection of the mirror. "I'll ask if Alexander's got the time," she said.

"We're in suite three twenty," Jane said and turned to go, "It was really nice meeting you."

"Likewise," Veronica said.

Jane walked briskly back to her room, through the garden and past the pool. She felt good about how it went—the groundwork. Cooper was in the room waiting for her, watching television. He muted the volume as she sat down and recounted every detail.

He listened silently, nodding. Something was definitely wrong. He seemed angry.

"Everything all right?" she asked.

"When were you going to tell me about this?" he asked, motioning to the television. Jane turned and was astonished to see *Gemini*, the B-movie she performed in years ago. Amid explosions and gunfights rebel cyborgs battled mutant troopers. The movie's costumes, special effects and props came off laughably low-budget. On screen Jane was bent over a dying cyborg soldier prying the weapon from his hands. She wore leather pants the tight black-vinyl corset accentuated her breasts.

"I can't believe it," she said, sinking into the chair.

"Is that really you?"

"Oh shit."

"Why didn't you tell me? What if Alexander or Veronica sees this?"

"What are the chances they'll ever—?"

"It's a porno on the hotel pay-per-view!" he said, furious.

Jane was shocked to see another scene spliced in, a futuristic orgy of some kind. A space ship interior was crowded with satin circular beds. These actors were different from the original cast and she did not recognize any of them. It was clear this scene was shot later, or more likely cut in from another picture. An X-rated picture.

"That wasn't part of our movie!"

Jane explained that she'd performed in the low-budget movie years ago but the film had never seen the light of day. She assumed it had been shelved forever. "This other stuff, this porn stuff, that wasn't in the script."

They watched as a big-haired vixen in ridiculous shoulder-pads performed fellatio, servicing a well-endowed space commander.

Jane felt like crying.

"I checked," Cooper said. "There are only three skin flicks on the hotel pay-per-view. This is one of them. If they're into this sort of thing the chances they will see this are good, depending on their preference."

To think *this* movie was on her resume, stapled to the back of her headshot sitting in casting offices all over town. She wished she could call her agent and scream, but she did not have an agent. She felt so betrayed, dirty.

The movie returned to Jane and her leading man, Curtis, retreating through smoky, pipe-filled tunnels. This footage was part of the original script. It all came back to her, a wash of memories.

"We shot that scene at the water treatment plant," she said.

"The what?" he said searching the mini bar.

"The sewer."

"Why doesn't that surprise me?"

CHAPTER 12

The next morning Jane was back in the spa. There was no sign of Veronica. She sat in the lounge area because this gave her a good view of the spa's entrance. She read magazines and sipped green tea. The staff tried again to sell her on their assortment of options: aroma therapy, pedicures and exotic mud baths, but she politely refused.

Finally Veronica appeared, and Jane hid behind a *Vanity Fair* magazine. When it was clear she had moved into the dressing room, Jane gave it a few minutes before getting up. She found Veronica undressing.

"What a nice surprise," Jane said.

Veronica yawned. "Oh, excuse me. I couldn't fall asleep so I watched TV all night," she said.

"Must be jet lag," Jane said hoping Veronica had not explored the pay-per-view choices. They made a plan, decided on a light workout in the gym, a sauna and then the Jacuzzi. It wasn't until they were neck deep in wet beauty-clay, and there was a lull in the conversation, that Jane found the opportunity.

"The four of us *should* have dinner."

"I'll check with Alexander. Tonight is probably best. He's got a hectic schedule the rest of the week."

"Charles will be back early, and the restaurant here is quite good."

"Say eight?"

"Perfect."
She had pulled it off. Cooper would be happy.
A wave of accomplishment came over her, goose-bumps of excitement under the cake of therapeutic mud.

CHAPTER 13

"Damn it," Jane said when she noticed a run in her stockings.

"Slow down." Cooper went to the drawer and handed her a new pair. "You're going to be fine. Keep Veronica amused while Wolff and I talk business. At some point I'll cue you to prompt me. When I nudge you under the table, find a graceful way to urge me to talk about my diamond deal, just like we talked about. I'll play reluctant, but push it. Insist I tell the story. Got that?"

"Yeah," she said. Between the details of her privileged background, what she and Veronica had previously talked about, and now this extra stuff; there was so much to remember.

Jane took her time with the new pair of stockings. She clipped them carefully to the garter on her thigh. They felt so different than nylon. These retro silk-stockings did not cling the same but as nylon, but Jane realized "Kimberly" would wear classic stockings like these. *The costume completes the character.*

Cooper zipped the back of her dress and kissed her bare shoulder. "You're beautiful."

"You keep saying that."

"Because you are."

They walked through the hotel grounds, her heels a challenge on the uneven concrete. It was chilly and the clouds at dusk were a splash of bronze superimposed against a deep cobalt sky.

Jane and Cooper arrived at the restaurant a little early. He tipped the maître d' and requested a private table. He also made it clear that the bill was to come to him.

"Yes, sir, of course," the maître d' said and led Cooper and Jane to the table set inside a bay window overlooking the tropical garden. There was live music in the bar. She recognized the Billy Holiday jazz standard. *"All of me, why not take all of me, can't you see, I'm no good without you."*

The maître d' led Veronica and Wolff to the table. Wolff's bodyguard brought up the rear. Jane had not seen this intensely handsome man since the evening they checked into the hotel. He hung back as Wolff and Veronica approached.

Jane made the introductions. The men shook hands and exchanged pleasantries. Cooper edged up behind Jane and tended to her chair. He had never done that before. She could see this was Cooper's time to shine.

The waiter took their drink orders and Jane saw the bodyguard drift off. He found a seat at the bar.

"Veronica tells me you two met in the spa," Wolff started in.

"It's heavenly." She hoped that wasn't a stupid thing to say.

That hung there until Veronica broke the ice. "Kimberly and I have so much in common, like we've known each other forever."

Cooper and Wolff began to chat about the stock market. Veronica talked about the shopping she had done that day, what she had seen, and how the selection here in Los Angeles was so different than New York. Jane listened and nodded politely, but her ear was craned toward the men.

Cocktails arrived and the men made small talk about an assortment of things most of which Jane did not understand. Cooper spoke of his supposed background in the shipping industry, explaining that Los Angeles is the busiest port in the West. Jane could see this was his subtle prompt to get Wolff talking about what he did. Wolff admitted he was in commercial real estate investments, and Cooper said that technically he was too.

"The difference is," Cooper said, "my buildings float."

This made Wolff laugh. He sipped his single malt.

Jane could see that Cooper had made some headway. She spoke all the lies that Cooper had taught her, about their travels and the people they'd met. Cooper poured on the charm. He told crazy, fun stories and had the entire table laughing.

Jane caught Wolff's eye on a few occasions. She offered a polite smile and glanced away, fully aware that his gaze lingered.

She waited for Cooper's nudge, the signal to bring up the diamond deal.

Wine, entrees, dessert, finally coffee and cognac; still Cooper had not given her the cue. Maybe he would find another way to bring it up. Then, the dinner almost wrapped-up, the waiter brought Cooper the check. He intercepted the bill perfectly as Jane made conversation with Wolff.

Finally he nudged her.

She waited for a lull then leaned into him. "Darling," she said, "you've got to tell them about your friend Roger, the diamond thing."

"No, they won't be interested in—"

"Diamonds?" Veronica asked.

"It's nothing," Cooper said.

"It's fascinating," Jane said. "Come on."

Cooper played reluctant. Jane urged and he finally gave in. He told a story about a close friend, an old college buddy of from Princeton who moved to Brazil ten years ago and bought a diamond mine. "It turned out to be extremely profitable," he said. "He's built a significant market share but the political climate has changed. The Brazilian government is insisting that Roger pay enormous taxes, even demanding back taxes. In an effort to raise cash, and pay off the corrupt government officials, he plans to liquidate much of his inventory and get out of the business. Because the diamond market is controlled by a few major players, a sudden glut may adversely drive worldwide prices down. As a precaution, DeBeers has made an offer to buy everything from him, lock, stock and barrel, also agreeing to pay his tax bill. But they're only offering twenty cents on the dollar, and Roger is furious. He's convinced DeBeers has bribed officials in the government to chase him off. But at this point he has no choice."

Jane felt the need to improvise so added, "And he's just such a nice guy, really great. So smart and down to earth."

Cooper nodded. "It's a shame," he said. "He has to sell everything and leave the country immediately. So, to Roger's friends and family, whoever can come up with the cash, he's unloading the very best diamonds before they audit his inventory." In a dramatic pause, Cooper sipped his cognac.

Jane noticed that Wolff had leaned forward—interest piqued.

Cooper continued, "He's set aside the very best, flawless or nearly perfect stones. That being the case," Cooper reached across the table and took Jane's hand, "in a few days, it seems, we'll take possession of over two thousand diamonds."

Jane added, "I still don't know what we are going to do with them all."

"Stones of that quality," Cooper said, "A trip to Antwerp and they'll be sold within hours."

"Remember, I've been promised a diamond necklace out of this deal," Jane said to Cooper, another improvisation.

"Did I say that?"

She punched him in the arm. "What selective memory you have," Jane said, and then turned to Veronica, "But I'll settle for a tennis bracelet."

Laughs around the table.

"All of these stones are between one and two karats— engagement ring size, the backbone of the diamond trade," Cooper added. "Engagement rings demand the highest price."

"Well, I guess there's no price on love," Wolff said.

Cooper raised his cognac and proposed a toast. "Well said.

Let's drink to love."

"To love," Veronica echoed, raising hers.

They toasted and sipped.

Jane felt Wolff's leg brush up against hers—clearly intentional. She pulled her leg away, pretended not to notice.

CHAPTER 14

As they said goodnight Veronica suggested Cooper and Jane join them at the racetrack Saturday afternoon. Wolff's horse, a two-year-old filly named Turquoise, was scheduled run in her debut race at Santa Anita.

Wolff explained that Turquoise had posted solid workouts. "Bullet works," Wolff called them, "but she's yet to race."

Plans were set; a day at the races.

Cooper and Jane walked back to their room. He put his arms around her and kissed her forehead, complimenting Jane on the job she did.

She decided not to tell him about Wolff's leg brushing hers under the table, instead asked, "Is there any truth in that diamond story?"

"In Thursday's, or maybe Friday's *Wall Street Journal* there's going to be an article about the Brazilian government taxing and regulating diamond mines owned by foreigners," he said. "I've got an associate who's been holding the story until I cue him to submit it. If it runs, and our scheme works, I pay him out of our cut."

"How much?" she asked.

"He'll see a nice bonus. Trust me, it's not the first time a gatekeeper of financial information is slipped a kickback."

"Those flawless diamonds you talked about, where are we going to get them?"

"No diamond is without some kind of flaw. Even the finest stones have slight imperfections of some kind. It's just a matter of what can be perceived. A few of the diamonds will be real, the rest cubic zirconia."

She peeled off her dress, threw on the hotel's terry cloth robe, and plopped down on the duvet cover. "I'm exhausted."

"Hang that up," he said, pointing to her dress lying on the carpet. "That's professional equipment. Treat it right, damn it."

"Sorry." She got up and hung her dress in the closet. She gathered the silk stockings as well, folding them neatly.

"I feel like a nightcap," Cooper said while taking off his tie. He opened the mini bar and poured himself a scotch without offering her anything.

"Should I go to the spa again tomorrow?" she asked

"No, we don't want to wear out our welcome. Use the day to visit your mother. Take my car," Cooper said.

Jane was relieved. She needed a break.

He sipped his scotch in silence. His mind working, she could see he was in his element.

CHAPTER 15

The next morning Jane was behind the wheel of the Jaguar. The sensation of the luxury automobile gliding with precision felt so different than her Nissan. She cleared downtown and was somewhere near West Covina when a stone smacked the windshield with a loud pop.

"Shit," Jane screamed and changed lanes.

The stone left a dime-sized fracture in the glass. Gunning it, she passed the semi and glanced at the starburst shape—a thin crack on the windshield. Cooper trusted her and now she'd ruined his perfect car.

She was still lamenting the blemish by the time she reached Pomona Raceway.

Following the instructions her mother had given her, Jane maneuvered the Jaguar past the grandstands to a cluster of trailers. She slowed to see men hovering, tinkering with dragsters, some of them checking her out. She drifted through the camp until he found the trailer with "Danny Dobson Racing" painted on the side. Jane got out and her mother came running.

"My baby! My baby Jane!" she squealed, embracing her daughter. "Why look at you!" she said with tears of joy in her eyes. She turned to the trailer. "Danny, come meet my precious daughter."

Danny Dobson, a lean and tanned man in his late-fifties, emerged from the Winnebago.

"Danny, my daughter Jane."

Danny sized up the Jaguar before he approached. He offered his hand. "It's nice to meet you," he said with a soft-spoken drawl, a tinge of West Texas, Jane guessed.

"It's really nice to meet you, too," Jane said.

They made small talk, and Danny's casual manner put her at ease. She felt good that her mom was involved with a genuinely nice guy. There had been so many bad ones.

After introductions and pleasantries, Nancy and Danny opened the trailer and showed Jane the dragster. Danny explained they were here to attend the NHRA Pomona Winter Nationals. "A lucky qualifying round," he said, "could pencil-out to thousands in purse money and a guarantee sanction for next season." Danny checked his watch and excused himself, apologizing for having to attend a meeting. He grabbed a pack of cigarettes and walked toward the grandstands.

Jane and her mother took a stroll.

"He's good to me," Nancy said, "and we have fun, traveling the circuit, it's an adventure."

"I'm happy for you, Mom."

"Enough about me, tell me about you. You a movie star yet?"

"No."

"That car and your nice clothes. Must be doing well."

"I'm doing a little bit of work here and there."

"Do you have a boyfriend?"

"Yeah. It's his car, not mine."

"Is he good to you?"

"Yeah, he is."

"Then we'll all have to get together. We're here until Monday. You two have to come out Saturday and see Danny race. We'll get you pit passes."

"I can't, Mom, sorry. I'm working, and he's out of town."

"Oh," she said, clearly disappointed. "What's your boyfriend's name?"

"Cooper. I'm sorry we can't make it."

"Nonsense. You can find the time. I want Danny to get to know you."

"I can't," Jane said, getting agitated. Her mom had a way of getting on Jane's nerves. "I'm sorry. Matter of fact, I'll be going out of town for a long time, out of the country."

"Where are you going?"

"A lot of places."

"Sounds exciting."

"Yeah."

There was an awkward silence.

"You and your acting bug," Nancy said. "Just as long as you're happy. That's what's important. Are you happy?"

"I am, Mom."

"I'm glad."

They walked in silence for a while. Nancy pulled out a cigarette and offered one but Jane refused.

Nancy lit hers and said, "Let's sit down for a sec." They took a seat on the bleachers as engines revved in the distance. Nancy took a drag of her smoke. "I know I didn't give you the greatest childhood, moving around as we did. Never had much. I'm sorry."

"Mom, you did great."

"I have my regrets."

"You raised me good," Jane said, realizing she'd used terrible grammar. Her character Kimberly would never speak that way.

"Your father," Nancy said, "I've always told you he was a man who came and went." Nancy paused. "That's true, but only part of the story. Now you're old enough you should know everything."

"Everything what?" Jane asked, wondering where this was leading.

"Before you were born your father went to jail. And that's where he died. He got killed inside. Knifed in a fight. I'm sorry for not telling you sooner."

Jane swallowed hard then said, "For what?"

"I'm not sure what for. Prison is a horrible place."

"No, I mean, what was he in for?"

"He wrote a few bad checks. We were young and dumb. Reckon we partied way too much. I'm sorry I never told you, but I wanted you to know. Just so you can be assured that he won't be coming around. So you can put it to rest."

Jane looked into her mother's eyes, thought about the struggles the two of them endured together, the different men her mother had dated, young Jane in tow. She recalled the fights, the failures and the midnight evictions.

At that moment it became clear, why the desire to be an actress had been so strong. Acting had always been an escape from her dismal life—a better place to go. And her mother encouraged her every step of the way. The dream was both of theirs.

Jane leaned in and hugged her mom. "You did great, Ma, and I love you."

"Love you too, baby."

Jane sat back and wiped tears. "I have to go."

"So soon?"

"Work. I'm sorry."

"Stay. We'll have dinner. Work can't be that important."

"It is. I'm sorry."

Nancy glanced out over the pavement. The wind blew her hair back and Jane noticed wrinkles in her mom's face she had never seen before.

"Keep in touch," Nancy said, forlorn. "Call, email, or text, whatever." Nancy reached in her jeans and came up with Danny's business card.

Jane took it. "If I can."

"If you can? What's that mean? If you can?" Jane could see Nancy was getting angry.

"Like I said, I'll be out of the country for a while. But don't worry, I'll write, I promise."

Nancy eased, smiled, "I know you will."

They got up and walked back to the Jaguar, hugged a tearful farewell. The last thing Jane heard was her mother say, "Goodbye, my baby Jane. Make me proud."

Driving back Jane could see the chip in the windshield had grown. Like a cancer, she had a feeling this gruesome crack would spread more and more.

She thought about what Cooper had said, how each and every diamond has some kind of flaw, some more than others. Now the Jaguar was imperfect and she knew it was her fault.

She tried to imagine her father. Like a character in a play, or in fiction, she realized he was ultimately flawed—a tragic hero. It all made sense, why she was drawn to Cooper's deceitful plan in the first place. Her inherent flaws, her imperfections were like the crack in the windshield. She'd been born with them—stigma imprinted in her DNA. Immorality was passed down by a man she would never know.

Driving west on Interstate 10 Jane became more and more obsessed with the crack in the windshield. It lengthened more and took shape of a skeleton hand—wretched and cruel.

CHAPTER 16

The diamond necklace was magnificent.

"Where'd you get it?" Jane asked.

Cooper stood behind her at the mirror, clipping the sparkling pendant around her neck. "You claimed were getting a diamond necklace out of the deal, right?" he reminded her. "Well…"

"Yeah, but that was just an ad lib."

"I thought we'd do a little show-and-tell. Don't get too excited. It's cubic zirconia."

She tried to hide her disappointment.

"Let me do the talking," he said. "This time silence is golden, remember."

Jane examined the necklace as they continued to dress, not nearly as enamored now. *Costume jewelry—story of my life.*

She cut the price tags off a new backless dress while Cooper slipped into a freshly laundered shirt. He adorned cuff links and a red tie before reaching for his suit jacket. Moments later they were seated into the Jaguar outside the hotel. Cooper showed no emotion and said nothing when she explained how the window became chipped.

"Shit happens," was all he said.

The plan was to meet Wolff and Veronica at Heidi's, a restaurant in Beverly Hills. Traffic was light. They cruised up Sunset Boulevard into Beverly Hills. She tried her best to forget that hours ago she'd been visiting her mother at a greasy drag strip in the Inland Empire. She tried to imagine what carefree Kimberly would have done with her day, shopping like Veronica, or browsing art galleries.

They arrived at a club just off Rodeo Drive, its entrance hidden from the street. The place was nondescript with a simple brass plaque and a few valets standing at attention.

Inside black marble dominated the modern decor. The space suggested sex and power, track-lighting illuminating delicate orchids, abstract and erotic art hanging on walls of lacquer-black tile. Although Cooper and Jane had arrived early, Wolff and Veronica were already in the bar. The lustrous clientele was predominantly fashion-clad men, and Jane figured most of them were probably gay. She noticed a small dance floor with musical instruments awaiting the band on a stage.

Wolff took Jane's hand and kissed it lightly. "Good evening to you," he said. It seemed so formal and old-fashioned. The Asian hostess led them to their table. Jane spotted Wolff's bodyguard taking a seat at the bar.

Fine wine was carefully poured. Flaming, wondrous gourmet dishes were prepared at their table. The evening felt magical. Cooper made everyone laugh, spinning outrageous stories and Jane marveled at his warmth and ease. After the main course Veronica suggested the women excuse themselves and led Jane to the powder room.

Veronica was touching up her lipstick in the mirror when she complimented Jane on her necklace. "That's an impressive piece you're wearing."

"That Brazilian diamond business my husband is so wrapped up in."

"It's radiant," Veronica said.

"Thank you."

As the women emerged from the restroom the Latin jazz band was starting their set, an upbeat dance groove.

That's when she saw him. Jeremy Sands, her acting coach,

was at the bar, out cruising, no doubt.

At that instant Jeremy Sands spotted Jane. He raised his hand in a wave.

Jane turned away and quickened her step.

Veronica noticed this. "Everything all right?" she asked.

Jane knew her knee-jerk reaction was too obvious.

"What is it?" Veronica asked.

"That man," she blurted, nodding to Wolff's bodyguard, also at the bar. "I noticed him at our hotel. I think he's following us."

Veronica turned to the bar and laughed. "That's Buddy. He works for us. He's Alexander's security consultant."

"Security consultant?"

"Bodyguard."

"Oh," Jane said, acting surprised.

"There have been threats," Veronica said, "I told Alexander it's crazy but he's a very cautious man sometimes. He claims it's for my safety too, but I think he's overreacting."

"I'm really not paranoid. It's just..." She could see Jeremy eyeing her.

"Since his name is Buddy, I call him our *buddyguard*," Veronica said, "but he doesn't like that."

Jeremy Sands was still staring.

Jane took her seat and nudged Cooper under the table. Mid-speech and without missing a beat, Cooper picked up on it and glanced to the bar. When he turned back it was obvious that he'd seen Jeremy.

Jeremy got up from his barstool, grabbed his vodka soda and walked to them.

Veronica, meanwhile, was explaining to Jane the differences between her yoga instructors. Jane feigned interest, but her eyes were on Jeremy. Buddy was also on his feet and right behind Jeremy, stride for stride. Both men approached the table at the same time.

"Jane." Jeremy said.

Jane pretended not to notice him. Cooper stood.

"Jeremy, what a surprise," he said. "Excuse us a moment, will you? An old friend," Cooper put his arm around him and led Jeremy away. Buddy stayed where he was, watching them go.

After a few seconds Buddy peeled off, apparently convinced Jeremy was not a threat.

"I love this song," Jane said, then to Wolff. "Would you care to dance?"

Veronica encouraged him with a nudge, "Sure he does. Go."

Wolff seemed surprised. He stood, took her by the arm, and guided Jane to the dance floor. As they blended into the crowd Jane searched for Cooper.

Hips swaying to the Latin rhythm, she could smell his cologne and feel his eyes on her. She wondered where Cooper had gone.

The song came to an end. Cooper was there when they returned to the booth.

"You missed the fun," Jane said.

"Apparently."

"Who was that man?" Jane asked out loud, for the benefit of the others, but then realized it was a mistake because Jeremy had called her by name.

"An old friend. Crazy bastard."

As a round of drinks arrived Jane noticed blood on Cooper's cuff.

"Now it's our turn to dance," Veronica said to Cooper before Jane could clue him in.

"Is that so?"

"Yes, that's so."

They moved to the dance floor leaving Jane and Wolff alone.

"That's a wonderful necklace," Wolff said to her. "Beautiful."

"Thank you," she said. *Less is more,* Jane thought. *Don't say anything.*

She turned and watched the dance floor, fully aware Wolff's eyes were upon her.

CHAPTER 17

In the hotel bar over a nightcap Cooper convinced Wolff to take a look at the stones. It appeared Cooper's charm had taken affect and Wolff was interested in the diamond deal.

"But if we're going to see the stones," he said, "it will have to be in the morning since on Saturdays the bank closes at noon."

"The earlier the better," Wolff said. "Remember, we've got the races tomorrow." He turned to Jane. "I expect you to bring me luck."

"Turquoise," Jane said, remembering the name of his thoroughbred racehorse.

"What time does the race go off?" Cooper asked, as if not interested but entertaining the thought. Jane sensed he was playing hard to get.

"Three or so, but you'll want to get there early. We'll be in the Turf Club."

"Why don't we carpool?" Jane suggested.

"Because we have to be at the stables at eleven," Veronica said, clearly not as enthused.

At this point Wolff waved Buddy over. He introduced him to Cooper and Jane as his "driver and assistant."

Veronica said, "Buddy is like family."

Buddy shook their hands. He was soft-spoken and mannerly, with an accent Jane could not place. After Wolff insisted Buddy join them for a drink he sat and barely said a word. Jane sensed he was never at ease. He kept watching the door, observing all who entered. The waitress came and Buddy ordered an Amstel Light. When it arrived he never took a sip.

"Turquoise is a first-time starter," Wolff explained. "She's got exceptional pedigree, solid workouts, and if she can hit the board I plan on pointing her towards a race at Del Mar this summer. She's got speed, so if she can get a good post and a clean break from the gate she's got a chance. As a first-time starter, she should go off at a good price."

"Price? Your horse is for sale?" Jane asked.

"No, a good price at the windows."

"Windows?"

"Her odds," Cooper explained. "She should have good odds because she's unproven." And then to Wolff he said, "What do you expect the morning line to be?"

"At least fifteen to one."

All this was Greek to Jane.

"How much are we going to bet?" Veronica asked.

"Enough to make it interesting," Wolff replied with a wink.

Cooper proposed showing Wolff the diamonds in the morning before they set out for the races. "And if you're game," Cooper said, "after the races we could take a sunset cruise on my yacht."

Wolff seemed hesitant at first.

"Let's do it," Veronica urged.

"Alright. I'd like my friend Buddy to join us too," Wolff said.

"There's plenty of room," Cooper said. "The more the merrier."

"The races, then yachting," Veronica said. "It's a plan."

Jane saw that Buddy did not seem happy about the decision but he said nothing.

Walking back to their room Jane wanted to ask Cooper about his bloodstained cuff but decided to wait.

In their room, Jane kicked off her heels as Cooper removed his jacket. The blood had dried on his sleeve, now hardened and dark burgundy in color.

"What happened to your hand?"

"Nothing," he said and rolled up his sleeve. He went to the bathroom and ran water over his knuckles. "I told Jeremy I'd take care of the balance you owed," Cooper said before he dried his hands with a towel and went to the mini-bar.

"But we paid that," she said.

"He insisted on speaking with you. I explained that the people we were having dinner with can't know that you're an actress. He said that was ridiculous, and that both of us should be proud of our craft. I led him outside. I think he's jealous that we're together."

"But that doesn't make sense," she said.

"What do you mean?" Cooper said, pouring himself a scotch.

"Jeremy's gay. He wouldn't be jealous."

"No, not romantically jealous. Professionally." He sat in the plush chair and kicked up his feet. Cooper used the ice-cold glass to soothe his wounded knuckles. "When he asked why we hadn't been to class, I told him you were studying with someone else. He demanded to know who it was. I don't know who's-who when it comes to acting coaches, so I refused to tell him and he became belligerent. He started back inside, claiming that *you* would certainly tell him. I had to stop him. Damage control."

"Weren't you afraid he'd call the police?"

"He was in no condition."

"But you weren't outside that long. What if he called the cops and pressed charges?"

"He won't," he said with quiet confidence.

"How do you know?"

"Because I told him not to."

This was a side of Cooper she'd never seen.

He continued, "Jeremy's got one big-ass ego. What does he care if you're studying with someone else? All he ever did was criticize you."

"I guess I let him," Jane said, removing her necklace, "and I came to expect it. Since my career was going nowhere, and I was so unhappy, I probably felt I deserved it."

Cooper joined her at the mirror. "Are you now?"

"What?"

"Unhappy? Because you shouldn't be. You did great tonight, thinking on your feet. You're a natural. I'm impressed."

He ran his hand along her snow-white slip and down the curve of her back, pressing against her.

Men had fought over her tonight, she thought. Cooper was the victor.

"Does it hurt?" she said, touching his hand.

"No."

She could smell the scotch on his breath and feel him getting hard. He kissed the top of her shoulder. Then he ravaged her neck, working his way down to her breast. The warmth and pleasure gave her goose-bumps.

He pushed her on top of the bedspread and went to work. It was rough sex, primal. Another part of him she'd never seen. For a moment she wondered if he was fantasizing about someone else.

Afterward, catching her breath as if the wind was knocked out of her, Jane was barely able to move. She dug out a turn-down-service mint from underneath the pillow, unwrapped the chocolate and broke it in half. They shared the treat, kissing afterward, tasting the mint on each other's lips.

CHAPTER 18

Cooper got up before Jane to meet Wolff at the safe deposit box. She was sipping room service coffee when he returned from the bank.

"How'd it go?" she asked.

"As good as can be expected. Thank God he liked the real stones and we never got to the cubic zirconia."

"Think he'll take the bait?"

"Hard to say," he said then sized her up. "You're going to need a hat. Ladies at the track wear hats."

Jane pictured glamorous images of Southern belles at the Kentucky Derby in wide-brimmed hats. "Another piece of equipment?"

"Precisely."

They drove to a store in Beverly Hills. Jane liked the smell of the place—expensive leather. Cooper picked out a sundress and a hat to match. He shot down the sunglasses Jane picked out and instead went for an over-sized pair. Jane thought they were something an old lady would wear.

"These are for yentas. Forget it."

"Trust me on this."

"I'll look goofy."

"No second guessing."

Most of his decisions she agreed with but this one Jane was not so sure. She figured they could make the purchase but she didn't have to wear them.

Stepping from the Jaguar at Santa Anita Racetrack Jane's first impression was the art deco mural of running horses along the entire length of the massive grandstands. It evoked images of old-Hollywood, the era of men in fedoras and women in minks drinking cocktails and smoking. They made their way to the entrance. The crowd was mostly middle-aged men, many of them with the *Daily Racing Form* tucked under their arm.

They entered glass doors to the air-conditioned Turf Club and gave their names to an elderly woman at the counter. Jane noticed a sign requiring jackets for men. They pushed through turnstiles and rode an escalator into the grandstands. Jane felt silly because no other women were wearing hats. *Why did I listen to him?*

They were escorted past tables draped with tablecloths, napkins propped like miniature tents.

Wolff was standing as they approached. Veronica and a few others were seated at their table and Veronica was wearing a hat too, bigger than Jane's. *Thank God,* Jane thought. Buddy also sat near and greeted them with a nod.

"Thank you for coming," Wolff said, and hailed the waiter. Cooper ordered two Bloody Marys.

Jane sat next to Veronica.

"Alexander is a nervous wreck," Veronica confided. "I've seen him negotiate million dollar deals, ice in his veins. But horse racing somehow gets him crazy." Veronica then made introductions around the table. The others were apparently business associates of Wolff. They greeted Jane with polite smiles but were clearly more interested in chatting among themselves. It seemed Veronica was bored with them and glad to have Jane by her side.

Wolff refused to sit. Veronica begged him to relax but he paid no attention. When it was time Wolff escorted all to the paddock. He chatted with a man in a blue blazer, his trainer. Then a jockey arrived and mounted the impressive black horse.

After all the thoroughbreds were led to the track the party returned to the Turf Club.

"I'm off to bet," Cooper said, money clip in hand.

"This is a tough field, and there's no guarantee," Wolff said to him.

"I believe in beginner's luck." Cooper marched off to the windows.

Less than twenty minutes later all watched the television monitor at their table as the horses were loaded into the starting gate. At first Turquoise protested going in, the track handlers having to walk her around to calm her down.

"Waiting on Turquoise," the track announcer said.

The tension at the table was thick. All eyes were on the television as the horse was finally loaded into the gate.

"The joy in life is anticipation," Wolff said aloud.

"That's poetic," Cooper said.

Wolff offered a smile.

"The flag is up," said the track announcer. The starting bell sounded and they were off. The horses grouped together at first and then spread out on the backstretch. Jane had a hard time discerning where Turquoise was. When it became clear the filly was not up front. Jane felt bad. She wondered how much Cooper had bet.

When they rounded the turn the track announcer cried, "And here comes Turquoise, four wide!"

She could see the horse gaining ground, in contention, but definitely not with the leaders. But the horses surrounding Turquoise were tiring. The filly broke out of the pack and was closing in.

"Get up there!" Wolff shouted. "Go!"

"Turquoise with a sudden burst of speed," the announcer said.

Turquoise reached the lead horse and nosed past at the wire.

"Turquoise gets up to win!" the track announcer sounded.

Wolff threw his hands in the air. Everyone was patting him

on the back, congratulating him. He placed his hand on Jane's shoulder, "See, you brought me luck."

Even Buddy came out of his shell, beaming, smiling, and waving his winning ticket in the air.

Finally Veronica grabbed Wolff's arm and pointed everyone towards the escalators.

"To the winner's circle," she said.

Jane followed until Cooper took her arm. "Not us," he whispered.

"Why not?"

"They take a picture."

"Right." She had seen winner's circle photos before, in sports bars, friends and family beaming with pride. She wondered what Wolff and Veronica would think when they noticed that neither she nor Cooper were along for the crowning moment.

After everyone moved on she asked, "How much did you bet?"

"Nothing."

"Nothing? Why not?"

"Because only suckers bet on horses." He turned and moved back to their seats.

She took off her hat and followed.

CHAPTER 19

Jane's first thought was that Buddy was not properly dressed for boating because he wore his usual dark attire: black blazer and grey slacks. The outfit was appropriate in the hotel, nightclubs and restaurants they frequented, but awkward here. She wondered what kind of violence he'd be capable of if she or Cooper were to blow their cover. Would Buddy be the one to track them down? There was something about him that made Jane feel uneasy.

Veronica teased Buddy, commenting on his attire.

"Aren't you hot?" she said, the double meaning obvious, and more a statement than a question.

"Hot?" he asked playing along.

"You know what I mean. Aren't you warm in that jacket?" Veronica asked, trying to play innocent.

"Not really."

"You look hot," she said, playfully.

"I'm fine. Thank you."

Veronica leaned over to Jane and whispered, "He's afraid to take off his jacket in front of you guys because he carries a gun."

Buddy grinned and stared out at the water.

Jane had only the one pair of sunglasses, the ones Cooper bought her. Even though she hated them she put them on out of necessity. Veronica complimented them, but she still thought they were ugly.

The yacht set out and glided along the smooth water of the marina. Cooper pointed out the vessels owned by celebrities as Jane busied herself serving refreshments. Setting the sails, they moved beyond the breakers. Cooper handed the wheel over to Wolff who seemed to like the responsibility. Veronica found hats down below. She placed a captain's hat on Wolff and took a white sailor cap for herself, playfully snuggling up against him. Jane thought the cap worked on Veronica. The sun glistened off the water behind her—looked like she belonged in a Ralph Lauren ad.

It was clear Veronica had "sea legs," able to move around the deck with grace and ease. Sailing, skiing, and tennis were skills the privileged learned at a young age, Jane thought to herself. Kimberly would have these skills too.

"You're good on a boat," she said to Veronica.

"A regular Anne Bonny," Wolff said.

"Who's Anne Bonny?" Jane asked.

"A famous woman pirate seduced by the sea. Fearless, reckless and mysterious," Veronica explained.

Jane caught Wolff checking her out again. She smiled back, turned away and felt his gaze linger. It gave her the creeps. She wondered if Veronica had noticed—was pretty sure she had.

CHAPTER 20

Back at the hotel Cooper suggested they get a drink in the bar. Veronica claimed she was too tired, "Besides, I desperately need a shower."

Jane thought it would be best for Cooper and Wolff to talk business alone, so she said goodnight and headed for the room. She glanced back to see the men move into the bar. Buddy trailed them.

Jane took a hot shower, slipped into a robe and turned on the television. The TV offered the usual menu of the hotel's amenities. Out of curiosity Jane chose movies and clicked on the pay-per-view menu, then "adult entertainment." She curled up on the bedspread.

As if on cue a trailer for *Gemini* appeared but the picture had been re-titled as *Saturnalia*. Jane cringed at the image of herself in her revealing costume juxtaposed with the harshly lit orgy scenes, not part of the movie she'd signed on for, abstract enough to suggest she was engaging in these acts.

It made her so mad.

She went to Cooper's laptop computer and researched *Saturnalia*. Jane learned that Saturn was the Roman god of sowing and seeding. The feast of Saturnalia was a Roman celebration of the winter solstice. It was described by historians as a lavish orgy wherein slaves and masters switched places for the day. She searched numerous links until she found the porn movie

Saturnalia, and a link to Zipper Video, the producer and distributor based in Chatsworth, California. Maybe she could sue them. She remembered signing a photo release and short-form contract but could not remember if she still had a copy or where it might be. Jane scanned Zipper's other movies, titles including *Sorority Sister Sodomy Soiree III* and one movie featuring obese performers in a historic New Orleans setting by the name of *Fat Tuesday*.

Jane hopped into bed and switched to an old black-and-white movie, *The Postman Always Rings Twice*, until Cooper returned an hour later.

"How'd it go?" she asked.

"Wolff is sniffing." He sat on the end of the bed. "Do you remember when I mentioned that this job may take certain sacrifices?"

"Yes."

"This is one of those times. Wolff has a certain request."

Jane jumped to her feet. "Forget it! No way!"

"Calm down."

"How could you even consider—?"

"It's not what you think."

"Yeah, well, I've seen the way Wolff looks at me. He's weird."

Cooper's tone became very businesslike. "What's important is that we close this deal. Don't you agree?"

Jane said nothing.

He took her by the arms. "We've come too far. We have to play into our mark's quirk and do whatever is necessary."

"What do you want me to do?" she asked, crossing her arms and pulling away.

"Wolff likes to watch."

"Watch what?"

"He likes to watch women."

"Who?" Then it became clear. "Veronica."

"I have a feeling they've done this kind of thing before."

Jane's mind raced. She remembered moments, in the spa or during evenings out, in which Veronica's touch lingered. Was she so naive that she hadn't picked up on it?

"How do you know Veronica wants to?" she asked.

"Wolff said so. It turns him on to watch her with other women. It's some kind of game with them."

"I won't do it. Forget it."

Cooper released her and walked away. "I can't force you. And I won't try." He sat at the desk and checked his email.

She could tell he was mad. A headache was coming on. "You're going to be pissed at me if I don't, right?"

"No," he said, but she didn't believe him.

CHAPTER 21

Jane tossed and turned, not able to sleep that night. Cooper was rolled to one side of the bed, snoring loudly, his back to her. She listened to the noises of the hotel; the plumbing knocking in the walls, a distant television somewhere. It seemed like such a long time ago when she first met Cooper, but it had only been a month or so. Her world was so different now.

Daylight was creeping through the curtains by the time she drifted off to sleep.

She woke to discover the drapes wide open, sunlight spilling across the tangled sheets. Cooper was gone. She dressed, put her hair up and headed for the hotel restaurant.

A waitress moved from table to table offering freshly squeezed tangerine juice and wedges of chilled cantaloupe. Another passed out complimentary newspapers. Jane chose a *USA Today*, not really what Kimberly would read, but Jane liked the pictures and concise stories. She thumbed to the entertainment section.

Minutes later Jane looked up to see Veronica crossing the lobby and waving at her. "Good morning," she said and sat down. A waitress approached and Veronica said she'd already eaten, would just have coffee.

"I slept late and I have no idea where Cooper went."

"I understand your husband spoke with you."

"Spoke with me?" Jane asked.

"About…us."

Jane leaned back, said nothing.

"I just want to say if you're not interested, I completely understand. I just hope it doesn't come between us. I mean, I've had such a great time with you, and I don't want you to think any less of me."

"No, I…If anything, I was sort of flattered, but it's just…not really my style."

"I understand," said Veronica just as the waitress appeared with her coffee. There was an awkward silence as the server poured.

After she left Veronica confessed, "Honestly, I don't really have that many friends."

Jane tried to imagine what Veronica's life was like, so different than hers. She seemed lonely.

"I really like hanging out with you," Jane said. "You're fun."

"I haven't been with that many women before," Veronica said, "but when Alexander suggested it, I thought to myself…Let's just say I trust you, so…"

At that moment Cooper, Wolff, and Buddy walked into the restaurant together, looking like old friends. They approached the table.

"Well, good morning," Cooper said.

"Where have you two been?" Jane asked.

"The bank for a little business," Cooper said.

"I was wondering," Wolff said as he took a seat, "are you an actress, by chance?"

There was an uneasy silence. Jane looked to Cooper but his face was a mask. "What makes you think that?" Jane asked.

"I couldn't sleep last night, and I thought I saw you in a movie."

"What movie?"

Wolff shrugged. "You just look like someone. It's not important."

Jane could see Buddy was listening. Something told her Buddy had seen *Saturnalia* as well.

"He knows," Cooper said, back in their room. "He was asking me on the way to the bank, and I told him I was certain whoever he saw, it wasn't you. Obviously he didn't believe me."

Jane wanted to cry. "What should we do?"

"Deny it. He can't prove it's you," he said.

"What happened at the bank?"

"He seems interested, but I can't get him to commit. He's hesitating for some reason, and asking a lot of questions. I can't put my finger on it."

Jane asked, "Do you think it will help if I agree to be with Veronica?"

Cooper studied her without saying a word.

"Okay," she said. "I'll do it."

CHAPTER 22

Jane decided against wearing panties and slipped naked into a spaghetti-strap dress. Cooper buttoned the back. She put on her sexiest heels, kissed Cooper, and without saying a word left him in the room.

Under a full moon she made her way across the meticulous grounds to Wolff and Veronica's bungalow.

She passed Buddy sitting near the pool, reading a paperback under a garden light. He gave her a nod.

The door was cracked open. She entered, hesitant. The bed was neatly turned down. A bottle of champagne sat iced atop a chrome stand. She could hear the shower running.

"Veronica?" she called out.

"Just a second." The water shut off and Jane could hear the glass doors open and close. Jane wondered if Wolff was in the bathroom but then spotted him beyond the sheer drapes covering the French doors. He was out in the private courtyard and she could barely make out his silhouette behind the translucent veil. The wind blew the curtains. She could see the burning red cherry end of Wolff's cigar illuminated in the darkness. Jane turned away, went to the champagne and poured herself a glass.

Wolff coughed. She pretended not to hear it. As an actor she was trained to never break the fourth wall.

She'd finished her first glass and was pouring a second when

Veronica emerged from the bathroom wearing only a black silk robe.

"Hi."

"Hey."

Jane resisted the urge to glance beyond the French doors.

Veronica crossed the room and stood beside Jane, pouring herself a flute. Jane could smell her shampoo.

"Pretend he doesn't exist," she whispered. "He'll stay right there and won't say a word, I promise. Are you nervous?"

"A little."

"Don't be."

Veronica put her hand on Jane's neck and caressed, then unbuttoned the back of the dress.

On the bed Veronica's skin was warm as if a fire burned deep within. Jane was embarrassed one moment, intoxicated the next, then back to feeling uneasy and even full of shame.

She found Veronica hypersensitive and easily aroused. Legs tangled. Hands explored. Lips caressed. Veronica may have been the most responsive lover Jane had ever been with.

Jane somehow knew what to do.

When Veronica reached orgasm Jane felt powerful. For a moment she was in control, and the feeling excited her. Then Veronica did her best to reciprocate. For the benefit of her audience, Jane feigned hers.

Afterward they held each other.

"You were fantastic," Veronica whispered softly and kissed her on the cheek.

Jane got up, pulled on the dress, found her high heels and decided to carry them. She crossed the hotel grounds barefoot, past the pool and was back in her room.

"Pour me a drink."

Jane took a hot shower and when she emerged Cooper handed her a glass of wine.

"Thank you." She sipped. "Perfect."

"How'd it go?"

"Good."

"What'd Wolff do?"

"I hardly saw him. He was watching from the patio."

Cooper seemed relieved. He kissed her on the forehead. Then the phone rang and he answered. After a few moment he said, "I'm glad you're aboard. We'll talk more tomorrow. Great."

He hung up, looked at her and said, "Whatever you did tonight...he's in."

CHAPTER 23

The next morning when Jane awoke, Cooper was already dressed and at the computer. He printed a picture of a streamline aluminum briefcase from a manufacturer's website and two plane tickets.

"I need you to take a cab to this luggage store and buy two of these suitcases," he said. "Make sure they're identical, same model, so you can't tell one from the other." He handed her six hundred-dollar bills. "When you return, have the valet bring them to our room. Don't risk Wolff or Veronica seeing you with them. Understand?"

"Okay," she said, and then glanced at the plane tickets.

"I'm going to switch cases on him," he explained. "We're booked to Tahiti on an open ticket. I need you to pack some of your things and put them in the Jag today, including your passport. Bring only a few changes of clothes and necessary toiletries. We've got to be able to pull out at a moment's notice. Got it?"

"Alright."

They ate a quick breakfast in their room. Jane packed a bag, including her toiletries, and put it in the Jaguar. Afterward she set out for the luggage store in a taxi.

Jane felt the driver's eyes on her in the rearview mirror. They were pulling onto Santa Monica Boulevard when he finally spoke.

"You're clown lady, no?"

"Excuse me?"

"I pick you up before. You take off clown costume in my cab."

Jane recognized him. He was the same cabby that picked her up from the children's birthday party the night she met Cooper.

"No, I'm not from around here," she said.

"I never forget face. You undress in my cab. I take you to Hollywood. No?"

"You must have me mistaken for someone else."

There was an awkward moment until finally the man laughed. "Funny how some people look so much alike. You remind me of one of my customers."

They drove the rest of the way in silence.

Jane thought it best to not have the cab wait outside the luggage store. She tipped him well and thanked him. She could feel his eyes on her back as she moved to the store.

Inside she showed the print-out of the briefcase to the cheerful woman. She assured Jane they had plenty in stock. Jane purchased two briefcases, still in the cardboard boxes and asked the saleswoman if she could call a taxi.

A half an hour later Jane delivered the boxed cases to the hotel bellhop. Minutes later the staff brought them to her room.

Cooper returned. "We're in luck. Wolff claims he can come up with the money this afternoon. His bank offers a special service for its key account customers, large amounts of cash available immediately."

"Banks do that?" she asked.

"Beverly Hills banks do, ones with celebrity clients, or customers with business interests in Mexico or South America. In case of kidnappings they keep millions on hand in emergency reserve."

She wondered what a million dollars in cash looked like.

"An armored car is supposed to deliver it to his bungalow," he continued. "That's where we'll supposedly split up the diamonds."

"What do I do?"

"Keep Veronica occupied. Is your passport in the car?"

"Yes, I did everything."

"Good." Cooper began to pack.

Twenty minutes later the phone rang. It was Veronica. She wanted to talk about last night. Jane did not feel like seeing her, needed more time to digest what had happened between them, but Veronica was persistent. With Cooper coaching her silently, Jane agreed to meet.

"They have a wonderful tea in the lobby," Veronica suggested. "Alexander has some business this afternoon so we can meet there."

"A tea?"

Cooper nodded, urged her.

"Sounds good," she said.

Finger sandwiches, pastries and cookie-biscuits accompanied the civilized English convention of afternoon tea. Jane tried to mimic everything Veronica did and hoped her inexperience at such a thing wasn't too obvious.

Jane saw the Brinks armored car guards cross the lobby with a grey metal strongbox in tow. She pretended not to notice.

"I wanted to say that last night was extraordinary," Veronica said. "You were incredible."

"Thank you," Jane said, blushing. She studied the pattern of the china, an old English fox hunt, hand-painted and ornate. Men, horse and hound closed in on the elusive fox.

"I won't say another word," Veronica said, "because I can tell it makes you uncomfortable. It's just, I wanted you to know. It was special for me."

"I'm flattered."

Veronica lightened the tone and went into details about how Wolff had other kinky requests, some of them absurd. Jane laughed. Together they came to the conclusion that, deep down, men are pigs.

They made conversation with some other women at the afternoon tea, most of them grey-haired and elderly. All of them, it seemed, were guests of the hotel. Jane saw the Brinks crew return with their strongbox. She was dying to know what was happening with Cooper and Wolff.

Waiters served more delicacies. Little bits of decorative greens were arranged to perfection on every ornamental dish. Jane had never seen these kinds of cookies before and assumed they must be European.

When the other women were out of earshot Veronica took a serious tone, confiding in Jane. "I also want you to know that, beyond Alexander, I really want to stay in contact with you. As friends."

Jane could tell Veronica was sincere but wondered aloud, "Beyond Alexander? What's that mean?"

"When he tires of me, or when our agreement ends. Whichever comes first."

"Agreement?"

"You don't get it, do you?"

"Get what?"

"Oh, I'm sorry," Veronica said with a condescending tone, as if Jane were a child. "I thought you knew."

"Knew what?"

Veronica leaned in and whispered, "Alexander is..." she paused, searching for the right words, "my client."

"Client?"

"I'm Alexander's girlfriend for now, because he can afford me."

The hotel concierge approached them, a thin young man. "Phone call for a Miss Van Cise. At the concierge desk," he said. Since Jane was not used to being called Miss Van Cise it took a second to figure out that he was talking to her.

"Excuse me," Jane said to Veronica, getting up, grateful for the interruption. She followed the man to his desk, wondering

Veronica is a call girl? Jane couldn't believe it. She was too perfect, *too* beautiful. The concierge transferred the call from his desk to the house phone on the wall.

"I've distracted Wolff enough to make the switch," Cooper said on the phone, "but he's holding me up and I can't seem to get past Buddy. Get the car. Take it to the airport. Park it at the international terminal and leave the keys in it. When I get the chance to duck out, I'll hop a cab and join you there. We'll meet in the airport bar, the one closest to our gate. Got that?"

"Yeah."

"Your ticket is in your name. Go now. Get away from Veronica."

"Okay."

"You alright?"

"Yes." She wanted to tell him what she just learned but figured it could wait. "Be careful," she said.

She hung up the phone then turned to see Jeremy Sands enter the hotel lobby followed by a man she did not recognize.

You've got to be kidding. She ducked behind a pillar.

Jeremy wore a neck brace and had a cast on his arm. They approached the man at the front desk. Jane spied as the man accompanying Jeremy displayed a police badge to the desk clerk. Jeremy had a photo and showed it to him. Jane could see they were looking at her acting eight by ten headshot.

The desk clerk nodded. He motioned to another clerk and they both studied the photo, even turning it over to scan Jane's resume on the back.

Jane thought about running but decided that it would only attract attention. She had to cross the lobby undetected, get outside and retrieve the car without Jeremy and the cops seeing her.

She glanced to Veronica who was still sitting, now thumbing through a magazine. Jane decided she would need to walk right past Jeremy and the cop, their backs to her at the counter. But then the men pivoted. They were walking her way.

Shit! Jane picked up the phone and pretended to dial.

The detective saw her. "Jane Innes?" he said.

Jane shot a desperate glance to Veronica. Veronica looked from the men and then back to Jane, confused.

"Jane!" Jeremy called out, limping beside the cop.

Jane turned on her heels. She briskly walked the other direction.

"Jane?" she could hear Jeremy calling out. "That you?"

She burst through the door and found herself in the kitchen. Steam and chaos reigned. Cooks shouted. Busboys clanged bustubs. She sidestepped a waiter and ran past. She almost lost a heel in the thick, wet rubber mat. Looking back, Jane saw Jeremy and the cop enter. They spotted her. Jeremy pointed, and they advanced.

Jane turned the bend and found herself at the walk-in freezer. A dead end. She could hear Jeremy calling her name again. The freezer was her last refuge. She decided to duck inside, but then got an idea.

Instead of entering, she hid behind the open door, outside the freezer. It was just like when she was hiding in her room as a little girl. None of her mom's crazy boyfriends ever looked behind her door.

She pressed herself up against the wall. The chrome door pressed cold against her face. She hoped they would walk past. Instead she could hear they stopped.

Her heart was pounding.

"Where'd she go?" she heard Jeremy say.

"Jane?" a voice called out. She assumed it was the detective. "Are you in there?"

She could hear the two of them push through the plastic transparent partition and enter into the freezer.

With a hard shove, she slammed the door. She placed the pin, dangling on a chain, into its hole of the latch-handle. She could hear muffled shouts from inside but they were barely audible compared to the noise of the bustling kitchen.

Success, Jane casually walked back the way she came.

"You cannot be here, lady!" a chef screamed.

"I'm leaving."

To avoid Veronica, Jane slipped out the side door near the restrooms. She circled the building and dug out the claim check plus a five-dollar tip. She handed the ticket to the valet, found cover behind a planted shrub and watched the door.

It seemed like an eternity.

Finally the Jaguar appeared and the valet hopped out. She handed him the ticket wrapped in the tip and got in. She took one last look back at the hotel before driving off.

She wondered how long Jeremy and the cops would be locked inside the freezer. She laughed about how she outsmarted them. She imagined sitting in First Class, the plane lifting off, toasting with Cooper to their success, while Jeremy froze his ass off in the freezer.

Minutes later she was dropping down onto Sunset Boulevard on the way to the freeway. She thought about the bewildered look on Veronica's face as Jeremy and the cop came at her. She hoped Veronica didn't run to the bungalow, tell Wolff about it and spoil everything for Cooper. He did say he was on his way, didn't he? Maybe he managed to get away. There was so little time.

Traffic was heavy on Sunset. When she reached the 405 Freeway, the crack in the windshield caught the light—the skeleton hand reaching out at her, horrifying and freakish.

Jane took the freeway and got off at Century Boulevard heading for the airport. Her heart was racing. She wished she had a cell phone so she could call Cooper to make sure everything was okay. Once in the terminal she'd find a payphone.

More traffic near the historic restaurant at the airport with its retro-futuristic *Jetsons* design. She wondered how long it would be until she would see it again. This was the beginning of a new chapter in her life. No looking back.

Near the Bradley International terminal Jane pulled the Jaguar into the parking structure, as instructed, and found spot on the top level. She jotted down the parking space number figuring Cooper would need to pass this information on to the car leasing company. She took one last look at the chipped windshield, so ugly.

As she stepped out of the car, a pock-marked man approached her.

"Jane Innes?"

She stood frozen.

"Detective Myers, LAPD Robbery Homicide," he said.

She saw there were other men flanking him.

"Please open the trunk, ma'am."

"Why?"

"We need you to open the trunk," he said bluntly.

Trying to appear calm, Jane circled the car and put the key into the lock. She turned the latch the trunk sprung open.

Alexander Wolff lay dead inside, shot in the forehead, his tongue swollen and protruding.

He was staring at her, eyes bugged out, glaring.

Jane staggered and lost her balance.

The next sensation was hitting the concrete—an explosion of pain up her tailbone.

CHAPTER 24

"Like I could possibly have lice!" Jane screamed at them. She stood naked in the shower. There was a dispenser of foamy, pungent disinfectant on the wall.

"Everybody gotta' delouse, princess," the female jailer said. To enforce the point the guard made sure Jane vigorously scrubbed her pubic hair.

Earlier during the interrogation at the police station she explained to them that she was the shill, an actress playing a role, but they kept asking about Wolff. She insisted the cops go to Marina Del Rey to track down Cooper's yacht. She told them her friend Carla would know all about it, or the gay couple Louis and Jim that had the boat in the next slip, but the detectives kept asking the same questions over and over. It was clear their only concern the murdered billionaire.

Jane realized she should ask for a lawyer. Once she made the request they stopped their questions, read her the Miranda Rights and booked her.

They took her to the Twin Towers Correctional Facility in downtown L.A. Jane thought it strange they would call a building the Twin Towers in this day and age, summoning images of 9/11.

Having surrendered her clothes before the shower, Jane was dressed in a bright orange jumpsuit, itchy and stiff from starch. The white, flat-soled shoes were too big and had Velcro straps instead of laces. She assumed no laces meant she couldn't hang herself.

They escorted her to what the guard called "K-ten Keep-away"—concrete-walled cells in a one hundred and eighty degree semi-circle. Each cell was visible from the jailer station in the center. Jane was told that since she was booked for murder she'd be partitioned here.

In the tiny cell she found the vinyl-cushion bed incredibly hard and the blanket was horrible, nothing like the Bel Air hotel's king-size luxury bed and goose-down comforter.

When she closed her eyes Jane could not shut out the image of Wolff's morbid death-face. It was like he wanted something from her—beckoning from hell.

Where was Cooper? Had he killed Wolff? What happened?

Some of the prisoners in the surrounding cells tried to engage her, a few spewing insults, but she ignored them.

She was allowed one phone call but she didn't have the phone number for her mother at Danny's garage. And she couldn't remember Danny's last name. So much had transpired since she'd driven out to see her mom. She could remember the racing insignia on his trailer, and that his garage was out of Sarasota, Florida. Instead she called her answering service hoping Cooper left a message. There was nothing. Next she called her neighbor Carla. She explained her predicament.

"I told you he was no good," Carla said.

"I know. I should have listened."

"The rat set you up to take the fall."

"You saw his boat," Jane said. "Do me a favor. Go to the marina. See if Cooper is there."

"And what if he is?"

"Then call the police."

"Okay."

"Thank you."

"You fell in love with a killer, girl."

"Tell me about it."

Carla promised to help, and Jane was grateful.

Only after lights out that night did Jane remember her mother's boyfriend last name was Dobson. Danny Dobson Racing, but it was too late. Lying on the bunk her throat ached and her head throbbed. She felt like she was coming down with the flu. To make matters worse, a woman's distant scream echoed in the darkness. The screams grew louder, pure madness boiling to the surface.

The next morning Jane conversed with the other inmates in the surrounding cells, even though she couldn't see them. Latisha was to her right and Kathy on her left. Neither seemed friendly, and Jane didn't answer when Latisha asked, "What they got you in here for?"

Breakfast was served on Styrofoam plates. The oatmeal was tasteless. The orange juice was undrinkable. The thought of yesterday's chilled cantaloupe and Kona coffee made it even worse.

She told a guard she'd remembered Danny's last name and wanted to make the phone call.

"Later," guard said and disappeared.

Throughout breakfast Latisha pestered with questions. Jane said nothing so Latisha offered her own narrative. "They got me here 'cause the cops found my man's stash at my place," she confessed.

"That must have been one hell of a stash if they put you in county ward," Kathy called out from the other side.

"Yeah, well...it was the stash, and 'cause I gave my man the Ginsu."

"What Ginsu?"

"The Ginsu Knife, like on TV."

"You stabbed your man with a Ginsu?"

"Damn right. It wasn't no *real* Ginsu...Just a steak knife, but he got the point."

"I bet he did." Kathy laughed. Latisha joined her with a hearty, commiserating chuckle.

K-Ten Keep-away, Jane reminded herself. Probably best to remain silent.

After a while the jailer escorted her to the same room where she'd been processed the day before. Jane called information and found a listing for Danny Dobson Racing in Sarasota. She dialed that number but nobody picked up so she left a message.

"Someone here to see you," one of the jailers said, pointing to a pathetic man in his mid-thirties behind the partition. He carried a briefcase, wore a cheap suit, and his thinning hair was parted in a comb-over.

"Jane Innes?" he said, bad posture, shoulders hunched.

Something told Jane this was her public defender.

CHAPTER 25

"You're looking at capital murder," Paul said matter-of-factly.

Paul Nance was indeed the public defender assigned to her case. They sat opposite in the sterile room designated for confidential attorney/client jailhouse meetings.

"I didn't do it."

Paul said nothing and dug into his briefcase.

"Are you assigned a lot of cases?" Jane asked him.

"What do you mean?"

"Cases like mine. Do you have a lot of them?" Jane remembered from school that most public defenders are swamped with clients—spread thin and never able to spend much time on any single case.

"My share," he told her, glancing at his papers and wiping his nose with his sleeve. "Not many murder cases, though. You're my first."

She noticed his collars were stained brown, his jacket sleeves frayed, and his tie didn't match his shirt.

"But I went to Loyola with the Deputy District Attorney assigned to this case," Paul said producing a manila file. "So I've pulled a few strings and got an advance copy of the evidence they have against you. Our arraignment is Thursday. It doesn't look good."

"What doesn't look good?" Jane could smell cigarette smoke on him.

He pulled out a yellow legal pad, "Seems a .32-caliber pistol was found in Alexander Wolff's suite. Tool markings match the discharged shell casings. Coroner pulled .32 caliber slugs from Wolff's chest and those are in the lab now. Latent fingerprints on the pistol are being analyzed, presumably the murder weapon. The gun is registered in your name, purchased by you, only a few weeks ago."

"That's right. He forced me to buy it."

"Who?"

"Cooper."

"Who's Cooper?"

Jane explained how she'd met Cooper, how she fell in love with him, and how he convinced her to assist him in the intricate scam. Paul listened silently while taking notes, encouraging her to continue with little nods and affirmative grunts from time to time.

"A con man," he said.

"And I was the shill."

"There's more," he said going back to his briefcase. "Detectives are making inquiry into whether strands of hair found in Wolff's bed sheets belong to you. Forensics has requested both hair and saliva samples."

"Wouldn't they have changed the sheets?" she asked.

"There was no maid service that morning, before the body was discovered. A Do Not Disturb sign was on the door."

"It's my hair, and probably Veronica's too. I was there."

"In his bed?"

"Yes."

She could see Paul was taken aback. There was painful silence as Jane bit her lip.

"Interesting…in his bed?" he offered. "Please explain how that came to be."

Jane told him how she was coerced into sex with Veronica. She felt herself blushing as she told him. Although Paul was clearly uncomfortable, she could tell she had definitely piqued his interest.

When finished, Paul dropped his pen and leaned in. "You need to tell me everything," he said. "Is that understood? Keeping secrets from me will only hurt you in the long run. So please, help me help you. Helping me..." he said motioning to himself first and then pointing to her, "...helps you. Understand?"

"I'm sorry?" she muttered.

He shifted in his seat and continued, "A witness, the bodyguard Buddy Fahlderberg, claims he saw you coming out of Wolff's hotel room. Mr. Fahlderberg has been cooperating with the investigation. He says you seduced Alexander Wolff. He contends you two had sex before you killed him for his money."

"I didn't have sex with him, and I didn't kill him."

"Can you explain the missing three million dollars?"

"I was set up."

Paul rubbed his eyebrows, clearly distraught.

"You have to believe me. I didn't kill him."

"There's more. A man who claims he's your acting coach, a Jamie, uh...Jim..." Paul thumbed through his legal pad.

"Jeremy Sands," she said.

"That's him. He's a frequent customer at Heidi's in Beverly Hills."

"I saw him there."

"He claims you had him beaten up outside."

"Cooper did that."

"Jeremy spent two nights in the Cedars Sinai recovering but was able to track your whereabouts through limo service records.

"It was Cooper's idea, so Jeremy wouldn't blow our cover."

"The detective on the case accuses you of resisting arrest at the hotel and then locking him in a freezer."

"Yeah, I did that," she said.

"Another detail you chose not to tell me?" Paul produced another piece of paper. "The timeline suggests that's when you murdered Alexander Wolff."

"Do they actually think I had time to kill Wolff and place him in the trunk?"

Paul set the legal pad down and sized her up. "Do you know where Cooper is?" he asked, clicking his ballpoint pen for emphasis.

"No."

"If your fingerprints match the ones found on the weapon, and this other evidence stacks up, what makes you think a jury is going to believe you?"

"I swear to you I have no idea where Cooper is. I was set up!"

"Okay, okay...As I said, our arraignment is scheduled for Thursday. How do you wish to plead?"

"Plead?"

"Guilty or not guilty? I'm obligated to ask."

"Not guilty! I didn't do anything!" Jane said, trying to get him to look her in the eye. "You've got to believe me."

"Let's take a short break." Paul stood, fumbling in his pockets. "I can use a smoke."

She watched him go. Feeling vulnerable, all Jane wanted was her pillow, not the pillow from the hotel but rather the one from her apartment, the down pillow she put in the storage with the rest of her stuff. She wanted her old life back. She wanted to be a poor, out-of-work clown again.

Finally Paul returned, but this time with one of the men she recognized from her arrest—the pock-mark faced Detective Myers.

"Jane," Paul said, "Detective Myers and his team have a request."

"Miss Innes, can you identify Cooper's yacht?"

CHAPTER 26

After Detective Myers asked Jane to accompany them to Dana Point, Paul took her aside and said, "I don't think it's a good idea."

"Why not? I've got nothing to hide," she said.

"It's not necessary. If it is indeed Cooper's yacht they'll find another way to identify the boat. Besides, I'm due in court and can't be there with you."

"Tell them I'll do it," Jane said.

"As your attorney it's my recommendation that—"

"Tell them I'll do it."

She could see Paul was offended but didn't care.

"Jane, please..."

"Don't worry. I won't say anything to incriminate myself."

"This is complicated, and you don't understand the ramifications—"

"Tell them I'll do it."

Thirty minutes later Paul was gone and Detective Myers escorted Jane out of the jailhouse. For the trip they were accompanied by Deputy Sheriff Ling, a squat, no-nonsense Asian woman.

"Did my lawyer tell you about my arrangement?" Jane said.

"What arrangement?" Detective Myers asked.

"The deal I made."

Officer Ling hesitated with the handcuffs.

"A deal?"

"I get a good cup of coffee for the ride," Jane said, improvising. She never mentioned this to her attorney but figured she'd give it a shot. "Real stuff. Not gas station swill, but Starbucks."

Ling started in, "I don't think we have time for—"

"I'm not asking for a latte or espresso," Jane cut in, "just good, plain all-American drip. Dark roast. With a splash of milk."

It was a complete bluff but good coffee is one of the things she missed the most.

"That's not a problem," Detective Myers said. "Anything else?"

"That'll do."

Officer Ling continued cuffing Jane.

"I'll need my hands in front to drink it."

Detective Myers nodded his approval and Jane's hands were re-cuffed in front.

Emerging from the basement of the Twin Towers, the warm sun hit her face and Jane felt invigorated. Minutes later the vehicle was double-parked outside a Starbuck's near the Dorothy Chandler Pavilion. Myers went in for the coffee as Officer Ling waited with Jane, the motor running. The car radio squawked unintelligibly.

Myers returned with her coffee. Jane thanked him and took a sip through the white plastic cover. It was strong, like coffee was supposed to be. Although she knew the excursion would be brief, to be out of that horrible jail with a good cup of coffee warming her hands was heaven.

"I saw on TV," Jane said as they made their way onto the freeway, "that for every day that passes after a murder, the chance of finding the killer becomes more and more difficult. Is that true?"

"There's truth in that, yes," Detective Myers said.

"You think I did it, don't you?" she asked.

"You're a suspect," Detective Myers said. "My job is to

simply gather evidence. It's the district attorney's job to build the case."

"What if this isn't Cooper's boat?"

"Then we'll continue to search for him."

Traffic became heavy. The longer this took the better. She wondered if she could get lunch out of the deal.

The cops made small talk. Ling said her daughter sold Girl Scout cookies to officers in the department and someone she called "Captain Crunch" bought twenty boxes, all peanut butter. That got a laugh from Myers. It was clear they were friends. Jane, the outsider, didn't get the inside joke.

As they drove she gazed out the window. She felt like a goldfish in a bowl, not part of the real world anymore, only able to watch it all pass her by. And like a goldfish, she was bright orange in her starchy prison wear.

The traffic lightened as they drove through industrial City of Commerce. By the time they reached Anaheim they were cruising briskly in the carpool lane. Jane craned her neck looking for the peak of Disneyland's famed Matterhorn ride but had no luck finding it.

As they exited the freeway and curved toward Dana Point Jane could see the ocean, sparkling in the distance. Myers made a call to the Orange County Sheriff's Department and told them to meet at the dock.

They turned off Pacific Coast Highway into the Dana Point Marina surrounded by steep ocean cliffs. They pulled into a parking lot and got out. Detective Myers produced a trench coat and draped it over her shoulders. She was grateful. The garment warmed her from the cool ocean breeze and cloaked the awful prison orange.

Momentarily a patrol car arrived. Two deputies got out and made introductions. One of the men was about Jane's age and completely bald. The other was older, African-American with graying temples who went to the trunk and retrieved a set of bolt-cutters.

A crusty dock tender emerged from a nearby office wearing a faded nautical cap and Bud Light T-shirt. He put out his cigarettes and led the way. As they approached the yacht Jane knew immediately.

"It's Cooper's boat," she said.

"You sure?"

"I'm certain."

The dock tender rolled portable steps over and the two Sheriffs boarded the yacht. Even though there was a padlock, the bald one knocked on the door and called out, "Sheriff's Department."

There was no answer. After a few more knocks they wedged the bolt-cutters in the door jam. With one yank it split the lock. They opened the hatch.

"Oh, God," the bald cop said, staggering back and covering his nose.

Myers stepped up to the door and peeked in before making a face. "We've got a bogie. Take Miss Innes back to the car," he said to Officer Ling.

"What's a bogie?" Jane asked, fearing the worst.

Myers did not answer and immediately got on his cell phone.

"What's a bogie?!" she repeated to Officer Ling as Jane was led back to the car. She was not given an answer and it made her mad. "What's going on?"

Moments later, sitting in the car, Jane saw the dock attendant stagger back, looking queasy. He took off his sailor cap, leaned over the railing and vomited. After wiping his mouth on his T-shirt sleeve he lit a cigarette and moved to his small office.

When a van marked Coroner arrived Jane was certain there was a dead body.

She witnessed the bald officer drape yellow crime scene tape across the gated entrance. More cops arrived. Coroner techs dressed in white pulled a gurney out of their van and stood by.

Finally Detective Myers appeared. He opened the car door.

"Are you certain that's Cooper's boat?"

"Yes. Who's dead?"

"I'm hoping you can enlighten us," he said. "Game?"

"Of course."

"It's not going to be pleasant. We've got to wait on forensics, so this may take a while."

"Is it a man or a woman?" she asked.

Without answering he closed the car door and moved on about his business.

"Let me out of here!" she yelled. She hated being left in the dark. Who could be in there?

Later, the setting sun cast a golden hue across the water and seagulls floated above. Detective Myers reappeared.

"It's time," he said.

Jane got out of the car to see techs wheeling the gurney down the dock ramp. They wore masks and rubber gloves. A blue tarp was draped over the body.

Detective Myers reached down and pulled up some grass, letting it fall so he could determine which direction the blades descended.

"What are you doing?" she asked.

"We'll want to be upwind," he said, and escorted Jane to the opposite side of the railing.

The gurney stopped before them with a human shape under the tarp.

"She the one?" one of techs asked.

"Yeah."

They folded the plastic back.

Cooper's jaw was wide open, gums black. His face was puffed-out and eyes frozen in a perpetual glare.

She had to look away.

"It's Cooper," she said meekly.

"You sure?"

"Yes." Her heart pounded. Tears streamed. This was the man she loved.

Then she could smell the rotting flesh. It made her gag. She fell to her knees and vomited. All went blurry, the taste of coffee in her bile.

How could I have been so stupid?

She hated herself. She hated it all.

The second wave of vomit came. Then the painful dry heaves.

CHAPTER 27

Carla sat across the glass in the visitation room and said, "I went to the marina like you told me. The boat's not there."

"I know," Jane said. "It's in Dana Point. They found Cooper dead, and no sign of the money."

"He's dead?"

"Yeah."

Carla took that in. "I learned something more."

Jane studied her friend.

"Remember those two guys we met that night, coming out of the gate?"

"Louis and Jim."

"Yeah. I asked them how long the boat had been gone. They said only a couple of days, and then told me about a woman who used to come around, and another guy."

"What other guy?"

"I don't know. Someone other than Cooper. They didn't like this dude, thought he was an asshole. Didn't like her much either. I guess one day they got into it with them, some kind of conflict. They were shooting pictures on the dock. One of the guys is a model."

"Who?"

"Louis or Jim, I forget who. But they said this woman and this other guy got all up in their face about it."

"What was this other guy like?"

"I've got a picture."

"A picture?"

"They were super helpful, texted it to me so I printed it out at Walgreens. You can see them in the background." Carla held the photo up to the glass.

Jane recognized Veronica and Buddy, arm in arm, obviously lovers, cool and collected, masters of the universe. She had newfound clarity. "I think I figured it out," she said. "Veronica killed Cooper. She masterminded it all."

"What makes you so sure?"

"I didn't realize it until now, but it was Veronica we saw that night on Cooper's boat, the night we drove out to the marina. You saw her too."

"I remember."

"She, Buddy and Cooper planned this together from the very beginning. And then they killed Cooper so she didn't have to split the money," Jane said, devastated.

"Who's Buddy?"

"Wolff's bodyguard. Now it all makes sense."

"How?"

"Because she fucked me!"

Carla said nothing in return.

"And her performance was flawless," Jane said. "Perfect. I'm an actress. I ought to know."

KILL THE SHILL

CHAPTER 1

The heavyset jailer was different. Jane had never seen the woman before. She led her from the exercise yard of the Twin Towers Correctional Facility and through corridors she'd never been. They went up flights of stairs, and Jane wondered if this hulking guard had confused her with another inmate. She led her into the small anteroom, mumbled "wait here," and closed the door.

It smelled like disinfectant. Fluorescent lights buzzed overhead. Jane paced for what seemed like an eternity. She called out, but nobody came.

The room fell into darkness.

The masked man came in from the other door. A pillow case was yanked over her head, and Jane screamed. He slammed her to the concrete floor. He was strong, pulled her arms back and drove a knee into her vertebrae.

The next sensation was the pillow case pulled tight at the nape of her neck. Something slipped over her head then cinched around her throat—a noose of some kind, cutting into her windpipe.

She screamed and fought with all her might. His hand reached around to muffle her, so she bit hard. He tried to free his fingers locked in her teeth, punching her head, so she bit even harder.

Something cracked in her mouth.

She heard him grunt, knew it hurt him, and bit even harder.

She bucked, rolled, tried to pull off the pillow case but the snug garrote made it impossible. Next came the kicks to her ribs. It knocked the wind out of her. She gagged, gasped for air, and was certain she was going to die. She felt him tighten the garrote around her neck again, then she heard the door slam, and Jane was alone.

Her cry of anguish came from somewhere deep, a dark and primal place she'd never been before. By the time the staff came to her rescue she was shivering, adrenaline spent, teeth clattering. They consoled her, snipped off the band around her neck and removed the bloody pillow case.

Only then did Jane realize the noose was a flex-cuff. On television she'd seen cops use these plastic strips in lieu of handcuffs—zip-ties impossible to loosen. She figured the prison guards probably have drawers of these things, as common as ballpoint pens or the mace they carry on their belts.

Jane got the picture—no need to smuggle this murder weapon into the jail.

She swallowed through the mucus and it hurt like hell. An inch tighter would have been certain strangulation.

CHAPTER 2

Eyes bugged out, jaw gaping in rigor mortis, lips peeled back exposing blackened gums; Cooper's death-face still haunted her. This was the man she'd loved. The horrible image was what Jane saw when she closed her eyes at night.

After the attempt on her life Jane was moved to the prison's medical ward with twenty-four hour watch. The other inmate's hacking coughs and the smell of death put Jane on edge. She hated hospitals. She hated herself for being so stupid—for agreeing to be the shill.

She was expecting her mom in the visitation room but instead a preppy guy in a pin-striped oxford sat behind the glass. He produced identification and held it to the window, "Special Agent Brendan Gallagher, FBI," he said. "I need your help."

Jane thought she was done talking to the cops. "For what?" she asked.

"To find the woman who burned you."

Veronica had indeed burned her—in the third degree. The beautiful Veronica appeared to be the fiancée of a billionaire, but in reality she masterminded a brilliant scam. Only now did Jane see she acted as Veronica's puppet, a pawn sacrificed, and three million dollars was missing. Jane was accused of murdering the billionaire and even Cooper, Jane's lover, betrayed her and was found slain. She could even remember the smell of his rotting flesh.

"I've already told the cops everything," she said, eyeing him with suspicion.

"Veronica is watching you."

That gave Jane pause. *Watching?*

"Hear me out," he said. "I've been tracking Veronica for quite some time. She knows all about me. I can't compromise my cover because her influence runs deep. More than you can imagine."

Jane didn't know what to say. She wondered if Veronica could have had something to do with the attempt on her life. Not offering too many details, she explained how she narrowly escaped the assassination attempt.

He nodded and asked, "You've heard about jailhouse suicides?"

"I guess."

"Death by hanging is most often the MO."

Jane read into what he meant. "You're saying if I died they would have covered it up, claimed I hanged myself?"

"The Los Angeles Sheriff Department has had its lion share of corruption, especially in the jails."

"My lawyer is working on moving me to Central Regional, in Lynwood."

"There's no guarantee you'll be safe there. Like I said, her influence runs deep."

She tried to wrap her mind around it, asked, "She can arrange a murder behind bars?"

"Draw your own conclusion. Now tell me, where do you think Veronica may have gone?"

"I've told everyone a thousand times," she said, "I don't know."

"Maybe we can figure it out together."

She feared she'd said too much. "My lawyer wouldn't want me to talk about this."

"Every day Veronica slips further away. Help me catch her before she's gone forever."

She really didn't trust him but ventured, "What do you want to know?"

He started with many of the same questions the detectives had asked, but he was clearly more focused on Veronica. He cared less about Cooper, the boyfriend who coaxed her into the caper. He asked nothing about Alexander Wolff, the murdered billionaire. Instead he focused on Veronica and Wolff's bodyguard Buddy.

"Did Veronica speak of any specific cities or destinations?"

"Not really."

"Buddy?"

"He rarely said anything."

"How about Cooper?"

The recorded voice sounded informing them they had only three minutes left, so Jane proposed question of her own. "What's his real name?" she asked. "Cooper must have been an alias."

"Didier Boucher," he said.

"Tell me about him."

"His father passed down the trade to both he and his brother. They ran successful boiler rooms up in Canada, cold calling people in the United States and claiming they've won a sweepstakes. But in order for the sucker to claim the prize they needed to first send a fee to, supposedly, cover government taxes. It's an age-old scam. Nobody wins the grand prize. Everybody gets third place. When it arrives in the mail it's nothing but an inflatable raft."

"A raft?"

"Worth maybe twenty bucks at Walmart. Technically a boat, but nobody reads the fine print."

"Cooper did that?"

"He and his family, among other scams, targeting the elderly mostly. At one time they were flying high, but no longer. His brother gambled most of the fortune away. Cigarettes took their toll on the father, and now he's in a Quebec City nursing home."

"Cooper, I mean Didier, was French?"

"French Canadian. But you must have known that."

"He said he was from Chicago, went to school in Boston or something," she recalled. Jane reeled at the thought. She knew nothing about this man she had fallen in love with. Everything was a lie. She said, "Since you know Veronica is behind all of this, get me the hell out of here."

"I can help you, but it's not like in the movies where police and FBI work hand-in-hand. Bureaucracy is incredibly inefficient. They took me off Veronica's case, but I still work it when I get the chance. It's sort of…my baby."

Gorgeous Veronica—she figured he was drawn by her beauty. "If Cooper was French Canadian," she asked. "Why didn't he have an accent?"

"He's a pro."

Jane explained how he could sit in front of the television for hours watching hockey, cursing, kicking furniture, and he always checked his iPhone for scores.

"That's good. Those are the details I'm looking for," he said. "Think back. What about Veronica? Anything stick out?"

Jane was at a loss, asked, "Do you think she killed Cooper?"

"I'm certain."

"Why?"

"Because she's done it before."

She's done it before.

The phone cut them off, meeting over. He nodded and mouthed "thank you" through the glass, then departed without looking back.

She worried that she'd said too much.

CHAPTER 3

The bus of female prisoners weaved through downtown Los Angeles and pulled into the basement of the 60's era courthouse. This was the day of Jane's preliminary hearing.

Jane realized it was only temporary, but swapping out her prison orange for the plain skirt and blouse her mother purchased at Ross Dress for Less made her feel human again. There was no access to scissors, so she had to bite the plastic tags off with her teeth. This endeavor cut her lip. She dabbed it with toilet paper, but it was still bleeding, salty to taste.

They escorted her and a few others into an elevator. They walked the long hallway, fluorescent lights illuminating cinderblock walls. They placed her in a holding area and removed the handcuffs. From a water cooler Jane took a drink and had to refill the tiny paper Dixie Cup a few times in order to quench her thirst. She remembered this space from her arraignment. For some reason it seemed different now.

The first person she recognized in the courtroom was her mother, Nancy, seated with her boyfriend Danny. He wore jeans and a Bud Light T-shirt, in contrast with Jane's mother, dressed for the occasion in a navy blue suit. There was a small crowd in the courtroom, mostly people waiting for other cases, Jane assumed.

She saw Paul, her long-suffering public defender, emerge from the judge's chambers followed by Assistant District

Attorney Noonan, the man she recognized from her arraign-ment. Paul sat beside her. He nervously rubbed his nose aggressively and wiped his fingers on his slacks before he said, "We're in luck."

The bailiff announced the judge, and all in the courtroom stood. A gray-haired woman appeared and sat at the bench in the high-backed leather chair.

"This court has come to order," the bailiff announced before reading the docket number. The judge cleared her throat and spoke. "In the matter of the State of California versus Jane Innes, the state is unable to proceed at this time." The judge shot a glare at D.A. Noonan before she peered over her bifocals, "Miss Innes, you are released forthwith."

Jane heard her mother gasp.

"Bear in mind, however," the judge continued, "because this dismissal is without prejudice, the district attorney may file charges at a later date, at their discretion. Is that understood?"

"Yes," Jane said.

"You are ordered to report your whereabouts on a weekly basis with the Sheriff's office. Is that understood?"

"Yes, Your Honor."

The woman sized Jane up for a moment before the gavel came down. Paul said, "Let's speak in the hallway."

Jane turned to her mother. They embraced over the railing. The bailiff read the next docket number. As they left the courtroom another case had already begun.

In the hallway Paul pulled Jane aside. "Your case was dropped because evidence the prosecution was counting on fell apart," he said. "If they can bring more, they'll charge you. It's their strategy to buy time."

"What evidence?"

"The timeline once hotel's video surveillance was reviewed. It shows you were nowhere near Wolff's room before he was last seen."

"Then who was?"

"They haven't determined."

"Veronica," she said.

"Realize they'll have you followed."

"Why?"

"To lead them to the missing money."

"I don't have it."

"They don't know that."

"Misdirection," Jane said.

"Miss who?"

"No, misdirection, like a magic trick. I was Veronica's decoy. To throw everyone off her scent."

He rubbed his nose again, said, "Do yourself a favor, stay out of trouble."

"I'll try my best."

CHAPTER 4

To celebrate Jane's release Danny took everyone to lunch. He insisted on Tam O'Shanter, a classic L.A. meat-and-potato eatery styled after a Scottish pub. With its drooping Tudor style architecture and stained-glass windows, Jane thought the place could be something at Disneyland—like *Mr. Toad's Wild Ride*—but with a well-stocked bar.

They were led to their table by a young waitress in a short plaid skirt. For drink orders Danny and Nancy chose beer. Jane opted for wine. She really could use a drink—*and keep 'em coming.*

The lunch arrived and her prime rib was magnificent. Combined with the hearty Napa cabernet, Jane was in pure heaven. "Oh," she exclaimed, "this is good."

"Better than that jailhouse slop?" Danny asked.

"Absolutely."

While playing her role as the carefree heiress, Cooper had not allowed Jane to eat red meat. He decided the character she played, Kimberly, would only indulge in seafood selections, salads, or gluten-free pasta.

She tried to forget what her lawyer Paul had said, that cops may be following her, but paranoia won out. She couldn't help but watch the door and wonder if someone in the restaurant was spying them.

"I've been in the joint a few times myself," Danny admitted.

"When?" Nancy asked with an elbow to his ribs.

"For stupid things when I was young."

"Like what?"

"You don't want to know."

Her mother had been with Danny for almost a year now. It seemed as if she'd found her perfect soul-mate. Jane liked Danny's laid back manner. He was authentic, and didn't care what anyone thought of him.

Her mother turned to Jane and said, "Danny and I had an idea. We thought you could be a big help to us. We need a secretary, a Girl Friday, but it's more than that. When we're on the road we need someone who can hold down the fort back home. Send us stuff, set up hotels and make travel arrangements, that sort of thing. You'll be our coordinator and live with us in Sarasota. We're only on the road three or four months a year, so the rest of the time we'll all be together."

"Florida?"

"Oh, Jane, it's so beautiful there. You're going to love it."

This proposition did not thrill her. It was moving back home, and that meant failure. Besides, this would stall her acting pursuits. As Jane chewed on her prime rib she entertained visions of pink flamingos, alligators, and orange groves—all the iconic images of the Sunshine State. The more she thought about it, the more she realized there was very little keeping her in Los Angeles. No job, no boyfriend. Nothing.

"And there's a clown college there," Nancy said.

"What?"

"A clown college. Maybe you can study there."

Danny offered an explanation. "It's associated with Barnum and Bailey. The circus spent their winters in Sarasota, back in the day. Their headquarters are still based there."

Jane was horrified. Film, stage, and television were her true passion. Working as a clown was just a way to make a few bucks. She sipped her wine and tried to fathom what clowns could possibly study. *Balloon animals? Bullshit.*

Her mother added, "A lot of circus folks retire in the area. There's a darling midget couple in the neighborhood. Very nice people. And they have two normal-sized children. All grown up now."

"We're supposed to call them *little people*," Danny reminded her.

"Why?"

"Because that's what they prefer to be called these days." Danny waved to the waiter for another round, then in a lowered voice, "It's politically correct, *little people*, not midgets."

Nancy laughed to herself and leaned into Jane. "Go figure. I guess I'm not PC."

"Hell no," he said, teasing her.

Having eaten the meal combined with two glasses of wine Jane was suddenly very tired. The plan was to get her a room at the Best Western where Danny and Nancy were staying. The three of them climbed into Danny's pickup and drove to the motel.

"We've already missed qualifying rounds in Denver." her mother said. "So we'll drive back home on Tuesday because Danny has some business to attend to on Monday."

"I've got to meet some top fuel people, out in Lancaster," he explained.

"How long will it take to drive back?" Jane asked.

"About two days if we drive it straight through," Danny said.

Jane turned back and considered the large bed of his pickup. With the exception of her futon, she was certain she could fit most of her things back there.

They got Jane the adjoining room at the motel and Danny drove Jane to see Yuri, the mechanic who had her Nissan in his shop. She was surprised to learn her car had been sold.

"I'm sorry to say," the soft-bellied Ukrainian said, "I had to put a mechanic's lien on your car since I couldn't find you. Your phone is disconnected, and I mailed the notice but it came back."

Jane was furious. "You sold my car!?"

"Pick-A-Part. Yes, Pick-A-Part junkyard, in the Valley. They were kind enough to pick it up, but I lost money on the deal," Yuri said then ducked into his garage.

"I'll sue you!"

Danny tried to calm Jane down, explaining that Yuri had every right to sell her car.

"But that was *my* car!"

"What year was it?"

"I don't know."

"Ninety-six Nissan Sentra, with over two hundred thousand miles," unseen Yuri informed from the shade of his garage.

Danny took Jane's arm, "The thing couldn't have been worth more than eight hundred bucks."

"It's got sentimental value."

"How much did you owe him?"

"I don't know. Maybe seven hundred. I forget."

"Then it sounds like it's time for a new car," he said. "I've got a Chevy back home. You can borrow it until you're back on your feet."

Jane had owned the Nissan since high school and was sad she'd never see it again. Getting back in the truck, Jane saw a Dodge Charger with darkened windows across the street. She got the feeling whoever inside was watching her. They pulled away, and after a few blocks, she could see the car was following, her suspicions confirmed.

"Someone's following us," she said.

"Where?"

"Behind us. That black car."

Danny studied the rear-view mirror.

"My lawyer said the cops may be watching me," she said.

"They think I can lead them to Veronica."

"Cops? I better clean those beer cans out of my truck bed, don't ya think?"

Jane could see there were no cans in his truck bed and wondered why he was teasing her at a moment like this. The car followed for a few blocks but then veered off. She wondered if it was the cops, a coincidence, or someone working for Veronica?

CHAPTER 5

Jane felt the presence and sat up in bed. She trained her ear, listened intently without moving a muscle. There was someone outside the door of her motel room. As her eyes adjusted in the darkness, she wondered if it was a dream. Her mother and Danny were in the adjoining room.

She heard the plastic key enter the lock and someone work the knob.

"Hello!?" she shouted.

The person hesitated, and she could see a shadow move past her window. She heard the beep from the electronic lock next door before it opened and closed.

Danny pushed through the adjoining door and peeked in, "You alright?"

"Someone was trying to get in."

He moved to the window, parted the curtains, and looked out.

Jane said, "It sounds like they mixed up rooms."

"Why don't you sleep with your mom. I'll take this room."

"No, I'll be alright."

"We'll keep the adjoining door open. No big deal."

Jane got up, taking her pillow. She could see Danny was holding something low, a snub nosed revolver. Jane pretended she didn't see it, and moved into the other room. She climbed into bed next to her mother, felt her warmth in the linen. She heard Danny settle in and was glad he had a gun. Her mother's snoring kept Jane awake, but somehow it was comforting.

"Come on, honey. Lancaster will be fun."

"No, Ma, I'm tired," Jane said. "I just want to chill. And Danny's got important business, so I'd only get in the way."

"You won't be in Danny's way," her mother insisted. "You can keep me company."

"I just want to sleep, watch TV, do nothing for a change."

Jane had spent the previous day sifting through her meager possessions and clearing out the storage unit. What she decided to keep was packed in boxes and placed in the back of Danny's truck.

When Danny was in the shower, Jane asked her mother about the gun.

"When we're on the road, Danny thinks it best to pack a pistol." Nancy explained that they were staying in a motel in Oakland when someone tried to climb in their bathroom window in the middle of the night while they were asleep. "You never know," her mother said.

After Nancy and Danny set out for Lancaster, Jane crossed the street to the Norm's diner for breakfast. She bought the *LA Times* and arranged it on her table when Agent Gallagher surprised her, sliding into the booth.

"Morning, beautiful."

"You're following me," she said.

"The sheriff's department so rudely interrupted our last meeting."

"Do you drive a Dodge Charger?"

"Can't say I do." He took off his aviator sunglasses, pulled a paper napkin from the dispenser, and began to clean them. "Do me a favor," he said. "I want you to start writing down details about Veronica. She may be good at what she does, but she's not perfect. I'm banking she's made mistakes."

"Seems to me like the perfect woman committed the perfect crime," she said.

"No, Veronica is deeply flawed," he said, with edge in his voice. "She may be easy on the eyes, and charming, but believe me she's a heartless bitch," his voice raising, "rotten to the core, with maggots crawling around inside. You have no idea."

It was clear he hated her. Jane looked around hoping nobody overheard his little tirade. There was an awkward pause before she asked, "How long have you been after her?"

"Long enough for my *stupid-visors* to take me off the case and assign someone else. It's Bureau policy, after two years, but I always get my man, or in this case, woman."

A wrinkled-faced waitress approached wearing a splattered apron. Jane sensed this woman had seen a lot in her life, and not all of it fair. She took Gallagher's order of a Diet Coke and he asked it be, "served in *only* glassware, by no means a plastic tumbler, please." After she left he produced a manila file from his shoulder bag. "First I need you to confirm that this is her," he said, indicating a color Xerox of Veronica's passport photo.

Jane was certain. "That's her," she said. "What's her real last name?"

"Tatinger."

"Like the French champagne?"

"I suppose." He handed her a wallet-sized photo of a teenage Veronica. It was a swim meet photo, a medal around her neck. Jane sensed a hint of sadness in Veronica's youthful eyes. "She grew up in Atlanta. Her father was an oil exec, her mother Junior League."

The waitress returned with Gallagher's soda and Jane's breakfast. "Can I get ya' something to eat, honey?" she asked Gallagher.

"Just the Diet Coke is fine, thank you," he said. She pulled a straw from her apron and Gallagher held up his hand, "I don't need a straw. I hate straws."

"Okay," the waitress said, "no straws then, not a problem."

To Jane she said, "Can I get you anything else, sweetie? More coffee?"

"No, looks good, thank you."

The waitress gave her a smile and was off. Jane wondered if she would be waiting tables at this woman's age, dealing with the public, pretending to be nice. "Why do you hate straws?" she asked.

"They bug me."

"Why?"

"Because I don't like plastic against my teeth."

"Even straws?"

"Straws, cups, disposable utensils."

"Like sporks?"

"All that shit, yeah. What's wrong with that?"

"Nothing."

"You think it's weird, don't you?"

"No."

"Admit it, you do."

"I think you've got some obsessive compulsive stuff going on, but I'm not one to judge."

"Yeah, you're probably right," he said with a laugh. "But other than that, I'm a great guy, really." It was clear he was trying to make her feel at ease. Jane noticed he wasn't wearing a wedding band.

"Now where were we?" he said and searched the file. "Veronica ran away from home at seventeen, moved to Manhattan. To pay the rent she became an exotic dancer and apparently she was quite good. That paved the way."

"Paved the way to what?"

"She became a Fifth Avenue call girl, quite sought after because she was so young and beautiful, and one hell of a seductress. She moved up the food chain," he said and sipped his Diet Coke. "She apprenticed with a couple of old-school swindlers who worked Wall Street hustles. They took her under their wing, and her beauty opened a lot of doors. They had Veronica seduce rich married guys, claim she was pregnant, and then they would blackmail these dudes. It's an age-old scam, called the badger game."

"She would have to sleep with them though, to claim she's pregnant?"

"All part of the scam. She's a whore."

"Yeah," she said, remembering the night she'd spent with Veronica as Wolff watched them. She swallowed back the anger and humiliation. Veronica's like a black widow, Jane thought to herself, she mates and she kills.

He continued, "The two old guys got caught in a Ponzi scheme. They were sentenced to Federal prison and that's when she hung her own shingle. No longer the hired hand, she started to mastermind her own capers, assemble her own crews. And she was quite inventive. But what I don't get is how Alexander Wolff ends up dead. That's not like her. There should have been a blow off."

"What's a blow off?"

"A setup so after the mark gets burned he won't go to the police."

"I don't get it."

"Let's say you come across a three-card monte game. You know what that is, right?"

"Three cards tossed around. Find the queen." Jane knew the routine from her experience performing magic in her clown act.

"It looks easy, one guy standing there making money. But what you don't realize it's a team and they're all in it together. So, say you're fool enough to get in on the action and they take your money. Just then someone, the lookout, claims cops are coming and they all scatter. You can't go to the police and say you were swindled because you were illegally gambling in the first place. When a blow off is done right the mark doesn't think he's been swindled."

"The art of deception," she said.

"Precisely."

Jane studied Veronica's high school photo before handing it back. "If things had gone as planned, do you think she and Cooper always intended on cutting me out?"

"You would have found yourself abandoned with only the clothes on your back. Tell me the truth, would you have gone to the police and admitted you were an accessory to grand larceny?"

"Probably not," she said.

"That's how it's supposed to work."

Jane felt so foolish.

"When are you leaving town?" Gallagher asked.

"Tomorrow."

"Great golf courses in Florida."

"I don't play golf."

"Maybe you should pick it up." He pulled out his wallet and dropped a twenty on the table. "Write stuff down when you think of it, and have a safe trip." He was off.

Jane wondered how he knew she was moving to Florida. She'd never told him. She had left a forwarding address at her old apartment, maybe he'd gone there. Through the window she saw him slip into a white sedan and drive away.

She paid the check with the twenty dollar bill—left a ten dollar tip.

CHAPTER 6

Danny had only one type of music—traditional Country & Western. Standards included tunes from Hank Williams, George Jones, and Loretta Lynn. Most of these narratives were about loneliness and heartbreak. Jane had never really cared for country, but now this music spoke to her. The beauty was in the simplicity.

As they traveled East on Interstate 10, she gazed out over the desert landscape and relived the events with Cooper and Veronica. There was a moment, she realized, that she could have walked, a crossroads after Cooper confessed he was a con man in search of a partner. Instead, she chose to be his shill— her fatal move. The weakness stemmed from her love for him, sure, but also her greed. Jane came to realize her troubles began with that one fateful decision.

They pulled over at a rest stop in Arizona. Sparse trees providing scant shade. Emerging from the cinderblock restroom she got the feeling she was being watched. Jane scanned the parking lot but didn't see anyone.

She noticed the young man on the park bench looking at her. He wore a black sweatshirt with the hoodie pulled over his head. He produced a phone and pecked away at the screen.

Jane couldn't see his face, but her first thought was that it was too hot to have the hood of his sweatshirt pulled up. She hurried to the truck, but it was locked. Danny was not there, and her mother was still back in the restroom.

The young man got up, carried a hockey stick, and came toward her. *Hockey in Arizona? What the...?*

Black jeans, black hood, the stick with its curved arch; Jane thought he looked like a modern day Grim Reaper. She ran toward the roadway. When she looked back he wasn't following, instead gliding on the pavement in rollerblades in the opposite direction. He joined a few others she hadn't noticed before. They had a rag tag hockey goal set up on the concrete basketball court—local kids playing roller hockey.

Jane realized her imagination was playing tricks on her.

Danny and Nancy soon joined her. "Everything alright?" her mother asked.

"Yeah," Jane lied.

Arizona, New Mexico, it was dark by the time they reached Texas. The roadside diners all melted together in Jane's mind, as if they were all the same. Los Angeles, and her acting dreams, were a world away, and getting further by the hour.

"Jane is so talented," her mother bragged when the subject of her career came up. "She got all the leading roles in her high school plays."

"No, I didn't."

"Almost all."

"Yeah, well, I didn't have much luck in Hollywood," she said.

"You were in that science fiction movie. Whatever happened to that? Can we see it on Netflix?"

Jane confessed the complications that arose from her supporting role in *Gemini*, the low budget film that went nowhere. She explained how a company calling itself Zipper Video had repurposed the footage, mixing it in with an X-rated title to create something entirely different. She knew nothing about it and was surprised to discover the porno, now titled *Saturnalia*, playing on pay-per-view.

"One of the girls sort of looked like me," she said, "hair

done the same, costume alike, clearly intended to be my character, but they renamed her Lieutenant Vixen."

Danny listened without saying a word. She could tell the subject bothered him.

"How can they do that?" Nancy asked.

"I signed away my 'name and likeness' in a contract, and I cashed the check. Legally they can do whatever they want."

"That doesn't seem fair," her mother said.

"No, it doesn't."

Her mother encouraged. "Don't give up your dreams, honey. I believe in you."

"Thanks, Ma."

"Zipper Video, huh?" Danny asked.

"Bastards," she said.

CHAPTER 7

Jane could immediately see that Sarasota was divided into two parts; the Longboat Key section lined with lavish, gated estates, and the other side of town with its mundane strip malls and trailer parks.

Danny lived on the other side of town.

His house was a simple tract home. Given the tour, Jane could see both his home and business were meticulously clean. She did not expect that, had images of a hound dog and a rocking chair on the porch. She complimented Danny on the garage being so organized. He explained that his sponsors expected it. "It's show business, really, all about spit-and-polish. Fools 'em to think I know what I'm doing."

Danny excused himself and Nancy further explained that much of the funding comes from sponsors. "That's how the racing game works. So when the benefactors come around," her mother instructed, "set out beers and heat up frozen snacks in the toaster oven." She showed Jane a pantry full of provisions, including coffee, and cartons of cigarettes. Nancy unwrapped one of the packs and demonstrated. "Make up a tray, take the cellophane off the cigarettes and set them out like this." Even though Jane didn't smoke, the presentation looked so inviting she considered trying one.

"How often do your sponsors come?" Jane asked.

"No telling. Fridays and weekends mostly. Sometimes it goes

late into the night, gets sort of like a country club around here, especially before a race.”

Jane got the picture. She would be a receptionist, office manager, travel coordinator, shipping and receiving clerk, caterer, and cocktail waitress. Without admitting it to her mom, Jane doubted she’d be in Florida for very long.

Getting settled into the desk Danny assigned to her, Jane considered calling the number the Los Angeles Sheriff’s Department gave her to report her new location. She hesitated since Gallagher warned her that Veronica’s “influence runs deep.” Instead, she phoned him.

“There’s something I thought of along the drive,” she told Agent Gallagher. “When Cooper was trying to hook Wolff, he mentioned he had a friend at the *Wall Street Journal.* On cue, the friend would run a news story about the Brazilian diamond trade. It was intended to justify Cooper’s information as legit, coming from an outside source. He called it a clincher.”

“Go on.”

“The idea was if he published the story when Cooper told him to, the journalist was supposed to get a piece of the action.”

“Interesting,” he said.

“Since we know Veronica was pulling the strings, I’m thinking maybe this writer is connected to her. And just maybe, as we speak, he’s wondering where his bonus is.”

“Assuming he never got paid?”

“Because there was a double murder and things didn’t go as planned.” From the silence on the other end of the line she could tell he was thinking about it.

“When did the story run?”

“I don’t know the exact date. I think it was the day before Wolff was found dead.”

“I’ll look into it and get back to you.”

She could tell by the urgency in his voice he was excited by this new lead. Find the journalist.

CHAPTER 8

Over the next few days Jane took on her new responsibilities. She met Danny's pit crew and a few of the benefactors, including the three hundred pound bearded guy by the name of Jeremiah, a former college football star whose family owned car dealerships. They were polite, good-ol' boys with Southern charm, and she found one of them, a guy her age named Luke, to be very attractive. But other than an occasional "hello," none of them approached. She figured they viewed her as the boss's daughter, off limits, and that was fine. She was in no place to start a relationship.

As promised, Danny lent her one of his cars. He called it his Chevy back in L.A. but Jane was surprised to see it was a restored 1969 Super Sport Malibu.

"It's better to drive it than let it sit," he assured.

"But what if I wreck it?"

"You won't. Give it a whirl."

The car was loud and powerful. Jane was scared of it at first, but found it exhilarating, like nothing she'd ever driven before.

As Memorial Day weekend approached Danny and the crew worked into the evenings preparing for a race at the Las Vegas Motor Speedway. Jane had plenty of spare time and began searching the Internet for *Veronica Tatinger*, plus other key words like deception, larceny, and fraud.

Her search produced nothing.

She remembered that at one point Veronica talked, at length, about fine linen. She was quite opinionated about it and detailed thread count, organic cotton, and washing techniques. Since Veronica was a former call girl in Manhattan, Jane decided to call the high-end linen stores there.

Dusting off her acting skills, she pretended to be Veronica. "This is Veronica Tatinger. I have a charge on my credit card I'd like to verify." Store after store had no record of the name.

The last on her list was an establishment named Versailles on Second Avenue. From their website it was clear they specialized in European linen. As Danny and the men were loading the dragster onto the trailer, Jane called.

"Veronica, how are you?" a man's voice warmly replied.

"I'm sorry, who is this?"

"It's me Giavanni."

"Oh, yes, Giavanni. I didn't recognize your voice." she faked.

"I'm glad you called. I have the complete sets, in your pattern," he said. "I tried to reach you, but your phone sends me to voicemail. Where have you been?"

"Travelling," Jane said, trying her best to mimic Veronica's voice.

"I was afraid your special pattern may have been discontinued, Vee, but that's not the case, thank God. Can you hold on while I see how many I have in stock?"

"Of course," Jane said. She made note that he called her by the nickname *Vee* and wrote it down.

Giavanni returned. "I'm sorry, Vee, I only have six sets in store, but I can get more. Now what's the credit card charge you mentioned?"

"I want to confirm you've got my current address. What do you have on record?"

"I'll have to look it up. Should I order your usual twenty sets?" he asked.

Twenty sets? Jane wondered. *Why would Veronica need*

twenty sets of sheets? "Yes," she said. "When do you think they'll be available?"

"Maybe three weeks. Your seashell pattern is custom, as you know."

Seashell Pattern?

At that moment a pair of police officers came through the door. "Jane Innes?" one of the officers asked, checking against his clipboard.

She said into the phone, "Please tell me what address you have," while motioning to them to hold on.

Giavanni said, "Give me a minute."

Jane could tell the officers did not like waiting. She cupped the phone and said, "How can I help you?"

"I'm Officer Hernandez and this is Officer Munroe of the Sarasota County Sheriff's Department. We're here to confirm the whereabouts of Jane Innes."

"I'm Jane."

"Can I see identification, please?"

Jane reached for her purse and gave them her driver's license, phone still wedged in her ear. The officer gave her ID a glance.

Danny noticed the officers and approached. He introduced himself, and Jane was glad for the distraction. At that moment, the other line rang.

"Dobson Racing," Jane answered.

"It's me," she recognized Gallagher's voice. "I found him."

"Who?"

"The journalist, Jason Fischer. Does that name ring a bell?"

"No, but let me call you back," Jane said, eyeing the officers.

"Veronica or Cooper never mention the name Fischer?"

"No." She could hear traffic and sirens in the background and asked, "Where are you?"

"In the City," he said.

"New York?"

"Miss Innes, we need to ask you a few questions," Officer Hernandez said.

"I'll call you right back," Jane said, and hung up on Gallagher.

She got back to Giavanni's line. Light opera music still played in the background so she put it on speaker and addressed the officers.

"Sorry, it's really busy around here," she said.

They asked for the address she was staying, and Danny supplied it. They asked how long she intended on being in Florida.

"Indefinitely," Jane said.

Giavanni returned on the line. "Sorry, Vee," broadcasting aloud for all to hear, "I have customers in the store and can't pull your invoice. Give me your number, Vee, and I'll call you back. Wait, I've got it here on my phone. Dobson Racing?"

Jane picked up the line, "Something just came up. Let me get back to you."

"Chao," he said before she hung up.

"Who's Vee?" Officer Hernandez asked.

"It's a nickname," she lied.

He shared a look with his partner who jotted that down. "Sign here, please," the officer said.

Jane was leery, signed the form as instructed, and they were off.

"I want you to keep the door locked," Danny advised.

"Okay. Why?"

"I've lived here for over twenty years, enough to know what doesn't smell right."

"What do you mean?"

"Cops around here...following up for the District Attorney out in L.A....seems out of place to me."

"How so?"

"Can't put my finger on it." Danny went back to the dragster.

Jane tried Gallagher, but only got his voicemail. She didn't leave a message.

***

After dinner, as her mother was doing the dishes, Danny said to Jane, "I want to show you something," and motioned her to follow.

In his study dominated by racing trophies Danny pointed to a cabinet. "If it makes you feel safer, this is where I keep my gun." He pulled out a hidden key and opened it. The revolver she had seen before sat on top of a box of shells. He explained, "It's a Smith & Wesson .38 Special, hammerless model 442, five rounds. Normally I take it on the road, but with you being all alone…"

"I'll be alright," she said, nervous at the sight of a gun.

"I know you will, but just in case. Maybe keep it in your purse when you're at the garage. Can't hurt."

"But it *can* hurt," she said.

"This model is safe. Double action only so you really have to pull the trigger back, with true intention, for it to fire." He popped open the cylinder to show her it was empty. "It's unloaded now, try firing it."

Jane took it. With the barrel pointed to the carpet she pulled the trigger. The chamber spun and the gun clicked. Danny took it back and loaded the revolver with long, silver shells. "What if I kill someone?" she said.

"You won't. If you're called to use it aim for the legs. Maim, then run. And whatever you do, don't let your mother know anything about this. I don't want her worrying."

Jane swallowed, said, "I won't."

"Deal?"

"Deal."

CHAPTER 9

The next morning, at the crack of dawn, everyone except Jane set out for Las Vegas. They would be on the road for three weeks. Jane knew she'd be lonely, but also liked the idea of being alone for a while.

She bid them goodbye, finished the pot of coffee, and waited until it was after nine to call Gallagher. Again she got no answer. She paced, felt incredibly restless, and made her decision. Since the crew would be on the road for two days, and she'd have very little to do, Jane figured she had a short window of opportunity. She got on the Internet found a discount flight. Nancy had left Jane her credit card in the event her daughter needed anything. Jane used it to purchase the plane ticket. She figured she'd pay her mother back the cost of the trip from the meager salary. A few hours later Jane was waiting at the Sarasota-Bradenton Airport to board a jet bound for Kennedy International.

It was something she had to do.

She slept for most of the flight, and awakened as she felt the jet descend. Out the window Jane could see the white, puffy clouds dissolve to reveal the Manhattan skyline. She had only seen the skyscrapers on television and movies, but now here they were, for real.

Her plan was to check into the midtown Holiday Inn, where she had a reservation, and call Gallagher. Together they could go to the linen store. She asked the middle-aged woman reading a romance novel next to her what was the best way to get into the city. She suggested the commuter bus that drops passengers off outside Grand Central Station.

She found the bus, and as it made its way through Queens Jane's first impression was that everything seemed so old. There were endless brick row-houses. The roads were so much narrower than she'd seen before, and she was amazed how the bus driver maneuvered the massive vehicle through the maze of traffic. As the bus entered a tunnel she realized, since Manhattan is an island, she would be passing under the East River. What struck her odd was that the road's descent did not seem steep enough. In the darkness she wondered just how far over her head the river flowed.

Her room in the Holiday Inn was small, but clean. Out the window she could see people working in cubicles in the building directly across the street and wondered what type of business they were engaged in. She took a moment to hang a few garments and freshen up before she texted Agent Gallagher.

"I'm here, Manhattan."

Her phone rang immediately. "What were you thinking?" he said.

"I found a cheap, last-minute flight."

"You shouldn't have come."

She could tell he was angry, "I want Veronica to pay for her sins just as much as you. Until she's caught—"

"—You're no use to me here," he said. "Go home."

"Say this journalist leads us to Veronica, that's great. If we come up empty, then it wasn't meant to be. But something tells me she's near."

"What makes you think so?"

"Call it woman's intuition." Jane explained her conversation with Giavanni at the linen store and how she impersonated Veronica. "We'll go there together. Tomorrow."

"Why not now?"

"They're closed by now. Where are you?"

"In a bar downtown. The Raccoon Lodge. It's a place Fischer hangs out. I'm rolling the dice that he makes an appearance."

"I'll meet you there," she said.

He reluctantly agreed.

Rain pelted the windshield as the cab driver weaved through cross-town traffic. Ballywood music chimed, and it smelled like pine air freshener. The LCD video screen in the back seat played New York City public service announcements.

The taxi turned on Warren Street and pulled over. Jane paid the cabbie and checked out the neon sign for The Raccoon Lodge, a tavern-style establishment. She was starving, but doubted there was much of a menu.

She found herself standing in front of The Mysterious Bookshop. Inside there was a gathering of some kind, a young woman signing books. Those standing around were drinking wine and chatting. She wanted to go in, browse, and discover something good to read, preferably private eye fiction. But business came first. Standing in the cold rain, she worked up the courage to face Gallagher, and crossed the street.

The Raccoon Lodge had a young crowd. Most were dressed in work attire, ties loosened, jackets hung over barstools. Gallagher sat at the end of the bar. They spotted each other, and he waved her over. She took the stool next to him.

"Welcome to New York," he said.

"Thanks."

"You shouldn't have come."

"I'm an actress, I live by impulse."

He sized her up, said, "Alright. What are you drinking?"

Since Gallagher had the remnants of a beer, she said, "Guinness." He raised his arm and caught the bartender's attention, an old school professional that fit this blue-collar establishment like a glove.

"Two pints of Guinness, please," he said.

"Right," the barkeep said with an Irish brogue.

Gallagher explained, "Fischer does his business socializing a few blocks north of here, a place called The Odeon. Afterward, he comes here to relax."

"Why's that?"

"Wall Street doesn't drink here, so he's off the clock. Plus he lives around the corner. The superintendent of his building tipped me off," Gallagher admitted, "and since it's Friday..."

"So tell me about him."

"He's had his fair share of exclusives, and he's made a good living leveraging financial information."

"Leveraging?"

"Breaking stories about corporate maneuvers that affect stock price. He finds underlings at a company, targets people who feel underappreciated. Or he pays cleaning crews to install spyware. Then he sells tips to insiders."

"So he's a spy?"

"He's an investigative journalist but doesn't expose injustices, necessarily. He leverages messages, creates stories that appear to be financial news. It's all about the stock price."

Jane didn't quite understand but nodded anyway. Their drinks arrived. She could see the bartender created a cloverleaf pattern in the frothy foam. "How much do you think Veronica paid him to publish the Brazilian diamond story?"

Without answering Gallagher perked up, eye on the door. "That's him, yellow tie."

She turned and was surprised that Fischer was much younger than she'd expected, in his early thirties, and good-looking. She had imagined a gray-haired, pot-bellied, sports writer type of guy. Instead he was lean and clean-cut. It appeared he knew the couple at the end of the bar and engaged them in conversation.

"So what do we do now?" she asked.

"Watch."

Fischer took the seat next to the couple and ordered.

"When he goes to the head, I'll approach him," Gallagher said. "I'm going to say you're with the Securities and Exchange Commission. Follow my lead."

"I can play a bureaucrat."

The bartender served him. After a few sips of his whisky, Fischer got up and walked past on his way to the restroom. Gallagher stood, pulled his leather from his pocket and unfolded it revealing a badge.

"Jason Fischer, Special Agent Brendan Gallagher with the Federal Bureau of Investigations, and this is Sarah King from the Securities and Exchange Commission. We're wondering if you can help us with a matter. I promise it won't take long." He motioned to a table, "Please, have a seat and I'll explain."

Jane could see the color drain from Fischer's face. He shot a quick glance to her, and then back to his friends before he said, "What do you want?"

"Have a seat. This won't take but a minute."

With reluctance he complied.

Jane joined them at the table and Gallagher continued, "We're trying to protect someone from harm, Veronica Tatinger, and we need your help finding her."

Protect her? Jane thought. That was the last thing they planned to do. But he said it so convincingly she almost believed it.

"Doesn't ring a bell, my friend," Fischer said.

"I have a feeling you're not being entirely truthful."

"Why do you say that?" he said, darting a look to Jane.

"Because we know she hired you to break a story."

"What story?"

Gallagher leaned in, "Don't play dumb, the Brazilian diamond piece in the *Journal*."

"I really don't know what you're talking—"

"—Insider trading is a felony," Jane blurted out. "Want to talk about that?" It was a bold move, but she went for it. Jane could see Fischer's shoulders deflate, his bravado cracked.

"Who said I know anything about inside trading?"

"Being truthful is in your best interest," Jane said.

He sat back, scratched the back of his head, and said, "Okay, I know Veronica, but I don't know where she is."

"How do you know her?" Gallagher asked.

"I was doing a story featuring Anne Bonny, the female pirate. You've heard of Blackbeard or Captain Morgan? Anne was a female version, and just as ruthless. I was writing a business-rag piece, drawing a parallel between corporate raiders and historical pirates. Veronica found me, somehow, and shared her expertise on the subject. She set me straight on historical details and sent photos of her artifacts."

"What kind of artifacts?" Gallagher asked.

"She's got a collection of nautical relics, letters, all stuff from that era. She was living at the Millennium Hotel at the time, but that was two years ago. She's obsessed with Anne Bonny."

"Why?" Jane questioned.

"Veronica claims she's a descendant. Anne was in prison and sentenced to be hanged for piracy. But the Governor of Jamaica granted her a stay of execution when they discovered she was pregnant, 'Pleading her belly' as they called it in the day. Veronica claims she's related to that child."

"So how did you end up placing her Brazilian diamond story?" Gallagher asked.

"There's no fiction in that piece," he said, defensive. "It's totally legitimate. There's big turmoil in those mines."

"I believe you."

"She emailed me, clued me in, and I did the research."

"The plan was to wait for her cue to run it?" Jane asked, knowing his answer but curious how he'd respond.

"A lot of people give me story ideas."

"But they don't necessarily pay you to publish them," Gallagher said.

"Look, I wish I could help you, but I have no way to contact her. Maybe the hotel has a forwarding address."

Gallagher pulled a card out of his breast pocket. "Please have her call me if she contacts you."

"I hope she's not in too much trouble." Fischer said,.

"Me, too. Thank you for your time," Gallagher said.

"No worries," he said, stood, and moved to the men's room.

"What next?" Jane asked.

"He'll try to contact her."

"And?"

"That's how we'll find her. Let's go."

It was dark by then and raining harder as Jane followed Agent Gallagher down the street. He spoke into his cell phone and she overheard him saying, "I'd like to report a stolen phone," then after a moment, "Jason Fischer." He responded to a few security questions reading from a soggy note. They slowed in front of a Tribeca loft apartment building. "Thank you," he said, before hanging up. "He lives here, in apartment 3F. I've put a tracer on his home phone. If he calls Veronica, we can track the number."

"A tracer?"

"Yeah, interprets the numbers dialed and transcribes the conversation."

"Think he'll call her?"

"We can only hope," he said eyeing the building before he turned to her and said, "Good work back there."

"Thanks."

"Pirates, now there's a new twist. Somehow I'm not surprised," he said, and guided her to the shelter of an awning.

"What's that old saying?" Jane said. "The apple doesn't fall far from the tree."

"Maybe you have a point." He explained he'd look into the Millennium Hotel, and they made plans to meet for breakfast the next morning before they went to the linen store. Gallagher hailed a cab and held open the door for her.

"Until tomorrow," he said.

It felt good to be back in the game.

Twenty minutes later, at the hotel front desk, she made arrangements to use the business center computer. She searched the name "Anne Bonny" and a number of hits came up including an illustration of Anne aiming a flintlock, garment flowing. The bio read:

Some call Anne Bonny a feminist who chose piracy as way of rebelling against a male-dominated world; others portray her as a tomboy who never grew up. Whatever her motives, Anne Bonny was history's most infamous woman pirate.

Born in Kinsale, Ireland, in the late 1690's, she was the daughter of a house maid. Her mother's employer, a well-to-do lawyer who was respectfully married at the time, took a liking to young Anne. When their forbidden tryst was discovered the lovers ran off to America and established themselves as plantation owners in South Carolina. The comforts of plantation life were far less alluring than the action in nearby port Charleston, and Anne soon ran off with a dashing pirate named Calico Jack Rachman.

Because the pirate code forbade female crew members, she disguised herself as a man and fought alongside his crew. It was only a matter of time before she was discovered, however, and according to legend, the first fellow shipmate to express anger at having a woman aboard paid for his opinion with his life. Anne stabbed him through the heart.

However incredible a woman's presence on board may have seemed to Calico Jack's crew, amazingly, Anne Bonny was not the only female on board. Also disguised as a man was a woman named Mary Read. The two became fast friends, and later lovers. Alongside Calico Jack they wreaked havoc throughout the Caribbean for nearly a year, until Anne Bonny became pregnant. She gave birth in Cuba, then returned to the ship, abandoning the child. Ironically, it would be another unwanted pregnancy that would later save her life.

In 1720, Calico Jack's ship was captured by pirate-hunters. During the fight, and hung-over from a night of revelry, Calico

Jack apparently cowered in the hold while the two women stayed on deck and attempted to fight off the attackers. After their capture, legend has it that Anne said to Calico Jack on the eve of his execution: "I'm sorry to see you here, Jack, but if you'd have fought like a man you needn't hang like a dog."

Calico Jack and his men were hanged for their crimes.

Because Bonny and Read were both pregnant, they escaped execution. Before giving birth Mary Read suffered a fever that took her life. Anne was heartbroken, but her life was spared by Jamaican Governor Woodes Rogers who granted her a stay of execution.

Afterward, no one knows what happened to Anne. Some say she went back to her plantation, some say she resumed the pirate's life, and others say she set out for the West. Using sex as a weapon, and never afraid to kill, Anne Bonny was a true femme fatale.

A femme fatale, Jane thought. Deceitful and deadly, just like Veronica. The apple doesn't fall far from the tree.

CHAPTER 10

Her phone rang early the next morning.

"He called her," Gallagher said. "She called back and told him to come to room 510 at the St. Regis Hotel. Can you meet me there in twenty minutes?"

"I'm on my way."

She pulled on jeans and a sweater, put her hair in a ponytail, and was down on the street hailing a cab before she realized she'd forgotten to brush her teeth.

Less than ten minutes later she was standing across the street from the St. Regis Hotel on 55th and Fifth. A doorman, wearing a white Royal Guard uniform, stood at the entrance. Jane thought he must be an actor. This gig is probably his day job, kind of like hers as a clown.

Gallagher found her. "Fischer just went in," he said.

They walked past the doorman who said good morning and tipped his stove-top hat. Definitely an actor, Jane thought.

They entered the lobby. When it became clear they would need a key card for the elevators, they avoided them and instead ran up flights of stairs until they reached the fifth floor. In the hallway they paused to catch their breaths. Gallagher found the room, pressed his ear against the door.

"Nothing," he said.

A few doors down the middle-aged maid emerged from a room and tended to her cart. She pulled up her reading glasses attached to a silver chain around her neck to consult the clipboard.

"Should we knock?" Jane whispered so the maid could not hear.

"I don't think so," he said.

"Why not?"

"We don't know who else is in there."

Jane remembered back in L.A. when Veronica showed her that Wolff's bodyguard Buddy carried a gun. "Maybe Buddy?" she asked.

"Possibly."

"So what do we do now?"

"We wait."

Jane could see the maid had noticed them so didn't consider waiting an option. Besides, she had come too far. Veronica was behind that door, and Jane was in no mood to play it safe. Over her reading glasses, the maid eyed them with suspicion.

"You strapped?" she whispered to Gallagher.

"Am I what?"

"Do you have your gun?"

"Sure. Why do you ask?"

"Follow my lead," she said before moving towards the woman. "Excuse me," Jane said, "I locked myself out of my room. I think I left the key on the dresser."

The maid looked to Gallagher who simply shrugged.

"You're going to have to call security," the housekeeper said, all business.

"Please," Jane said, bending her knees, "I really, *really* need to pee."

"I'm sorry, but I can't let you in, it's policy. There's a phone near the elevators," she said pointing over her shoulder. "Call the front desk and security will send someone up."

From years of performing magic tricks Jane knew exactly what to do. "I can't wait," she said. "If you don't mind…" she said trying to wedge past the maid.

"I can't let you do that, ma'am" the maid protested.

The pickpocket routine was part of her clown act, but it was always was a crap shoot. Sometimes the volunteer from the audience is easy to manipulate and Jane could successfully lift their wallet without them knowing. Other times the volunteer would feel her. At that point she'd default to plan B in her routine and hold the wallet out to the audience, take a bill, make a joke out of it, and use the cash for another trick. This time the housekeeper had no idea Jane snatched her key card. She said, "There's a ladies room in the lobby."

"Okay," Jane said, backing away, the key card tucked. After the maid collected towels and went back into the room, Jane spun the card around the retractable key chain, flaunting it for Gallagher's benefit.

"Look at you, Houdini," he said, clearly impressed.

The coast clear, Jane slid the key into the slot and quietly pressed the handle. She could see Gallagher had his gun out, a sleek automatic.

They entered the room together.

First the scent of marijuana hit her. Then she heard sounds of passionate moans as they made their way into the suite. From tangled sheets her leg was propped high. Fischer's naked ass was visible. He cradled one of her thighs with one hand and enthusiastically went about his business. This appeared to be rough sex because his other hand pulled her hair.

But her hair was not black—it was red.

Fischer noticed the intruders and spun around, eyes wide. He pulled the sheets to cover himself. The woman emerged from the bedspread and screamed, recoiled against the headboard with a loud thud.

It was not Veronica.

Fischer yelled, "What the…Get the fuck out of here!"

"Who are you?" the mystery woman asked.

"Feds," Fischer answered.

The redhead eyed Jane. Pleading, she asked, "Does my husband know?"

Jane was at a loss. She turned, was almost out the door when she realized Gallagher was not behind her. Turning back she saw him place his foot on the coffee table, return his weapon to its ankle holster, and then finally join her in the hallway.

The maid was there with a walkie-talkie. "Excuse me. Is everything alright?"

Jane tossed her the keycard.

The woman caught it, surprised, then turned red with anger. Into the radio, she barked "Security!"

They darted into the stairwell, descending flights. They cut through the lobby and brushed past the doorman. They moved up Fifth Avenue and crossed the street. When it was clear nobody was following, and as if nothing had happened, Gallagher casually said, "So, Jane, tell me again the deal with this linen store."

"I'll explain on the way."

CHAPTER 11

Jane gave the cab driver the Upper East Side address and said to Gallagher, "I'll pretend to be Veronica's personal assistant, and you'll be her interior decorator."

"Her what?"

"The person in charge picking décor. We check their address against ours."

"But we don't have her address."

"They don't know that."

Gallagher was reluctant. "I don't know anything about interior decorating."

"You don't have to. You won't say a word. Just show contempt, like everything you see isn't good enough. Pretend to be gay, and like you'd really rather be someplace else."

"You're the actor, not me," he said. It had been a long time since Jane heard someone call her by her chosen profession. She thought about her acting class back in L.A., and her overbearing teacher Jeremy. She thought about Cooper. So much had changed so fast. It seemed like a lifetime ago.

Versailles was in a quaint, upscale storefront on Second Avenue. The window dressing featured a queen-sized bed draped with a golden-hued duvet cover. Decorative pillows framed the antique cast-iron bed frame. Jane got the impression everything inside was handmade and very, very expensive.

"Two of us working for Veronica doesn't seem realistic to

me," he said. "You go in alone."

Jane agreed, said "Okay, wish me luck," and then entered.

A paunchy man wearing bifocals approached. "How may I help you?"

"You must be Giavanni."

"At your service," he said with a smile revealing bleached teeth, much too white for a man his age.

"I'm Candice, Veronica Tatinger's personal assistant," she said with a slight Southern drawl so he wouldn't recognize her voice from the phone. "I believe she spoke with you. I'm checking on the twenty sets."

He sized her up over his bifocals, said, "Of course. This way, please." Giavanni led her to the back and pulled out linen wrapped in thick plastic. He peeled back the packaging to reveal the fabric patterned with finely stitched conch shells. When he had mentioned the seashell pattern on the phone Jane imagined something entirely different—her minds-eye seeing clamshells and starfishes. Instead the linen had only the conch shell, each framed by a threaded spiral. Jane remembered a conch from science class in school. She held it to her ear to hear the sound of distant waves and wanted to believe it was magic, a portal to some exotic beach somewhere. She remembered how disappointed she was to learn it was simply resonance, a sonic phenomenon.

"Yes, that's it," Jane said, pretending that she was familiar with Veronica's pattern. "And Veronica asked to confirm her address with you."

"Oh, yes," he said and moved to his computer. She fought the urge to hover and peek over his shoulder. Instead she sifted through an assortment of pillow shams waiting for him to bring up Veronica's page. Out the window she could see Gallagher pacing on the sidewalk, paper coffee cup in hand. She was glad he had not come in.

"It appears I don't have contact information," he said.

Jane's heart sank. She moved over to view the screen. With

the exception of Veronica's name there was no other information. "Oh, now I remember," Giavanni said, "here in the memo it says 'hold goods for pick up.' Vee sent a messenger for the merchandise. An international courier, I remember now, because I had to fill out the customs form."

"Oh sure," she bluffed, trying to appear informed. "And where did it go?"

"To the Institute, of course."

"The Institute?"

"The Turks and Caicos. How long have you been working for Vee?"

"Oh, yes," Jane bluffed. "Forgive me…The Institute."

"Shall I ship the merchandise when all comes available?"

"Please do. We'll send the same courier. And thank you."

She met Gallagher across the street and said, "He shipped her order out of the country, a place called the Turks and Caicos."

"You get an address?"

"Unfortunately he didn't have one. She used and international courier."

"Hmm," he said, chewing on that thought. "We don't have jurisdiction in the Caribbean."

"So what do we do now?" Jane asked.

He stroked his chin, and she waited for a response, until he finally said, "I know of a place where we can get the perfect bloody mary. Take a load off, and plan our next move."

Jane liked the idea.

CHAPTER 12

Jane and Gallagher got out of the cab in front of the famed Plaza Hotel. They moved up the carpeted steps and entered the grand lobby. "This way," he said, and led her into the Oak Bar. To Jane, the place felt timeless with its classic oil paintings and dark wood—everything seeped with history. A piano player warmed up the room with Chopin Etude.

They took seats in green leather-backed barstools and Gallagher ordered for the both of them. The bartender immediately went to work. To the frosted glasses he added ice, and to his cocktail shaker bitters and hot sauce. He squeezed lemon, and finished it all off with a celery-stick and dash of pepper.

"Can you put a straw in his, please?" Jane asked the bartender. "He really likes straws."

"No!" Gallagher said.

"Oh that's right, I forgot, you have this crazy thing for straws," she teased with a wry smile.

He nudged her, said, "So I'm a freak. Nobody's perfect." The chilled libations were set in front of them in a New York minute.

After a sip, Jane said, "This is the best bloody mary I've ever had."

"Told ya." Gallagher pulled out his phone. "Let's search Turks and Caicos." Together they huddled over the iPhone. From Google Maps they could see the tiny nation was a cluster of islands north of Haiti and the Dominican Republic. In Wikipedia they discovered the conch shell is part of the Turks and Caicos coat of arms. Alongside a spiny lobster and stubby cactus, the shell is displayed prominently on the nation's flag.

He read aloud, "*Although many governments have laid claim to this small province, throughout the eighteenth century the Turks and Caicos was known as a hideout for pirates.*"

Jane said, "And Veronica collects relics."

He continued, "*Much like Jesse James and his gang who found refuge in their 'hole in the wall' hideaway, privateers favored to the Turks and Caicos because of its unique geography. The islands are surrounded by miles of coral reef. Only experienced sea captains familiar with the waters dare to navigate a safe landing.* I remember reading about this place. It attracts worldwide attention for its tax haven status." He combined the search with the word "tax" and they learned that there are strict banking laws that forbid inquiry into financial interests.

"Veronica lives there to hide her money," Jane said.

"Possibly," he said, and sipped his drink.

Jane pulled out the celery-stick from hers, bit the end, and replaced it to stir the ice. All the time she felt his eyes on her. When she looked up it was clear—he had more than research on his mind.

Jane needed a distraction, recognized the tune from the piano, Cole Porter's "Let's Misbehave" and said, "Let's Misbehave."

"Excuse me?"

"Cole Porter." She didn't plan on the double-entendre. "He wrote love songs, lyrics with irony," she said.

"The Great American Songbook," he added.

"Exactly."

"Maybe we should misbehave," he said with an infectious smile.

Now it was crystal clear. He *was* coming on to her.

"I wonder what the rooms are like in this hotel?" he ventured.

The moment happened so fast. She pressed up against the backrest. On one hand she was flattered, but on the other hand she knew she couldn't go there.

"Probably not a good idea," she said. "This song's from his musical *Anything Goes*," she said.

"Anything goes?" he said, teasing her, "that's sort of what I'm talking about."

Jane couldn't believe she'd offered up two double-entendres in a row. *Damn Cole Porter.* "Look, I…" she stammered until she found the words, "I'm not in a place to start a relationship. I have to stay focused. And I know nothing about you."

"You're right, and I'm sorry, it's just…you're so beautiful, and I can't help myself. I totally understand. Please don't judge me for being so forward. I have these feelings and…I guess I'm impulsive too."

Another place, another time, Jane would have considered it, but she was still recoiling from Cooper, even though he burned her. She sipped her drink and after a moment said, "You must have a girlfriend."

"I don't."

"I find that hard to believe."

"I'm in the middle of a divorce," Gallagher said. "And the lawyers are drawing it out, and costing me a fortune."

"Kids?"

"We tried, but it didn't happen, which is probably for the best." He explained how the separation was his wife's idea. "Annette gets what she wants, and she wants me out of her life."

"The demands of your job must have been a strain," she said, having read that the divorce rate is high among law enforcement professionals.

"Maybe that had something to do with it, or maybe we just drifted apart. The clincher was we had investments go bad. The loss was primarily her family's money, what she inherited from her grandparents, and she'll never forgive me. Neither will her mother."

"So...your wife came from money?"

"Let's just say Annette went to Vassar. I went to John Jay."

Jane got the picture.

He explained how he used to live in a well-manicured home in Summit, New Jersey, and commute to the FBI field office in Newark. Now he lives in a shabby one bedroom apartment in East Orange, "with rented furniture, and half-eaten cartons of Chinese food in the refrigerator."

Although wounded, she had a feeling he'd land on his feet, and told him so.

"You seem so certain about my bright future," he said.

"My gut tells me you're the kind of person who will bounce back."

"Thanks for your confidence."

Jane's flight was later that afternoon so they retrieved his BMW from the garage where he'd parked uptown, and he drove her to the Holiday Inn to get her things. Crossing the Williamsburg Bridge, on the way to Kennedy Airport, Gallagher said, "I'll look into this Turks and Caicos more, but realize we don't have jurisdiction in the Caribbean. If we find Veronica it may take some time before we can arrest and arrange extradition."

"I don't have time. You said yourself that she's watching me. And she tried to kill me."

"I'm just saying if becomes an international matter then—"

"—I know what you're saying," Jane snapped. The thought of going back to Florida, and being alone, saddened her.

"First we need to confirm Veronica is there," he said. "And if she is, I'm certain she won't stay forever. Sooner or later she'll come back. We'll arrest her at the airport."

"In the meantime what happens to me? Witness Protection? I tie her into two murders, and she knows it."

"Let's first determine Veronica's location before we make a

plan," he said.

"How?"

"The Bureau has its resources."

Jane imagined him at work in his office while she was sitting alone in a humid Florida garage. They reached the curb at Kennedy and she said, "Thanks for the ride to the airport."

"Be patient," he said. "These things take time." Their conversation was cut short as an airport cop was upon them and threatened with his leather-bound ticket book. Jane got out.

"Let's talk later," he said. "Hang in there."

She gave him and nod, closed the door, and headed for her plane.

CHAPTER 13

The flight back to Florida was uneventful. Jane ordered a bloody mary but it paled in comparison, nothing like the super-deluxe libation she sipped with Gallagher. She paid for the headphones to watch the in-flight movie, but her mind was somewhere else. The history of Anne Bonny is what stirred Jane's imagination. If Veronica really was a descendent, could a heart of larceny be inherited—passed down through generations? Does Veronica feel compassion and empathy, or is she truly a heartless psychopath? According to the mini biography, Anne left a baby behind in Cuba and returned to a life of crime. What was that parting moment like? Who cared for her abandoned child? Did Anne's maternal instincts tug at her on cold nights at sea?

It was dark by the time she drove the Chevy past Danny's home. She figured she'd play it safe and took her time—didn't see anything that raised concern. She parked down the street and approached the house from the backyard. When satisfied no one lay in wait, she entered the empty home through the back door.

In the darkness Jane retrieved Danny's revolver, just in case. She was careful not to turn on many lights, and heated up a microwave dinner. When her mother called, Jane didn't mention her trip to New York and the costs she'd have to repay from using her mother's credit card. Jane figured she would tell her mom all about it later. Exhausted, she placed the revolver under the pillow and crawled into bed.

"There's only two types of hotels in the Turks and Caicos," Oscar explained to Jane while filling a scuba tank. It made a tremendous hissing sound so he had to shout over his work. "All-inclusive luxury resorts, like Beaches or Club Med, or rum-soaked fleabags where us serious divers stay."

Jane was outside Oscar's Dive N' Mariner, a shop devoted to all things diving. Since diving is such a draw to the Turks and Caicos, that morning she had called over a dozen shops to ask if anyone who worked there had been to the islands. Oscar's Dive N' Mariner was owned and operated by the namesake proprietor, a seasoned dive tech who knew the Turks and Caicos well. He was everything Jane had imagined after speaking with him on the phone: ragged T-shirt, cigarette dangling, face prematurely wrinkled from excessive sun.

She'd borrowed one of her mom's suit jackets and brought a notepad to complete the costume. "It's now in the preliminary stages," she said, "but we're putting together a business plan to present to investors to build luxury condominiums. I'm curious to hear about the islands from people who've spent time there, like you."

He was clearly not thrilled, but abandoned the tanks and showed Jane a photo album—pictures he had taken while on the islands. The images were striking with white sand beaches in dramatic contrast with the greenish-blue Caribbean ocean. Many of the photos featured tile work of kitchens, patios, decks and stairways. Others were of underwater flora, fish, sharks, and turtles.

Also in the book was a map of the islands. Oscar explained, "The big resorts and condos are all on Grace Bay Beach, in Providenciales," he pointed to the largest island. "The locals call it Provo, but don't mistake it for the Provo in Utah. There's no Mormons there, that's for sure," he said with a laugh. "It's the only island with an airstrip long enough to land a commercial jet. A few of the others are accessible by small plane, the rest only by boat."

He explained that years ago the place was "a diver's nirvana," but now, with recent development, "the prices keep us dive bums away."

She cut to the chase, asked him, "Did you ever meet Veronica Tatinger?"

"Name doesn't ring a bell," he said.

"Ever heard of Anne Bonny?" she asked, a shot in the dark.

"No." Oscar pulled a pack of cigarettes from his breast pocket, offered one.

"No, thanks," she said.

He produced a novelty lighter attached to a key chain and put flame to his next Marlboro. The intake of tobacco appeared to put him as ease, and he fondly recalled, "The diving is epic, unbelievable. The water's so clear, and the sea life's intense. The shelf drops off into a literal abyss," he said, motioning with his hands downward.

"A shelf?"

"Not far offshore the ocean goes really deep. In the sixties the U.S. Navy used the island of Grand Turk as a listening post to track Russian subs. Ever read *Hunt For Red October*, or see the movie?"

"No." Jane was familiar with it but hadn't seen it. "Tell me about Grand Turk," she asked.

"There's not much there other than abandoned salt ponds, a shanty town, the prison, and a half dozen hotels that cater to divers, like the ones I told you about."

"Nothing upscale?"

"The only fancy joints are the resorts and condos in Provo. When I left they were building vacation homes, places like you'd find along a golf course, but not ultra-luxury."

From her research Jane was familiar with the developments

he was talking about. She had a feeling Veronica would choose to live in a much more extravagant setting. "How long were you there?" she asked.

"On and off, about two years. I'd come back to the States during hurricane season."

"You work in a dive shop there?"

"Nah…I had a tile business," he said, pointing to his photo album.

She paged through the photos. "Nice work."

Oscar beamed with pride. "Thanks. I refuse to install crap, like tile you'd see in a McDonalds. I've got my standards."

"You're an artist.

"A craftsman," he corrected.

"What else did you do there?"

"Between tiling and diving, I drank a lot of rum," he said, laughing at the memory. He explained, "After a while I got really bored and came back to the States. A lot of my friends, ex-pats who still live there, they didn't have the option to come back, at least not yet."

"Expatriates?"

"Yeah, most of them have to stay to wait out the hurricane season, or travel to Europe or something. They're counting down their seven years, before they can return."

"I don't understand," she said.

"Statute of limitations."

"Oh." She figured just as the Turks and Caicos is a tax haven, it made sense the nation would also harbor its share of criminals, bail jumpers, and ne'er-do-wells. She thumbed through the images of sunsets, smiling locals, and beaches. "How about pirate relics?" Jane ventured.

"Pirate shit. Hell, yeah. At the Institute."

"What's that?" Giavanni had mentioned it, and now Oscar.

"It's on a private island, Stingray Cay."

Bingo. Jane waited for him to elaborate.

"The only way to get there is by boat. They've got a ferry

that goes back and forth from Provo. I did some stone and tile work there, showers in the new bungalows, and a patio off the main house. You can see in there."

His calloused hands flipped through the album, stopping on the appropriate pages. Standing closer now, she could smell tobacco on him. Although most of his pictures were angled downward, framing tile, she could see structures and recognized the style of architecture as French Colonial—windows dominated by large white shutters.

"I installed slate too, in the kitchen" he said. "The ferry brought me in the morning and then back to Provo at the end of the day."

"Tell me about the pirate relics."

"There's some cool stuff, old canons, marine hardware, muskets and anchors, most of it salvaged from sunken ships. The place feels historic from the pictures, but it's actually quite modern. It's built with an impressive infrastructure."

"In what way?"

"There's a diesel generator and water purification system hidden inside the light house." He thumbed to another page and pointed out a light house perched on rocks.

"What do they do at the Institute?" she asked.

"They teach New Age, artsy-fartsy kinda shit. I heard it's some kind of think-tank, whatever that's supposed to be."

"A think-tank?"

"Professors, CEOs, but it's all very secretive, private, and discreet. The place is locked down."

"Why do you say that?"

"They've got their own security team, bad ass Haitian dudes. They've got nothing better to do but monitor the boats coming and going."

"Why?"

"I don't know."

"You ever meet the director of the Institute?"

"Lady Vee?"

Lady Vee! Double bingo. "Yes, Veronica," Jane said.

"Nah, I dealt with a coordinator out of Provo," he said. "Pops is his name. He supervised my work, and ferried me back and forth. But some of my friends have met her."

"Your statute of limitations friends?"

"Yeah. Those guys."

Figures. "How long is the boat ride from Provo?" she asked.

"Twenty-five minutes or so."

"Do you have Pops contact info?"

He gave her a once over, dug into the folder and produced a worn business card. It read:

Xavier "Pops" Pena
Project Manager Conch Institute
Singray Cay, Turks and Caicos, BWI

There was an email address and the word "cell" with a number scrawled by hand. "Perfect, thank you." she said, and copied the information.

"You ever dive?" he asked.

"Can't say I do."

"First session is free," he said, and gave her his card, eyeing her breasts. "Or...if you need tile work for your hotel project...We can grab lunch and talk about it."

She could see he was making a pass, thanked him, and said, "You've been very helpful."

"All good," Oscar said, crushed his cigarette, and returned to his tanks.

Moments later, while sitting in the Chevy, Jane called the number. The dial tone rang once. "This is Pops," a voice answered.

She realized she should have come up with more of a plan before calling. "Are you the Project Manager for the Institute?" she asked.

"Yes, ma'am. You be asking 'bout the little boy's party,

then?" he said, his Caribbean accent thick. "You catering or entertainment?"

"Entertainment, I'm the clown," she responded, and wondered why she said it—a conditioned response, she assumed.

"Ah. All entertainment goes through Debra in Miami."

"Not Veronica?" she asked.

"Who?"

"Lady Vee."

"No, no, ma'am...Please, *do not* bother the mother," he said. "Debbie at Book-A-Look in Miami has all the details. Wait a minute," he said, and she could hear him shuffling. "I don't see a lady clown on my paper. When are you supposed to arrive?"

"Not certain. I'll call Debra to find out. Thank you," she said.

"No worries," he said and hung up.

Don't bother the mother? Little boy's party?

Jane tried to fathom it. Could Veronica have a child?

CHAPTER 14

Driving home, Jane texted Gallagher, *"Learned stuff. Call me."*

She was making tea on the stove and searching the address for the Book-A-Look agency when he called back. "It's not her," Gallagher said before she could tell him the news. "I had my guys do a search. There are photos of this Vee woman, and it's not Veronica."

"What kind of photos?"

"Images from social media mostly. I'll forward them."

"In the Turks and Caicos?"

"She's the director of the Conch Institute. Check your email, I'm sending them now."

While waiting she told him what she had learned from Oscar, about Stingray Cay. The email finally arrived with images of a studious-looking blonde woman in her forties. To Jane, she appeared to be a school teacher, or a librarian.

"You sure this is the one they call Vee?"

"Yes, and she's British."

"The director?"

"Lady Vee is the nickname the islanders gave her."

"Shit!" she said, her theory smashed to pieces.

"I realize it's disappointing, but it's better for us that Veronica's not out of the country. It would have been difficult to extradite from the Turks and Caicos."

"What about the pirate relics? And Anne Bonny?"

"I'm figuring Fischer lied, and sent us on a wild goose chase."

It didn't sit right. After a moment, she said, "I'm going there."

"That would be an incredible waste of time and resources."

"I have a feeling it's her."

"These photos prove it's not. Don't do anything stupid."

"Maybe it's a ruse. Maybe Veronica created this Lady Vee persona as a stand-in to throw people off."

"Jane—"

"—Veronica is there. I can feel it."

"Let's concentrate on what we *do* know, and not conjecture." She could tell he was getting angry. "Assuming everything Fischer told us was a lie, let's go back to the drawing board.

There was a moment of silence on the phone before she said, "I've got to go."

"Jane—"

"—I've got to go. I'll call you later."

Jane hung up, angry, and viewed the photos he'd sent in more detail. The blonde was captured alongside what appeared to be academic types, older men with greying facial hair, and graduate students. She recognized the French Colonial architecture and the lighthouse, what she'd seen from Oscar's photos.

That's when she heard the creek on the deck outside.

In the reflection through the decorative mirror over Danny's couch, she saw the man standing outside the sliding glass window working the lock with a pick. He hadn't noticed her. She could see one of his hands was bandaged, his fingers taped. She wondered if this was the same man who tried to strangle her in jail.

When he slid the door open and entered she screamed. Jane knew the Smith & Wesson was under her pillow. She made a break for it.

CHAPTER 15

The man was fast. He had her by the hair, but she twisted away. Jane cut into the bedroom. She dived onto the bed, grabbed the gun under the pillow, and spun around.

He reared back, not expecting a snub-nose revolver aimed at his face. Only then did Jane see him, an olive-skinned man with a flat nose. He stood at the end of the bed and studied her with squinty eyes. To Jane, he looked like a laborer, or a construction worker of some kind, dressed in dark fatigues. There was a crude wire garrote in his hand, handles wrapped in duct tape. Although she had the gun, Jane felt incredibly helpless.

"Did Veronica send you?" she asked.

He said nothing, studied her.

"You were the one in L.A., weren't you?"

He brought up his hand, displayed the white tape on his crooked finger.

"So it was you," she said.

The killer smiled to reveal yellowed teeth. As fast as lightning, he ducked down and flipped over the mattress. Jane tumbled to the carpet, squeezed off a random shot that missed by a mile. It was incredibly loud.

Rolling across the floor, she squeezed the trigger again without finding her mark. He had a hunting knife and was coming at her.

Maim? Kill? She aimed for his heart.

The third shot hit him just below the neck. The impact sent him back on his heels. Blood sprayed the wall behind him, and she could see shock, then panic in his eyes.

She was squeezing the trigger again when the man stumbled out the bedroom door. Her next shot took out the door frame. White plaster filled the air. She heard him running down the hallway. Jane jumped to her feet, and went after him.

She chased him outside to the deck, fired again, then click, click—she was out of bullets. It was only a five-shot revolver, Danny had told her that.

The man disappeared into the thick foliage.

Her ears ringing from the deafening gunshots, she ran to the study, reloaded from the box of shells, and cautiously returned to the porch.

The killer was nowhere in sight.

Jane figured the neighbors would certainly call the police. It must have been the cops that leaked her whereabouts. She didn't trust them. She went back inside to pack her things. It wasn't long before the phone rang. Jane had a feeling it was the police—her suspicion confirmed when she saw a squad car on the street.

She made a mental note not to rush. *Take everything I needed, including passport.* When she was sure she had it all, she slung the bag over her shoulder and slipped out the back door.

She could hear the police knocking at the front door as she cut through the neighbor's yard. She hopped over a fence, avoided a yappy dog, went through the side gate, and calmly walked to the Chevy while seeing another patrol car drive past and pull up in front of Danny's house.

She climbed in and started the car. She'd call Gallagher from the road, on the way to the Turks and Caicos.

CHAPTER 16

For fear of getting pulled over, Jane was careful not to speed on Interstate 75. She'd left two messages with Gallagher. He didn't call back, and that made her angry. It was hot and humid, and the air conditioner in the 70's muscle car was weak. Three and a half hours later she reached Miami.

The unimpressive two-story office building was wedged between a Sizzler and a Circle K. She changed into her costume inside the Chevy and applied the clown make-up in the rearview mirror. She was running low on clown-white and reminded herself to order more. She prepped a few magic tricks, put the gun in her clown pants, and climbed the stairs to a small office tucked around back. Auditions always made her nervous. This cold-call was the most brazen of her career.

Book-A-Look specialized in celebrity look-a-likes. There were autographed black-and-white eight by tens of famous people on the walls, Marilyn Monroe, Groucho Marx, Hillary Clinton, and Elvis. Debra, the frenzied proprietor, waved Jane in as she finished a phone call.

"So let me get this straight," Debra said into the phone, "you've got a billy goat, a Shetland pony, three rabbits, and a donkey? Oh...it's a mule? What's the difference?"

Jane wondered what this woman could possibly be talking about. The air conditioner was blasting—almost too cold, but a welcome relief from the car. She bided her time examining the photos. It was obvious that they were not images of real celebrities but rather performers who looked like these personalities, some more than others.

"Uh, huh…okay, darling. Sounds wonderful. Don't do anything until I get back to you. I need to run it by my client." Debra hung up and yelled out to someone unseen in an adjacent office, "Janice, scratch the Dominican with the petting zoo. We're going with the Jamaican guy."

"Gotcha," a voice rang out.

Debra fingered a wedge of chocolate out of gold foil. "Can I help you, sweetie?" she said, before popping it in her mouth.

"I'm Karen, or, uh…Koo-Koo Karen the Clown, and I understand you're booking a children's birthday party in the Turks and Caicos."

"That I am," she said with a mouthful.

"Well, I'm going to be in Provo over the weekend, seeing an old friend, and I thought I'd drop in to see if you needed another performer."

"You're going to be in Provo?"

"That's right," Jane said, "so I thought I'd see if I could pick up a day gig while I'm there."

"How'd you find out about it?"

"Pops mentioned it."

"Here, have a seat." Debra struggled to her feet and moved around her desk to clear old newspapers and junk-mail from the vinyl padded office chair. "You're not from around here, are you?" Debra said as she reclaimed her seat behind the desk, seemingly exhausted from all the effort.

"I'm from L.A., but now I live in Sarasota. Just moved there."

"Studying at the clown college?"

"I live with my mom in Sarasota, so I applied there," Jane said, thinking it best to weave in a few truths but keep details to a minimum.

"That's nice, to live with your mother." Debra sighed. She

pointed to a framed picture on the wall, "That's my daughter."

Jane considered the photo of a young woman in a white sundress embracing a tattooed guy wearing a Hooters T-Shirt with the sleeves cut off. The lights of Las Vegas were behind them. From the bouquet of flowers in the girl's hand Jane assumed this was their wedding photo. "She lives in Yonkers with her husband Patrick. Patrick's a stereo salesman." By her tone Jane got the impression Debra was not particularly fond of her son in law. "Dark chocolate?" Debra offered. "It's supposed to be good for ya. Plenty of antioxidants."

"No, thank you."

"You sure?"

"Yes. But thanks anyway."

Debra took a slurp from her coffee and sampled another piece of chocolate. She chewed and studied Jane's clown regalia. She sat up in her chair to peek over her desk and took in Jane's over-sized shoes.

"So...you place look-a-likes?" Jane said, stating the obvious in an attempt to keep the conversation going.

"I do. For parties and corporate events, mostly. I also handle prank performers, strip-o-grams, female impersonators, and plus-size burlesque acts." Debra handed Jane the Book-A-Look brochure. There were no clowns or magicians featured in the marketing material. Jane wondered where the children's party operation fit in.

"You must be branching out, handling children's events too?"

"Just this one. As a favor, really. As you see I'm geared toward an adult audience, which makes sense in this demographic."

"Demographic?" Jane asked.

"I don't know if you've noticed, sweetie, but most people in South Florida are old. Know what the state bird is? Florida's bird, know what it is?"

At a loss Jane offered a shrug.

"The *early* bird." Debra threw her head back in a cackle. Jane laughed with extra enthusiasm for Debra's benefit. Debra placed the rest of her chocolate in her desk and wiped her fingers on her terry cloth sweat pants. "I could probably use another clown, as long as I don't have to pay for transportation and housing. The rate is three hundred cash, and my fee is twenty percent, including a quarter of your tips." Debra handed Jane an application on a clipboard. "If you're interested just fill this out."

"Sounds great, but I thought agents get ten percent," Jane said.

"I'll be your agent and your manager on this one."

"That's fine. Do you want to see some magic tricks?"

"Save it for the kids. I can see by your shoes that you're good. Just keep the little brats happy, and you'll do fine. There'll be another clown, like you, and a ventriloquist."

"How many children will be at this party?" Jane asked, starting to fill out the application, hoping Debra wouldn't ask for identification.

"God knows. Maybe thirty or so, maybe more. If you know of any other kiddie acts, ones where I don't have to supply airfare, let me know."

"You must know Lady Vee, then?" Jane asked her.

"Who?"

"Lady Vee. Veronica. She runs the Institute."

"Never heard of her. Everything's gone through Pops," Debra said.

Jane hoped she and Pops didn't compare notes.

"You ever consider taking on a celebrity persona?" Debra asked. "Can you sing?"

"I'm tone deaf," Jane lied. "But thank you."

"Seriously think about it, honey. I can see you're very talent-ed."

Debra had given her instructions to meet Pops and the rest of the performers at the boat docks. Jane pretended she was familiar with the island and knew exactly where the docks were, figuring she could ask when she got there.

Jane changed out of her costume in the car and searched the Internet on her phone for flights. There was one flight left that day. With luck, she could make it.

She drove to Miami International and parked the Chevy in the long-term lot. She knew she couldn't take the revolver, so reluctantly put it in the glove compartment. All she had was her passport, costume and make up, a few toiletries, and a change of clothes.

Next she found the American Airlines counter and stood in line for a good twenty minutes, thankful she did not have luggage to check after seeing a sign that informed bags were required to be tagged no later than two hours before international flights. Finally given her boarding pass, Jane left another message for Gallagher but didn't tell him her plans.

She got in the security line and it took another twenty minutes to reach the checkpoint. After she passed through the metal detector an overbearing TSA agent brought her bag to a stainless steel table. "May I open your bag?" she asked.

"Sure."

She pulled Jane's jar of clown-white from her carry-on. She opened the container and looked inside, sniffing it. "What's this?" she asked.

"Clown white. It's make-up. I'm a clown."

"You're going to have to check this."

"But I'm not checking any baggage."

"I can't let you carry this on. It's a gel."

"It's a cream."

"Close enough."

"If I go back to check it, I'll miss my flight."

The emotionless TSA agent said, "You're going to have to check it or dispose of it here."

"It's just make-up," Jane insisted, figuring the woman had singled out the clown white because it was in the largest of her containers.

"It could be a flammable substance." She pointed to a placard detailing carry-on restrictions. Jane realized even if she had time to go back, and check it for the next flight which didn't depart until the following day, the clown-white would still not get there in time.

"Give me a break. I really need this first thing tomorrow."

"There's nothing I can do."

"It's just clown white."

"Step aside, please."

Jane dropped her jar of clown-white in the trash container. Feeling vulnerable, she realized she was parting with a key element of her disguise as she ran to catch her flight.

CHAPTER 17

"We're going to the Bermuda Triangle," the acne-faced fifteen-year-old boy declared, the passenger sitting next to her. "It's also known as the Devil's Triangle. I've seen shows on TV about it."

The boy was traveling on vacation with his parents and sister, or "bratty sister," as he affectionately referred to her. He'd spent most of his time reading from a stack of graphic novels while listening to heavy-metal in earbuds. But now, to Jane sitting next to him, he was making it clear he had great knowledge. "Many aircraft has been lost," he continued, "ships have disappeared, and there are confirmed reports that the basic laws of physics, for no apparent reason, go off the charts."

Jane wondered what charts he was referring to. "Think this jet's going down?" she asked, pretending to be worried.

"Not going down, going up," he said pointing to the ceiling, "alien abduction." The boy filled her in on an assortment of conspiracy theories about Area 51, Roswell, and the elusive Chupacabra. Jane gave plenty of non-verbal cues that she was not interested, but the boy went on and on. Finally he fell silent and returned to reading his comic books.

Leaning her head against the glass, Jane stared at the vast ocean below and thought a place named Devil's Triangle was somehow appropriate for Veronica. She began to doubt herself. Was a small, secluded island in the Caribbean Veronica's style?

She wondered what she would do if Lady Vee was indeed the studious blonde woman from the pictures Gallagher sent her.

Two hours later, as the jet descended, she could see white-caps topping the waves. Suddenly the tarmac appeared just before the jet touched down. As she scanned the landscape, her first impression was the island appeared barren, covered in low scrub-brush.

It was Jane's first experience deplaning by a mobile staircase wheeled up to the jet. It felt like something out of the 60's, like Jackie O, or The Beatles. She pulled the brim of her hat low to not be recognized and descended to the tarmac.

The customs agent, an officer in a white short-sleeved uniform that only heightened the contrast of his dark ebony skin, asked her, "Business or pleasure, ma'am?"

"Pleasure," Jane said, even though she knew there would be little time for that. He stamped her passport. She could make out the conch shell in the official stamp, part of country's coat of arms.

Minutes later, standing at the curb, she purposely chose a cab driver who was not as aggressive as the others. "Hotel Columbus, please," she said.

The cabbie with nappy dreadlocks blew his horn and maneuvered his taxi out of the small airport, barely missing other drivers who, Jane could see, had reckless disregard for rules of the road.

"Do you know a place where I might be able to get clown-white," she asked, "I need base make-up, what a clown would wear?"

"No, ma'am," he said.

She wondered what she was going to do. She considered the possibility of mixing white paint with Vaseline but feared it would dry and crack. She asked the cabbie to make a stop at the hardware store. He veered off the dirt road and pulled up to the strip mall. Jane purchased a half-pint of flat white paint, a screwdriver to open the can, and Vaseline.

Returning to the dusty, washboard-grooved dirt road, they passed through a run-down shantytown. Discarded litter was caught in weeds. Chickens pecked the gravel in front of squalid homes. Clusters of old women found refuge from the sun under a corrugated tin shelters. At one point her driver had to stop because a feral horse, incredibly scrawny and malnourished, blocked the road. The pathetic animal took its time before relenting right of way. Jane's heart went out to the poor animal.

Back on a paved road, she could see resorts in the distance. Drawing nearer, the Hotel Columbus was set back near a cluster of bars and restaurants.

Jane paid the cabbie and checked into her hotel. Her room had decorative tile in the bathroom, and she wondered if Oscar had done the work.

Next the test—she mixed the white paint with the Vaseline until it felt like it had the right consistency. She applied it her cheeks, and it seemed to work, but time would tell. It didn't take long before the makeshift white dried. It became more and more transparent, and she looked terrible. She washed if off and wondered what was she was going to do. How was she going to keep Veronica from recognizing her?

She decided to take a walk on the beach, donned her hat and sunglasses, and strolled the shore. At one resort a steel drum band played to a crowd of tourists. Jane slowed to watch.

"Whatcha drinking?" he said to her.

She turned to consider a guy her age wearing a silly straw hat, his nose covered with sunblock. "I'm drinking this here El Presidente," he said with a drunken smile, showing her the green bottle. "It's Dominican, but tastes just like Heineken. Better than Heineken, I'd say. I've been sippin' these bad boys all week, and I suggest you try one, because it's on me."

Ordinarily she would have accepted, especially since he was kind of cute, albeit a little drunk. Jane missed socializing with people her age but work needed to be done.

"Uh, no, thanks, I..." then it hit her—zinc oxide, the white protective stuff on his nose could work as clown-white. "Where'd you get your sun-block?" she asked.

"Oh, yeah, well…I burned my beak on my first day out. They sell it at the gift shop, but I think the lady gouged me on the price."

"Thanks for the offer, but I can't stay." She moved on and could hear his friends jeering him that he struck out.

At the resort gift shop she purchased two tubes of the sun-block, and he was right, everything was overpriced. Back in her room, and testing it in front of the mirror, it was an acceptable substitute. Problem solved, she relaxed, if only a little, and realized she hadn't eaten all day. She was famished.

The small restaurant was adjacent to her hotel, and practically empty. She sat at the bar and ordered jerk chicken and a Ginger Ale. Her server was an outgoing, local Caribbean woman by the name of Dorothy. Jane found her to have a great sense of humor and in between duties Dorothy joked about current events and poured herself a rum and Coke behind the bar. When Jane probed for details about the Conch Institute, Dorothy's jovial manner disappeared. "Why do you ask, child?" Dorothy said.

"A friend, back in Florida, was telling be about it. He'd done construction work out there. Have you ever met the owner, the one they call Lady Vee?"

"No, but I've heard of her."

Jane sensed resentment in her tone, asked, "What have you heard?"

"I am not one to gossip," she said, then moved to the end of the bar to sip her drink.

In an attempt to keep the conversation going Jane said, "Maybe I'll sample some of this Caribbean rum. What would you suggest?"

Dorothy pointed to the shelf and explained there are two types, dark and light. "Both are good."

"Which brand do you prefer?"

"For the money, Sailor Jerry is my favorite." Dorothy pulled the bottle down to show her. An illustration of a hula girl adjourned the label.

"Should I have it on the rocks?" Jane asked.

"It's good with Coke, or I can mix it with juice like pineapple or orange and cranberry. Or I can make a mojito."

"That sounds good."

Dorothy grabbed a glass and began to mash mint.

"My friend back in Florida," Jane continued, "he said the place is all secretive."

After a moment, in a lowered voice, Dorothy said, "Those in-the-know suspect the Institute turns girls out."

"What's that mean?" Jane asked.

"They train girls to be prostitutes."

"No!" Jane said dramatically to encourage her.

Dorothy nodded, "Afraid so. The word is Lady Vee combs the world to select her students, beautiful young girls, some come from poverty but not all. She brings them to the island and teaches the trade. After they graduate, I hear she keeps a percentage, like a race horse, or oil well, know what I'm saying? She's got a piece of the action as long as the girl's working."

Jane didn't know what to say. Dorothy set the frosty glass in front of her and Jane sipped. It was strong, but good. "Nice," Jane said.

Satisfied, Dorothy returned to her drink. "But it's not just sex I'm talking about," she continued. "I hear it's much like a finishing school. They teach the girls manners, and social skills, sort of like..." she searched for the right words, "how to hold a fork, and shit like that. But that's only what I've heard. Who knows if it's true. I'm just an old barkeep, so what do I know?"

"What does the local police think of all this?"

"The police?" Dorothy laughed. "Those damn fools, they don't bother with Stingray Cay. I hear select gentlemen fly in to visit and assist in the training. I reckon some of our police train these girls too."

"Who are these select gents?" Jane asked.

"I don't know. It's seems to be a sex tourism thing, all very hush hush. But if anyone asks, you didn't hear it from me."

"Hear what?"

"*That's* what I'm talking about," Dorothy finished her drink.

Considering everything Jane had learned about Veronica's sordid past, this new information fit like a glove. She could not wait to call Gallagher and fill him in.

Back in her room Jane called, and finally got him, "Hey, I was worried when you didn't call back. Everything alright?" she said. The connection was bad, but it was nice to hear his voice.

"I've been on assignment," he said. "I can't talk about it, and certainly not on the phone."

"FBI business?"

"Another case."

When she explained how she'd battled the assassin, and had flown to the island, Gallagher became very angry.

"You left the scene?" he asked.

"I wasn't going to stick around and wait for him to come back. And I don't trust the cops there."

"Don't be foolish. Take the next flight home," he snapped.

"I've come too far," she said. "Don't be mad at me, please. I'm going to identify Veronica and get out of here, and then you'll find a way to arrest her."

"It's not Veronica."

"I think it is." As she informed him about The Institute training girls to be prostitutes their cell phone connection worsened. There was a beep and the call was cut off. When she dialed him back it went into voicemail.

"Hey, we got cut off. Call me."

She plugged the phone into the charger, and after laying out her clown costume for the next day, she turned on the television and tried to relax. Besides the bad connection there was something strange about the phone conversation with Gallagher. She couldn't put her finger on it, wondered if maybe he was back with his ex-wife.

What if he was right and Lady Vee is not Veronica? Jane doubted herself. She wondered if her impulsive nature had tricked her into believing only what she wanted to believe. She wedged the chair under the doorknob and made sure the bolt was secure before turning off the light.

In darkness the sound of distant Reggae kept her awake.

CHAPTER 18

The pillow was hard, and Jane never got comfortable. Finally drifting off, she was awakened by the cry of a rooster. After a quick continental breakfast provided for free in the hotel lobby, Jane showered and got ready. She applied her make-up, wig, nose, and put on her clown costume with great care. She prepped a handful of magic tricks and placed them in her satchel. Assuming she would be sweating, she brought her sun-block and make-up touch up kit, plus a bottle of water. Last item was her cell phone. That went in the pocket of her clown-pants. She wished she had Danny's gun.

The cab got her to the marina in plenty of time. A handful of fishing vessels, diving skiffs, and sailboats lined the dock. A rusty barge was beached, a casualty of hurricane season, she assumed. She could feel the humidity and was now sweating in her clown costume.

A crew was unloading ice and party supplies from a truck. She could see cases of Grey Goose Vodka, Peter Luger dry-aged steaks, seafood packed in ice, fresh bread, pastries, and cases of French wine. No doubt the guests were in for first-class treat-ment.

A bald man with a clipboard addressed her. "You clown Karen?"

"Koo-Koo Karen," Jane said recognizing his voice, "and you must be Pops."

"Pleasure to meet ya, Koo-Koo," he said, his smile revealing a gold plated front tooth. "Please have a seat with everyone else and I'll gettcha when we're ready." He motioned to picnic benches with a group seated in the shade, some smoking cigarettes. Jane thanked him.

She joined the others; assorted caterers, bartenders wearing bow ties, musicians with their instruments, and entertainers. Jane said a collective "hi" to everybody and found a seat next to Nate and Al, a black ventriloquist team. She could tell the dummy Al was just a painted Charlie McCarthy model, complete with mini afro. She was familiar with the dummy from magic catalogues she'd browsed.

She made small-talk with Nate and learned he was signed with Debra's Book-A-Look agency. He confessed that most of his gigs were nightclubs and comedy venues so the majority his jokes were bawdy. Nate was worried that occasional profanity might slip out of Al. "Sometimes I can't control this little bastard," he said.

The ferry arrived and the crew loaded supplies before Pops waved everyone over. As Jane boarded, she noted the vessel was named *Calico Jack,* Anne Bonny's pirate husband.

Pops explained to all passengers that the ferry would be going back and forth all day, bringing guests to the island and then returning them to Provodenciales. Under no circumstances were the staff to return on the trips with the guests. There would be designated runs at the end of the day for staff only, and only after most of the guests had returned. He explained a handful of guests were staying overnight, and Pops would let everyone know when the boat was ready.

Jane's heart raced. She would be trapped for the duration of the party which meant there would be more of a chance she'd be recognized. She willed herself to stay calm and focused. The ferry set out. The wind-blown spray was refreshing but Jane made sure to keep her face turned away as not to smear her clown make-up.

Ten minutes later, on the horizon, she could see Stingray Cay. As they got closer she could make out a cluster of palm trees surrounding a scatter of buildings. There was a central compound structure and the familiar lighthouse she'd recognized. The island's docks came into view, and a large power yacht overshadowed smaller sailboats. White event tents surrounded a swimming pool, and inflated puffy-castles swayed in the breeze.

As the ferry neared the docks, Jane could see more detail. The main house, styled Colonial, was exquisite with large shutter windows and a wrap-around porch. There were isolated buildings set back from the white sand beach, and quaint bungalows scattered on the coast.

Jane searched for any sign of Veronica.

As the ferry slowed Jane checked out an impressive yacht on the dock, Veronica's cabin cruiser no doubt. Rounding the bow she could see the vessel's name: *Anne Bonny*. No surprise there.

The sight of the security staff on shore gave her pause. They were hard-looking, dark-skinned men who stood at attention, the Haitians Oscar had told her about. In her research Jane learned that the poverty-stricken nation of Haiti is a mere ninety miles south. If she was caught as an imposter these were the men who would deal with her. Her throat clinched and went dry. She dug into her satchel and stole a sip from her bottled water.

Just stick to the plan.

Craning her neck, she did not see anyone resembling Veronica; however, beyond the security staff she could see Debra from Book-A-Look waiting on the shore.

Jane could not help but notice the vintage canons lining the bank. The black-iron antiques were set behind stone turrets and aimed out to sea. She wondered if these canons actually fired as opposed to the Civil War memorials she'd seen in parks, their canon barrels filled with cement. She could see a small petting zoo off to the side.

Book-A-Look Debra came to them. "Nate, darling, thank you for coming."

"Anything for you, love," Nate said, and hugged her with his free arm.

"You and Karen set up over there, in what we're calling the 'kiddy zone.' Debra pointed to an area near the house where white folding chairs were arranged before a shaded riser. "You'll share the stage with Dippy, another performer. Work out the schedule amongst yourselves. In between, roam the crowd and keep the kids entertained. We expect the first guests to arrive in about an hour. The main house is strictly off limits, so if you have to use the facilities please do so only in the conference center," she said, pointing to the largest of the buildings.

Jane took another opportunity to look around. There was still no sign of Veronica.

"The birthday boy is Billy," Debra continued. "He's on the shy side, so you may need to draw him out a little bit."

Debra's eyes caught something over Jane's shoulder. Jane turned to see a barefoot Elvis impersonator, white cape draped over his shoulder, wandering up the beach.

"Excuse me," Debra said and rushed off to wrangle The King.

Jane glanced around again but there was still no sign of either Veronica or the blonde woman she'd seen in the photos. She heard the boat engines roar and turned to see the ferry heading back to Provo.

As Jane was setting up her tricks on stage she met Dippy, a hobo-styled clown with a thick New Orleans accent. Juggling was his specialty. He'd spent years working the French Quarter as "Dippy the Cajun Clown."

They agreed on rotation plans for the stage, Nate and Al would go on first, then Dippy, and finally Jane—twenty minutes or so on stage. Jane realized they would be short-handed once she feigned sick. Not the end of the world.

A half an hour later, out on the horizon, Jane could see the ferry returning with the first group of guests. Staff and performers took their places. She caught sight of a young boy coming out of the house. Could this be Veronica's son? She guessed the birthday boy was about six years old and searched for a physical resemblance. Once he saw them the boy ran up.

"Billy! Happy birthday," Jane said in a high-pitched clown voice, kneeling down to his eye level.

"You're a lady clown!" he said.

"I am, indeed. Koo Koo Karen the clown. And I bet you like magic." She pulled a sponge ball from her pocket. "See this spongy," Jane said, embarking on one of her close-up standards. Jane made the ball vanish. His eyes widened. "Oh, look here it is!" Jane said, pretending to pull it from behind his ear. He reached up and felt his ear, amazed at first, but then furrowed his brow, suddenly very concerned.

The boy drew back and slugged her in the face.

Jane's clown nose fell off.

"Ha!" Billy said. He turned and ran away.

What a brat. She figured he was probably never disciplined. *Is he afraid of clowns?* Retrieving her rubber nose, she felt a presence followed by, "Come on, Billy."

Jane stood to see the woman. It *was* Veronica.

Jane didn't have her nose on as Veronica smiled to her and then returned her attention to the boy. "We've got to greet our guests," she said. "Come on, sweetie." Veronica took the boy's hand.

Jane studied Veronica as she moved to the dock. She was relieved when Veronica did not glance back. Jane thought Veronica appeared older than she'd remembered, even though it had only been a couple of months.

Wolff's former bodyguard, Buddy, joined them. He glanced at Jane and held his look.

She turned away, pressed her nose on, and pretended to busy herself with her magic tricks. *He recognized me. Shit!* Out of the corner of her eye she could see Veronica urging Buddy to follow. He obeyed.

Jane sensed he did not make the connection and breathed a sigh of relief. She watched as Veronica, her lover Buddy, and little Billy graciously greeted the first wave of guests—the perfect nuclear family.

Jane peeled off.

She ducked behind the jumpy-castle, pulled out her cell phone, and dialed Gallagher. There was no signal. *Shit!* She would have to get back to Provo before she could call Gallagher. Behind her the jazz band kicked in with a rendition of Henry Mancini's "Peter Gunn." The party was officially underway.

Jane recognized the Bermuda Triangle kid from her flight, his parents, and his little sister. She wondered how they were connected to Veronica. The boy saw her and waved. "Beware of the Devil's Triangle!" he said before he pressed his hands to his face and screamed in make-believe terror. It was clear *he* recognized her, even with the nose on. *I've got to get out of here.*

She thought maybe she could weave through the new arrivals and get past the security staff, but the boat kicked up exhaust and shoved off, obviously returning for more guests.

Jane decided to be patient and stick to her plan—avoid Veronica and Buddy, fake sickness, and get back to Provo to call Gallagher as soon as possible. She was sweating enough now to appear convincingly ill, and considered putting her finger down her throat to induce vomiting.

Jane spotted Debra near the buffet and figured she's give it a shot. She marched towards her, holding her stomach.

It was time to improvise.

CHAPTER 19

"Do you have a medical condition you didn't tell me about?" irritated Debra said, arms crossed.

Jane shook her head. "No, it's just…"

Having just been summoned by walkie-talkie, Pops joined them. "What's up?" he asked.

"Our clown is sick," Debra said.

"It must have been something I ate," Jane feigned. "I had chicken last night, or maybe it was the hollandaise sauce on my eggs this morning." Jane bent over holding her belly, adding a whimper to her performance. "Please, get me back to Provo."

"If we take her back now she may get sick on the boat and make a mess," Pops said. "I think it's best we wait until all the guests have arrived."

"I won't get sick, and if I do, it will be over the side," Jane said.

"Where's the ferry now? Debra asked Pops.

"Just set out. Won't be back for another hour," he said.

"Hmm," Debra's forehead was in a wrinkle.

"She can rest in one of the bungalows," Pops suggested. "There's a bathroom in there, and she can lie down if she wants."

"The bungalows are reserved for the overnight guests," Debra said with growing irritation.

"I'll have it serviced, no problem," Pops assured with a wave of his hand.

Jane gave Pops a grateful nod. "That would be great. Thank you." If Jane couldn't get off the island yet hiding was the next best thing. The bungalows were set apart from the compound, away from the party, and Veronica and Buddy would be too busy entertaining. Debra reluctantly agreed and went back to her duties.

Pops escorted Jane down a path. "You gonna be all right?" he asked.

"I think so, thank you," she said. "I'll be careful not to make a mess."

They entered the impressive guest cottage, the last one of a dozen of them nestled along the shore. Jane saw the familiar linen on the bed. It was now obvious how the conch shell pattern complemented the room's tasteful design, its wallpaper, carpet, and drapes all working together in nautical a theme.

Pops opened the French doors and said he'd return when the ferry was ready to take her back. Jane thanked him again. When he was gone she searched for a phone but there was none. This seemed odd since every other amenity was there, television, mini bar, a high-end sound system. She checked herself in the mirror. The sun-block was wearing off so she applied more and used a towel to dab the sweat off the back of her neck. Satisfied, she took a seat on a high-backed chair and waited, scanning the horizon for the ferry's return.

That's when she noticed something coming across the water, an inflatable Zodiac boat with an outboard motor. A lone figure piloted the craft as the boat chopped through the waves. It appeared the man aboard had a fishing instrument of some kind strapped to his back.

Curious, Jane got up and aimed the brass telescope, one of the nautical themed amenities in the room, out across the water. When she finally adjusted the focus she caught sight of the pilot, Agent Gallagher, powering the craft. *What the hell?* It wasn't a fishing rod on his back but an assault rifle.

He's coming to my rescue was her first thought, but then wondered where everyone else was, helicopters, FBI agents, other boats. It seemed so weird. *Could Gallagher be working for Veronica?*

Her knees began to quiver and Jane felt sick, for real.

CHAPTER 20

Gallagher was hunched low in the boat, in commando mode, and he rounded the edge of the island.

What's going on? Jane was confused. Gallagher had to have been in Provodenciales last night when they spoke on the phone. He must be in cahoots with Veronica. She was expecting me. It's only a matter of time before they come.

She sprang across the deck and ran though the scrub brush. The thorny branches caught her costume. They painfully scraped her arms but she pressed on. Minutes later, sweating and out of breath, Jane reached a remote beach on the other side of the island. Neither the boat nor Gallagher were anywhere in sight.

There was the sound of a gunshot.

Jane took cover. She came across an electronic device on a metal stake. At first, she thought it was a mini video camera. Upon closer inspection she could see it was a motion detector. Realizing she had probably already set it off, Jane panicked and moved behind it. There were, unfortunately, others; one on a stake about twenty yards away, another on the trunk of a palm tree.

Jane came across a Haitian guard face down in the sand, motionless. Blood soaked his shirt. It appeared as if a chunk of flesh was missing out the middle of his back. *Did Gallagher shoot him?* She ran for cover, ducked into the thick mangrove, and came across Gallagher's hidden Zodiac boat.

More gunshots sounded. She dropped to the ground and heard men shouting. There was screaming—a man in pain. She rolled into the scrub and hid deeper with the sound of approaching footsteps.

They were coming.

She dug further into the underbrush, pressed down, and could recognize Gallagher's voice. He was the one in distress. Peering through the leaves, she could see a half-dozen armed men, one carrying a machete, another with Gallagher's rifle. They escorted him, now handcuffed, past her. Jane was certain she would be discovered, but they moved on. After a moment the only sound was that of the lapping waves against the coast and the party in the distance. *He did come to rescue me.*

Jane got up, moved to a vantage point. She could see Gallagher and the Haitians as they forced him into the lighthouse. It appeared the oldest of the men gave orders, and they split up. A young man stayed behind, the one to stand guard.

Jane knew she had to get off the island. On the way back to the Zodiac she came across an exposed hole in the ground. She could see it was a trap complete with bloody Punji sticks. It was clear this is what snared Gallagher.

She was struggling to drag the boat into the ocean but stopped, torn, she couldn't leave him behind. Jane scanned the horizon but there were no other boats.

Near the bullet-ridden corpse flies had begun to swarm. She pulled a pistol from the dead man's holster, hid the gun in her pants, and set out for the lighthouse.

The guard was sitting on a concrete bench, his back to her, smoking a cigarette. Wires from ear-buds dangled. The rock she found was about the size of a cantaloupe. She snuck up behind him, lifted it over her head, and brought it down hard. He dropped to the sand, out cold.

She pushed through the door.

Machinery dominated the dark space. Gallagher was on the

concrete floor. Handcuffs bound his arms wrapped around pipes in front of him.

"What are you doing here," she said over the loud generator, removing her clown wig.

He looked up, squinted, warned, "You need to get out of here."

She knelt. "I saw them, Veronica and Buddy."

"I know," he said, clearly in pain.

The sight of blood gave her pause.

"I told you not to come," he said, teeth clinched. "Why didn't you listen to me?"

She wondered why there were no back up agents with him. Why was he all alone on this mission? Thinking back, Jane realized she had never been to his office. She never had seen him associating with other law enforcement professionals. The only proof was a badge he produced, and that could have been a prop. She felt foolish. "You're not FBI, are you?"

"No."

"Then who are you?"

"One of Veronica's victims."

"Nobody's coming?"

"We're hundreds of miles away from anyone who can help, or anyone who would care."

As hot as it was in this room, she felt a chill. She had hoped the cavalry would charge in and save the day. She said, "I don't get it."

"I had a lucrative career on Wall Street until I met her," he said. "Veronica seduced me and talked me into a deal I couldn't refuse. I lost everything, all of my firm's assets, all of our holdings. I tried to make up the losses with my own money, but I lost that too. That's when I was arrested for embezzlement and my wife left me. I jumped bail and have been trying to get Veronica ever since."

"So...it's about revenge."

"I had no idea where Veronica was until you figured it out.

Those photos I emailed, the blonde woman, that was supposed to throw you off so you wouldn't get in my way."

"Let's get out of here," she said, and tried to pry the handcuffs free. It was no use. They were clinched tight, and his blood was warm and oily. When she wiped sweat from her eyes she didn't realize her sleeve was also drenched in blood and it brushed across her lips. The blood tasted like copper—nothing like the bloody mary back in New York. "I'll go to the party and scream my head off," she said. "Somebody's got to help."

"There's a number in my wallet. Get it." She reached into his pocket and pulled out his billfold. "There's a card in there, Kenny Lang, FBI. He's the guy I impersonated. He's the one who's been tracking Veronica."

She found the card.

"Call him. Tell him I've been kidnapped. Demand he contact the American Embassy in Provo. He'll know what to do."

"There's no cell reception. I tried."

"There has to be a phone somewhere. In the main house."

She so hated seeing him in pain and reached into her pocket for the automatic. "Here," she said, and handed him the gun.

"Where'd you get this?" he asked.

"From that guard on the beach."

He looked to her with his piercing blue eyes, glassy now, "Brilliant. You found her, Jane, a needle in a haystack."

"We both did."

He slid the carriage of the pistol to chamber a round. "Go now."

Tears streaming, she was out the door.

CHAPTER 21

Jane moved quickly along the sandy path. She could hear the music up ahead mixed with shouts and cheers—jovial commotion of the party in full-swing. She reached the compound and headed toward the main house, cutting through the garden and patio. Debra said the house was off limits. As far as Jane could tell nobody had seen her.

She entered through the French doors. There were voices coming from the kitchen. She cautiously peeked to see chefs adding finishing touches to a massive birthday cake.

Avoiding them, she moved down a hallway and past a wood paneled sitting-room. Colonial era antiques were everywhere. Dramatic nautical paintings filled the walls, many depicting ships in battle. It all felt like a museum, or something out of *Architectural Digest*.

There was no phone.

The portrait of Anne Bonny caught Jane's attention, hanging over the mantle. Her hair and dress were flowing in the wind, a musket pistol in hand. A medallion hung from her neck, and her eyes were intense. Even though it was a painting, Jane could see there could be a resemblance.

She heard voices coming her way. There must be a phone upstairs, in one of the bedrooms. She climbed the steps.

It was considerably cooler upstairs as the air conditioning raised the hair on her arms. Jane tip-toed across the thick carpet and entered the master bedroom. An imposing, four-post bed was draped by Veronica's signature conch shell linen.

Gingerly picking up the phone on the nightstand, she pulled out the business card and dialed. As it rang she considered the framed pictures of Veronica as a young girl, her mother and father beside her. Another picture was familiar, something Gallagher had shown her, Veronica in her teens emerging from a pool—all glimpses into Veronica's childhood.

Where did it all go wrong?

A stern receptionist answered, all business, "How may I direct your call?"

"I need Kenny Lang. It's extremely urgent," Jane said, hushed.

"One moment please." Jane was put on hold.

She went to the window and peeked through the wooden blinds. The band finished a swing number and the guests on the dance floor applauded. Didn't these people realize their hostess was a black widow? A young woman in heels stepped up to the microphone. The band kicked into a vintage number, something familiar, but Jane couldn't place it. All became clear when the woman began the lyrics of Cole Porter's "Love for Sale." Cole Porter again? What are the chances? A song from the point of view of a prostitute—Jane wondered if Veronica had chosen the playlist.

"What are you doing in here?" the voice sounded behind her.

Jane spun to see Buddy at the bedroom door. She was caught red-handed, phone in her hand.

"Who are you calling?" Buddy approached her.

Jane froze. "I'm, uh, can't get reception and..." she realized her voice was not disguised. She began all over again, as another persona, "I can't get reception on my—"

"What's with the blood?" he said, pointing to her sleeve. Buddy snatched the card from her hand and read it, "FBI? What the...?" He ripped her wig off, sneered at her, and clamped her arm, nostrils flaring, "How'd you find us?"

Jane had to think fast. She wished she hadn't given Gallagher the gun. In that split second she made the decision—*don't let him see fear*. "I want my cut," she said with determination, pushing him off. "Either I get what's coming," she said, "or the FBI shit-storms this place." Much like performing her magic, the art of deception is much about manipulating expectations. *Remain in control.*

Holding up the card he asked, "Who's this?"

"Gallagher's in the lighthouse and needs medical attention. See to it immediately. Get him out of there."

"Who's Gallagher?" he said with furrowed brow.

"In the lighthouse. Do it!" She heard a radio squawk from a walkie-talkie. Jane turned to see Veronica in the doorway. Pops and a few of the Haitian guards stood behind her.

"What a surprise," Veronica said.

"Who's this Gallagher she's talking about?" Buddy asked Veronica.

Veronica ignored him, asked Jane "How did you find us?"

"We'll talk about that after I get my share," Jane said. "But first, tend to Gallagher before he bleeds to death."

Buddy turned his palms up, seeking clarification, "Who the fuck is this Gallagher?"

"An old mark," Veronica snapped before moving into the room with a cool expression on her face, "What is it you want?"

"A third."

"A third of what?"

"What we took from Wolff," Jane said, and caught the slightest smile on Veronica's face. "You didn't have to kill him," she added.

Distant gunshots rang out. The lights in the ceiling dimmed and the electricity cut off. Jane feared Gallagher had used the gun she'd given him.

A radio on Pop's belt squawked with panicked voices in

French. "The generator in the lighthouse," Pops translated. He was off followed by the Haitians.

The three of them alone, Veronica gave Buddy a knowing nod. Buddy grabbed Jane by the arms and slipped into a chokehold. She clawed, trying to break free but his grip tightened.

Veronica stepped closer, cool as ice.

His arm clenched tight. Jane gagged, the taste of bile in her throat, and she tried to bite. Her lungs began to burn and she elbowed. She kicked for her life, but he clamped down even harder, like a vise.

Meanwhile Veronica studied Jane, calm and clinical. *This is it*, Jane thought, *I'm going to die*. She gave it another desperate shot, sinking her nails into his arm.

Colors burst in her mind's-eye, much like fireworks. Then all went black.

CHAPTER 22

The vibration against her cheekbone woke Jane. Her head throbbed, throat burned, and everything hurt. She tried to wipe the drool from her face but couldn't because her hands were bound behind her back. From the sound of the engine Jane assumed she was on the Anne Bonny, Veronica's yacht.

She heard a "bah."

Jane spun to see a goat standing over her. The animal startled and scurried back, its hooves clambering on the varnished deck. It lost its balance and fell before scrambling back up again. The goat snorted in defiance, then sniffed at her from a distance, a little bell clinking on its neck.

"I don't give a shit!" Jane recognized Buddy's voice from behind the door, and then Veronica in response. They were clearly arguing, but she could not make out what they were saying other than occasional bursts of profanity.

Footsteps. Someone was coming.

Jane pretended she was still passed out. She heard the door unlock and peeked to see Buddy's boots step up to her face. The goat tried to escape but he kicked it back. With a grunt, he lifted Jane and dragged her through the bulkhead. Although the rope cut into her wrists, Jane pretended to be unconscious.

He wedged her against something to keep her upright and Jane opened her eyes to see Veronica sitting across from her at the boat's dining table. Buddy mumbled to himself before stepping out on the deck and climbing the ladder to the wheel-house above.

"How did you find us?" Veronica asked.

Feign confidence. Jane said to her, "I've already contacted the FBI."

Veronica sat back. "You have one hell of an imagination, I'll give you that."

"They know I'm here."

"I don't think so."

"They'll come for me,' Jane said. "And Gallagher."

"I don't think so," Veronica scoffed. "How did you two pair up?"

"Where is he?"

"Unfortunately he, uh…" Veronica stroked her chin searching for a way to put it, "lost a gun battle with my capable staff."

Jane swallowed hard, asked, "So, back in L.A., the plan all along was to kill Wolff for his money?"

"Hey, Buddy," Veronica yelled above. "Did we kill Wolff for his money?"

A voice came from above in a faux British accent, "Precisely, love. We killed the wanker for his bleedin' shillings." Then back to his own voice added "the pig."

"Wonderful, darling," Veronica said, forcing a Russian accent that reminded Jane of the character Natasha from the Bullwinkle cartoons.

Jane said. "So I was the shill, and all along the plan was to pin Wolff's murder on me."

"We didn't plan on killing Wolff, but things got complicated."

Buddy shouted from above, "Just fucking find out how she found us!"

"Shut up," Veronica yelled back.

"How'd it get complicated?" Jane asked.

"Don't tell her shit!" Buddy barked.

"Fuck you, Skipper! How much longer?"

"Ah…five minutes."

Veronica shook her head, exasperated. "What was supposed to happen," she confessed, "was Wolff would discover me dead, as if I overdosed."

"You?"

"I'd appear that way, and a doctor would confirm it, well…a fake doctor, and guys posing as paramedics."

"I don't get it," said Jane.

"Wolff was the perfect mark because he was not a U.S. citizen. Since he had a criminal record himself, his only choice would be to flee the country. Cooper would agree to meet up with him at a later date, to split the diamonds. So in his haste, Wolff was supposed to rush to the airport thinking he's carrying his cash with him. What he wouldn't know is that by then we'd already done the ol' switch-a-roo."

"That's why Cooper had me get two suitcases."

"Wolff wouldn't go to the authorities for fear of being implicated in my death, and he wouldn't report the missing money. It was a perfect blow-off, and it should have gone that way."

"So what happened?"

With a raised voice Veronica shouted, "Buddy got jealous. Didn't you, Buddy?"

"I wasn't jealous!" Buddy yelled.

Veronica leaned in, as if confiding, "Buddy shot Wolff, with your gun. He spoiled everything, and we had to change the plan."

"Why?"

"I don't know, macho bullshit between men. Because he was afraid Wolff fucked me better than him."

"I killed him because he was a pig," Buddy persisted.

"Because you're a pathetic, Eurotrash piece of shit!" Veronica shouted back in anger, and then to Jane, "men are *so* incredibly stupid. It's such a cruel travesty that males rule the world. Not the case for many of nature's other species."

"He deserved to die," Buddy added. Jane could hear him spit.

"What about Cooper?" Jane asked.

Veronica sat back and studied her. "You were in love with him, weren't you?"

"No," Jane lied.

"I can tell you were," Veronica laughed. "Love's a bitch, sister," she taunted. "He became a liability, so it had to be done. But trust me, he wasn't your type."

"So what happened?"

"Well," Veronica said, "after our fatal mishap with Wolff, Cooper got paranoid and then belligerent. He became *difficult*."

"He was a royal pain in the ass!" Buddy added. "One hundred percent."

"Was Buddy jealous of Cooper, too?" Jane asked.

"Were you, Buddy? Jealous of Cooper?"

"No!" Buddy boomed from above. "I am telling you, he was a complete pain in the ass. Pompous, too. I hate Canadians!"

"I killed Cooper," Veronica confessed with a tinge of pride.

"Why?"

"Because I couldn't trust him."

"How'd you do it?"

"It's not important."

"I need to know"

"I slit his throat."

"Because you were afraid he'd go to the cops?"

"No, he wouldn't have done that. I couldn't trust him when the cops got to him, which they would have. He lost his edge. He was done."

"To take a life?" Jane asked, "Does that bother you?"

She could see Veronica's jaw tighten. "I killed him on his boat, and I'm going to kill you on mine unless you tell me how you found us."

Jane bit her lip. It was her detective work that uncovered Veronica's whereabouts, but she could not admit it, not as long as Veronica wanted something.

"There's obviously a breach," Veronica pressed. "Someone's talking. Who?"

"Who do you think?" Jane asked, not having an answer, wondering where it would lead.

"I don't have time for games. Tell me, or you're going in the water."

Realizing that Veronica had made a career out of deceit, Jane knew she had to be perfectly convincing at this moment. She needed pure confidence. This would be the performance of her life. "Cooper is not dead," Jane bluffed. She studied Veronica for her reaction.

"Impossible," Veronica said.

"You didn't kill him, back in Dana Point," Jane said. "He's alive."

Buddy jumped down from above, startling Jane.

"What do you mean?" he asked.

"Veronica failed," Jane said.

"Wait a minute, he—" Veronica started in.

"He survived," Jane said.

"Where is he?" Buddy asked.

"I can't tell you where Didier is," she said, using Cooper's real name, what she'd learned from Gallagher. Buddy and Veronica shared a look of concern.

"Didier is alive?" Buddy asked. She motioned him to step outside. They climbed to the wheelhouse and Jane could hear them arguing in hushed tones—not happy. Jane searched the galley for a knife, something to cut the ropes behind her back, anything. She struggled, and felt them loosening, but not enough to free her hands. She remembered reading in one of her magic books that Harry Houdini expertly wriggled his hands out of ropes by applying constant pressure, but not enough to swell the wrists.

Buddy shut off the engine, came back. He went past her and into the forward cabin. Jane craned her neck to see Veronica on the bow, turned away smoking a cigarette, deep in thought. She had never seen Veronica smoke before. The boat rocked gently. The only sounds were of waves lapping against the hull. Jane continued to struggle against the ropes.

Cursing in a foreign tongue, an angry Buddy emerged from the cabin with the goat on its leash, dragging the reluctant animal out to the bow.

"The fucking thing pissed all over me," he griped. "And it smells!"

"This was your idea," Veronica shouted.

Jane could see Buddy tie a rope around the goat's collar. He wrapped the other end to a tie anchor on the side of the boat. "You want to see what's going to happen to you?" Buddy said to Jane.

With a knife he cut a long slash along the goat's leg. The animal squealed in pain and thrashed about. Buddy picked the goat up and tossed the animal overboard. The goat hit the water with a splash and Jane's heart sank, feeling sorry for the poor thing. Buddy wiped blood from his hands as Jane could see the goat trying to swim, dog-paddling, its head just above water. It was working its way back to the boat but Buddy grabbed the harpoon and pushed the animal away.

Then it hit her, blood in the water. Sharks. The goat was the appetizer.

CHAPTER 23

Veronica pulled a bottle of Vodka from the freezer. Without saying a word, she filled a glass with ice and poured heavy.

Although weakening, Jane could see this goat had resolve. Buddy kept busy with the harpoon, pushing the animal off the hull.

"Stop him," Jane pleaded.

"Too late for that," Veronica said before sampling her drink and climbing back up to the wheelhouse. Jane struggled with the rope that bound her wrists. She could feel it loosening, but not enough to free her hands.

Beyond the goat, Jane saw a shark fin break the surface. Buddy saw it too.

"Thar' she blows!" he said with a laugh.

Shark teeth clamped. The goat screeched. The rope pulled taut before it was yanked below.

"Did you see that?!" Buddy exclaimed, charged with adrenaline.

In the bloody whitewash the goat came up again, still alive, until a larger shark sank its teeth. Thrashing, it pulled the animal below.

"Outstanding!" Buddy said, pacing at the bow, loving it. Buddy pulled the rope aboard. At the tether's end Jane could see the frayed goat collar with remnants of fur. Somehow the little bell was miraculously intact.

Next Buddy was in the cabin. Jane flinched as he brushed past her. He entered the bathroom door and struggled with something inside. With a grunt, he lifted and emerged with Gallagher's body wrapped in a transparent, blood-smeared plastic tarp.

Jane screamed.

"Shut up!" Buddy said as he struggled with Gallagher's lifeless mass. He dragged him past. It took great effort, but he maneuvered the cumbersome corpse over the railing. Then Buddy flopped Gallagher over, tarp and all.

Air bubbles in the plastic tarp kept the body buoyant, but it didn't take long before the sharks tore Gallagher to pieces—like a pack of starved wolves devouring grocery store meat, packaging and all.

Veronica surprised Jane, dropping down from the wheelhouse. "Where's Cooper?" she asked.

"A hotel."

"Where?"

"I'll show you, but untie me first," she said, trying to appear calm even though she felt like throwing up.

Veronica turned back to Buddy who was now making a sport out of prodding the sharks with his harpoon. "Will you cut that out, for Christ's sake? Come here!"

Buddy set the harpoon down and came up behind Veronica, breathless. "Tell us where Didier is," Veronica calmly said to Jane, "or you're going in the water."

"In a hotel. I'll take you there."

"No, you'll tell us."

"If I tell you, you'll kill me. Pay us both two hundred thousand each and you'll never hear from either of us again."

"We're wasting time," Buddy said. He grabbed the drink from Veronica and took a healthy swig before handing it back to her. "Let's get this over with."

"Listen," Veronica said to Jane. "You've seen my island paradise. I've spent a considerable amount of time and effort making it my sanctuary, and peace of mind is very important to me. I'm not going to compromise that, especially now, because of a nuisance like you. I need to talk with him." Veronica picked up the receiver of the ship's radio. "We'll call him ship-to-shore."

"I don't have his number with me, but I'll take you to him."

Buddy grabbed Jane by the arms and lifted her. "Tell us where he is or you're shark bait."

Now on her feet, Jane was able to twist behind her back, just enough to pull out one of her hands. She kept it hidden. "You're going to kill me anyway," Jane said.

"No we won't," Veronica said. She took another sip and licked her lips. "If you tell us where he is, we'll let you live. We'll set you out on the life raft, but we won't harm you. Someone will pick you up, probably a fishing boat, but if you don't tell us we'll definitely toss you in."

Jane tried to gauge Veronica. Was she telling the truth? She knew she had to buy more time. "Inflate the life raft first."

Veronica and Buddy shared a look. He gave her a shrug as if asking if he should. Veronica returned a quick shake of her head—no.

"Inflate the raft," Jane demanded.

"Can't do that," Veronica said.

"Then I'm not telling you shit," Jane said, still trying to appear in control, backing into the cabin door so they could not see her loose hand. "That's the deal, take it or leave it."

Veronica sighed heavy. "Have it your way," she said, and stepped back. "He will find another way to contact us, and I'll take care of him then."

"Why are you so threatened by him?"

"Like you, he knows too much."

"About the island?"

"That, and other things."

"Your boy," Jane said. "He knows who the father is." Jane could see she hit a nerve. "Or maybe...he *is* the father," she added.

Veronica sneered. "Did he tell you that?" she asked.

"I'll take you to him. The four of us will discuss what all we know," Jane said.

Veronica studied her, wheels turning. Jane could see her weighing it for a moment before she said, "I don't think so." She nodded to Buddy. He clamped his hands on Jane and led her to the bow.

"Inflate the raft!" Jane persisted, struggling against him.

"Not a chance," Veronica said before she started the engine. The motor kicked to life and a steamy exhaust drifted off the hull. Jane could see a shark fin glide past. "The raft shoots a flare and sends a radio distress signal with GPS coordinates. It's a shame 'cause I like you," Veronica said, reflecting in thought. "You weren't a bad shill for me. Come to think if it, you weren't all that bad of a fuck either," she said with a laugh. "Maybe I could have enrolled you as one of my students, and taught you a few things."

Buy more time was Jane's only thought. "They'll come for you. The FBI. Let me go, and I'll lead them astray."

Veronica shook her head in disbelief. "You have been such a pain in the ass." She nodded to Buddy. He bent down and took Jane by the waist. He wrapped his arms around her, lifted her off her feet, and carried her out.

In his grasp, Jane yanked her hands out. She clamped both sides of Buddy's head and sank her thumbs deep into his eye-sockets.

Buddy grunted, struggled blindly, and then lost his balance. They both went over the edge and hit the water at the same time.

CHAPTER 24

Below the surface Jane felt a tug on her arm. She flipped over in a summersault. The loose end of the rope, which was still bound to one of her wrists, was snared to something onboard. This enabled her to pull herself to the surface, and back to the fiberglass hull.

She could hear Buddy cursing and splashing behind her. With both hands on the rope, she climbed up. Then back on deck, she rolled to her knees and coughed, the salty sea water burning her throat.

Veronica crashed the glass of vodka over her head. It sent Jane face down, and she could feel the ice and broken glass wedged in her hair. She could smell the alcohol and saw Veronica retreat into the cabin.

Jane stood to see Buddy about to pull himself aboard when there was a ripple in the water behind him. Something stopped his progress. That *something* was a shark.

Fear in his eyes.

Buddy kicked below the surface. First he was thrown hard against the hull, his face turning a deep purple. Then he tried to pull himself aboard. Jane could see one of his legs was sheared off below the knee. Back beyond him sharks fought over the severed appendage.

"Help me," he said to Jane, frantic, reaching out to her, his eyes pleading. She couldn't just watch him die. She stepped forward to assist, holding out her hand, but then another shark appeared and he was yanked back into the sea. The ocean became a crimson, bubbly whirlpool, and he was gone.

Jane turned back to see Veronica standing up in the wheel-house having witnessed Buddy's demise. Jane could see Veronica considering her next move before she jumped down, grabbed the harpoon, and charged. The metallic hook grazed Jane's side.

Jane was able to grab the other end with both hands. It became a tug-of-war and Veronica's end hit the chrome throttle. The boat engine thundered to life and the yacht surged forward, kicking up a mighty wake.

Jane struggled to gain control of the harpoon. She pulled herself forward, making her way up to the middle of the shaft. The advantage gave her more leverage, and she was able to wrestle the harpoon out of Veronica's grasp. Victorious, Jane tossed the harpoon overboard.

"Enough!" Jane screamed.

The yacht was racing, unmanned. Veronica darted inside the cabin. Jane thought it best to slow the yacht and steer it towards land. She climbed to the wheelhouse. Jane was searching for the throttle when a sharp pain shot up her leg. A kitchen knife was embedded deep into her thigh. Veronica pulled it out and was about to plunge again when Jane jumped away. "Bitch!" Jane screamed.

Veronica came after her, knife swinging.

"Get away from me!"

Veronica lunged, and Jane dodged her again. She escaped around the outside of the cabin. She tried to keep her balance, holding the handrail as she made her way to the front of the boat. Veronica came after her, so Jane rounded to the other side, leaving a trail of blood. Every time Veronica came around one side, Jane retreated to the other. It was a deadly game of musical chairs.

"It's over!" Jane shouted, trying to reason with her.

Veronica said nothing, and kept coming. Jane considered

jumping overboard but could not risk it with the sharks. The boat rocked violently and pounded the waves. The spray soaked her, and rounding the boat again Jane slipped on her own blood. Veronica was upon her. She slashed again with the knife, slicing Jane's arm.

Jane kicked at her and was able to get away again. She rounded the cabin once more. Whatever side of the boat Veronica advanced, Jane would retreat the other until finally she found herself trapped at the bow.

Nowhere left to go, Jane steadied herself at the railing.

"Why do you do it?" Jane asked, still trying to buy time, an attempt to engage Veronica.

"Do what?" Veronica said, pausing to catch her breath.

"Kill."

Veronica seemed surprised by the question.

"You've got everything," Jane continued over the roar of the engine, "beauty, brains, you'd be a success in anything you choose, so why destroy lives?"

Veronica said, "Admit it, back in L.A., you felt the thrill, am I right?"

It was true. Jane had never felt more alive when then she was on the inside the caper, teamed with Cooper, and living on the edge.

"Am I right?" Veronica asked again.

Jane didn't know what to say.

A buoy whipped past the boat. It was a point of reference, and for the first time Jane could see how fast the boat was going. Veronica saw it too and glanced back over her shoulder. By the look on Veronica's face Jane could see something was wrong. Veronica began to climb back to the wheelhouse.

Buoys warn boaters, was Jane's thought the second before a deafening crunch.

Both she and Veronica were violently thrown forward. It was as if the boat hit an unseen wall. Jane hit hard against the cabin.

The boat listed and Jane could hardly breathe, the wind

knocked out of her. Finally getting her bearings, she looked inside to witness water pouring into the cabin. Sparks rained from the ceiling. The engine was driving the boat forward, filling the cabin with water.

Jane rolled see Veronica pull the kitchen knife out from her side. She looked to Jane and said, "I'm bleeding," utter disbelief in her eyes.

"What was that?" Jane asked.

"Coral," Veronica said through clinched teeth.

A coral reef, of course—one of the underwater hazards that made the region a hideout for pirates. The scent of fuel hit Jane's nostrils just before KABOOM!

Jane could feel the percussion in her chest. Heat washed over. The craft listed even more and Veronica slid across the deck leaving a bloody smear. Veronica climbed to her feet and entered the burning cabin, fighting against the rushing water at waist level.

Reaching out, Jane tried to grab hold of something. Below the seat she found a hatch with a yellow caution sticker. She pulled the lever. Compressed air hissed, and the inflatable raft ballooned out into her face. She wrapped her arms around it and held on. She could feel the heat of the fire as she pushed off.

The yacht was still under power and left her in its wake.

Just as Veronica said it would, a flare shot into the sky. A flashing strobe-light pulsed. After the raft was fully inflated, Jane climbed over the edge and flopped inside. She turned to see the yacht half submerged. Black smoke filled the air.

There was no sign of Veronica.

In the distance Jane could see the peak of the coral reef they'd hit crest the water. She thought how ironic it was that a boat named Anne Bonny would come to such an end. She watched as the yacht sank leaving a bubbling, foamy mushroom on the surface.

Did Veronica go down with the ship?

Minutes later, a hundred yards away, the burning flare

descended on its tiny parachute before extinguishing into the water. It was getting dark, the water turning black, and the flashing strobe cast strange shadows across the surface.

Jane scanned the horizon but there was still no sign of Veronica.

She felt woozy, and could see the water on bottom of the raft was red with blood. She ripped the top off her clown costume to wrap her bleeding leg. She considered making a tourniquet but didn't have a stick. She tightened the crude bandage and worried the sharks would smell the blood in the raft and bite through the flimsy rubber bottom.

Jane stared into the dark water. Could Veronica be just below the surface? She could see her own reflection—mirrored in the blackness. So much had passed since the day she met Cooper. Things were so simple then, so what happened? Where would I be now if I hadn't agreed to be his shill?

Then her reflected image transformed to Veronica's face. Jane jumped back in panic. She wondered what she would do if Veronica tried to climb into the raft.

CHAPTER 25

The thundering noise came first, and there was a shimmering light in the sky. Jane tried to stand in the raft to wave the helicopter down but her wounded leg gave way and she stumbled back. The helicopter approached, deafening, the light blinding. Windy chop from the whirling blades kicked up spray in a wicked, deafening mechanical monsoon.

She was overcome with joy.

A figure dropped out and hit water with a splash. It was a man in an orange jumpsuit and he swam towards her. She could see his face—a guy in his twenties. He took hold of the raft.

"You alright?" he shouted over the roar of jet engines above.

"Been a lot better," she shouted.

"United States Coast Guard," he said and climbed into the raft.

"I'm American," she said. "From New Mexico."

"Missouri. Glad to be of service."

He was rugged and handsome, and at this moment saving her life. She entertained a split-second fantasy—their blissful life together, kids, a golden retriever and picket fence. Jane was so happy to be rescued she figured *what the hell* and kissed him on his cheek. The microphone on his headpiece scraped against her teeth.

All business he asked, "Anyone else?"

"One, but she went down with the ship."

"When?"

"Maybe three hours ago."

He relayed, "One in the raft, one in the water," into his radio before going about his business. A metal basket descended from above. They climbed in, and he instructed her to hold on to the cable. "And don't look down," he said. He took her in his arms and motioned above before they were both hauled upward.

Inside the helicopter a man introduced himself as the medic and examined her wounds. She tried to tell what happened, her teeth chattering, voice hoarse. The medic wrapped her wounds. "Consider yourself lucky," he said. "We're only out here because we responded to a distress call, a vessel of Haitian refugees. With the severity of these wounds, you may have not lasted through the night."

"Kenny Lange, he's an FBI agent in Miami. I need to talk to him immediately," Jane said. The medic wrote Lange's name on his notepad.

An ambulance was waiting for her at the Provodenciales airport. As they placed her in a stretcher Jane searched for her savior, the Prince Charming who saved her life. He was gone. She was sad she did not get his name. *Missouri.*

By the time she got to the hospital the staff was waiting. Little time was wasted before Jane was prepped for surgery. The doctor, a paunchy Indian man with a toupee, said something about trauma and internal injuries just before she drifted off.

The next thing Jane remembered was waking up in a hospital room. She was told there were both stitches and medical staples under the wraps on her arm and leg. An IV dripped above her head. The nurse brought her breakfast, orange juice and soggy toast, just like L.A. County jail.

After breakfast the phone rang in her room, Kenny Lange of the FBI. Jane explained how Gallagher had given her his card.

"I know who you are, and I am familiar with the Alexander Wolff case," Agent Lange said. "Tell me what happened."

She did.

CHAPTER 26

The next morning Agent Lange was standing at her bedside. Jane's first impression is that he looked like Buddy Holly, thick-rimmed glasses, button-down shirt. He asked more questions about her involvement with Veronica, and Jane told him as much as she could remember. Agent Lange recorded audio of their conversation and took copious notes.

Jane learned Gallagher was indeed a victim of Veronica who had stayed in touch with Lange. "He never gave up," he said. He spoke with the local police and arranged a search of Stingray Cay.

"I'll show you," Jane volunteered. "Her house, and where they killed Gallagher."

"I don't think you're in any condition—" Lange started in.

"You need me there. I can do it."

As the police boat arrived Jane could see the guests, party rentals, tents, and attractions were gone. Only Pops and a handful of caretakers were left on the island. The scary Haitian guards were nowhere to be seen. Jane showed them the lighthouse. There was dried blood on the concrete floor. The police took pictures, and Jane made them aware of the motion detectors and Gallagher's hidden Zodiac boat.

Inside the house she pointed out the portrait of Anne Bonny and told them about the significance. Jane led the team upstairs. In Veronica's bedroom the bed was made, the plush carpet vacuumed with care. She explained how she tried to call Agent Lange from there but was caught by Buddy. Then a strange feeling overcame her. "Wait a minute," Jane said, "something's missing."

She could not put her finger on it. She noticed the pictures she had seen the other day were gone. The jewelry box was on the bureau, but not centered. Another picture frame was missing from the nightstand.

"There were photos, her life, but now they're gone."

"What kind of photos?" Lange asked.

"She took them," Jane realized.

"Who?" Lange asked.

"Veronica. Have they found her body yet?" Jane asked.

They said nothing. It was clear the answer was no. Then finally, "We have not seen Lady Vee since the party," Pops informed.

"She was on the swim team," Jane explained. "There was a picture, proof she's good in the water."

Agent Lange asked Pops, "Did someone take these photos she's talking about?"

"Not that I know of, sir," he replied.

Then it hit her. Why hadn't it come up? She asked, "Her son, the birthday boy, where is he?"

The Montessori school on the island of Provodenciales was a quaint, white stucco structure. At reception, Agent Lange summoned the principal. A middle-aged woman emerged from her office and, upon seeing the police, became very concerned. The woman led everyone down the hall to a classroom, Jane's injuries slowed her, so she was the last to arrive. Through the window on the door, the principal waved to a teacher who came out. Lange asked her where the boy was.

"Oh, Billy's not here today," the young teacher said.

"When last did you see him?" Lange asked.

"Yesterday. His mother picked him up."

Jane felt a headache coming on. Her leg was throbbing, and

she had to sit down. Anne Bonny had abandoned her child, but not Veronica. She came back.

CHAPTER 27

Accompanied by Agent Lange, Jane caught the next flight back to the states. When the stewardess took drink orders, Lange asked for coffee, but Jane opted for a virgin mary, a bloody mary without alcohol since she was on pain killers. A can of Mr. & Mrs. T's arrived, and she poured it over the ice. Against the window, over the Atlantic, she toasted Gallagher.

She caught herself in a surge of emotion. Another time, another place—there was something between them.

Jane realized she forgot to inform Lange about the assassin who twice tried to kill her. As she started to tell him he produced his digital recorder and pressed "record" to make it official. She detailed both the attempt on her life in Los Angeles, and the incident at Danny's house.

When they arrived in Miami another man met them at the airport, and he followed Jane and Lange in Danny's Chevy for the drive back to Sarasota. At Danny's house, officers and detectives from the Sheriff's Department were waiting.

Dried blood was on the wall. Jane reenacted the events in her bedroom and explained that after she shot the intruder he ran outside and into the trees. The cops found more blood on the deck, and took many photos. Jane was given an iPad with a mug shot of the man.

She confirmed it was the same man, the assassin. "You know who he is?" she asked.

An officer informed her that the Highway Patrol found this man dead on the side of the highway in a stolen car. "The victim suffered from an apparent gunshot wound with trauma to the carotid artery, and he bled out," he read from the police report.

She swallowed hard, remembering the feeling of his brutal chokehold back in Los Angeles. *Better him than me*, she thought, and asked "What kind of car?"

"Dodge Charger," the officer said.

"Black?"

"Yes. Stolen in Los Angeles."

She remembered the Dodge Charger following her and told them about it. They asked for the gun. She told them it was in the glove compartment of the Chevy. More cops arrived and she asked Agent Lange, "This man, was he Veronica's assassin?"

"I'm not sure, but I'll look into it," he said.

"Am I going back to jail?"

"It appears you acted in self-defense during a brazen home invasion. This is Florida, you have nothing to worry about."

Hours later the police packed up and left. Afraid Veronica might track her down at Danny's, Jane got a room at the Motel 6, a short walking distance from the house. Her plan was to sleep, and recover, watch TV. She took her pillow because she figured the ones at the motel would be shit.

In the darkened room watching old movies Jane finally fell asleep. The nightmare came. She was back in the raft. Veronica dark face stared at her just below the surface. She awoke in a sweat. When she realized it was only a dream she wondered why her mind was playing tricks on her.

The next morning she marched to a Starbucks across the street. After waiting in line behind professionals on the way to work, Jane finally got her coffee. She stepped outside and that's when she saw *him*.

It *was* him. Her stomach flipped.

"Jane," Cooper said.

Jane dropped her coffee on the concrete. "You set me up!" she shouted.

"Listen," he said, "Veronica tried to kill me, but she got my brother instead. It was my brother they pulled from my boat. You were there. I was watching from a distance."

Jane recalled the grotesque, bloated face she saw that day. It had to have been Cooper. But then she also remembered Gallagher telling her about Cooper's family, and vaguely remembered something about a brother, a gambler underwater in debt.

"I saw Veronica leaving the boat. I saw her toss a knife in the water. I discovered my brother but couldn't go to the police. So I got out of there, and by the time they did find him he was so decomposed everyone assumed he was me. I was there. I saw you there that day. I was watching from the cliffs in Dana Point."

The image of that bloated face returned to her memory.

Cooper continued, "He knew I was coming into money so he came down for a loan. I was out running errands, and he was sleeping off a drunk in the forward cabin. Veronica came aboard and slit his throat, thinking he was me."

"You betrayed me," she said.

"It wasn't my idea. Once Wolff was murdered, Veronica needed a diversion for her getaway. You were it."

"But she got away again, and with her son."

"I know."

"The boy...is he yours?"

He swallowed, said, "Yes."

"She tried to murder the father of her child?"

She waited for his response until he finally said, "You know how evil she is."

"You're evil," she said. "And I hate you." She turned but he grabbed her wrist. "You have every right to hate me, but I need your help. Please."

"With what?"

"Help me make Veronica pay for my brother's death."

Common sense told her to run the other way. This was the time she needed to scream at the top of her lungs and call the police. But something tugged Jane the other way—impulse. She wrestled with both the desire to stay in the game, or to get the hell out of there.

Curiosity won over. She asked him, "How?"

"By helping me kill her, that's how."

BEWARE THE SHILL

CHAPTER 1

Jane could feel the stitches on her leg tear. Blood streamed but she pushed through the pain, running for her life. She looked back, couldn't see him—wasn't sure if he was following.

She had just seen a ghost.

Only moments ago Cooper had surprised her. The man she thought was dead asked her to help him kill Veronica. She had said, "I won't be an accomplice to murder."

"I'm not asking you to," he replied.

"Sounds like you are."

Since the day she'd identified Cooper's corpse she couldn't get the image of his rotted face and shriveled hands out of her mind. But that was his brother, a mistaken identity, and now here Cooper was, alive, the lover that betrayed her—Jane's partner in crime.

"You lied to me," she'd said. "You set me up. Why would I help you?"

"Because unless we get to Veronica first, she'll kill you."

That gave Jane pause. She thought about the assassin, who failed to strangle her in the Los Angeles jail; the one hired by Veronica. The same man followed Jane to Florida to finish the job. If it wasn't for the .38 Special under her pillow, and a little bit of luck, she realized she'd be dead. She backed off and tried to distance herself from him.

"She won't stop," he pressed.

"I'll go where she can't find me."

"But she will find you. She'll kill your mother to draw you out," he said.

The thought clinched her heart. Her mother Nancy was the only family she'd ever known—the one person in Jane's life who truly loved her. Cooper added, "We both know who you're dealing with."

To Jane he seemed older and far less handsome than she'd remembered. He was unshaven. His hair was long, and his clothes disheveled. This wasn't the master of the universe she'd fallen in love with. She said to him, "But you and Veronica were lovers at one time."

He nodded, said, "Technically we're still married."

"You're asking me to help you kill the mother of your child?"

"We won't kill her. We'll nail her for good so Billy doesn't grow to become a monster."

She recalled Veronica's boy. He had punched Jane in the nose at his lavish birthday party when Jane was disguised as a clown. He seemed beyond spoiled and a total brat. She said, "So he doesn't become a monster? It's too late for that."

"You have every right to hate me. I had to let you know I'm still alive. I had to warn you."

"Warn me?"

"And ask for your help. We don't have much time."

"I wish I would have never met you," she said. Jane yearned to be the pathetically broke, out-of-work actress once again. Sure she was lonely back in Los Angeles, and miserable, but at least there was peace in her life. At least people weren't trying to kill her.

With regret, he said, "I should have never groomed you to be my shill."

"This is your war, not mine."

"War. That's exactly what it is," he said with a nod. "And you're on the front line."

"Leave me out of it."

"Ever read Sun Tzu?"

"Who?"

"He wrote *The Art of War* in 500 B.C. Do you know what I'm talking about?"

She vaguely knew what he referring to. She'd heard the book mentioned in military shows on Discovery Channel.

"Sun Tzu claims 'All warfare is based on deception,'" Cooper said.

"You're the one who taught me all about deception."

"I suppose, but you were exceptional," he said with a glimmer in his eye.

"I'm just an actress," she said. "It's craft."

"You're much more than that. You're smart and determined. You found Veronica. You cracked her world wide open and she's back on her heels now. But she won't lick her wounds forever. She'll counterattack. That I know."

"What makes you so sure?"

"Because I know her, and I know how she thinks. About the enemy Sun Tzu wrote, 'When we are near, we must make the enemy believe we are far away; when far away, we must make the enemy believe we are near.'" He paused and then continued from memory, "'Hold out baits to entice the enemy.'"

"I won't be your bait," she said with anger.

"You won't be. Realize you're the one person that has stripped virtually everything Veronica owns. You deceived the master of deception. Veronica will avenge."

"Not if she can't find me."

"You've been lucky so far," he said, "but you can't count on luck forever."

"I'll take my chances."

"Listen, Veronica's got one last card to play and I know exactly what it is. She needs money, desperately. When we were together we tried to pull a caper together. The time wasn't right, but now it is. She's finally got the break she's been waiting for, and Veronica's going for gold…literally."

"Fool's gold?"

He laughed. "No. Her plan is to retrieve hidden treasure off the California coast, lost gold from a sunken steamship."

"Is Anne Bonny part of all this?" she asked, remembering that Veronica claimed to be a proud descendant of the notorious female pirate.

"This tragedy at sea was long after Anne Bonny's time."

Jane remembered and said, "I saw Anne Bonny's portrait over her mantle on Stingray Cay."

"Yes. Veronica cherished that."

"What's this tragedy at sea?"

"We discovered it together when Veronica and I were looking to entice suckers into a scheme. She was researching priceless coins from shipwrecks and we came across a treasure map. It checked out, buried gold on government land, impossible to get because it's so heavily guarded."

"Where?" Jane questioned.

"Vandenberg Air Force Base on California's Central Coast. Any day now permission will be granted and she plans to excavate the gold under the guise of scientific study, as if she's leading an expedition, like Jacques Cousteau, saving wildlife under the cloak of animal welfare. We don't have much time."

"Sounds crazy…buried treasure."

"Jane, listen to me," he said, "You and I made a great team, and I need you." Cooper placed a hand on her arm. His physical touch was like a jolt of lightning to her. It sparked a conflict of memories, thoughts both good and bad. "And believe it or not," Cooper continued with a squeeze, "you need me."

She backed off, angered. "Get your hands off of me!"

"Jane, listen I—"

"I don't need anybody. Stay out of my life!" Jane broke into a run. She crossed the six-lane highway, cars swerving to avoid her, blaring horns. When she turned back she couldn't see Cooper.

Where'd he go?

Pain surged from the knife wound Veronica had inflicted, bleeding now, a not-so-gentle reminder of their life-or-death struggle. Jane avoided the Motel 6 she'd stayed in the night before. She cut through a used car lot. She didn't know if Cooper was following, and wondered how he'd found her. Danny's garage was about a mile or so away. Full of fear and adrenaline, she could make there in less than ten minutes.

CHAPTER 2

Jane knew her mom's boyfriend Danny kept a hide-a-key in the planter outside the office door. She entered the business park, slowed to a brisk walk, and found Danny's shop. Still looking back over her shoulder, Cooper was nowhere in sight, so she dug out the hidden key and entered the through the office door.

The stitches on her leg felt prickly now. She could see blood seeping through the gauze bandage as she went for the water cooler to quench her thirst. Jane was gulping from the paper cup when she heard a voice call out, "Jane?"

She spun to see Danny standing beside the trailer. She hadn't noticed the rig when she came in, nor had she seen his truck. "You're back?" she said, surprised.

"We got home late last night. Where were you?" Danny asked, a look of concern on his face.

"I stayed at a motel. Where's Mom?"

"We've been calling you for days, and worried sick," he said, angry. "Your mother insisted we rush back to make sure you're all right."

Jane hadn't filled them in on everything that had happened in the Turks and Caicos. She knew how her mother worried and didn't want to inflict her with anxiety. And then, exhausted from her travels, she'd put her phone on mute and forgot that she'd done that. She hadn't taken her cell phone to Starbucks that morning and realized it was still on her charger on the motel room's bedside table.

"Are you okay?" he asked.

"I couldn't stay home last night."

"A neighbor said police cars were there all day yesterday. What happened?"

"I killed a man," she confessed in a quivering voice, "with your gun." Saying the words made Jane realize the gravity of what she'd done—taken a man's life. Sure it was self-defense, but he was dead.

"Who?"

"He broke into your house and tried to kill me. Veronica's assassin."

"Where's the gun now?" Danny asked.

"The police have it."

"Why didn't you call us?" he asked.

She didn't know why she hadn't called, realized she should have, but so much had happened so fast. Maybe a part of her didn't trust Danny, she thought, or any man for that matter. She wanted to run away and hide. "I'm sorry," Jane said.

Danny's eyes traveled down to her leg, now bleeding below the bandage.

"What happened there?" he asked.

"That's where Veronica stabbed me."

"Where is she?"

"I don't know," she said, tears of frustration filling her eyes.

"Let's get you home."

She handed Danny the hide-a-key back. "I remembered you had this hidden, that's how I got in."

"There's a hide-a-key for the Chevy too," he said. "Under the left fender. Always a good idea to have backup."

"Your car's back at the motel."

"Don't worry about that. We'll get it later."

Less than an hour later Jane was sitting at the dining room table in Danny's suburban home. Her mother tended to Jane's stitches with cotton swabs and a tube of Neosporin. Danny had gone to the Motel 6 to get her things, including her cell phone, and the pillow she'd brought. He now stood at the sliding glass door smoking a cigarette.

Jane told them everything, how she discovered Veronica living in the Turks and Caicos, how she infiltrated the birthday party disguised as a clown, and how former victim Gallagher impersonated an FBI agent only later to storm Veronica's island, fall into a trap, and get himself killed.

Jane explained all the steps she'd taken to survive including her battle in shark-infested waters. She explained how the sharks went after Buddy instead of her, and how she and Veronica battled on the deck of her speeding yacht. Jane explained how the boat ran aground and how Veronica, an experienced swimmer, escaped the wreckage and vanished from the island with her son.

Lastly Jane told them about Cooper. She was certain he was dead before he somehow reappeared at a nearby Starbucks. She feared she was being watched. "We need to hide out," Jane said, "until they can catch Veronica or she'll kill me."

"Oh, Jane," her mother said, "why didn't you call us?"

"I should have, I'm sorry, but it was only yesterday that I got back from the Turks and Caicos. I told the cops what happened and figured they were going to put me in jail. But they didn't. After they left I was alone and got really scared because Veronica knows I live here. She sent that assassin."

"Oh, Jane," her mother said, near tears.

"I went to the Motel 6 where nobody could find me, even you guys, because I just wanted to sleep. But somehow," Jane said, "Cooper tracked me down. He must have been watching the house."

"And the police took my gun?" Danny asked.

"That's right."

Nancy questioned Danny, "Will that be a problem?"

"Hopefully not," he said, drawing on his cigarette and tossing the butt into a Folgers can on the concrete porch.

"You seem concerned," Nancy pressed.

"That .38 Special has the serial number filed off," he said. "So there's a good chance they'll be back to ask me about it."

Jane vaguely remembered a scratch on the face of the pistol below the barrel. She asked, "Where do you get a gun with the serial number filed off?"

"It had the number when I got it," he said softly.

"You filed it off?" Nancy asked.

"Yes."

Jane ventured, "Why?"

Danny and Nancy shared a look. Her mother nodded to him before he confessed, "I didn't buy that snubnose. It was my friend Smitty's and registered in his name. But he's not around anymore and I was afraid if it fell into the wrong hands they'd trace Smitty, through this gun, back to me. Should have thrown that damn thing in Gulf."

Jane said, "Who's Smitty?"

"You're going to have to tell her," Nancy said to Danny.

He considered that for a moment, a somber look on his face.

"Tell me what?" Jane asked.

"She's my daughter, Danny," Nancy said. "And we're your family now."

That surprised Jane. She sat back in the vinyl padded dining room chair. "Are you guys married?"

Nancy held up her hand to show Jane the diamond wedding ring. "Yes, honey, in Las Vegas. We've been meaning to make the announcement but...it was spontaneous."

Jane didn't know what to say so simply blurted out, "Congratulations."

"We'll have a proper wedding reception," Nancy affirmed. "I promise."

It was Jane's turn to ask, "So why didn't *you* tell *me*?"

"Well...Danny and the team set the track record at the Las Vegas Motor Speedway while we were qualifying for the NHRA Toyota Nationals. We celebrated that night by getting married. Well, maybe we celebrated first," she said with a smile, "and then we got married."

"I'm so happy for you," Jane said, a little hurt that she wasn't invited to at least witness the ceremony. The image of a cheesy Vegas wedding chapel and a gaudy Elvis preacher flashed in her mind. Maybe it was better she wasn't there.

"I'm a lucky man to have met your mother. It's been a long, long time since I've had love in my life. Way too long."

Nancy reached out to him. He stepped over and they held each other's hands, like teenagers. "I've been honest with your mother and I suppose she's right. You have a right to know, especially now that we're family. There was a time when I did a lot of flying, back in the eighties."

"Danny's a pilot," Nancy said.

"*Was* a pilot," he corrected. "I let my license lapse long ago." He moved from the glass door to the kitchen and poured himself a cup of coffee. "I'm not proud of it, but as a young man I flew special cargo from South America and the Caribbean to the U.S., no questions asked."

Jane shot a look to her mother who gave her a nod.

"My part was to simply land the aircraft and walk away," Danny continued. "In a couple of days I'd get a package delivered to my front door, my fee, in cash. That's how it worked, and that's what I did for many years."

Jane had images of *Miami Vice* with Don Johnson wearing a pastel blazer, mirrored sunglasses, and his sleeves rolled up. She asked, "Cocaine?"

He sipped his coffee. "Mostly that, and sometimes guns from here to there."

"Guns?" Jane asked.

"Weapons delivered to the Contra rebels in Nicaragua," he confessed. "We freelanced for an outfit that became to be known as 'The Enterprise.'"

"What's that?"

"A covert operation run by the National Security Council

and the CIA. Oliver North kind of stuff."

Jane vaguely knew what he was talking about from segments she'd seen on TV. The image of Oliver North on the witness stand dressed in full uniform came to mind. It was a part of recent history she knew very little about.

Danny continued, "It was never political for Smitty and me...just a paycheck. We flew under the radar, got really good at skimming the water," he said as he demonstrated with his hand over the Formica table.

Jane looked to her mother.

Nancy nodded and said, "But this was a long time ago."

"Long before I knew your mother," Danny said. "That .38 was registered to Smitty. He'd bought it in San Antonio as a hideaway and kept it in an ankle holster in case things turned melancholy."

"Melancholy?" Jane asked.

Danny nodded. "That's right. We were a great team but then Smitty met a young lady, fell in love, and got married. He had himself a kid and wanted to get out of the business. I'd made enough money by that point, so agreed. It made sense. We'd pushed our luck far enough and it was only a matter of time before we'd crash into the ocean or get caught. But the problem was we were good at what we did. Getting out of the trade is difficult. We tried to break off, but..."

"Things turned melancholy," Jane said.

"Unfortunately, yes. What was supposed to be our last run, on an abandoned tarmac overgrown with weeds, we landed to make a drop. That's when they killed Smitty."

"Who?"

"The Columbians. If it wasn't for that .38 strapped to Smitty's ankle they would have gotten me too."

Intrigued, Jane asked, "What happened?"

"I shot my way out of there. It was a mess. I hid out for years, but that's no way to live, believe me, watching my back the entire time, scared of my own shadow." Danny squeezed

Nancy's hand and said, "I found work as a mechanic and that's how I got into the racing business."

"This drug cartel, are they still after you?" Jane asked him.

"It's been so many years…most of those guys are either dead or incarcerated. But the police and FBI don't necessarily let it go. It's complicated."

"FBI?" Jane questioned with Agent Lange coming to her mind.

"They've always suspected I know something about it, which I do." He paused and continued, "That's why I filed the serial number off, so I can't be connected to the carnage of that day."

Jane looked to her mother who said, "We've all made mistakes."

Danny affirmed with a nod. "And I regret it every day. So this going away and hiding…I don't do that anymore. Like I said, it's no way to live."

"You don't understand," Jane tried to explain, "Veronica has incredible connections."

Danny considered that, stood, and with a smile said, "Come here, darlin'. Let me show you a little something."

Jane stood and followed Danny into the foyer, Nancy behind her. He opened the hall closet and reached for a hidden latch beneath the shelves. A false door revealed a hidden compartment. Jane was shocked to see an assortment of pistols, even a compact machine gun. *Machine gun?* Her jaw dropped.

Danny explained, "Most of these were gifted by some of my former clients."

"The Columbians?" asked Jane.

"Not them. Reagan-era arms dealers I worked for, most of them long gone by now, too." He reached in and pulled down a flat black machine gun pistol. A wire shoulder stock folded into the pistol's handle. "This here is the American made MAC-10, illegal for civilians to own, for obvious reasons."

To Jane, the gun appeared like something Chuck Norris would blow bad guys away in a bad '80s action movie, or maybe Steven Seagal. "Wow," is all she could think to say, hiding her trepidation at the sight of all these weapons.

"If this Veronica decides to send more of her friends…" Danny said, and let it hang there.

245

CHAPTER 3

Jane couldn't help but peer out the windows of Danny's home. Although she couldn't see Cooper out there, she suspected he had not gone away. She felt he was still watching the house and it made her uneasy.

Meanwhile Danny hid an assortment of guns in drawers and under furniture. He methodically showed both Jane and Nancy where each one was stashed, and later, when Jane was helping her mother make breakfast she asked her, "When did you find out about all of this?"

Nancy made sure Danny was out of earshot before she confessed. "After we'd been with each other for a while, and I'd moved in. He wanted me to know if something happened to him..."

"So," Jane said, "my late father went to prison for writing bad checks." She remembered from what her mother had said. "And now my stepfather worked for the drug cartel and was somehow involved in the Iran-Contra Scandal? You sure know how to pick 'em, Mom."

"When Danny told me about his past, I was naturally cautious, but it was such a long time ago, and we've all made mistakes. With your father, I wasn't oblivious to what he was doing. I'm guilty too, but they didn't throw me in jail, maybe because I was pregnant with you. I was fully aware of what your father was doing," she confessed. "Hell, I think I encouraged him."

"Really?"

"We were so naïve back then. All we cared about was ourselves. It caught up with us. But I believe in second chances, Jane. We learn from our mistakes. I've faltered, so has Danny, and now so have you."

Jane remembered the moment when she visited her mother attending the Pomona Winter Nationals back in California. At the time Jane was in the midst of the scam that started it all, impersonating Cooper's wife, playing the part of a carefree heiress while living in the plush Beverly Hills hotel. That day Nancy revealed that her father wasn't the handsome stranger who rode off into the sunset, what she always thought he was. Instead he had been incarcerated and tragically knifed to death in prison. At the time Jane wondered if her own criminality had been passed down from her father's DNA. Now she learned more about her mother's penchant for larceny. If it was a heritable trait, Jane's fate was in the cards from day one.

Jane wondered aloud, "Can we ever really escape our past, or does it follow us forever?"

"I don't know, honey," Nancy said. "But we can change our ways, and make amends."

The doorbell sounded. Danny entered the living room and somberly said, "Sheriff's here."

Jane and Nancy shared a look.

"Don't say a thing. Let me handle this," he said.

At the door, Jane recognized FBI Agent Lange, plus the pair of Deputy Sheriffs from the day before. These were the two officers that had come to Danny's garage to confirm her whereabouts after she'd been released from jail and moved to Florida. Jane didn't trust them.

Agent Lange made the introductions. He gave Jane a nod and said, "Jane, how are your holding up?"

"Okay," she lied.

"Please let me know if there's anything I can do," he said.

There was an edge in his voice and it made her uneasy. Was he an ally or someone to be feared? He held out a color photocopy for Danny, images of a .38 Special. "Mister Dobson, concerning the unfortunate incident at your home the other day," Agent Lange said, "Miss Innes used this weapon to defend herself and claimed she'd gotten it from you."

"That's right," Danny said. "Since she was going to be here alone I showed her where I stashed it."

"Can you tell me where you acquired this weapon?" Agent Lange asked.

"Is there a problem?" Danny returned.

"Well…" Agent Lange looked to Jane before returning his attention to Danny. "It appears the serial number has been filed off."

"I'm aware of that," Danny said deadpan. "That's how it was when I got it."

"And where did you get it?" he asked.

"Gun show, as I recall. It was a long time ago," Danny said.

"The thing is…" Agent Lange said, "according to our lab, the numbers weren't shaved off with a common metal file. It was clearly done in a machine shop, with sophisticated equipment, by a machinist or expert metallurgist. You own a speed shop, am I right?"

"I race top fuel, that's correct."

Agent Lange said, "One can never really shave off a serial number, not on a gun anyway. Through X-ray there's a way to extract the number, and we've done that."

"So what's the problem?" Danny asked.

"It appears this gun was owned by Lyle Smith of Beaumont, Texas."

Danny shot a look to the two sheriffs, then confessed, "Now I remember. I knew Smitty, and I didn't get that pistol from a gun show. He gave it to me after his daughter was born, to get it out of the house and so his wife wouldn't know about it."

"He gifted it to you?"

"Smitty and I were buddies."

"Were?"

"He's dead now," Danny said eyeing Agent Lange. "What's this all about?"

"If you don't mind, I'd like to show you a few more photos, but we don't have them here. Do you mind taking a few minutes out of your day and following us down to the field office here in Sarasota? I promise it won't take long."

Nancy clutched Jane's arm. She could feel her mother's nails dig.

Danny calmly responded with, "Whatever I can do to help."

"Thank you," Agent Lange said, and stepped back.

Danny turned to Nancy. "Honey, turn off the tea kettle for me. I won't be long." With that he crossed the threshold and stepped outside.

CHAPTER 4

"Shit," Nancy said as they watched from the window. Jane could see Danny climb into his pickup, back out of the driveway, and follow the government vehicles before the sheriff's car brought up the rear. "Danny said he knew this day would come," Jane's mother said. "He claims they have a dossier on him, whatever that means."

"This is all my fault," Jane said, feeling horrible.

Nancy bit her lip. "Now what did he say to...?" Then she snapped her finger and marched into the living room. From the bookshelf Nancy pulled down a leather-bound Bible. She thumbed through the pages and a business card fell out. She picked it up from the carpet, tossed the Bible onto Danny's crushed-velvet Barcalounger, and went for the phone.

"Our savior," Nancy said as she punched numbers.

"A pastor?" Jane questioned.

"No, honey. Danny doesn't drink tea, never has. Saying there's a kettle on the stove, that's code to call his lawyer."

"Code?"

"So it wasn't obvious in front of mixed company," her mother said, and then into the phone, "Good morning. Avery Weeks please, it's urgent."

Jane wondered what other secrets her mother and Danny shared.

***

As instructed, Jane and Nancy waited in the air-conditioned comfort of the Courtyard Marriott, a hotel just around the corner from Sarasota's Sheriff Station. Her mother explained that Danny's lawyer, Avery Weeks, had spent years in the prosecutor's office before he crossed the street to hang his shingle as a criminal defense lawyer.

Nancy had met Avery at his annual Derby Day party, a dressy garden affair where, as Nancy explained, "They serve mint julips in iced pewter mugs to the ladies while the men sip twenty-year-old Pappy."

"What's Pappy?" Jane asked.

"Pappy Van Winkle's a bourbon," her mother explained. "A twenty-year-old bottle is very hard to come by, but not for Avery."

"How's that?"

"Apparently there was some kind of heist of this bourbon years ago, from the Buffalo Trace Distillery in Kentucky. Many pallets of the stuff went missing worth hundreds of thousands of dollars."

"A bourbon heist?" Jane questioned, intrigued by the thought.

"I know it sounds crazy, but Danny suspects one of Avery's clients was involved in this caper, so in lieu of the lawyer fee..."

"Why does Danny suspect that?" Jane asked.

"I don't know. It's just what Danny said. Avery is his insurance policy in case something comes up unexpected."

"Like his past?"

"Please don't judge him. He's a good man. We've all made mistakes."

"He's great. I'm happy for you, Mom. I just feel horrible that I've brought this all upon him."

"We're family. We'll get through this together," she said, a hint of emotion in her tone.

The automatic doors slid opened and a portly middle-aged man made his grand entrance. Jane's first impression was that

Avery couldn't be more of a cliché: bow tie, cane, puffy grey sideburns. The only thing missing was a seersucker suit and he could have stepped right out of central casting.

Nancy introduced her daughter.

"It's my pleasure, Miss Innes," he said in a Southern drawl, "and I'm sorry we have to meet under these unfortunate circumstances." As silver-tongued lawyers come, Jane could see Avery was the real deal.

They took a seat in high-back padded chairs in the corner of the lobby and Avery, in his genteel manner, explained, "Ladies, I'm happy to report that I've just spoken with Danny and he is doing just fine. Fortunately he didn't say anything to incriminate himself, but unfortunately it appears they've made an arrest."

"Oh my," Nancy gasped.

"It's merely a formality. I sense they don't have much of a case."

"A case for what?" Jane asked.

Avery looked to Jane and paused before Nancy said, "It's okay. She knows about Danny's past."

Avery nodded, then started in. "Many years ago, at a private airport near Corpus Christi, there was a shootout with a number casualties, including Danny's acquaintance Smitty. Unfortunately an undercover federal agent also perished that day, and since there's no statute of limitations on murder..."

"Why was there a shootout?" Jane asked.

"I'm sure it had something to do with the cargo found in one of the planes."

"And they feel Danny was involved in the killing?" asked Nancy.

"Yes, my dear. Since an undercover agent fell in the line of duty they're compelled to take action." Jane could see her mother's face turn pale. Avery continued, "Fortunately Danny set aside a trust to handle emergencies such as this, and he entrusted me as the executor."

"A what?" Nancy asked.

"A trust, my dear, a fund set aside for a rainy day. He's never had need for my professional services until now and I very much applaud him for his foresight. Luck comes to those prepared. However, because it's Sunday he's going to have to stay overnight, unfortunately, before a judge can set bail for his release."

"Overnight?" Nancy said with concern.

"Tomorrow will come soon enough, and he'll be all right."

"Oh…" Nancy lamented in a worried tone.

"I understand you two were recently married?"

Nancy nodded, "Yes. We've been talking about it for quite some time."

"Congratulations," he said, and then turned to Jane. "Miss Innes, I'm aware of your unfortunate incident, the home invasion in which you were forced to defend yourself…"

"Yes?" Jane said.

"And I understand you're in some sort of a heated dispute."

"I'm in a dispute, all right," Jane said.

"According to Danny," Avery continued, "you feel these hostilities are life threatening. Is that correct?"

Jane thought about what Cooper had said to her, how Veronica would stop at nothing to seek revenge. "Knowing who I've crossed," she said, "I'm concerned."

"And who is it, my dear, that you've crossed?" he asked.

"Veronica Tattinger. Do you know of her?"

He shook his head and said, "Can't say I do."

"Lady Vee?" Jane ventured, using Veronica's nickname from the island. "Does that ring a bell?"

"I am not familiar with that, either," Avery said, stroking his mutton chop sideburns.

"That man who came for me was a hired assassin," Jane explained. "She'll send more, or come herself."

Avery asked, "Is there anything I can do to help?"

"Yes. You can." Jane turned to her mother. "Mom, I can't

stay in Florida. I'd be putting you at risk, and looking over my shoulder every minute. I've got to lay low for a while."

"But we're family," Nancy said. "And at times like these we need to stick together."

"Veronica knows all about me, and until she's caught..." Jane turned back to Avery. "Can you help me get a new identity?"

"I'm not one to..." he started in.

"With all due respect, counselor," Jane said, referring to him by his profession to make her point formal, "you're a criminal lawyer and I'm sure you know how do it. Please, set me up with a new identity. You can have it back when Veronica is caught, or dead."

"Dead?" Nancy questioned.

"According to Cooper she'd rather die than rot in jail," Jane said.

"Coming from a man that faked his own death?" Nancy quipped.

Jane ignored her and turned to Avery. "Can you get me a new identity?"

From the look in his eye she knew he could.

CHAPTER 5

Jane and her mother returned home, and although there were an assortment of guns recently planted around the house, Jane still felt insecure. To make matters worse, when she checked her phone Jane saw that Cooper had texted her.

Why did you run? Call me.

Sitting at the dining room table again, Jane echoed her concerns. She told her mother how deeply she felt she needed stay hidden, now more than ever.

"Where will you go?" Nancy asked.

Jane had already thought about it and said, "The semester I spent in college, one of my friends encouraged me to work in dinner theater. She did it, but at the time I thought it was below me because I wanted to act in film and TV roles and needed to be in Los Angeles. But now it makes sense. She's still working there and says there's always need for help."

"Doing what?"

"I'd start by selling tickets and concessions, work as a stage hand, and be available as an understudy. The Wild West Melodrama in Santa Maria, on California's Central Coast." Having driven the area a few years ago, Jane knew Vandenberg Air Force Base was not far from there.

Nancy proposed. "Assuming Avery can spring Danny like he says, we can meet at Sonoma Raceway in Sonoma, California. You can see us race."

There was a knocking noise coming from outside and Jane flinched. She jumped up and darted to the hallway. She tried to remember where the closest gun was stashed.

Nancy remained at the dining room table, asked, "What are you doing?"

"What was that?"

"What?"

"That noise."

"What noise?"

"Outside."

Nancy got up and went to the sliding glass door. She looked out and said, "I didn't hear anything."

"A bump or something," Jane said. "It sounds like someone's out there." She heard the noise again and said, "That!" She remembered there was a pistol under the couch and considered going for it.

Nancy explained, "That's just the air conditioning kicking on."

Jane concentrated on the noise until she realized it was the air conditioning and not a threat. "They know I'm here," she said.

"Who?"

"Veronica. Cooper. I have to leave."

Her mother reluctantly agreed. She made tacos for dinner, a dish Jane always loved as a kid, and they spent the evening on the couch watching TV. Convinced someone was watching the house, Jane had a hard time falling asleep that night. At one point she got up and, without turning on the lights, peered out the windows. The neighborhood was dark and silent.

The next morning Avery called Nancy and explained Danny's hearing was scheduled for early that afternoon. Over the receiver Jane overheard him say, "Once the judge determines the bail, I'll have him out in a matter of hours."

Nancy jotted down the time and courtroom location of the hearing. She then explained Jane's plans to leave immediately.

"Can you pass that on to Danny?"

Avery agreed.

Since it would be a few hours, Jane climbed into Danny's Chevy Malibu and backed down the driveway. To ensure that nobody was following, she got on the freeway and opened the car up, the speedometer pushing past one hundred twenty miles per hour. Then she got on the frontage road and double-backed the way she came. She found Avery's office in downtown Sarasota.

Jane could see Avery's law office was also a cliché with its antique, dark wood furniture and leather-bound law books arranged on shelves. She noted a vintage safe in the corner and a wet bar complete with a bottle of Pappy Van Winkle's Family Reserve Bourbon. On the label was the namesake Pappy himself, an old man with a cigar in his mouth.

Avery sat in a leather-upholstered chair across from his polished mahogany desk and explained that he had spoken to Danny and relayed her request. Then he handed over a North Carolina driver's license of a woman a few years older, Lynette Foster, a curly haired brunette. There was no resemblance in the photograph. The mousy looking woman wore thick glasses and Jane said to him, "This won't work. She looks nothing like me."

"It's going to have to work, for now," Avery said.

"Who is she?"

"Victim of aggressive breast cancer, I'm afraid. But the driver's license is not critical as long as you don't get pulled over or take a flight." Avery handed over a MasterCard. "It's this credit card that you'll need more than anything else. Be conservative with it." He gave her his business card with a PIN number scribbled on the back. "You can draw cash at any ATM using this number, and the credit card bills will come to this office. I'll pay them from Danny's trust."

"Was this hard to get? I mean…a false identity like this?" she asked.

"Everything is available at a price, my dear. But if you get arrested, just remember, you didn't get this from me. If they ask, you found a wallet."

"Thank you," she said.

Avery sat back and said, "You should know Danny was resistant at first and would rather have you all together. But I looked into your adversary, this Veronica Tattinger character, and what little I found...let's just say I convinced Danny that your plan to lay low is undoubtedly best."

Jane had no intention of telling him that laying low was not her plan at all. She'd continue to chase Veronica, no matter what, and finish the job she'd started. She asked, "What have you heard about her?"

"That she's ruined many lives."

"Who said so?"

"I have sources on both sides of the law," he said. Then he handed her a cell phone still in its plastic case. She could see it was nothing fancy, a model you'd see in a supermarket. "Stay in touch with this phone, registered as Lynn Foster, your new alias, and stop using yours."

At that moment it dawned on her. "That's how Veronica has been able to track me. Through my cell phone."

"Quite possibly. Turn off your old phone and remove the battery for now," he advised. "And please use this one until further notice." He stood and said, "Now if you'll excuse me, I've got to prepare for Danny's hearing."

Jane got up and said, "Thank you. I'll see you there."

"I suggest you do not attend the hearing."

"Why?"

"Just in case."

"Just in case of what?" she asked.

"Worst case scenario."

Back at home her mother helped Jane pack her suitcase. In addition to toiletries she added a photo of them smiling together taken at Jane's high school graduation.

"What are you doing?" Jane asked her mother. "You should keep this."

"So I'll always be with you," Nancy said, burying the frame under a sweater. Her mom then pulled a Colt .380 Mustang from under the bed and packed that too.

"Mom?" Jane said.

"Just in case," Nancy said. She added a second clip loaded with copper-headed bullets.

From her old cell phone Jane jotted down the numbers she'd need, Cooper's included. Jane gave her mother her new phone number and they made plans to meet in Sonoma. They hugged, pledged their love for each other in a tearful goodbye.

First she drove to Danny's garage. She used the hide-a-key to get in, went to the kitchen, and pushed the old refrigerator away from the wall for the outlet. She put her old cell phone's ringer on mute, plugged in the charger, and wedged the phone into the coils in the back of the appliance. She figured this was a place nobody would ever look. If Veronica was indeed tracking Jane's location through her cell phone, keeping the phone powered would make it appear as if Jane was still in Florida. Avery suggested she turn the phone off, but Cooper had said something outside the Starbucks that stuck in her mind, about the writings of Sun Tzu from the *Art of War*, something about, "When we are near, we must make the enemy believe we are far away." She leaned into the fridge and pushed it back.

On the same stretch of highway, Jane repeated the Chevy's blistering speed before she double-backed, the procedure to make sure she wasn't being tailed.

Lastly, she saw the nursing home and pulled off the highway. She drove through the concrete parking structure and found a non-descript Honda Accord that looked like it hadn't been driven in a while. She parked alongside the vehicle and swapped out the Florida license plates. The Honda got the Chevy's, and vice versa. It was a gamble the owner of the Honda wouldn't notice but a risk she felt she had to take. Now the Chevy could not be traced back to Danny.

An hour out of Sarasota, at a payphone in a nearly vacant Denny's, she called Cooper. His voicemail picked up so she left a message, "It's me, call me at this number." She had just finished the wedge of pickle and was about to take bite out of her club sandwich when the phone rang. She got up from the counter and picked up the receiver.

"Where are you?" she asked.

Cooper said, "Not far from Vandenberg Air Force Base in California. Where are you?"

"Listen to me. This is the deal, take it or leave it. We work as a team finding Veronica, but we don't kill her," Jane said. "Is that understood? We hand her over to the cops."

"Okay," he said.

"Say we won't kill her," she persisted.

"We won't kill Veronica."

"You have to promise me."

"I promise."

"I don't believe you."

"Eating jailhouse slop will be hell for Veronica, I assure you."

"What do you mean?" Jane asked.

"Over the years with her high-priced lawyers she's managed to slip out of every noose, but not this time. I have a plan that's going to put her away for a very, very long time."

"We're not together anymore," Jane said, "No intimacy whatsoever, or I won't help."

"I understand," he said.

"Because of you I'm running for my life," she said.

"I had no choice."

"I don't believe you."

"You have every right to hate me," he said, "and after we snag Veronica you'll never see me again. I agree, we work only as partners, but we don't have much time."

"How do you plan on catching her?" she asked.

"It's complicated. I'll explain everything. Where are you?"
"On my way."

CHAPTER 6

Jane carried the camera bag, Cooper the tripod. She'd brought along a portable umbrella but left her gun in the car. They walked the campus of California Polytechnic State University nestled in the rolling hills of San Luis Obispo. There was a heavy fog and the concrete pathways were damp.

Jane couldn't help but notice the students going about their day and wished she could turn back the clock. It wasn't that long ago that she was in school. Other than keeping up with her busy social calendar and getting to class on time, she hadn't a worry in the world. As she walked among the students Jane felt old even though the age difference was only a few years. She figured what separated her from these students was that she had real world problems, with life or death consequences. Her carefree days were gone forever.

Fueled by coffee and Red Bull, she'd driven straight through from Florida and only stopped for gas, food, and occasional shut eye. With the Colt .380 Mustang in her hand, she'd taken brief naps in the backseat of the Chevy parked at twenty-four-hour diners, curled up under a polyester throw blanket she bought at a roadside truck stop.

She'd arrived in Pismo Beach the day before, exhausted, and checked into a kitschy Polynesian-themed motel along the cliffs. She parked in an adjacent motel's lot just in case. The room overlooked the ocean across an uncrowded beach. Jane rewarded herself with a take-out pizza, took a long shower, then slept like a baby as the sound of the waves crashed beyond her balcony.

This morning she grabbed a cup of coffee in the lobby before she tended to her injured leg. She could see the wound was healing. Although annoying to deal with, at least the pain was gone. She thought the wound looked like a Frankenstein scar and it would be a long time before she could wear a dress. This was a battle scar for life, thanks to Veronica.

With the .380 Mustang in her purse, she headed out to meet Cooper. She was not entirely comfortable with him knowing where she was staying so she walked the shoreline and met him at entrance to the Pismo Beach Pier. He was there waiting and Jane reminded him theirs was strictly a working relationship.

Cooper nodded and said, "Fine. Understand the reason I need you is I can't do this myself. This gold is Veronica's escape hatch, and she desperately needs it." Then they set out for the campus in his nondescript rental car.

Jane and Cooper entered the university campus and followed the engraved signs before they found the history department. Professor Ricardo Gomez rose from behind his cluttered desk to greet them. "So nice to meet you," he said, extending his hand. The energetic, middle-aged professor sported a grey beard and wore round, John Lennon-style glasses.

"So kind of you to find the time on such short notice," Cooper said.

"I'm honored to be included in your project," Gomez said.

Cooper introduced Jane as his cinematographer. Having acted in low-budget movies, Jane was familiar with what the camera department did but never thought she'd masquerade as one of them. Jane considered the black and white photographs in the office, miners panning for gold in old-time San Francisco. There was a California history book on the professor's desk, his name as the author. This made sense since Cooper explained Gomez's expertise was the California Gold Rush.

"I've set aside a classroom," Gomez said. "Right this way." He grabbed his laptop and led them down the hallway asking, "So…why such interest in the *SS Yankee Blade?*"

"As I explained," Cooper said, "there's newfound evidence that there might have been more gold on that ship than the ship's manifest claims."

"A likely scenario," Gomez said. "The California Gold Rush drew its share of ruffians. The railroads and steamship companies were known to create two manifests, especially when shipping gold."

"To throw them off?" Cooper asked.

"That's right, and since Captain Randall abandoned her…" he said shaking his head. "It doesn't make sense. A captain is supposed to be the last one off a ship, but that was not the case on the *Yankee Blade*."

The classroom had large windows that offered plenty of light. Jane suggested the professor sit in a chair with the classroom's white board partly in frame behind him. Cooper agreed and pulled up a chair beside the camera. Within a few minutes they were set up, a lavalier microphone on the lapel of the professor's jacket. Jane framed up the shot, confirmed it with Cooper, and they were ready to go.

"Rolling," she said, mimicking the lingo of an actual cinematographer.

After Cooper asked the professor to introduce himself, he asked, "What can you tell us about the *Yankee Blade?*"

"Most people think of steamships as Mark Twain-style paddleboats with tall smokestacks, like that one they have at Disneyland. But seafaring steamships of the time were much larger than riverboats, designed for speed, powered by sidewheels combined with sailing masts. The *Yankee Blade* was a state-of-the-art vessel when she was built in New York. Cornelius Vanderbilt, founder of the New York Central Railroad, purchased the boat. Vanderbilt knew a thing or two about steam-powered transportation. He'd built a monopoly in railroads and shipping, and he sent the *Yankee Blade* to transport gold, passengers, and cargo between San Francisco and Panama during the height of the Gold Rush."

Jane could see Gomez had prepared for the interview and admired him for it. As a performer, she knew preparation was key.

Gomez went on to explain that in the mid-19th century there were only three routes to travel between the east and west coast, "Train, but that was time-consuming with many stops and a risk of robbers poaching the cargo. The second was sailing around the tip of South America which took longer and could be treacherous considering the currents. The preferable route was steaming to Panama then transporting passengers and cargo by small boats and mule train through the mosquito-ridden Isthmus of Panama, then sailing north again on another ship. Mind you this was a good fifty years before the Panama Canal was built. The *Yankee Blade* served the Pacific Ocean leg of this journey."

"Fascinating," Cooper said to encourage him. "Tell us about the shipwreck."

"There were eight hundred and twelve passengers and a hundred and twenty-two crew aboard the *Yankee Blade*. She was traveling southward too fast considering the fog. There's speculation," the professor said, leaning forward for emphasis, "that a bet was made."

"What kind of bet?" asked Cooper.

"Also leaving San Francisco for Panama at the time was the steamship *Sonora*, and the captains may have engaged in an unofficial race to Panama, with five thousand dollars on the line, according to the newspaper *Daily Alta California*. Once both ships left San Francisco Bay, the *Sonora* took the longer, safer route further out to sea, whereas Captain Randall hugged the coast, waters considerably more dangerous."

"Five thousand dollars was a lot of money back then," Cooper said.

"It's a lot of money now, just imagine it back then," Gomez said. He continued, "The fog grew thick"—motioning to the windows—"much like today, with visibility extremely low, and the *Yankee Blade* struck a pinnacle of rock off Point Arguello. It tore a gash in the ship's hull and she was wedged at an angle on the rocks." Gomez demonstrated with his hand.

Cooper had told Jane some of these details, but Gomez made the story so much more interesting. This professor was a bona fide storyteller.

Gomez went on, "It was obvious to those on board it was only a matter of time before the pounding surf would push the listed ship off the rocks to a watery doom. But for some unexplained reason, Captain Randall took command of the lifeboats instead, leaving his unqualified teenage son in charge of the ship."

"His teenage son?" Cooper asked.

"Yes. A captain leaving a sinking ship doesn't make sense, but to make matters even worse for those on board..." The professor paused for dramatic effect. "California had attracted a large number of lawless men unable to find fortune mining for gold. Bear in mind the state was just four years old and lawmen were few and far between. Bad guys on board took advantage of the situation and began to rob and murder passengers. Mind you, some of the passengers had struck gold in the fields and were heading back to the east coast with their hard-earned treasure, probably carried in money belts. Captain Randall would later claim to have been seeking safety for the women and children, but conflicting claims confuse whether he ever returned to the shipwreck and instead spent the night onshore while most of the passengers were on board fending for their lives. In the disorganized rescue effort a few of the lifeboats full of women and children sank, apparently loaded with too much weight. Drowned bodies of mothers clutching their children washed ashore."

Images of drowned children came to Jane and she felt a sudden pang of sadness. *How tragic.*

"Could these lifeboats been loaded with gold?" Cooper asked.

"Presumably."

Cooper shot a knowing look to Jane before he said, "I understand the San Francisco Mint was brand new at the time so, according to the manifest, there were gold coins aboard."

"That we know for sure. Back in the seventies divers salvaged some of these coins from the shipwreck, high-grade 1854 double eagle twenty-dollar pieces. Today, a standard twenty-dollar double eagle piece is worth over twelve hundred dollars, but the same coin traced to the *Yankee Blade* is worth well over ten thousand dollars at auction. Collectors authenticate the shipwreck coins from both a subtle die crack imperfection traceable to the first stamps of the San Francisco Mint, combined with the damage of sand and sea water over the years."

"So what happened next?" Cooper asked.

"With the stern of the ship underwater, throughout the night the *Yankee Blade* slipped lower and lower which forced the passengers to the aft of the already crowded boat. Fortunately the next morning the steamship *Goliath* came to her rescue, and the *Goliath*'s skipper, Captain Haley, risked his own ship drawing close enough to transport the surviving passengers to safety. Because of the limited capacity of the *Goliath* some of the passengers were left behind. They camped onshore and local ranchers supplied them with food and supplies until they were eventually rescued."

"And Captain Randall?"

"Captain Randall stood trial for his role in the disaster in a kangaroo court almost a year after its occurrence. A panel of his peers acquitted him of all charges."

"Acquitted him?"

"Yes."

"So he got away with it?"

"So much so that years later the *Santa Barbara Gazette* reported that a Captain Randall, commanding a small schooner, had succeeded in recovering gold from the wreck; his share penciled out to over eighty thousand dollars at the time."

"He got to keep the gold?" Cooper said.

"Yes. That's maritime law regarding shipwrecks: finders keepers. Randall retired but not before he returned to the site a few more times. He even helped chart maps of the area, his career apparently unblemished by the incident."

"What a rat," Cooper said.

"Indeed."

Indeed, Jane thought. *Who uses that word*? Professors, she guessed.

Gomez continued, "Thirty souls perished, some of them having jumped ship or were murdered by the ruffians. Call it cowardice, greed, or a combination of both, but Randall's negligence is what makes the wreck of the *Yankee Blade* such a tragic event."

"What's your opinion?" Cooper asked. "Is there gold still out there?"

"I wouldn't be surprised. Reportedly the ship's vault was underwater only minutes after she struck the rocks. Although pieces of the ship have been salvaged over the years, including a brass canon, the vault has never been found. And since 9/11 salvage efforts are impossible."

"Why's that?"

"The wreckage is off Vandenberg Air Force Base and security strictly prohibits access to the area."

They wrapped up the interview and Cooper thanked the professor. As Jane put the camera away, Gomez opened his laptop and he and Cooper explored Google Maps. From the satellite image bird's-eye view, Gomez pointed out where he approximated the ship sank, rocky clusters near small islands he said was the Vandenberg Marine Reserve. The satellite imagery depicted brown topsoil contrasting the shoreline of blue ocean. There were curvy lagoons and cliffs with the whitewash of crashing waves, evidence that there were many rocks just under the water's surface. Jane pointed out a cluster of white buildings and asked, "What's that?"

Gomez zoomed in for more detail, "Vandenberg Space Launch Complex 8."

She looked to Cooper. *You've got to be kidding.*

He gave her a subtle nod and Cooper thanked the professor again.

On the drive to Morro Bay Cooper explained that the long lost, hand-drawn map Veronica has in her possession does not necessarily detail where the ship sank but rather the caves onshore where, supposedly, Captain Randall hid the gold. Apparently the ship's purser drafted the map. But then he disagreed with how Randall handled the tragedy and kept it from him when Captain Randall returned to the scene. By then violent storms had altered the coastal geography and covered up the shoreline caves. "When Captain Randall returned," Cooper said, "he only salvaged a portion of the hidden gold. Gomez is right, he returned a few more times over the years but wasn't successful until finally he gave up. Treasure seekers have long searched for the ship's vault, but according to the purser's map, the one Veronica has, the vault was emptied before the ship went down."

"So the gold is in these caves?"

He nodded, "That's right."

"After all of these years?"

"Everyone has always focused on the shipwreck, not where the gold was stashed."

"How is Veronica going to find these caves?"

"Aided by sophisticated geological equipment used in the oil shale industry. It may take a while, a few weeks."

"A few weeks?"

"Unless they get lucky. Veronica is convinced she knows

where to dig."
"All under the cloak of scientific study?" Jane said.
"That's the plan."
"And what if the Air Force finds out?"
"She plans on deceiving them but I have a plan."

CHAPTER 7

When they arrived in Morro Bay Jane was struck by the massive rock that overshadowed the bay. It looked like a giant molar tooth that stuck up at the edge of the shoreline, black, and seemed so out of place. She didn't realize how large it was until they drew closer.

Cooper parked the rental car on Embarcadero Street. Through binoculars they spied men on a yacht. "The trawler arrived from San Diego last week," Cooper explained, "and as you can see they're preparing it now. Once Air Force Space Command grants permission, they'll set out and anchor just off Vandenberg. They're supposed to be graduate students studying sea life but in reality they're nothing but scavengers."

Jane watched as one of them behind a welder's mask worked on the arm of a crane at the bow of the ship—the hot glow of the torch visible from a distance.

Cooper added, "Veronica will be on that boat."

She turned to him and asked, "When?"

"Could be any day now, could be next month. What I need you to do is a little reconnaissance."

"How so?"

Cooper produced a photo of a short-haired, tattooed guy that appeared to be in his early thirties. "By befriending Brendan Cassidy, the boat's captain."

"Me?"

"That's right."

"Why me?"

"Because he knows me. When Veronica and I were together I found Brendan for this job. He owns that yacht and has a lot of diving and salvage experience. You're going to be the girl he meets in the bar."

"What bar?"

Cooper thumbed over his shoulder. "A craft brew place he hangs out in just around the corner."

Jane craned her neck to look for the establishment he was talking about, "So I'm just going to walk up to him and say, 'Hey, sailor, when ya shoving off?'"

"You're an actress. Improvise."

"How do I do that?"

"Get him to open up. You'll find a way. I've seen you in action," he said, respect in his eyes. "You're a natural."

Jane felt a mix of both anger and sorrow. She had loved Cooper once. What was he suggesting? "You don't expect me to sleep with him, do you?"

"I'm not saying that."

"It sounds like you are."

"Just befriend the guy. Distract him enough so I can get on that boat for five minutes. That's all I ask."

"But you're implying—"

"I'm not implying anything," he said, cutting her off. "He's not going to tell you what he's doing here, but he may clue you in to when they're heading out. We need to know that."

Jane returned to the binoculars just as the welder pulled up his mask. It appeared to be the same guy from the photo Cooper had shown.

"Is that him?" she asked.

"That's Brendan."

He was lean and sported a close-shaven beard, a ruggedly handsome surfer type. "What's he like?" she asked.

Cooper cleared his throat. "A crazy party boy with larceny

in his soul."

"How so?"

"His father was a safe cracker and jewel thief, currently serving a stint in Rahway."

"Rahway?"

"It's a prison in New Jersey. As a young man Brendan wanted nothing to do with his father and joined the Navy to get away from the life. He excelled, became a SEAL, saw action in the Middle East, did a few tours, and then after an honorable discharge he started buying and selling boats. But he's had a hard time adjusting to civilian life. If there's ever a poster boy for post-traumatic stress disorder, you're looking at it. He's unpredictable and lives on the edge, his lifestyle far more extravagant than what a common boatyard broker can afford. His racket is insurance fraud, but on a Lloyds of London scale."

"How does that work?" she asked, watching as Brendan and one of the men moved an acetylene tank.

"He finds yacht owners who need to get out from under their...investments."

"Out from under?"

"The accessories and electronics, everything on a yacht, all are extremely expensive. He orchestrates it all so the boat owner purchases all sorts of upgrades that never make it on the vessel. He returns or resells them, then waits for the perfect storm and sets the stage for a disaster at sea. They sink the yacht and split the insurance money."

"So he's a pirate, like Veronica," Jane said.

"Precisely. He's got a clean record except for a few instances of physical abuse."

"What kind of abuse?"

"He's been known to slap around a girlfriend or two, that sort of thing. More than one has pressed charges. He has anger issues."

"So he's a bastard."

"Yes, he's a bastard," Cooper said. "And these men he's

brought on, they're not boy scouts either, most of them ex-soldiers gone bad, or mercenary washouts."

She set the binoculars on the console, turned to him and said, "And much like you, a life of crime is in his family."

"That's right."

Jane didn't know how to phrase it so just dived in. "How about you? You ever try to get away from the family business?"

"So you know about that?"

"I understand your father ran boiler rooms in Canada, sweepstakes scams that preyed on the elderly."

"Among other things," he said.

"Did you ever try to do something else?"

He shrugged, took a moment to think about it, then said, "I went to college. Concordia in Montreal. Studied economics."

"And?"

"Do you remember the old-school ventriloquist Shari Lewis? She had a white sock puppet named Lamb Chops, back in the fifties and sixties, *The Ed Sullivan Show* era."

Being an amateur magician Jane was familiar with Shari Lewis and her signature puppet. "Sure," she said.

"She was the only female ventriloquist in her day," Cooper said. "Well...I saw an interview with her and she told a story. She was just barely out of school when she found success on television, and eventually NBC gave Shari her own show. It replaced *Howdy Doody*."

Cooper telling *her* a show business story? That's a first. Jane said, "*Howdy Doody* creeped me out. All marionettes are freaky."

"I agree. Sock puppets are better. The way Shari tells it one day she met Queen Elizabeth, who apparently really liked her act. The Queen asked, 'How does a young girl become a ventriloquist?' Shari explained that she grew up in New York and that her father was a magician. Mayor LaGuardia named him New York City's official magician, and Shari had learned the basics of ventriloquism from him."

"Okay…" Jane said, wondering where this was leading.

"So, the Queen considered this and said, 'Dear, I suppose we *all* tend to do what our parents do, don't we?'"

Jane laughed. "Okay, but Queen Elizabeth doesn't have a choice. She's born into it."

"I was born into it too," Cooper said.

Jane thought about her mother, wondered how she was doing, and then trained the binoculars back on the yacht.

"After we confirm Veronica's on that boat," Cooper continued, "and it's anchored outside Vandenberg, we blow the whistle, claiming they're preparing for an act of terrorism."

"Terrorism?"

"Because of something special I'll plant, everyone on that boat will go away for a very, very long time."

"What will you plant?" she asked.

"I'll show you," Cooper said and opened the car door. Jane emerged from the passenger side while keeping an eye on the yacht. Cooper opened the trunk of the car to reveal a black plastic Pelican case.

"What's that?"

He snapped the handles and opened the large case to reveal the military-grade weapon and said, "It's a FIM-92 Stinger."

Jane was shocked at the sight of the single-shot bazooka fit snuggly into the foam of the case. "Holy shit," she said.

Cooper explained, "A shoulder-fired, surface-to-air missile launcher. When the crew is off that boat, and you've distracted Brendan, I'll sneak this aboard and hide it in the engine room."

"So that's the plan? Get the surfer off his boat?"

"He won't leave his yacht unless one of the crew is on board. The rest of the guys don't sleep on the yacht, so…"

"I don't get it."

"You'll make his acquaintance then distract him enough so he'll be forced to leave the yacht. That's when I'll move in. Then, once Veronica gets on and they're sitting outside Vandenberg we tip off the feds."

Realizing the weapon had to be extremely illegal Jane asked, "Where'd you get it?"

"Everything's available for a price, and this didn't come cheap, believe me. I had it smuggled from Chechnya by way of Montreal," he said. "It's questionable if it actually works, but that doesn't matter because it doesn't have to. The government just has to find it in their possession."

"So that's the plan, frame Veronica?" she asked.

"For starters. Then we let nature take its course."

It seemed so elaborate and she asked, "Why not just grab her before she gets on the boat then hand her over to the cops?"

"Because for the first time in her life she won't be able to snake out of it."

"How can you be sure?"

"Bail is rejected in cases of domestic terrorism," Cooper said. He slammed the trunk and added, "She'll be fucked."

CHAPTER 8

Jane smiled at Brendan.

He smiled back.

Moments ago she and Cooper were watching as Brendan left his yacht. She went to the bar and then, as if on cue, Brendan entered the Libertine Pub, found a stool, and ordered an IPA. The bartender, a woman with tattooed arms, poured his draft and they chatted for a moment. Jane could see they knew each other. The smell of fried fish wafted from the kitchen.

Cooper had explained this was Brendan's daily routine, a couple of hours off the boat for dinner and a few beers before he'd return to the yacht and relieve the last of the crew.

Before he got there she'd ordered a Sprite and lime in a highball glass to make it look like she was sipping a gin and tonic. Even though she had the .380 Mustang in her purse, Jane was nervous.

One exchange of smiles became two. It wasn't long before Brendan moved over, introduced himself as "Brad," and took the stool next to her.

Jane played along. "I'm Sarah. Where are you from?"

"The Bay area."

"I moved here from L.A.," she said, weaving a little bit of truth into her narrative. She'd already invented her backstory. She was a traveling nurse recently hired at the local hospital.

When she asked what he did, Brendan boasted, "I'm a skipper."

"A what?"

"Owner/operator of a commercial vessel. You can see it from here," he said and got up from his stool. "I'll show ya."

"Luxury sailboat?" she asked, following him to the window.

"Not a sailboat, but it's got its comforts."

She thought of her purse and the gun back on the bar. She considered turning back to get it but thought it might look suspicious, like she was hiding something. "It's a research vessel," he explained, pointing it out. Jane could see two of the crew working on deck as Brendan went on, "We're a scientific team studying ocean mammals for the Marine Life Protection Act."

"That's cool," Jane said. "What kind of mammals?"

"Whales and dolphins mostly," he said.

"Awesome," she said with a smile, knowing it was all a lie, his fictional cover story. Since Veronica had named her pleasure yacht the *Anne Bonny*, Jane asked him, "What's the name of your boat?"

"*Maenads*."

Jane raised an eyebrow.

"In Greek mythology maenads are female worshippers of Dionysus, the god of wine."

"Worshippers?"

"Think of it as his lady posse. Through the ages Maenads are depicted as scantily clad maidens."

"God of wine, huh? Sounds like they're party girls," Jane said.

"Got that right. My vessel was named by the previous owner. Since it's bad luck to change the name of a boat, I kept it."

"So you're the captain of a boat named after a half-naked party girls," Jane teased.

"I didn't name her."

They returned to the bar and he offered to buy her a drink. Jane agreed on a Chardonnay but wished she had eaten more of a lunch. He elaborated on what it was like captaining a boat and added that he had served as a Navy SEAL. Jane could see he was trying to impress her. By the way Brendan looked at her it was clear sex was on his mind. Although men in flannel weren't necessarily her type, she found him attractive, and charming. She'd never think of flirting with a guy like this had she not been undercover. The fact that he'd been physically abusive to girlfriends came to mind.

She could see Brendan was fishing to find common interest. When a guy wearing a leather jacket and sporting wide mutton chop sideburns strolled past reeking of marijuana, the subject of legalization came up. It wasn't long before he asked if she wanted to duck out to sample a bit of, "Da kine indica," as he phrased it.

Jane explained, "I wish I could but I work in a hospital, so…drug tests."

"Seriously?"

"Random, supposedly, but I've never been asked to take one. It's because we work around pain killers."

"Oh, I see, like some nurse sneaking a patient a placebo while keeping one or two for herself?" he said.

"I'm sure it happens," Jane said.

"OxyContin? Morphine? Tylenol with codeine?"

"I administer all that stuff."

Brendan then said, "Can I ask you something? And please don't take this the wrong way."

"Sure."

"Got a boyfriend?"

"It's complicated," she said and found herself blushing. She tore the fringe of her cocktail napkin out of nervousness. It was clear he had sex on his mind.

"That a yes or no answer?" he playfully inquired.

Jane knew she had to keep his prospects alive in order to distract him and said, "I'm not seeing anyone. I was, but…he betrayed me."

"Cheated?"

Jane thought of Veronica and Cooper together before she said, "So to speak. But he was with this other woman before me. Then when he went back to her she betrayed him, so…c'est la vie."

"No way."

"Yes way."

"As beautiful as you are…he was a fool," he said.

"She was very persuasive, this other woman, and far more beautiful than me."

At that moment her phone buzzed with text from Cooper, *"How's it going?"* Jane replied with a thumbs up emoticon. "A nurse friend," she said for his benefit. After she felt she'd made enough of a memorable impression, Jane excused herself by claiming she had to meet her.

"Ask your friend to meet us here," he proposed.

"She's making dinner at her apartment."

"Okay then. What's your number?" he asked. "We can meet for lunch. I'm not going to be in Morro Bay long, but if you can find the time…?"

"Sure," she said before realizing she hadn't memorized the new phone number on the throw-away phone Avery Weeks had given her. "Better yet," she said, "let me text you. What's yours?" she asked.

Brendan offered his number as she pecked it into her phone. Then she texted out the name she'd given him, "Sarah," and pressed send. Seconds later his phone chirped and he said, "Cool. Got it."

"Really nice meeting you," she said getting up and grabbing her purse.

"Seriously, let's grab lunch or another drink sometime," he said and nudged her arm. "Whenever it works for you and your schedule. It would be great to see ya again."

"I'd like that. Thanks for the drink," she said.

"Cheers."

Jane could feel his eyes on her back as she walked out the door.

On the drive back to Pismo Beach, Jane filled Cooper in. The wine she had with Brendan put her in a good mood. "I'm certain I made an impression," she said.

"You always make an impression."

"What does that mean?"

"You have charisma. I saw it when we met in Jeremy's acting class."

"Charisma?"

"A spark."

On the one hand Jane liked the compliment, but on the other she didn't want to encourage him. She changed the subject and asked, "So tell me again, how do we plan to get this rocket launcher on Brendan's boat."

"After the crew leaves for the day, and he's alone, you're going to feign distress. Car trouble."

"Aren't you afraid," Jane asked, "that we'll get pulled over and the cops discover that thing in your trunk?"

"They'd have to be tipped off, and nobody knows I have it, except you."

"When do we plant it on the boat?"

"As soon as possible."

"And where do you think Veronica is now?"

"No telling. She can't be far. She'd feel compelled to supervise the expedition."

"And after the feds arrest her, what will happen to Billy?"

"I'll take him home to Canada. The story I told you about Shari Lewis, the ventriloquist...I'm determined to break that chain. Setting him on a straight path is my stab at redemption."

"Having a midlife conscience, are you?"

"My brother is dead, my father has advanced dementia. Billy is the only family I've got left. I'd be happy to just live a quiet, suburban life."

Jane asked, "Is Billy going to play hockey?"

"Damn straight."

"You'll teach him?"

"He's my son."

"You'd have to kidnap him, though, right?"

"What do you mean?"

"The cops will want answers and you're supposed to be dead."

"Veronica lives off the grid, and so does Billy. He's not a U.S. citizen because he was born in the Turks and Caicos. Nobody will lay claim to him, except me."

They drove the rest of the way in silence.

To put herself at ease, Jane still felt it best Cooper not know which one of the many motels she was staying at so she had Cooper drop her off at the Pismo Beach Pier. They made plans to meet back there the next morning.

She walked up Pomeroy Avenue and ordered a takeout sandwich at Mo's Smokehouse BBQ. Then she walked around downtown Pismo Beach to make sure she wasn't being followed. She slipped into a nail spa and cut out through the back door. When she was satisfied nobody could be tailing, Jane walked back to her motel room at the Kon Tiki Inn. She sat on her private balcony to eat her tri-tip sandwich as the sound of waves crashed in the distance. Then she called her mother.

"We're on the road, driving to California," Nancy said. "Avery took care of everything, like Danny said he would. Where are you?"

"Working at my friend's melodrama near Pismo Beach," Jane lied.

"Are you going to be in the show?"

"Just working the box office and serving concessions for now. I've got to pay my dues there. That's how it works. But everyone's been really nice."

"We'll come see you!"

"Wait until I'm in a show," Jane said.

"The racing team is just a few points shy to qualify for Nationals. Danny's certain we can get them in Sonoma."

Familiar with the region from its wine, Jane had never been

to Sonoma County but knew it was north of San Francisco. She held images in her mind of mountainside vineyards, but not necessarily a dragstrip. She asked, "When do you get there?"

"We're driving straight through without stopping so probably tomorrow. Where's Pismo Beach?"

"South a few hours," Jane said.

"You have to come see Danny race."

"Okay," she said, even though she wasn't sure if it was possible.

"How ya doin', Jane?" she heard Danny pipe in.

"Let me put you on speaker," her mother said.

A second later Danny's voice became clear and he asked, "How was the drive?"

"The Chevy served me well. I made really good time. That thing's got guts."

"I knew she would. You doin' all right? Your mother misses you."

"I miss her too. Both you guys. How was jail?"

He teased, "You know as much as I what it's like to be in the pen."

"I bet Florida's jailhouse slop is better than what they serve in California."

"I highly doubt that. When we get together we'll compare notes."

Jane heard her mother's nervous laugh before she said, "That's all behind us now. We're family and nothing is going to keep us apart."

Jane hoped her mother was right and said, "Call me when you guys get settled."

"We will. Love you."

"Love you, too."

After she hung up Jane finished the sandwich and washed it down with the rest of the bottle of wine she'd bought the night before. She thought about what her mother had said, *we're family*, and then Cooper's plans to rescue his son. *What's more important than family?*

Out of curiosity, Jane searched on her phone and pulled up a satellite geography map of Vandenberg Air Force Base, similar to what the professor had done on his laptop. It featured an overlay grid which displayed the base perimeter. On another site a map denoted both active and abandoned missile sites along the thirty-five square miles of restricted coast. From the photos she could see many of the silos were decaying remnants from the Cold War.

She learned that the tracks of Amtrak's Pacific Surfliner cut through the base and hugged the scenic coast.

This all seemed so crazy, long lost gold on restricted government land, buried for over one hundred and fifty years. After searching legitimate sites, Jane came across the conspiracy theory ones that claimed there was a labyrinth of underground tunnels connecting Vandenberg's launch pads, all remnants of decaying infrastructure from the Cold War.

Exhausted from the long day, she put her phone on the charger on the bedside table then pulled down the Tahitian floral bedspread and crawled into bed.

CHAPTER 9

It was late afternoon when Jane and Cooper sat in the rental car parked up the hill. As to not be noticed, they had moved around a few times. This position offered a good view of the yacht, but not too obvious. Earlier that same day Jane found a skin-colored bandage to cover the ugly scar on her leg. She purchased a snug, mini-cocktail dress, a pair of leather high-heels, and a matching purse big enough to fit the Colt. Again she'd call on her acting skills. This ensemble was the right wardrobe for a scene about seduction.

"It's freezing," Jane said to Cooper, fighting off a chill. "Can you turn on the heater?" A damp, cold mist hung in the air.

Peering through binoculars Cooper said, "Not a good idea. A running car might draw attention."

"Easy for you to say, you've got a jacket."

"You wear it," he said, and started to remove it.

"No," Jane said, angered. "Forget it."

"Why not?"

"Because I don't want it."

"If you're cold then—"

"I don't want your jacket," Jane snapped. The idea of wearing one of his garments did not appeal to her.

"All right. Let me know if you change your mind." He considered the yacht again and said, "Looks like everyone else is gone," before he set the binoculars on the dash.

Jane caught him sneak a peek at the top of her thighs below the hemline before he said, "Let's see if you can coax Brendan off his boat."

"This dress is too short," Jane said, pulling it down.

"You picked it."

"You told me to get something sexy."

He looked at her and said, "You are."

"Stop it!"

Cooper raised his hands in surrender, "I know, strictly business, as you said. I'm just saying…"

"Why did I allow you to talk me into this?"

"Look, we're almost there. Get him off the boat, I'll plant the weapon, and then you're done. Once Veronica shows up…"

"I should have gotten a shawl, or something. And this hemline is too short."

"Just have confidence that you look great."

Jane felt a sense of déjà vu. It was as if she was back in L.A. where she and Cooper were attempting to hook Alexander Wolff into the diamond scheme. It brought back the memory of Cooper's betrayal. But now here he was again complimenting her on the way she looked, stirring up memories of their romance. She considered telling him to shut up but instead dug out her phone. "So how do I phrase it?"

"Keep the text simple. Say your car won't start. Give it a minute to see if he responds. Then call him."

"And if that doesn't work?" she asked.

"Then we'll find another way," Cooper said and started the car.

"Can you turn the heater on now?"

"Okay." He obliged, fumbled with the controls on the dash. They drove down the hill and parked on Embarcadero Street near a cluster of shops and restaurants. Cooper searched below until he found the latch and released the hood of the car. They both got out of the car, Jane finding her balance in her new high heels. Cooper popped the hood and, near the ignition wires, pulled out an electronic chip. He put it in his pocket, slammed the hood, and went around to the back of the car to open the trunk.

Jane followed, her heels wavering on the damp pavement.

Cooper struggled with the bulky black case, and Jane could see the weapon was heavy. He pulled it out, handed Jane the keys and said, "Give me a few minutes to get near the boat, then call."

"Okay."

He carried the black case toward the water.

As instructed, Jane sat behind the wheel and waited a few minutes before she texted Brendan, "*Help. My car won't start.*" She waited but there was no response. After a few minutes she dialed. From this vantage point she could not see the boat.

"Hello?"

"Hey, it's me Sarah. From yesterday."

"Sarah the nurse?" She picked up on his enthusiasm.

"Yeah, that's right. Hey, sorry to bother you, but I'm on my way to a fundraising event and my car won't start. I was shopping for shoes over here, not far from your boat."

"Where?"

"I'm parked outside a bunch of shops. I've got nobody else to call. Can you lend me a hand?"

"Now?"

"Yeah."

"Where are you?"

"Like I said, not far from your boat."

They stayed on the phone until he found her. When Jane stepped out of the car his eyes lit up. She could see he didn't expect her to be dressed up. "Thank you so much, I'm going to be late for this thing and I don't know what happened," she said handing over the keys. After smiling at her for a second he climbed in the car and tried to start it. The starter turned over but the ignition did not fire. He got out and popped the hood.

"Weird that it won't start," Jane said.

"Where are you headed?" he asked.

"A cocktail reception near the hospital."

He looked over the engine and said, "The starter works so it's not the battery. These new cars…"

"Just my luck."

"I'd drive you but I don't have a car. I've got a moped on the boat."

"I'll just Uber it, I guess," she said and pulled out her phone, "Or maybe I just blow this whole thing off."

"Nobody's expecting you?" he asked.

"Donna, a nurse friend of mine, but I'm so new over there nobody will miss me." She let that hang for a moment then proposed. "I'll call a tow truck from the bar."

"A mighty fine idea," Brendan said, "but we'd need to go to a place where I can keep an eye on my boat," he said pointing to Dutchman's Seafood, a restaurant at the edge of the water.

"I could use a drink," Jane said. "Give me a second." She took her time going through the car to collect her things, figuring she needed to delay him as long as possible. "I'll call my friend and let her know not to expect me," Jane said. Brendan waited as she feigned a phone conversation with the fictitious co-worker Donna telling her she had "car trouble" and "may or may not make it." Then she texted Cooper to let him know Brendan was with her. She could see Brendan was getting impatient, and when she felt she couldn't delay anymore Jane grabbed her purse and joined him on the sidewalk.

Dutchman's Seafood was a nautical-themed, waterfront eatery with old-school brass fixtures and paintings of clipper ships on the walls. Brendan chose a bar table which afforded a view of his yacht. Jane gazed but could not see Cooper near the boat.

The cocktail waitress arrived and Brendan ordered a beer. Jane ordered wine and then, to buy time, fried calamari. After the waitress left she asked him, "When we met you asked me if I had a boyfriend,"—attempting to divert his attention from the yacht—"so, what about you? Seeing someone?"

He gave her a smile. "It's been a long time since I've had a girlfriend…or been with anyone for that matter."

She didn't believe him and teased with, "I doubt that. I'm willing to bet you have a girl in every port."

"Hardly."

"Yeah, right."

"Seriously. The sea is my mistress."

"Where'd you get that?" Jane questioned with playful cynicism, "From a Gordon Lightfoot song or something? 'Brandy?'"

"If you're talking about 'Brandy You're a Fine Girl,' Looking Glass recorded that tune," he said, "Lightfoot wrote 'The Wreck of the Edmund Fitzgerald.'"

"You know what I mean," she said, "sailors breaking their girl's hearts because they're called to the sea."

"You've had yours broken, haven't you?"

She didn't expect that and said, rhetorically, "Haven't we all, at some point?" She glanced out to the yacht and was surprised to see Cooper on the docks. When Brendan followed her gaze Jane was quick to distract him, "You haven't answered my question. Are you seeing someone or not?"

"I'm not," he said.

Jane gave him a flirtatious smile and held her gaze for an extra moment before she looked away. It was the same non-verbal exchange she'd shared with Cooper on the first night they'd made love. She twirled her cocktail napkin as she felt his eyes upon her. She looked back to find his eyes were still locked and said, "What?"

"Nothing." He glanced to the bar for a moment, then returned his attention and said, "I'm no Casanova, that's for damn sure. Just an average guy out there saving seals."

"Navy SEALS?"

"No, the real thing now."

"I'm just teasing," she said.

"So tell me, who broke your heart?"

"Someone I used to work with," Jane confessed.

"A doctor?"

"No. A salesman," Jane said, considering the profession a realistic portrayal of Cooper—a con man and master of persuasion.

"He was a fool to let you go," he said.

"There was someone else."

"He made a mistake," he said, and sipped his beer before he proposed, "What do you say I show you my yacht?"

Here it goes Jane thought, *he's asking me back to his place.* She wondered what the captain's quarters on the yacht could possibly be like before she said, "We've got calamari coming."

"No rush," he said and looked out to the boat. Jane followed his gaze to make sure Cooper wasn't there. She could not see him.

"When are you setting out?" Jane asked.

"It depends on…" he started to say just as his cell phone rang. He reached into his pocket and pulled it out. He looked at the display, furrowed his brow, and said, "Sorry, I've got to take this." He got up and accepted the call with a formal, "This is Brendan."

Jane realized he'd made a critical mistake. He'd spoken his real name into the phone as opposed to alias the "Brad" he'd claimed to be when they first met. Brendan excused himself and searched for a quiet spot near the men's room to take the call.

She texted Cooper, "*Still with him.*"

After a moment she overheard Brendan say, "I've got it covered, Veronica. We're all set."

Veronica.

The realization hit her. He was talking with Veronica. Jane didn't know what to do. She got up to eavesdrop, approached the alcove to the restrooms and overheard him say, "Equipment is on board and my crew is standing by," before he turned and noticed her.

Jane gave him a forced smile and pointed to the door of the

woman's room. He stepped aside and she brushed past him. Once inside, she stood at the door and trained her ear on the conversation. Jane caught a few snippets before Brendan asked, "A rocket launch? How long does that take? Okay, if we have to come back to Morro Bay and wait it out that's okay, I won't give up the boat slip."

Jane texted Cooper, *"He's on the phone with Veronica!"*

There was a moment of silence, and she wasn't sure if he'd walked away or not, but then she heard him ask, "So you're saying we shove off Friday? Got it. I'll check the weather again but it appears clear through the weekend."

Jane did the math in her head. Friday was a few days away. Then her phone buzzed. It was Cooper's text response *"Done. Get away from him."*

She texted back *"Fix the car. I'll meet you there."*

Jane knew she had what she needed, a clear idea when Veronica would board the yacht. And now that the missile launcher was stowed on his yacht her job was done. She breathed a sigh of relief, gave it a few minutes, washed her hands, and then returned to the table to find Brendan picking at the fried calamari with his fork. He gave her a smile as she sat down.

"Everything all right?" she said.

"Yeah. Just business."

"Who was it?" she asked to gauge his reaction.

"A marine scientist I'm working with."

Marine scientist? Jane thought, *total bullshit.* "So when do you all go to save the whales?" she asked.

"Not sure yet," he said before he motioned to her wine glass and said, "Want another?"

Jane pulled her purse close and said, "Can't, the tow truck is on its way."

"You called a tow truck?" he asked, surprised.

"That was the idea."

"What about touring my boat?"

"Some other time."

"Look, I'm sorry I had to take that call, but…"

"It's not that. I'm worried about my car. I've got to get to work tomorrow."

She could see he was mad so Jane feigned that she received a text, pulled her phone from her purse. "Oh, there they are now." She gave him a smile and said, "Thanks for the drink."

"What's the rush? Let's have dinner together."

"You're sweet, but I've got to work tomorrow," she said getting up. She could see he was disappointed and said, "Call me," to soften the blow.

"Wait up, I'll help you," he said reaching for his wallet.

"Thanks, Brendan," she said, using his real name. Jane saw the surprised reaction on his face. "That's you're real name, right?" she asked. "At least the one you used on the phone?"

He stammered, not knowing what to say, face turning red with anger. She'd caught him.

Jane spun on her heels and strolled out, feeling his eyes on her back. She figured it would take a minute or two for the waitress to bring Brendan the check and hoped it was enough time for Cooper to put the chip in the car—and make a fast getaway.

CHAPTER 10

Although she was exhausted, Jane tossed and turned in her sleep. Something didn't feel right, but she couldn't put her finger on it. Morning came and she pulled up Google Maps on her phone. Sonoma County was about a four-hour drive. Since she had a few days, Jane made the decision to visit her mother. She'd call Cooper from the road.

She checked out of the motel and hit the road. Outside Pismo Beach she found a stretch of two-lane highway and floored it for a half a mile. She cut onto a dirt road off the highway, shut off the engine, and gave it a good ten minutes. Then she double backed. Only after she was confident she wasn't being followed, Jane pulled over under the shade of an oak tree and checked the map again. She had the time so decided to take the scenic route, the Pacific Coast Highway heading north.

She called Cooper, "I'm getting out of town for a few days," she said, not wanting to offer too many details. "But I'll be back before Friday."

"Your job is done here," he said. "You really don't have to stick around. Go back to Florida. It's a waiting game until she gets on that boat."

Jane said, "I want to see her in handcuffs. But more importantly, I want her to see me."

"Realize the arrest will happen on the base."

"There's got to be a perp walk, right? And they won't hold

her on the Air Force Base, will they?"

"I don't know."

"I want Veronica to see me, even if it's in the courtroom for her preliminary hearing."

"Why's that important?"

"She tried to kill me."

"She tried to kill both of us."

"I need closure. What are you going to do?" she asked.

"I've checked into a motel in Morro Bay with a view of the yacht. Watching it now. When Veronica boards, and I know they're anchored off Vandenberg, I'll drop the dime."

"Call me if you see anything," she said. "I'm not going far."

"Where are you going?"

"I'd rather not say," she said.

"You still don't trust me?"

"What do you think?"

He said nothing.

"I'm a phone call away," Jane said.

"Fair enough."

Winding north on Highway 1, she was in awe of the rugged natural beauty of the coastal drive—dramatic cliffs and rocky beaches. Maneuvering the vintage muscle car through the curves made it even more exhilarating. She stopped a few times to get out and take in the majestic view. She'd seen photos in magazines but never realized how magnificent it was. At one scenic overlook there was a patch of fog off the coast and she imagined the fateful *Yankee Blade* hugging the shoreline as it steamed past so many years ago.

In Big Sur she considered checking into one of the tiny roadside motels but it was not something she wanted to do alone, and besides, she'd already told her mom she was on her way. *Someday,* she promised herself.

She stopped in Carmel for lunch. At a quaint bistro Jane sat outside under the shade of a cypress tree and ate what she considered the best turkey sandwich she'd ever had. The sliced turkey breast was cut off the bird, and the sandwich had a smoky chipotle dressing spread on its crispy baguette.

Afterward she took a stroll, truly enchanted by the sleepy coastal town. It felt like something out of a storybook. She found a wine shop and picked up a couple bottles of red that she guessed her mom would like.

Above Monterey she segued onto Highway 101, the scenic part of the drive behind her. When she reached Sonoma Raceway later that afternoon Jane drove past the grandstands and found the cluster of campers and trailers near the pit sheds at the end. She recognized Danny's trailer from a distance.

"Oh, Jane," her mother said, giving her a big hug. "I was so worried about you."

"What are you worried about?" Jane asked.

"A mother worries," she replied. "Always."

"I'm fine."

Danny came from the pit shed with a rag in his hand, his crew tinkering on the dragster behind him. "How's the old Chevy treating you?" he asked.

Jane turned to the Malibu and wished she'd taken it to the car wash before she'd arrived, out of respect since his pride and joy was on loan. "It's been running really well," she said and went on to explain how beautiful the drive up Pacific Coast Highway was. What she didn't mention was that she'd often used the muscle car's speed to ensure nobody was following. Sure, there was always the chance of getting pulled over and the cops not buying her fake ID, but she took that risk for peace of mind.

"I'll change her oil," Danny said, thumbing to the pit shed behind him. "She's got to be overdue."

Jane thought it interesting that he called the Chevy Malibu a *she*. Jane had never thought of vehicles, or boats for that matter, to be gender specific. She remembered that Veronica's boat was named *Anne Bonny*, and Brendan's yacht christened *Maenads*, both named after women. She wondered if maybe the fate of the *Yankee Blade*, or even the *Titanic* for that matter, would have been different had they been given feminine names.

"We're having burgers tonight," her mother said, pointing to the grill and the prepared fixings.

"Sounds good," Jane said, even though she wasn't hungry.

While Danny went back to his work on the dragster, Jane opened one of the bottles of wine she'd brought and helped Nancy make dinner. She asked her mother why she'd set the gas grill so far away from the pit shed.

"In case of fuel spill," she explained.

Jane noted the no smoking signs all around them.

They cooked the burgers and set them on picnic tables nearby. The men arrived after washing up, most of them grabbing a can of beer as opposed the wine Jane had brought. She recognized most of the guys from the shop back in Florida. One of the younger ones, Luke, went out of his way to greet her and make small talk. He was nice, but she felt they had little in common. Her mother seemed to encourage Luke, and that embarrassed Jane. Aside, she accused, "Trying to get me married, Mom?"

"Grandchildren wouldn't be such a bad thing."

"I'm not ready for that."

"When the time is right, you'll know it," she said, then whispered, "But don't wait too long."

The thought of having a child and being responsible for another person's life while staying one step ahead of Veronica's vengeance brought a chill to Jane's spine. What if Cooper's plan failed? What would she do then? Where could she go where Veronica couldn't find her?

After dinner wrapped up, and as the sun was setting, the crew rolled the dragster into the trailer, locked it up, and they went back to the hotel. Just as he had before, Danny arranged an adjoining room in the hotel so Jane could be near them. She still had his Colt .380 Mustang in her purse and wondered what firearm Danny had brought along.

When her mother was in the shower, Jane asked Danny, "When you were on the run years ago, did you often feel like you were being watched?"

"What do you mean?"

"I feel like a dark shadow is hovering over me all the time. It's driving me crazy."

"I felt that way, too," he admitted, "for a long time."

"I don't know if it's real or my imagination." He said nothing and Jane pressed, "What do you think? Should I be worried?"

"Paranoia not such a bad thing if it keeps you alert."

"Why do you say that?"

"I don't want your mother to worry, so don't say anything to her."

She nodded.

In a lowered voice he said, "Back home...I noticed there were a few unannounced visitors, more than normal."

"Like who?"

"A UPS guy came to the garage and had me sign for something that was just junk mail, nothing I'd ordered. I got the feeling he was checking my place out."

"Looking for me?"

"Or checking on me. Hard to say."

"What else?"

"There was a door-to-door salesman came by the house one night selling Kirby vacuums. Nobody does that anymore, do they? Door-to-door vacuum salesmen? Maybe I'm being paranoid too, but at the time my gut told me these guys weren't what they appeared to be."

"I've got a confession to make," Jane said. "I silenced my old cell phone, put it on its charger, and hid it behind the refrigerator in your garage."

Danny raised an eyebrow.

Jane continued, "In case Veronica was tracking me through that phone, which I suspect she was. I didn't want to turn it off so it would go completely dead. I wanted her to think I was still in Florida."

"Clever."

Jane considered telling him about Cooper's caper to trap Veronica at the base but felt it best to not divulge those details. She was afraid he'd insist she stay with them and she really wanted to see it through. Instead Jane asked, "How about your case? What does Avery Weeks say?"

"He claims the government doesn't have much of a case and they won't necessarily pursue it because it was such a long time ago. If it had been a mid-level drug dealer instead of an under-cover agent who died in the line of duty they wouldn't have made a big deal out of it anyway."

"I'm sorry I brought this all down on you."

"Ah…I brought it upon myself," Danny said, "I didn't bank on my past catching up with me after all these years, but I suppose that's the one thing nobody can truly shed."

"What's that?"

"The sins of our past."

"But we can repent," Jane said, "Can't we?"

"That we can, darlin'. That we can."

CHAPTER 11

Jane awoke with a headache.

At first she attributed it to the red wine from the night before, then realized it was more than that—a sickness lingering, her body aching, possibly the beginnings of the flu. Nancy gave her a few Advil and made a cup of coffee from the single serve Keurig in the hotel room. While everyone else converged in the hotel's complimentary breakfast room, Jane took her time getting ready. She didn't have much of an appetite. She put her hair up and pulled on linen pants and a light cotton top. She put a few Advil in her pocket.

When they arrived at the racetrack and emerged from the air-conditioned comfort of Danny's truck, Jane could see it was going to be a hot day. The temperatures in Pismo Beach and along the Central Coast were mild with a gentle sea breeze. In comparison the inland air was dry and stagnant. The blazing sun made itself known early in the day.

"You'll need this," Nancy said as she handed Jane a credential badge. It was a laminated card to wear around her neck that read "Pit Crew." She then gave her a handful of foam ear plugs. "And you're going to need these, too."

"What are they?" said Jane.

"Ear protection."

Danny's crew pulled the dragster from the shade of the pit shed. They made last minute adjustments and everyone, including Jane and her mother, helped push the race car to the area behind the grandstands to queue it up for its first race. Other teams were doing the same, and Jane asked Danny, "Can't you just drive the car over?"

"She's not geared for that," he said.

There it was, *she* again. *So a dragster is a she, too?* Danny further enlightened her while pointing to the chrome engine block, "There's no radiator, and no starter on board either."

"Why not?"

"Extra weight we don't need. It's about speed and horse-power." Jane still did not understand. "Once she's warmed up," Danny continued, "we run her full bore for everything she's got. Then we get her back to the pit for some TLC."

"Tender loving care," her mother said in answer to Jane's quizzical look.

Jane knew that acronym and said, "Oh, right."

Danny continued, "Before she can even cool down we'll rebuild her for the next race. Pistons, rods, bearings, even the clutch; everything needs to be taken apart and put back together again."

"And all within seventy-five minutes," Nancy said. "These are the rules."

"I get it," Jane said, even though she didn't, but she came to realize why Danny needed the crew. This was obviously a lot of work. She could see the sport attracts guys who like to take things apart and put them back together again.

"You'll see," her mother said.

A large crowd had already begun to arrive and fill up the grandstands. She'd been to outdoor concerts and occasional college football games, but never anything like this. RVs filled the parking lot. Entire families swarmed in, braving the heat. The fans were primarily male, but there was a percentage of women too, girlfriends and wives mostly, and grandmas tagging along.

Feeling dehydrated, Jane bought a large Dr. Pepper from a

concession stand and found shade under a carport. When one of the dragsters started nearby it startled her. She couldn't believe how loud it was. The earth shook under her feet as she covered her ears. She remembered the hearing protection her mother had given her and dug out a pair from of her pocket.

"I need to sit down," she said to Nancy.

"The teams have reserved seats in the grandstand," Nancy said and led the way.

The smell of exhaust hit Jane like a ton of bricks, and she felt like she was going to be sick. They made their way over, and sitting down made Jane feel better. She washed down another couple of Advil with her Dr. Pepper and chewed on the ice.

That's when she noticed the man with the horn-rimmed glasses.

He took a seat near them and appeared to have his eye on her. Jane got the impression he had followed them to their seats. When an usher standing in the aisle asked him for his credentials it was clear the man didn't have a lanyard. The usher pointed him to the general admission seating, and the man obliged, but not before glancing at Jane one more time.

"Do you know that guy?" Jane asked her mother, pointing him out.

"No."

"He was checking me out."

"Because you're my beautiful daughter," she said with pride.

The horn-rimmed man talked to another man wearing a green visor. The man with the visor gave her look before they both blended into the crowd. Jane lost sight of them. She wondered if they were a threat, or if her lingering sickness was making her even more paranoid. She reached into her purse and adjusted the Colt Mustang into position for an easy draw.

After the announcer came on, welcoming race fans and reporting changes in the program, all stood for the national anthem. Her mother put her hand over her heart, and Jane mimicked her. During the last verse three parachutists appeared above them in the sky, each parachute the American flag. Red, white and blue smoke streamed from pods strapped to each of their ankles. All three landed in unison to roaring applause.

Two "funny cars" were introduced at the starting line. These were different from Danny's car. They had a stock car body and Jane asked her mother why they call them funny cars. She didn't know.

By the time the engines were warmed up, and the cars had burned tires back and forth at the starting line, Jane knew she couldn't take an entire day of this. The bank of lights between the cars cued the start. The dragsters blazed down the stretch. Even though Jane had protection, she still had to hold her hands over her ears. It was loud.

She suffered through a half dozen races until Danny's car was up. Jane could see he was dressed in a fire-retardant suit and thought it must be really hot wearing that thing. A few of the crew joined her and her mother in the grandstands. She could see Danny pull on his helmet and climb into the dragster.

Side by side, he and the dragster he was set to run against burned rubber preparing for the race. This was a ritual, Jane came to learn, that maximized traction off the line. The acrid smoke wafted into the stands and made Jane cough.

Nancy grabbed her arm. "I get so nervous," she said.

The bank of lights cued, and the dragsters exploded off the line. Flames jetted from the exhaust pipes and Jane could feel the sonic percussion in her chest. Side by side they thundered down the straightaway. When they reached the finish line, a mere three seconds later, parachutes popped out of the back of each car. It took a long distance to slow down past the finish line.

The crowd cheered with enthusiasm.

When the results lit up the board, Nancy did not appear happy.

"What's the matter?" Jane asked.

"Not the best time," her mother explained. "But it all depends on how the others run."

Everyone walked back to the pit shed. Danny soon met them there with the dragster. As the team descended on the machine, Danny explained, "Clutch failure in the upper gears. We'll get her in the next run." He pulled off his fire-retardant suit and joined the others to work on the car.

Nancy explained the team would rebuild the engine and race again in a few hours. Jane saw the opportunity and proposed she get the keys to Danny's truck so she could take a nap. Her mother was reluctant at first, wanting Jane to stay with them, but then finally agreed. "I'll come get you when we're ready to run again."

Jane figured she had at least an hour to nap.

The walk to Danny's truck was welcome relief from the noise, smoke and commotion. Jane removed the ear protection plugs and put them in her pocket. She climbed in the truck, rolled down the windows a few inches for air, and then adjusted the seat as far back as it would go. She pulled the pistol from her purse and curled up with the Colt just as she had while sleeping in the Chevy on her drive to California.

She closed her eyes and was drifting off when she heard footsteps on gravel. It sounded as if someone was close to the truck. Jane sat up but nobody was there. She scanned her surroundings. Nothing. After a moment she lay back again but kept her ears alert. Other than the racing in the distance there seemed to be nothing of concern. Jane finally closed her eyes. She figured she may not be able to sleep, but at least she could rest.

Exhaustion won out, and she drifted off.

In her dream came images of Big Sur's dramatic coast. She walked on the beach as waves crashed the jagged rocks around her. Then she came across an old wooden lifeboat full of gold bars. Strange. Beyond it there was a woman sitting at the edge of the water, her back to Jane, weeping. She could see the woman was hunched over a dead child, trying to revive her. The toddler's face was blue. She had drowned, a victim of the *Yankee Blade*.

Jane was startled by a strange sound and awoke. She sat up to see the plastic spout of a gas can wedged into the crack of the truck's passenger side window. Raw gasoline poured inside. Jane screamed.

She went for the driver's side door but it would not budge. Something was blocking it. She put her weight into it without luck. Out the side window she could see a thick strap, the kind used to hold cargo on flatbed trucks, snug over the door. Someone had wrapped this strap beneath the truck and around the top of the cab. Winched tight, it clinched both doors. The pink-colored gasoline streamed inside and the scent hit strong.

Then she saw the man with horn-rimmed glasses standing in front of the truck. He had a propane torch in one hand, the kind used to strip paint, and a Bic lighter in the other. He ignited the torch and adjusted the light blue flame.

Jane screamed again.

She raised her gun and fired through the windshield. The safety glass splintered but other than the fractured hole where the bullet had penetrated the glass remained intact. She couldn't see him beyond the fractured windshield so where had he gone?

She went for the passenger door, pushed the gas can out, and tried that door. It, too, wouldn't budge. The puddle of gas in the seat soaked her linen pants and she could feel the caustic fumes harsh in her throat. Then Jane saw the man in the rearview mirror. He had the propane torch raised.

She stuck the gun out the crack in the window and fired back, but was certain she didn't hit him. The she went for the ignition. The truck started, lurched forward, but there was little room to make the turn. Instead Jane smashed into the back of a SUV.

She was putting Danny's truck in reverse when she saw the man in the sideview mirror. He was closing in and poised to toss the propane torch.

Jane abandoned the wheel and fired through the rear window of the cab. Then she put her feet on the seat and pressed against the glass. Jane broke through at the same time he tossed the propane torch into the cab.

The gasoline ignited. An explosion rocked the truck and blew out the windows.

Sprawled facedown in the truck bed, she could feel the heat on her back. Shards of burning glass scaled the back of her neck. She spun to see the inside of the truck aflame and realized her pants were soaked in gas. A flammable wick, she had to get away.

With the Colt in hand, she jumped from the bed of the truck and ran with all her might. There were gunshots as car windshields shattered beside her.

She turned back and fired but after a few shots was out of bullets. She knew she hadn't hit him so cut through the space between parked cars. She glanced back. He was following.

She ran to the racetrack, the area just beyond the finish line. More gunshots sounded so she zigzagged—a changing target. She reached the track, hopped over the concrete barrier, then ran across the lane.

She jumped over the middle concrete barrier and found herself on the other track. That's when she heard the engines roar. She kept going and reached the outside but came across a wire fence. She turned back, realized she was trapped as the man moved toward her, adjusting his thick glasses, and took aim.

Then she heard the cars.

He had little time to react. The man stutter-stepped in an attempt to get out of the way but the dragster in his lane was traveling way too fast. It swerved sideways to avoid him, fishtailed at over three hundred miles per hour.

From Jane's perspective, when the dragster struck the man his body split in half. The torso flew skyward while the legs were yanked under the tires. The car slammed into the rail and exploded in a ball of fire.

CHAPTER 12

Jane instinctively ducked behind the concrete barrier and hugged the asphalt. She could hear the crashing metal and the crowd reacting with oohs and ahhs. The announcer barked something she couldn't understand followed by the sound of sirens. Jane sat up but because of the smoke she couldn't see anything.

She knew she had to get out of there. There would be an inquiry and police. The press surely would make a big deal about it. Then Veronica would realize Jane had survived another attempt on her life.

The thought came to her: *fake my own death.*

Danny's burning truck, this wreck, so much carnage nobody would know she was alive unless she stuck around.

There appeared to be room to slide under the wire barricade. As emergency vehicles blew past, Jane crawled on her belly under the fence. The veil of smoke gave her ample cover, a literal smokescreen. She climbed to her feet and slipped the gun in the front pocket of her linen pants. Getting as far away from the smoke and burning wreckage as she could, Jane stepped on something—shattered horn-rimmed glasses.

What are the chances?

She kicked them aside and made her way upstream against curious onlookers running to the crash. There was a cluster of recreational vehicles. When she got to the encampment it seemed like a ghost town. It appeared most everyone had gone to see the wreck.

Jane realized her purse containing her cell phone, credit card, fake ID, and keys to the Chevy were all in the burning truck and most likely incinerated by now. She did, thankfully, have the key card for the hotel room.

A teenage girl sat in a camping chair, bored, ear buds in and engrossed in her cell phone. It appeared she could not care less about the wreck and was far more interested in the content of her tiny screen.

Jane approached and said, "Excuse me."

The girl looked up.

"My mother is going to be worried sick," she said, thumbing back over her shoulder to the plume of smoke rising in the air, "and I don't have my phone with me. Can I borrow yours to tell her I'm okay?"

The girl sized her up, squinting, and said, "You smell like gas."

"Yeah...an accident."

"You all right?"

"I'm okay."

The girl studied her a moment, got up from the chair. She pulled the earphone jack out and handed the iPhone to her.

"Thank you," Jane said and dialed her mother. It rang and rang. She was afraid she'd have to leave a voicemail, but then Nancy picked up.

"Mom," Jane said. "I'm okay."

"Where are you?"

"Near the wreck, but I'm fine."

"Whose phone are you calling from? I don't recognize the number."

"A really nice girl was kind enough to lend me hers," she said, then stepped away out of earshot. "Mom, listen. That man from the grandstands tried to kill me."

"What man?"

"The one eyeballing me. And he lit Danny's truck on fire."

"What!?"

"He's the reason for this crash."

"They said there was someone on the track...where are you?"

Jane thought about the other guy she saw, the man with the visor she'd seen talking with the horn-rimmed assassin and said, "I don't know if he was alone or if there are more."

"More of who? Jane, are you all right?"

"Veronica got to me through you, Mom. Be careful. Watch your back."

"Meet me in the pit shed."

"I can't."

"Then Danny's truck."

Jane could see the separate plume of smoke coming from where Danny's truck was parked. She said, "I need to get out of here. I'll call you tonight. I love you." She hung up and walked back to the girl. "Thank you," she said and handed the phone back. "My mom will probably call back but you don't have to answer. It's probably better if you don't."

The girl's phone rang. She put it on silence, considered Jane, and said, "You, uh...okay?"

"I'm fine," Jane lied.

"Want water, or something?"

"That would be great."

The girl dug into a nearby cooler and handed Jane a plastic bottle.

"Thank you," Jane said, and twisted off the cap. Water was exactly what she needed at that moment. "Where's your family?" Jane asked.

"Went to see what happened, I guess."

"You're not interested?"

"Crashes scare me."

"Me too," Jane said.

The girl nodded and gave her a smile.

Jane marched on. She'd have to find a way to get back to the hotel and get out of the gas-soaked clothes. She needed a shower before she drove back to Morro Bay.

She remembered what Danny had said to her in his garage in Florida. *Backup* is what he called it. She recalled that after she'd run from Cooper to Danny's shop, and used the hide-a-key to get in, he'd mentioned there was also hide-a-key under the fender of the Chevy. She had never checked for it, but if it was true the muscle car would be her getaway.

Jane marched toward the highway, determined to get back to the hotel. She planned to stand on the side of the road with her thumb out.

CHAPTER 13

The scrawny trucker didn't ask Jane why she smelled like gasoline. By the time he'd pulled over to pick her up most of the gas had evaporated out of her clothes, but she could still smell it on her skin. The scent made her queasy.

Hitchhiking seemed so old fashioned, like from a bad '70s movie, but she had no choice. The moment after the tractor trailer pulled over, Jane hesitated. *Is this a good idea?* But the gun gave her confidence even though she was out of bullets.

Once she climbed into the truck she could see the lean trucker was more interested in talking about Christian values than anything else. She said little but encouraged with silent nods. In the half hour it took to drive Jane to the hotel, she learned his life story, once a wayward son of sin and debauchery before he was born again. He used the word "repent" just as she had with Danny the night before.

Repent.

When he dropped her off in front of the hotel, the trucker handed Jane a pamphlet for his on-line church. "God Bless, sister," were his parting words.

Jane thanked him, and after he drove off the first thing she did was check under the Chevy's fender for the hide-a-key. There was nothing. She tried the other wheel wells but it wasn't there either. Tears of frustration came to her eyes but she fought them off, knew she needed to stay focused. She went back to the front wheel well and tried again. She felt around inside. Sure enough Jane came across the magnetized, metallic case and pulled it out. Inside there was a spare key and folded twenty dollar bill.

She showered quickly and got dressed. The only thing clean to wear was the mini dress so it would have to do. There was second magazine for the Colt in her suitcase. When she swapped out the spent clip for the new one, Jane could smell the burnt gunpowder on the weapon. She left a note for her mother letting her know she'd taken the Chevy, then set out.

Her plan was to take the direct route down Highway 101 back to Morro Bay. Without her trusty credit card, she hoped there was enough gas in the tank to make it. The twenty dollar bill came in handy at a Chevron in Salinas. By the time she pulled into Morro Bay the needle on the fuel gauge was below empty.

When they last spoke, Cooper had mentioned he was staying in a motel close enough to spy on the yacht. Jane had no problem finding the place. Although it was getting dark, it was obvious what room he was in by the binoculars mounted on a tripod visible outside the second floor balcony. She found a small stone and threw it at the sliding glass door. After a moment Cooper emerged. "You're back," he said.

"She tried to kill me."

He motioned her to come up.

In the darkened motel room, Jane explained how she had barely escaped with her life.

"I don't think he was alone. There had to be others," she said with images in her mind of both the flat-nosed intruder she'd battled in Florida and the man in horn-rimmed glasses.

"Veronica probably put a bounty on your head," he said.

"A bounty?"

"The first man to kill you collects the prize."

"So there will be more?"

"As long as she's around to pay the bounty hunters." He

explained that there had been much activity around the boat. "The crew no longer goes home at night. They're now sleeping on the boat."

"Any sign of Veronica?"

"No."

She obsessed on the thought of hired assassins and wondered how much Veronica offered for her, dead or alive.

For most of the evening Jane watched the yacht from the balcony. Cabin lights were on, and there was little activity up on deck. It reminded her of the night she saw Cooper's yacht docked in Marina Del Rey. Her neighbor Carla had driven her, and that night she had seen him on his boat with another woman. Although Jane didn't realize it at the time, she knew now it was Veronica. Jane thought back on it. So much had happened so fast.

Cooper learned there were no other rooms available in the motel. Since there was only one bed in the room, without saying a word he took a pillow and blanket and made an impromptu bed on the floor. Jane was grateful and it put her at ease. He was holding up his end of the bargain. It wasn't that long ago, she thought, that the two of them had been lovers. She recalled the moments they shared and the feel of his embrace. She wondered what her life would be like if she had never met him and had never agreed to be his shill. Why hadn't she had the common sense to run the other way when he confessed he was a criminal? But no, she didn't. Because she loved him? *Love is blind,* she lamented, head on her pillow.

She couldn't sleep, and Cole Porter's tune "I've Got You Under My Skin" came to mind. Sinatra had made it universally popular but she favored Diana Krall's slow tempo version. Jane loved Cole Porter's songs, and this was one her favorites. His tunes all tended to be love stories with great irony. Thanks to Cole Porter, she had been caught in a double entendre having a drink with Gallagher in the Plaza Hotel with the lyrics to "Let's Misbehave." And then the band on Veronica's secluded island played "Love For Sale." Jane had memorized the lyrics to "I've Got You Under My Skin" long ago, and lying in bed the melody played in her head. One verse went, "I'd sacrifice anything come what might, for the sake of having you near, in spite of a warning voice that comes in the night, and repeats in my ear."

Of course the "warning voice" that "comes at night" and "repeats in my ear."

A *warning voice* was there when she first met Cooper. Jane realized she'd ignored it. The song continued in her head, "You can never win. Use your mentality...wake up to reality." Cole Porter had true wisdom and she wished she had taken it to heart.

Lights out, she heard him stir on the floor and wondered if Cooper would try to join her in bed. It didn't look like he was going to, but if he did Jane figured she wouldn't necessarily resist as wrong as it may be.

He kept his word. That was best.

After a while, she heard him begin to snore. She'd remembered it from the evenings they'd spent together, her lying in bed after he was asleep. Jane knew that Veronica was familiar with Cooper's snore too and wondered what she thought of it. This was the man they had both loved.

Or was Veronica capable of love?

CHAPTER 14

The next morning Jane heard Cooper get up. He tossed his blanket and went into the bathroom. She hadn't slept well. When she got up to peer out the window Jane was surprised to see much activity around Brendan's yacht. "Something's going on," she said.

Cooper emerged from the bathroom and peered through the binoculars. "Looks like they're getting ready to shove off."

"A day early?"

"We've got to make sure Veronica's on that boat."

They got dressed quickly, jumped in the rental car, and drove down the hill. Cooper parked on Embarcadero, the closest they'd ever been to the yacht. She could see Brendan supervising others as they brought provisions on board.

"I don't see Veronica," Jane said.

"She'll be here."

"What if she doesn't come?"

"She has to."

As if on cue, a black Audi with tinted windows pulled into the parking lot. Brendan walked from the gangway, went to the driver's side window, and was engaged in conversation with someone inside the vehicle.

"Could that be her?" Jane asked.

Cooper was silent.

Then the driver's side door opened and Billy came running

out. Jane could see Cooper tense at the sight of the boy and raise the binoculars for a closer look. His son ran around the parking lot then went to the railing to look at the yacht.

"That's Billy," Jane said, stating the obvious.

"Then it's definitely her."

Sure enough, Veronica emerged from the sedan. Jane could see she was dressed in black active wear as if she was going on a run or joining a yoga class. The last time Jane had seen Veronica she had slipped under the waves in the Caribbean. Now here she was—the proud descendant of pirate Anne Bonny about to board another boat.

She and Brendan spoke. There were nods and gestures before Brendan turned and barked orders to the crew. Veronica returned to the sedan and grabbed a small backpack. She went to the energetic Billy, kneeled down, and hugged her son as if he was heading off to camp. He shouldered his backpack and ran for the boat.

"Where's her bag?" Jane said.

Cooper said nothing. Then as Veronica stood on the dock, the *Maenads* shoved off, her son on board.

"Why isn't she going with them?" Jane asked.

"I don't get it," Cooper said softly.

Jane realized Cooper's scheme would only work if Veronica was on that boat—the yacht with the stashed missile launcher.

"What do we do?" Jane asked.

She could see Cooper was at a complete loss, his face pale. His carefully crafted plan had just crumbled before his eyes.

Jane said, "Start the car."

He simply blinked.

"Follow her," Jane demanded. She could see Veronica get into the sedan and pull out of the parking lot. "Don't get too close," Jane said.

The sedan headed out, and they followed. It swerved its way into a turn lane.

"Don't lose her!"

A flustered Cooper maneuvered the rental car to keep up. Jane felt as if she had to steer the ship now and tell *him* what to do. *What was the matter? Had he gone soft at the sight of his son?*

They followed Veronica as she weaved onto Highway 1 toward San Luis Obispo.

"If she's not supervising from the yacht, then where could she be going?" asked Jane, hoping to bring Cooper back to a tactical mindset.

"Why would she bring Billy along?" he wondered.

"She wants him with her when it's time to escape," she said.

After a fifteen minute drive, Veronica reached San Luis Obispo and pulled into the parking lot of the Amtrak station and parked. Cooper, keeping their distance, found a spot on the street. Jane checked out the California vintage depot with its signature Mission Revival architecture—stucco exterior and red clay tile roof before Veronica got out and walked to the station.

"The Amtrak Pacific Surfliner," Jane remembered, "the tracks cut through the base."

"But the train doesn't stop there."

"Close to it, right?"

"There's a seasonal stop at Surf Station in Lompoc, but that's miles north of Point Arguello."

"Let me see your phone."

He punched his code and handed it over. Jane searched. She pulled up a map and pointed it out, "Look, the tracks hug the coast and cross between Point Arguello and the launch facility."

Veronica emerged from the train station, ticket in hand, and returned to the sedan. At first Jane thought she was wearing yoga pants, but on closer inspection it appeared to be flat black triathlete clothing. Her tight compression clothing glistened in the sun. She opened the trunk, hoisted a sleek backpack on her shoulder, pulled dark sunglasses down, and walked to the platform. If there was ever a time that Veronica looked like a black widow, Jane thought, this was it.

"We've got to get on that train," Jane said.

"She'll see us."

He was right. There was little room on the concrete platform and no way they could stand there without Veronica noticing them.

"What's the next station south?" she asked.

He consulted his phone, "Grover Beach."

"She might not see us board there."

Jane could see the concept dawn on Cooper's hardened face. "Let's do it."

They sped south on Highway 101, past Pismo Beach, and pulled into the parking lot of the Grover Beach Amtrak station. This unmanned station, also Mission Revival, simply offered shelter and a seating area considerably more modest compared to the San Luis Obispo depot. Jane strapped on her purse and felt the weight of the Colt on her shoulder. Cooper grabbed his shoulder bag and pulled on a baseball cap. She grabbed the pocket umbrella from the back seat of the car.

At the electronic kiosk Cooper bought a pair of tickets as Jane found cover behind a Spanish-tile pillar. There were a dozen people waiting, evidence the train would be there soon. The idea came to her, and she said, "I wonder if the Air Force base runs everyone on the yacht through a check point."

"And taking the train Veronica avoids that," he said, finishing her thought.

"Exactly."

"She's obsessed with not leaving a paper trail so that makes sense. But nobody can get off the train on restricted government land."

"Unless someone pulls the emergency brake and jumps off," Jane ventured.

Cooper snapped, pointed to Jane and said, "You figured it out."

"We'll see," she said.

A train horn sounded. Jane could see the Pacific Surfliner round the bend up ahead. Veronica was on that train.

CHAPTER 15

Jane and Cooper waited behind the pillar of the Grover Beach station until the Pacific Surfliner slowed to a stop, brakes screeching. Jane popped up the umbrella in the event Veronica was seated on the right side of the train. Only one of the train's car doors opened and two conductors jumped out. One set a stepstool on the concrete platform. The other shouted, "All aboard."

Jane and Cooper shared the cover of the umbrella and moved to the train car. Once on board, Jane directed Cooper to seats nearby. Hunched low, she whispered, "We need to find Veronica without being seen. If she's seated in the cars ahead we can approach from behind, no problem. But if she's seated in the cars behind us she'll see us come through the car door."

"We need a disguise," Cooper said.

Jane racked her brain.

"Tickets?" the grey haired conductor said.

He punched them, tore off a piece of each, then wedged the receipt into the clip on the side of the seat.

"Where's the bar car?" Jane asked.

"Up ahead, ma'am," he said and moved on.

"I'll go forward first," she said, "and see if she's ahead of us."

"I'll go."

"No, she'll recognize you before she does me."

"She'll be on the right side," he said.

"How do you know?"

"It's got the ocean view."

"Makes sense," Jane took the baseball cap off Cooper's head and put it on her own. She dug sunglasses out of her purse. Not the greatest disguise, but it would have to do. She got up and entered the forward car, moving cautiously, upstream against a few passengers carrying cardboard concession trays coming from the bar car.

Veronica wasn't in the next car, so she moved on. In the vestibule between cars the deck rocked and Jane almost lost her balance. She took a moment to consider the hatch below on the diamond-plate deck. A hinged metal door allowed access to drop down to the tracks. She assumed that was how Veronica planned to get off.

Up ahead in the next car she saw the back of a brunette and drew close. Jane could see it was Veronica by the way she moved her head, like a cat: precise and graceful. She was sitting alone at a window staring out at the ocean, lost in thought. Jane wondered what was on her mind as she stepped even closer. A mere fifteen feet away, Jane could see Veronica held an electronic device in her hand. Jane recognized it as a GPS device.

She backed off but something else caught her eye. Not far, on the train bulkhead, the red latch for the emergency brake. She'd chosen her seat wisely.

CHAPTER 16

She showed Cooper the hatch between the train cars and they made their plan before they settled in and waited. When there were no homes or commercial structures in sight it was obvious the train had crossed onto Vandenberg Air Force Base, the landscape barren with low scrub. There were occasional buildings scattered here and there and Jane noticed large white towers. Upon closer inspection, she could see "Titan II" in black text on the side of one of them. She had read about these, the defunct launch pads. There were others that appeared fully operational.

"Once we get off the train we have to stay out of sight," Cooper said. "Air Force Security will probably respond to a stopped train. If we're caught we're going to jail, no questions asked."

"So once Veronica gets on the boat," she asked, "that's when you'll call?"

"You wanted to witness the perp walk? Now you'll see her arrest."

Jane had been meaning to ask him, and said, "You were married to her. Did you ever pick up on her treachery and second guess your decision?"

"Many times."

"But you stayed with her."

"We had a child together. If you want to understand think of it this way, Veronica is a cheat."

"A cheat?"

"She lives to cheat. She cheated in our marriage...hell she cheats playing cards. It's her nature. She can't help it. If she put the same effort into honest work Veronica could have been very successful. But she can't help herself."

They sat in silence for the rest of the trip. After a while Jane felt the train go around a slight bend. Then it finally happened. An electronic alarm sounded and the train came to an abrupt halt. The conductor ran past them into the next car, his radio squawking.

"Now," Jane said.

She grabbed the ticket receipts out of the seat and, for the benefit of the passengers around them, Jane said, "I can use a drink." She asked him, "You buying?"

On the spot, Cooper stammered for a moment before he said "Sure." She and Cooper went to the sliding door and entered the vestibule.

Through the window in the forward door they could see the conductor and waited until the he'd moved into the car ahead. Then she gave Cooper a nod. He pulled up the hatch and they dropped down to the tracks. She made sure to replace the hatch so it wasn't obvious they'd jumped off before they hid beside the train wheels.

Jane could see Veronica move out from below the train car ahead and, unbeknownst that they were there, she scrambled down into a ravine and darted into a corrugated metal drain tunnel buried beneath the tracks.

She heard the conductor open the side door near them and saw his legs drop down. Ducking low, they moved to hide in the space near the train wheels. She was so close her bare arm brushed against the wheel and Jane burnt herself. She suppressed the pain, gritting her teeth. She had no idea it would be so hot.

It appeared as if the conductor was searching for signs that someone got off the train, and another conductor met him. They conversed for a moment and then ducked underneath to examine the other side.

Jane saw the window of opportunity. Much like the tunnel Veronica had found, there was a similar one behind them. Since the conductors couldn't see them now, she said to Cooper, "Follow me."

They ducked into the dirt ravine and wriggled into the corrugated tunnel, barely wide enough to fit them both. It was muddy inside with spider webs and standing water. Jane wiped the webs from her face and pressed on. It smelled like something had died in there.

The proximity to Cooper felt awkward. This was the closest she'd been to him since they'd last slept together. She distanced herself as much as she could.

Just as Cooper had predicted, from their vantage point they could see a pair of Humvee vehicles arrive and a half dozen men of the Air Force 30th Security Forces Squadron jump out. The soldiers were dressed in full khaki camouflage and wore dark blue berets. A few carried M-4 carbines. She had been so focused on chasing Veronica she hadn't even thought about how they'd get off the base.

The commander spoke with one of the conductors as the others did their reconnaissance. Jane was certain they would look in the tunnels, but nobody did. After a few minutes, the conductors climbed back on the train and it continued on its way. The soldiers returned to their vehicles, took a moment to radio in their findings, and then departed. After they had gone, Cooper went to the end of the tunnel and pointed out a small airplane in the sky above them. "UAV," he whispered.

"What's that?"

"Unmanned Aerial Vehicle," he said.

"A drone?"

"It might circle for a while. We may have to wait until dark."

"What about Veronica?"

Jane peaked out to consider Veronica's tunnel. It appeared she, too, was laying low.

"We have to be quiet," Cooper said in a hushed tone. "This tunnel amplifies everything, like a horn."

She could see he was right and tried to settle in while keeping an eye on Veronica's tunnel. She concentrated on her breathing to slow her heartrate.

The afternoon dragged on and there was no movement as Veronica stayed hidden. Jane grew thirsty and wished she'd brought water. At one point she heard another train approach but it was unclear which direction it was heading. As it passed overhead she assumed it was northbound from the echo but couldn't see it to confirm.

Still, Veronica did not emerge.

Jane began to wonder if Veronica had slipped away without them seeing her, but then she saw her arm at the end of the tunnel tossing a wrapper out. Jane ducked back, and by the time she ventured another look she could see a silver wrapper blowing in the wind. The breeze brought the wrapper past and Jane could see it was a power bar. Veronica had come prepared. She had snacks, and probably water. *Damn.*

It was hot and Jane was so thirsty she considered sipping the standing water pooled in the corrugated pipe but knew that would only make her sick.

The wait was interminable.

At one point Cooper fell asleep. His snoring was so loud she had to wake him.

Two hours later another train passed. That one was clearly heading north and she wished she could jump on board and get a bottle of water from the bar car. Wasn't there a Johnny Cash song, she remembered, something about a prisoner yearning for freedom and every time the train passed by out his prison window it tortured him? Didn't the guy imagine passengers at ease sipping coffee and smoking cigars? She'd heard the song played in Danny's truck.

As dusk arrived Jane was even more vigilant in watching Veronica's tunnel so she wouldn't miss her. Finally, only after the sky had transformed from sunset gold to a dark blue, Veronica emerged.

"She's out," whispered Jane.

She and Cooper watched as Veronica stretched her muscles as if she'd just awakened from a nap. She sipped bottled water, gave the area a once over, then moved toward the coastal cliffs.

"Where's she going?" Jane whispered.

"To the yacht," Cooper said.

CHAPTER 17

Keeping a safe distance, Jane and Cooper followed Veronica. They took cover behind scrub brush as she made her way to the cliffs. Jane could see Brendan's yacht tied to a military vessel, gunmetal grey with clusters of antennas.

"Security running background checks," Cooper said.

Jane's lips were cracked and her throat parched from thirst. Meanwhile Veronica casually sipped water at the bluff. It was driving Jane crazy.

The military vessel pulled up anchor and powered away and Veronica got a phone call. Only then did she drop down from the cliffs to the beach below.

Jane and Cooper snuck up closer.

Veronica stashed her backpack on a cluster of rocks and then started to wade into the ocean. Jane realized why Veronica had chosen triathlon wear. "She's swimming out to the yacht," she said.

"Of course she is," Cooper said.

Jane remembered the framed photo of teenage Veronica adorned with gold swim medals. She'd seen the photo in Veronica's bedroom on Stingray Cay. Then, before Veronica got away, she snatched the framed picture. Jane wondered where the photo was now.

Although the sun had long set over the water, Veronica was backlit by the lingering light in the sky. She swam past the whitewash, her strokes graceful. Jane could see Veronica had the kind of athletic form only expert training buys. Much like an elegant tennis forehand, or perfect golf swing, you know it when you see it. There are some things not learned in public pools or city parks, where Jane had spent her youth. Veronica had come from a life of privilege and learned to swim at country club pools. So where did it all go wrong?

When Veronica reached the boat Jane could see Billy at the railing. Brendan and the crew tossed a rope ladder and assisted her on board. They had a towel waiting for the boss.

"Call base security," she said to Cooper.

"Tomorrow."

"But she's on the boat."

"After they dig up the gold."

"When did you decide that?"

"Just now."

"I'm not sticking around. Call them."

"Jane…"

"Besides, I'm dying of thirst here."

"I bet there's water in the backpack she left behind."

"This is crazy," Jane said, getting angry. "Call now and they'll turn that boat back around."

"There's no rush."

"We can't be here. Soldiers will find us. We'll be the ones arrested."

"There are caves in these cliffs we can hide in."

"Fuck that!" Jane said. She pulled the Colt from her purse. "I'm not staying around here. Get this over with. Call in the cavalry."

"Let's get some water and talk about it."

She aimed the .380 at his chest. "There's nothing to talk about. We had a deal."

He just looked at her before he said, "We can't risk it at night. That boat comes back and Veronica will jump back in the water. Nobody will see her at night, and she'll disappear again."

There was a degree of logic in that. Jane remembered the night she'd survived the wreck of the *Anne Bonny*. She was certain Veronica went down with the ship but the darkness of the night allowed her to swim away unseen.

Suddenly she heard a loud crack followed by a thunderous noise. They both turned to the source, a rocket launching. The earth rumbled beneath Jane's feet and she couldn't believe her eyes. The night instantly turned to day as the flaming contrail pulsated below the climbing projectile. She'd seen this sort of thing on TV but the sight of it so close was jaw dropping. As the rocket continued to climb and arch toward the ocean Jane heard cheers coming from the yacht. It was as if this was a firework show for their benefit.

"Did you know they were going to do that?" she asked Cooper.

He appeared as amazed as she. "No."

Jane swallowed hard. "Let's get that water."

CHAPTER 18

Under the cover of darkness they descended the cliffs and Jane found Veronica's backpack on the rocks. There were two bottles of Fiji water, one of them half gone. Jane took the unopened bottle and tossed Cooper the other. He could drink Veronica's backwash. *Hell, aren't they still married?*

"There's something I didn't tell you," he said.

"Now what?"

"I told you the truth, just not the whole truth."

"What a surprise," she said with sarcasm.

"Listen, there's not going to be a lot of prospecting and time wasted. These guys she brought in are going to have to dig, for sure, but Veronica has a pretty good idea where the gold is buried. She's been here before."

"When?"

"Both of us were here years ago, posing as surfers. We snuck in by boat, dug up a few gold coins in a collapsed cave right over there," he said pointing, "but only reached the tip of the iceberg before we were caught. This was before they ramped up security, before domestic terrorism and drones."

"So this is not about revenge for your brother's death, it's about padding your bankroll," she said.

"It's about getting my son back with a nest egg to ensure he'll grow up right and be a better person than me."

Jane lamented, "All this is nothing but a family squabble,

and I'm the sap in the middle of it."

"It's about stopping Veronica for good."

"Give me that phone," she demanded, gun raised.

"I'll throw it in the waves, I swear to God," he threatened, and held it up as if he were to toss it.

"Don't be ridiculous."

"Give me until morning," he pleaded. "And I'll split what we find fifty-fifty."

"You'll burn me again."

"I swear on my son's life...I can't hide from you, Jane. You're too smart, and too good. You found Veronica, and you'd definitely find me." He looked out to the yacht. "Think about it, this gold could be a leg up. You want to be a waitress in your old age?"

"I'm an actress!"

"Same thing."

"I don't care about money," she snapped with anger. "I just want my life back."

"Twenty-four hours. That's all I ask. Tomorrow night Veronica will be in jail and you'll be sipping a fine cabernet at the Biltmore in Santa Barbara."

"How do you plan to get the gold out of here?" she questioned.

"Once Veronica uncovers the cave we call in the Air Force. We wait until they're all arrested and hauled away, and then move in. Maybe we stash it in that tunnel under the tracks for now and come back later."

"And where do we hide?"

He pointed. "The caves in those cliffs. Nobody will be able to see us there."

Once again Jane realized she was at a crossroads. On one hand she considered shooting him in the leg, grabbing the phone, and calling the authorities herself. But on the other hand something tugged her the other way—impulse. In the end the fear of Veronica getting away in the darkness is what swayed her most. She'd come too far. She couldn't let Veronica slip away a second time.

"Show me," she said.

CHAPTER 19

Jane sat on a ledge under the overhang, gun in hand. The caves Cooper spoke of were nothing more than deep crevices within the cliffs. The one they were huddled in, the deepest, barely offered cover from the wind. She'd spotted a bat swoop past them, and it was getting cold. She said, "I'm going to freeze to death."

He slipped off his dark fleece REI pullover and gave it to her.

"What about you?" she said.

"I'll be fine."

She put the pullover on and sat on the ground. She curled up and stretched it over her knees, like she'd when she was younger. There was something metallic in the front pocket. Jane pulled it out—a pair of handcuffs.

"What the…?" she said.

He said nothing.

She pointed the gun at him, handcuffs in the other hand. "Are these supposed to be for me?"

"Of course not. Veronica."

"You've been carrying these around everywhere so when the time is right you plan on locking me to something to make your escape."

"That's not true," he said.

"Why do you have handcuffs?"

"Like I said, for Veronica."

"I don't believe you."

"Keep them. I don't care."

Jane said. "What's that saying? Fool me once…"

"Believe what you want. Those aren't for you."

They sat for a long time in silence. Finally Cooper broke the ice explaining where the gold was buried, inside a cave wall in a lagoon-shaped canyon within the cliffs. "At low tide you can enter the lagoon at sea level, but only for an hour or two before the waves make it impossible as the sea rises. The only way to get to it is to repel down from above."

Jane could hear music coming from the anchored yacht, its cabin lights glistening off the black water. Occasionally laughter echoed. "They're having a party," Jane said.

"And nobody realizes this is their last night of freedom."

Jane imagined what it must have been like for the survivors of the *Yankee Blade*. Maybe passengers fortunate enough to come ashore found shelter in this very same cave. She came to the conclusion that pure greed was ultimately the culprit, whether it be from Captain Randall or Veronica, unbridled greed is what bought on so much misery.

The hours dragged on and she spent the night watching both Cooper and Brendan's yacht. The distant wails of seals accompanied the pre-dawn light, much like birds welcoming a new day. Cooper decided to empty Veronica's backpack. There was a single power bar, peanut butter. He broke it in half, offered the meager ration to Jane, and said, "Breakfast."

She shook her head no.

Even before the sun was up the crew had inflatable boats aside the yacht and Veronica led the team ashore. Her son Billy was with them. Hidden back in the shadow of the cave, Jane could see Veronica go to where she had stashed the backpack and appeared confused why it wasn't there. Veronica looked down and studied the sand.

"She sees our footprints," Jane whispered.

The high tide had cleared some of their tracks away, but not all. Veronica scanned the beach. Jane ducked back further into the cave. "Get back," she said to Cooper. Laying in the dirt, they both watched as Veronica gave the cliffs a once-over. She held her gaze in their direction and Jane couldn't tell if she'd seen them. It didn't look like she had.

Getting back to business, Veronica tightened a sheath strapped to her leg. It appeared to be a diving knife.

Meanwhile Brendan and his men shuttled cases and equipment from the yacht. They all converged around a canyon wall. Pounding ocean waves crashed the rocks at the base of the crevice. The violent waves appeared to guard the entrance, nature's sentry at the castle gates. Cooper was right. The cave they had chosen was a good spot. They were close enough to see everything, but hidden in the shadows as to not be noticed.

With Veronica supervising, Brendan and his men built aluminum Speed-Rail and scaffolding at the top of the cliff. With a series of ropes they eased it down inside the canyon wall. At one point, a Coast Guard helicopter flew up the shoreline, low over the water. The men on the cliff paused for a moment, then went back to work after it had passed.

Jane could see Billy was bored by all of this. He began wandering up and down the coast, searching for seashells and skipping rocks in the surf. He found a piece of driftwood as a walking stick, poked at seaweed, and began exploring the rocks.

He was coming their way.

"Shit," Jane said. They both scrambled back into the cave.

Billy came closer. If he continued on his path he'd come directly to them, and sure enough, Billy did. The boy was startled and about to call out but Cooper cut him off with, "Billy! It's me."

The boy squinted at them.

"It's Dad," Cooper said. "Come here."

Jane saw recognition on the boy's face. He dropped his walking stick and came running, "Dad!"

They hugged. Cooper said, "We're playing hide and seek.

Don't say anything to anyone."

"Where have you been?" Billy asked.

"In Canada. I missed you so much."

"Mom said you guys had a big fight and you left us."

"I'm back now. Everything is going to be all right. I came back for you."

For the first time ever Jane saw Cooper emotional. He had always been so cool and collected, so in control. But now hugging his son, she could see, Cooper was nothing more than your average, run-of-the-mill father with prideful tears in his eyes.

Billy looked to Jane with caution and said, "Who are you?"

"That's Jane, Billy. She's Mom's friend."

Mom's friend? Jane thought. *There could be nothing farther from the truth.*

"Listen," Cooper said to him, "You can't say anything or you'll ruin our game. Can you keep a secret?"

He nodded.

At that moment Jane heard Veronica call out, "Billy?" She looked to see Veronica walking the shoreline.

"Shh," Cooper said to Billy, pulling him back. "Don't give us away."

"Billy?" Veronica continued, "Where are you, honey?"

Billy played along as Veronica searched. Jane could see Veronica was growing increasingly agitated.

"Billy!?" Veronica called, now with anger. "Come here right now or you're getting a spanking!"

Jane could see Billy flinch.

"Do you hear me? Come out right now or I'll pull down your pants and spank you in front of everyone! Is that what you want?!"

Jane could see Billy's face turn red. *Does Veronica do that?* From the look in the boy's face Jane could tell it wasn't the physical pain that he feared, but the shame and humiliation. That's what put him over the top.

Billy broke from Cooper and screamed, "Mom?!"

Oh shit. She turned to Cooper and said, "Call now."

He reached in his pocket for his phone, punched up his contacts, then said, "No bars."

"What?"

"Because we're in this cave. I've got to get up on the cliff."

Jane saw Billy run to his mother. He pointed back at them. Although she couldn't hear what he was saying, it was clear the boy was giving them up. *What's that kid's problem? Such a brat.* Jane wondered what he was saying to her, that he'd just seen his father? Veronica would doubt it, wouldn't she? She'd killed Cooper in Dana Point, or so she thought. Jane wondered what she was thinking at that moment as a confused Veronica squinted in their direction. She had a bitter look of concern on her face. Then she violently yanked the boy by the arm and dragged him back to the others.

Cooper ran from the cave and scrambled up the cliff embankment. Jane followed. It was steep and the gravel was loose. Jane kept sliding back and her progress was slow. She looked back over her shoulder and could see Brendan with a rifle coming their way. Jane realized had Cooper chosen another route up the steep cliff, with solid footing, they would have been up the embankment and out of sight by the time the men were there. But it was too late to turn back now and choose another path.

She heard the crack of rifle fire. Clods of dirt exploded beside her. Jane considered firing back but realized the short barrel Colt would be useless at this distance. A rock beside her cracked followed by the ping of a ricochet.

Cooper reached the top first. He reached back to help her as gunfire erupted on either side of them. Jane screamed. He dropped to one knee and pulled her up. She thought it miraculous they hadn't been hit.

Atop the crest, Jane ran for her life. It would take some time for Veronica and her men to climb the cliff. She figured they had a brief window of opportunity.

Jane could see, beyond the train tracks, there was a cluster of white buildings around the perimeter of the launch pad. *Make it there.*

She ran faster than Cooper as he struggled to keep up. She crossed over the train tracks, ran through dried weeds, and came upon the pavement. The buildings appeared abandoned. Jane went for the closest one. The door was open and she burst in. It was a dark, abandoned machine shop. Rows of lathes and drill presses lined the walls. Cooper followed her in, gulping for air.

"Call," she said.

Catching his breath, Cooper punched his phone. "This is an emergency. Vandenberg Air Force Base Space Launch Complex 8. There is a FIM-92 Stinger missile in the engine room of the boat anchored there." As he gave details over the phone Jane could see his shirt bloody, seeping from his side. His knees gave way and he dropped. She realized he'd been hit, probably when he turned back to helped her up the cliff.

In panic, Jane glanced out the door.

Veronica and her men were closing in.

She pulled the Colt .380 Mustang, chambered a round, and fired.

CHAPTER 20

Even though the Colt Mustang had limited accuracy at that distance, the sound of gunfire gave them pause. Veronica and her men stopped advancing on them and returned fire. Jane and Cooper dropped to the floor as bullets punched through the tin building in a deafening deluge—a hailstorm of lead just above their heads. Shafts of light now pierced the darkness.

Throughout the chaos Cooper continued to give coordinates to someone on the other end of the phone. Through the door Jane could see Brendan advance commando style and she remembered when he recounted his Navy SEAL days. She fired to keep him at bay, but stopped herself when she realized her pistol only held six rounds. She'd have to conserve. Jane thought she'd fired four already. With all the confusion maybe it was five.

She could see Veronica give orders before the team retreated. They moved past the dried weeds towards the cliffs. Soon they were out of sight, and it fell silent. Once Jane felt it was safe, she went over to Cooper and saw a puddle of blood had formed beside him. She yanked off the fleece pullover and held it against his wound.

"Bastards!" he said, clearly in pain.

Applying pressure, the pullover helped control the bleeding. She said, "The cavalry is coming, right?"

"They asked a lot of questions before I lost them. Let's hope they won't write me off as some crazy," he said.

"They'll be here," she said, trying to be positive. "Hang in there."

He looked to her and said, "I'm sorry…I'm sorry I made you my shill. You're a better person than any of us, me, Veronica, all these lowlifes."

Jane said. "What did they say on the phone?"

"I'm sorry. I shouldn't have used you in our scheme. But then I broke rule number one and fell in love." Jane could hear more gunfire in the distance as Cooper continued, "No matter what happens, just know it wasn't my idea to frame you for Wolff's murder back in L.A. That was all Veronica's idea plan. I fought her on it, but this was her caper from the very beginning."

"We'll get you to a hospital." Jane was making progress with his wound, having stopped the bleeding, before she saw his eyes look past her for a second. Then she felt a presence. Before Jane could turn something hard struck her in the back of the head. Her chin hit the concrete and she bit her tongue.

She rolled over to see Brendan standing over her. He'd struck her with the butt of his rifle. Brendan kicked her pistol away, turned to Cooper, and said, "What the fuck, bro? Bring along a nurse?"

How had he snuck up on her? Jane wondered. There must have been a door at the back of the building. The pain was overwhelming and her sight began to blur. There was the taste of blood in her mouth and it felt like she'd bit her tongue in half. She felt nauseous and was certain she was going to throw up.

To Jane, Brendan said, "You were a plant all along, weren't you, bitch?" He tilted his head and said, "And I thought you liked me."

Jane couldn't speak, checked her tongue, it was still intact. She looked in vain for her gun on the floor.

"Brendan," Cooper said through clinched teeth, "Listen to

me. Veronica will betray you."

"Dude," he said, "this doesn't concern you."

"You think she's going to split that gold? She cut me out, and she'll do the same to you."

At that point gunfire erupted somewhere in the distance and Brendan went to the door to see.

"Security Forces," Cooper said. "They know who you are."

"We'll see about that," Brendan said, his rifle poised to go into battle.

From the darkness behind them Veronica appeared.

Jane recoiled back. She must have come through the back door too.

Veronica sized both of them up before she turned to Cooper, eyeing him, and said, "Christ almighty...I thought I'd taken care of you. I could have sworn I slit your throat."

"That was my brother," Cooper said, "You killed him by mistake, and now you're fucked."

"Speak for yourself," she said before turning to Jane. "And you, Jane? Do you know how much money I've spent trying to get rid of you? The exterminators I've hired? You're like a cat with nine lives."

Jane remained silent and eyed Veronica with hatred.

"I planted a missile on Brendan's yacht," Cooper said with a hint of pride in his voice. "So it's only a matter of time."

"A what?" Veronica questioned.

"In the engine room, a surface-to-air missile. Security Forces know all about it, and they're on their way."

Brendan put two and two together and said, "You're framing us for treason."

Jane considered that for a second then snapped, "He's bluffing."

"You're right. I am," Cooper said.

Veronica and Brendan shared a look. He gave her a shrug. She sighed deeply then said calmly, "Go find it and throw it into the sea."

"Hooyah," Brendan said. Orders. He was out the door.

Jane found the strength to sit up. She searched for the Colt but couldn't find it. Veronica stood by the door for a moment as if considering what to do next. Jane could see Veronica's jaw was clinched in anger and she was pretty sure she was whispering to herself, weighing options. It was strange, obsessive compulsive behavior. This was a self-reflective moment, something she'd never seen in Veronica before.

Then Veronica took a deep breath and seemingly pulled herself together. She considered Cooper and drew the diving knife from the sheath on her leg. She said, "It's about time we break it off, once and for all." With that Veronica kneeled down and slashed his throat.

Jane screamed.

Cooper struggled, helplessly reaching up to Veronica to defend himself. Jane screamed again followed by the sound of the handcuffs ratcheting. Veronica pulled back from Cooper in confusion. In his last breath he had cuffed himself to her. Jane realized the handcuffs were in the front pocket of the fleece pullover.

It was Cooper's final act of defiance.

Veronica yanked, but she was anchored to him, and Cooper was barely alive. She cursed and tried to use the diving knife to slash his arm off. He struggled and blood sprayed her. She stabbed him more, then went back to his arm. The knife clearly could not cut through the bones in his forearm. She was now shackled and covered in blood.

"Mom?"

Veronica turned to see her son Billy standing in the shadows, the look of terror on his face.

"I told you to stay put!" she barked.

The boy had witnessed it all.

CHAPTER 21

Anchored by Cooper, Veronica shouted, "Billy, get the gun!" pointing to the Colt at his feet.

The boy hesitated.

Finally Jane saw where her gun had gone. She tried to stand but fell. The concussion was affecting her balance. Jane crawled towards the gun, and Veronica yanked Cooper, both of their progress slow.

"Give Mommy the gun, Billy. Now!"

Jane could see the boy still processing what he had just witnessed, tears streaming down his face.

"Billy…" Veronica used both hands to pull Cooper across the floor. She was making progress, and would get there quicker than Jane. Finally the boy stepped over and picked up Jane's Colt. "Shoot her!" Veronica demanded while still struggling with the single handcuff that anchored her to Cooper. "She's bad. She's going to hurt Mommy!"

Holding the pistol with both hands, a quivering Billy pointed the barrel at Jane, a look of confusion on his face.

Veronica barked, "Shoot her, Billy! Shoot her now!"

Jane tried to reason with the young mind. "No, Billy. Killing is wrong. You'll go to hell."

"Shoot her or bring me that gun," Veronica snapped.

"Billy," Jane said, "Nobody is going to hurt you, or your mom. Go get help."

Veronica shrieked, "Bring me that gun, young man, or you're getting a very hard spanking. Do you hear me!?"

Jane could see the boy was on the fence, true fear on his face, and thought *this kid is going to need some major therapy*. Jane said, "Billy, your father needs help. We need to get him to the hospital." The boy's eyes darted to Cooper sprawled next to Veronica, his bloodied arm chained to her wrist. "Be a hero. Run as fast as you can. Get help."

"Don't listen to her," Veronica shouted.

"You hurt Dad," he said to his mother, clearly heartbroken.

"He's not your father," Veronica said.

"But he said—"

"He lied!"

"Then who is?" Billy asked.

Jane could see Billy's question threw Veronica. To her son, she said, "Your father's dead."

"Cooper is your father," Jane said. "You need to get help for him. Run!"

"Okay," Billy said, convinced it was a good idea. He stepped up to Veronica and handed her the pistol, then ran out the door of the machine shop.

"Billy! Where are you going? Get back here!" Veronica shouted.

But the boy was gone.

Jane figured she could make it and jumped to her feet. She went for the open door.

Veronica fired.

Jane's knew she'd been hit. It felt like a red hot fireplace poker had been jammed in her armpit. Her knees buckled.

This is it, Jane thought, face down on the concrete, *I'm going to die*. But then something Cooper had said, something from *The Art of War*, the idea that all warfare is based on deception.

Her idea—*play possum*.

Deception.

Play dead.

She released the tension in her body and prayed Veronica wouldn't fire again. *Let her think she won.* Other than the gunshot still ringing in her ears, it was completely silent. After a moment she heard Veronica climb to her feet. Then she heard the clink of the handcuffs and Veronica's laborious grunts struggling to drag Cooper's body across the floor. Cooper grunted. He was still alive. The next sound was a machine turning on, a low hum of some kind. The mechanical sound was familiar to Jane, but she couldn't place it.

There were more efforts, Veronica cursing with lifting weight, and then the high-pitched whine made it clear.

Jane peeked. Veronica was at the band saw. It was the same kind of contraption from high school wood shop—much like what the butcher uses to cut steaks. Veronica had hoisted him up and had Cooper's arm draped over the table. Cooper was still conscious as she began to cut his arm off at the elbow. He screamed, squirmed and flailed about.

Veronica was successful and one-armed Cooper flopped to the concrete, his neck crimson red and his arm a stub above the elbow.

Meanwhile Veronica was trying to yank Cooper's severed arm out of the dangling handcuff. But his forearm was too thick. Neither Cooper's hand nor his meaty arm could fit through the opening of the cuffs.

Veronica went back to the saw, turned it on again and was preparing for a second cut when the sound of gunfire distracted her. Still bound to Cooper's forearm, dangling at her side, Veronica went to the door to investigate. She was only a few feet from Jane.

Play dead.

For a moment all Jane could hear was Veronica's labored breathing before the distant gunfire resumed.

Cooper was still moving, so Veronica returned to him and found a crowbar. She finished him off with violent blows to the head. His skull bobbed up and down off the concrete. Jane heard the crunch and was struck with pure terror. Even if she wanted to move, Jane was frozen. *I'm truly in hell. This is evil incarnate.* Jane had been stabbed, strangled, bludgeoned, and now shot. *Is this how it ends? Does Veronica win?*

Jane remained still. *Play dead.*

She heard Veronica approach and was certain she was about to get the same crowbar treatment but then a distressed Billy cried out from somewhere in the distance, "I want my mommy!"

The blow from the crowbar never came.

Instead, as if pulled by her maternal instincts, Veronica stepped over Jane and went out the door to attend to her son.

Mommy bear's cub needed help.

CHAPTER 22

When she knew Veronica was gone, Jane reached around to feel where the bullet had entered. The puncture was under her armpit and hurt like hell. She could feel the warmth of her blood and hoped the bullet hadn't hit vital organs. Maybe she was lucky. It seemed high enough on her torso. She could still move her arm.

Jane realized if she remained there she'd surely bleed to death. She struggled to her feet and went to Cooper. His face was a concave mess—once handsome good-looks gone forever. He was the man she had loved. He was the father of Veronica's child. How could she have done this to him? So brutal.

Out the door Jane could see Veronica moving towards the cliffs. *Is she trying to get back to the yacht?* A helicopter appeared in the sky, hovering over the water. *Does she think she's getting away?*

Jane staggered out of the machine shop.

By the time Jane crossed the train tracks the Air Force Security Forces had converged—a brigade of soldiers with assault rifles. A few of Veronica's men fired back but they were cut down, no match for the professionals. But somehow Veronica walked through it all, unfazed, as if she was completely unaware of the firefight surrounding her.

Hunched low, Jane kept following, holding her bloodied hand against the seeping wound in a feeble attempt to stop the bleeding. When Veronica reached the end of the cliff she turned back, looking for Billy, presumably, but was taken aback by the sight of Jane.

Jane just stared at her, hatred in her eyes.

Veronica shouted, "How does an utter nobody like you manage take everything away from me?"

"All warfare is based on deception," Jane said. "And you underestimated your opponent, bitch!"

"Not anymore," she said. Veronica aimed the Colt. But then shouts from the soldiers distracted her. There was much commotion. Jane could see Brendan standing at the stern of his yacht. He had the rocket launcher over his shoulder; not tossing it in the water as instructed, but rather aiming it to the sky.

Veronica saw him too.

Jane's thought at that moment was simply *don't* before she saw a wisp of white smoke. The projectile banked towards the helicopter. It exploded in a ball of fire. Debris flew in every direction. The aircraft crashed into the ocean in a massive ball of flame.

Brendan thrusted his fist in the air.

The Air Force Security Forces retaliated with the .50 caliber firepower.

Brendan was cut down in an instant, and his luxury yacht destroyed. The white, fiberglass hull was ripped to shreds as if it were a Styrofoam cooler. Pieces went flying. The gunners continued to unload, ripping the boat apart until a commander screamed, "Cease fire!"

Then silence.

Jane saw Veronica drop the Colt and hold her arms up in surrender. As the soldiers closed in, she backed up against the cliff.

From the look on Veronica's face Jane knew exactly what she had in mind. Veronica took a deep breath then, as if at the edge of a diving platform, she threw her arms out and leaped backward.

Jane lost sight of Veronica over the cliff but heard her body hit with a thud. She went to the edge.

Veronica was splayed out on the jagged rocks, arms stretched out, her head bent grotesquely to its side.

Jane watched from above. She expected the master of deception to get up. Veronica always had before.

Cheat death. Let's see you do it.

Veronica moved no more.

Jane decided she'd been there long enough.

It had been four days since she'd been admitted to the Lompoc Valley Medical Center to treat her gunshot trauma and concussion. Nancy and Danny had been there, and Avery flew in from Florida to defend her. She'd given her statement, and Avery made the case for her innocence, but there was still Air Force security stationed outside her door.

She hated hospitals and wanted out. She told the doctors she felt fine, but they insisted on playing it safe. It was when they were describing her next battery of tests that she planned her escape. The challenge was to get past the Air Force guy.

The smoking section in the courtyard gave her an idea. From her window she occasionally saw patients, wearing bathrobes and gowns, go out for a cigarette. Jane didn't smoke, but the guy outside her door didn't know that.

She'd bummed a cigarette from Danny to use as a prop, and when the time was right, Jane unhooked herself from the IV and got dressed. The flimsy bathrobe her mother brought covered Jane's street clothes just enough. Showing the cigarette to the security guard, he gave her a nod and she took the elevator to the first floor.

Her deception worked.

There was an old guy she recognized, a regular in the smoking section. He had a lighter in one hand and was searching planters for a butt. Jane figured either he was out, or someone was rationing his smokes. When she approached he stepped away from the planter and gave her a smile. "Can I trouble you for a smoke, little lady?" he said.

"Sure," Jane said and gave him her Marlboro prop.

When she felt the coast was clear, Jane removed her bathrobe and stuffed it into the trash container. The old man's eyes lit up and he said, "Looks like a perfectly good bathrobe to me."

"Not my style," Jane said.

She cleared the hospital grounds and walked up the avenue. She reached the commercial district and kept going.

Jane had her life back, her name back, and for the first time in what seemed like forever—the wind at her back.

ACKNOWLEDGMENTS

My love and gratitude to my beautiful wife Jennifer whose support, great ideas, and keen instincts helped shape this trilogy of novellas. Thanks to my supportive community of crime writer friends and filmmakers (ne'er-do-wells and otherwise) and those who encouraged me to tell stories.

JOHN SHEPPHIRD is a Shamus Award-winning author and writer/director/producer of television films. The Shill Trilogy was inspired by noir master James M. Cain's terse, tense, and twist-filled narratives.

John's short fiction has appeared in *Alfred Hitchcock's Mystery Magazine* and various crime fiction anthologies.

As director films include *Jersey Shore Shark Attack, Chupacabra Terror, I Saw Mommy Kissing Santa Claus* and *Teenage Bonnie & Klepto Clyde.*

Visit JohnShepphird.com